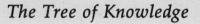

The Tree of Knowledge

EVA FIGES

The Tree of Knowledge

Minerva

A Minerva Paperback
THE TREE OF KNOWLEDGE

First published in Great Britain 1990
by Sinclair-Stevenson Limited
This Minerva edition published 1991
by Mandarin Paperbacks
Michelin House, 81 Fulham Road, London SW3 6RB

Minerva is an imprint of the Octopus Publishing Group,
a division of Reed International Books Limited

A CIP catalogue record for this title
is available from the British Library
ISBN 0 7493 9190 1

Printed and bound in Great Britain
by Cox & Wyman Ltd, Reading, Berkshire

The Tree of Knowledge

One

PRAY BE SEATED, sir, and pardon such humble
surroundings. This room must serve both as
schoolroom and for living in, and I fear it is but a
shabby place to receive visitors. You see how bare
it is, and lacking in comfort, but children make
rough work of household chattels, which consoles
me for having so few. I endeavour to keep the
bare boards clean, and the hearth swept. It is
uphill work, with but a child to help me. I teach
her gratis in return, her father having not the
wherewithal to pay for schooling, but the work
wearies her, and then she is not fit for study.
Or else I must turn a blind eye to dust in
corners, if she is not to be nodding off over her
alphabet.

You do me too much honour to say I follow in
my father's footsteps. Let me hang your hat on this
nail. The walls are but lately whitewashed, so all is
clean. This is a poor neighbourhood, and I teach
but the rudiments of reading and arithmetic to
children who must work their way through the
world in humble callings. They will have little need,
I fear, of such learning as my father had at his
command. If they can but keep accounts, so the
shillings flow in faster than they must needs spend
the pence, I shall have done them some service, I

1

think. Their parents will consider those few pence well invested, that they must find for me.

Besides, sir, what have I to offer them? I am but a poor weaver's widow, when all is said and done. Think you my father shared his learning with me, being but a woman? Alas, sir, I have more in common with these unkempt, oft hungry children who come to my door, wishing to learn their alphabet and master sums, though not akin by blood, than with my father.

You say I have his features? This is true enough. But a life of hardship gives us other kin, or so I think. Like my neighbours here, I have known want, and worked with my hands. I was taught to make lace, not to hold converse with scholars, or entertain fine gentlemen. And then, sir, I was denied a dowry. Else it might have been otherwise. It was ever likely I should sink in the world.

Would you have me shut the casement? The street is noisy, and the stench which comes from it in summer weather scarce to be endured. I must choose to have the window shut, and so be stifled, or let the breeze blow in, bringing foul odours with it. I will shut it, if it pleases you. No? Then pray, remove your coat. Let us not stand upon ceremony. I am no fine lady, that you should swelter in it. Pray do so, sir. I can lay it along this bench, and the silk will not harm. I can dust it first.

I would not have you think me bitter. I have long since forgiven him. All I have in my heart now is a kind of love, and much sorrow, that there should have been so little of it when he lived. But we cannot undo the past, can we, sir? Those regrets I have are rather for a kingdom of the mind unshared, too little understood, than aught of worldly wealth. So I am poor, and wedded a poor man. Yet he was fond of me, and did ever treat me kindly. Few can say as much.

I teach but the rudiments here. I have but few books, and time is lacking, had I more to share with them. Their parents, being poor, and mostly ignorant, can find but little purpose in reading poesie, or ancient classics either, had I the knowledge of them. And yet I would give them some little pleasure with their tasks, and not mere drudgery. The pill, being sugared, is taken with a will. I try to teach them Christian principles, and open up their minds to such simple delights as they will understand and I am mistress of.

For you must know – my cousin wrote of it – that though I am my father's daughter, he made me not his heir. I speak, sir, not of the dowry denied me, but of the learning in which he was so rich. Had I been his son, that died in infancy the year that I was born, it might have been otherwise. He was, as you have read, schoolmaster to my cousins, Edward and his younger brother John, for many years. They were taught much willynilly, so I was told, and oft went supperless to bed, with nought for their pains but a whipping.

Whether this be a good thing or no, I know not. What think you, sir, that have a scholar's mind? Is this the way to stir the appetite for higher things? My woman's heart says no. And if the consequence should be the judge, it must be said that neither of my cousins rose to greatness, in the manner of my father. Mere hacks of Grub Street, both, and their stepfather, Mr Agar, was much disappointed in them. He thought they had been better served, having no particular gift and no true calling, in the learning of an honest trade. For both died poor, and left the world no better than they found it.

Indeed, my younger cousin was thought to have brought disgrace upon the family, being dissolute of both habit and mind. Is it not strange, sir, that the pupil of such a master should turn out so?

I would not whip my pupils, no. I have not had necessity so to do. And I think I scarce have the strength for it, being old, and a woman. But I think, were I put to it, I would rather send a child away, telling his parents that he wastes their hard-earned pence. The poor cannot afford to keep their children idle, so such a threat would keep them studious.

But to tell the truth, I think my father used my cousins, though his pupils, as his eyes, much as he used my sister and myself. But on account of their sex, and being paid for his services, he did teach them to understand that which they read aloud. My cousin Edward has written of the many ancient authors he and his brother studied whilst in his house. Certainly I have heard him speak of it, with something less than fervour, as a time of hard study and spare diet, the ancient texts being chosen rather to increase my father's knowledge than to inspire young minds. Though he had the use of his eyes then, and might have spared them much tedious matter. 'Tis little wonder, sir, that they would not be obedient without a rod to their backs. I pity the young boy that must needs study Vitruvius, his *Architecture*, or Frontinus, his *Stratagems*. We must whet the appetite with tastier morsels, I think.

As for me, sir, and my sister Mary, it was all one to us, whether the text was dry as dust or heavenly poesie that might have lifted up our spirits, and made us glad. One tongue, he would say, was enough for any woman. And so, his eyes being then quite sightless, we must read to him in many, exactly pronouncing all such foreign tongues as he

4

would have read to him. A task, sir, that must try the patience of a saint, and I was but flesh and blood, and young also.

I see you have brought books with you, to try me. There have been several gentlemen who came to visit me with this purpose, finding it hard to credit such reports. But indeed, sir, 'tis true. I would it had been otherwise. Very well, let us go to it. But my cousin Edward was no liar, and had it at first hand, and not by hearsay, when he wrote of it.

Aurea prima sata est aetas, quae vindice nullo,
sponte sua, sine lege fidem rectumque colebat.
poena metusque aberant, nec verba minantia fixo
aere legebantur, nec supplex turba timebat
iudicis ora sui, sed erant sine iudice tuti.

Would you have me continue, sir, or shall I read to you in Greek perhaps, or Hebrew, or some modern tongue? This runs trippingly even now, being one of his most favourite texts.

Does it not speak of the golden age, when all mankind did live at peace with one another? I thought so. There was a lady once, took me to Ireland as her companion, after I left my father's house. Who would laugh at my reading in such parrot fashion, and told me something of the meaning. I would I had known this when I was wont to read aloud, for then I might have had some joy of it, and so performed my task more willingly.

I see that the flies vex you. Would you have me shut the window? Things putrefying in this hot weather, I fear they are numerous. Vinegar will not drive them off, though it was put on the panes this morning. I shall never be rid of them, I think, this being an old house, and a poor neighbourhood. I will try fanning, sir, that may drive them off.

She was most kind to me, the lady Merian, treating me like a daughter, having promised so to do. As I never yet had been by my true parent. She did teach me, so I got a smattering of learning, which made me hunger to know more. For appetite comes from feeding. I have seen it oft amongst the little ones I teach, how they will pester me with why and wherefore, so each reply provokes yet one more question.

Girls are as much imbued with eager curiosity as are their brothers. I know this, sir, both as a woman and a mother, and from this schoolroom too. See you that verse writ neatly on the wall? The pupil who did this, her name is Mary, and had she been born John, her father wealthy, she might have made her mark upon the world, as you did, sir, or even as my father. But she must fetch and carry for her mother, help mind the shop, and find herself a husband, and lose all other thoughts in household cares.

I wish that you might see her as she is now, so fresh and eager, with an appetite for all that I can give her. And more, much more, had I the means in this poor room. But soon her mother will be scolding, she reads instead of sewing, wastes much time by writing when she should be hemming sheets or making shirts. Then will she come no more, but I will think on her, and pray she finds contentment.

My father, sir, had no need to think on aught but study, though his appetite for learning was uncommon. We had an old servant who had been with him since childhood, having worked in his parents' house when but a child herself. She it was who had to sit up late, so he would not set the house afire with burning of his candle. And I but a child myself, so she would tell us, nodding with sleep and like to tumble from my stool with weariness. I took against learning even then, she said, for I must be up at dawn to sweep hearths and fetch water.

The apple of his doting mother's eye, the great hope of his father, being the firstborn son – when did he ever fetch and carry, hew wood, or clean his boots? His father was a scrivener, but of the middling sort, who came of yeoman stock and sought to have his sons rise far above him by spending on their education.

Such zeal as my father did show, even in youth, is a rare thing indeed, and some would say against nature. So our old servant would have it, who ever after maintained it had been the ruin of his eyes. If God had meant us to read books in the night, she said, he would have made the moon to shine like the sun. She was much given to such homespun philosophy.

The many books within our house were ever the bane of her life, making but dust and clutter in small rooms, and so breeding moths and flies to plague us, and worse also. This was her opinion, to be voiced out loud at times of cleaning. She thought that long service did give her a kind of licence.

I speak of her, since she made common cause with us, and with our grumbling. In truth, sir, I found it hard, in my youth, to be roused from sleep at my father's bidding, when the Muse was on him. And though it may be thought a rare honour now, to have heard his stick knocking on the wall in the small hours and go to him with a candle to write at his dictation, I cannot say it made me fond of verse. I would rather have stayed snug in bed, and my sister also. She, being my senior by several years, had done such tasks far longer, when I could not yet read or write. Much soured by broken nights and tedious days, her tongue grew tart, so she would wish him dead upon occasion, caring little who should hear her.

My sister is long since dead. Had she lived, as I have, into riper years, I doubt not she had wished those words unspoken. In ageing, we forgive our elders, is this not so? But such words were spoken, I will not deny it, in youthful, hasty rage. That they rankled with him, the whole world knows, our quarrels being made public after his death. I am sorry for it, yet was he unkind also, in thinking not on our youth.

Genius is exigent, you say? I know this, sir, but did not know it then. I knew him but as a harsh father, who cared not for us but as we could help him, since he was blind. He was never truly young, I think, as other men are. Indeed, I have heard my uncle say that he was much misliked whilst at the university, for being too earnest. And so he cared not how it might be for us under his roof, being young, and full of youthful high spirits.

Had he thought us worthy to share his labours, and get some profit from them, we might have lived peaceably enough together, but our sex made us unworthy. I find this mighty strange, thinking, as he did, that the purpose of education should be to redeem the faults of our first parents. Must we not be saved also? And Eve, being the greater sinner, has surely more need of saving by such means? But we durst not argue. Women and servants must obey, not speak their mind.

My grandfather, being a practic, who had got some standing by thrift and industry, thought the purpose of education was to rise in the world, and so he sent his sons to school, and then to Cambridge. My father was intended for the Church, his brother for the law, both worthy estates which do a man honour. And indeed, my uncle did well enough, and died with a Sir to his name, and was much respected. But my father despised the clergy. He was fortunate in having a loving father that let him continue so long at the university, when he but pursued learning for its own sake, and not to be ordained. For this was a great expenditure of capital, and generous in a careful moneylender, such as he was, being a scrivener by trade.

Such indulgence in a father is much to be envied, I think. Seven years he studied at the university, and then was able to study the world by travelling through it. This is no mean gift for a father to give his son, but the world knows he was worthy of it. I would I had been given mere crumbs from such a rich table, if not to keep my body from want, then my soul from hunger.

Would you have me shut the casement? I can scarce hear myself speak. The fishwife has a lusty voice, but her cod stinks. She goes first to wealthy houses, and seeks to fob us off with foul remnants, that are poor. I dine mostly on bread and cheese, having so few pence to spend. It is simple fare, and but little labour.

A few crumbs of wisdom from my father's table, as I told you, sir, if it kept me not from want, women's learning being frowned upon, might yet have made me richer far in spirit. I have heard it from my uncle, that the school at St Paul's where both he and my father did go, had a tradition that no more than one hundred and fifty-three boys were to be instructed gratis, since Simon Peter drew one hundred and fifty-three fishes in the miraculous draught. But we are not fish, sir, to be fried for supper, but Christian souls, all worthy of redemption, and a father should share with his children that which he has, whether it be gold or learning.

Aptitude, sir? I know not. But I can recite you Virgil even now, though it is but foreign sounds to me, and a lifetime since I read it out loud to him. I do not wish to boast. I am no genius, but yet no fool. It is true that not all minds are alike apt for study. Having kept school I know this well enough. But the fault lies oft in the teaching, not the pupils. If a pudding finds no favour at the table, 'tis the cook we blame, not those who will not eat. And then, if I am my father's daughter in feature, as you are pleased to tell me, would it not be strange if such likeness were all on the surface, and no similitude beneath? This I know: I had no aptitude for making lace, or stitching with gold thread, and yet I was put to it. It is hard labour, and but poorly paid, and will damage eyesight as surely as reading.

I doubt that every boy who went to school with my father had equal aptitude. Indeed, my uncle, being of a free and easy nature, and much unlike my father, has confessed to me and to his children, that he would oft wish himself elsewhere when in school, and dream of ball games, flying kites, and all such sports. But gazing out the window he would read the dread words there inscribed – AUT DOCE AUT DISCE AUT DISCEDE, which, being translated, warned 'either teach, or learn, or leave', and so sent his wandering eyes back to his books.

A stern warning, sir, but I think it apt. I teach no Latin here, but my children know they must apply themselves or go to harder tasks, and tedious labour. Their parents can but ill afford the few pence they pay me and, to tell truth, there are some who have not paid, but how can I turn their little ones away? Would you do it? I have not the heart to deny them the knowledge which is mine to give. I but wish it were more.

When they leave here they must work, and work hard. There are some who spare the labour of childish hands but grudgingly, being poor, and without hired labour. They would have results, sir, or else their schooldays are ended. The children, knowing this, are apt to work with a will, and look upon school as like to a holiday.

You see how I must live, being a poor man's widow. It is hard to come to this, after a life of much hardship, and sorrow also. I would not take charity, could I live decently without it, and have ever tried to survive by my own industry. But those who enter the world with nothing are like to die so, for all their toil. I have found this out, in a long life amongst the humble. Though a great man's daughter, I have sunk in the world, as a daughter must, not being heir to his learning, and having no dowry to recommend me. If we cannot rise by matrimony we are like to fall, having no other way.

I was married to a decent man, ever industrious. But times were hard, and now I must fend for myself. There was no surfeit to be put by, such as my father was heir to from his father. I would not have you think me bitter, for I have long since forgiven him his harshness to me, and to my sisters. I could do no less, it being our Christian duty so to do, and besides, I have much pride in him. But if the truth must be told, he got more from his father, to help him in the world, than ever we got from him.

There's a knocking at the door - what can it be? The child who works for me is deaf, I fear, and will

11

not go to answer. You must excuse me. I will return directly.

I cannot think who it should be at this hour. It is almost dusk. Few hawkers come so late and, besides, would call. Why, young Barnaby, what brings you here at this time – have you not had your fill of lessons? Your mother sent you, and with this? Bring it in. She is most kind.

This is young Barnaby, sir, one of my pupils, and amongst the brightest that I have coming to me. His mother keeps a shop, and sends this mutton pie, but freshly baked, for me. Will you not bow to this fine gentleman? I would not have him think I teach you no manners.

Truly, sir, I could wish his father had the means for it, to keep him at his studies, if a place could be found for him, to teach him more than I know. It grieves me to think such lively wits should not be led to higher things, but waste themselves.

He likes to read, sir, and has long since exhausted my little store of books. Can memorize a poem so speedily, word perfect, it would astonish you. And so I think he does it from love, and not from duty. And will ask such questions as I have no answer to, being but an unschooled woman, without benefit of university.

Why, he will do his sums, and learn by rote so speedily, he lacks diversion. And so he will plague me with questions – why do the stars shine? And what brings winter? What makes the rain to fall, and whence comes it? I am hard put to it, to satisfy him.

But I fear it will all go to waste, his parents being poor. Westminster will not take a mutton pie for their fees, nor St Paul's neither. Could you not use your influence, sir, to get him a place gratis? He is a good child, as well as gifted, and will repay your trouble. Think you do it for my father's sake, if not for his, the child being unknown to you. Who knows, he may be another such, and do his country service which shall last unto the end of time.

Now, Barnaby, let the gentleman hear the poem you learnt but yesterday. Do not stand abashed, for I know you can speak boldly enough. This fine gentleman knows more of poesie than you and I together, and it will please him mightily to hear one so young recite so prettily.

Come now, let us have it then. 'How doth the little busy bee' . . . He has it by heart, sir, I assure you, and the rest of Dr Watts also. I have had the children learn one poem each week, as the author recommends. It is indeed an easy way for them to imbibe great truths simply, and get some pleasure by it, as well as virtue. Come, child, what of the last verse then? Has the sun addled your brain this day? 'In books, or work, or healthful play' . . . how does it go on? 'Let my first years be past' . . . now you have it. I thought you would shame me, that are my prize pupil. It is the rhyme that sticks in the memory, though my father was much against it, and despised it so. That 'past' should rhyme with 'last' is a great help to the infant mind – you see how it tripped from his tongue with but a little prompting.

You may go, child. And thank your mother most heartily for the pie. I shall have it for my supper. And this gentleman also, if he will stay to sup with me. I am sure it will be to our liking.

He is a good child, and has quite won my heart with his diligence. Had he more schooling than I can give, he would surely profit from it. Not that I would have him so learned as my father, and the classics, I believe, are now but little thought of. Mr Clarke, my late husband, was wont to say that such learning had no uses but to make the poor think themselves more ignorant than in truth they were, and thus keep them humble. Which was why both law and Holy Writ had long been in the Latin tongue, so that the common sort might not know for themselves either truth or justice, but have it told to them by those who had been to school and university, this being a privilege of those who ruled us.

But we can all read the Bible now, and such classics as my father was wont to study, why, they are turned into English, so our fine young ladies, that now have so much leisure, may read them. And in rhyming couplets too, to ease the task. No, sir, there is more to be got from school than Latin grammar, and the child must earn a livelihood, when all is said and done.

Will you take supper with me, sir? His mother bakes a fine pie, and there is a little ale in the scullery, to keep it cool. I know it is but humble fare, but I think you will find the pie to your liking. She does a good trade, and works hard, his father being often without work, as much from vagaries of fashion and demand, as from uncertain health. I know how it is, being a weaver's widow. I have seen her weep, not for herself, being weary, but for her children, born to a world which holds nothing for them but fruitless toil, and little hope of better things to come.

To send her child to me, it is an act of faith. And it costs her dear, in losing of his labour. I fear, being quite untaught, illiterate, she thinks too highly of me, of the learning I can give him. This is a grief to me, sir, I confess it. I can scarce look in her eyes, for the hope I see in them. A kind of pleading, like unto a prayer, that I would not betray. You know the look a favourite dog will give you, his head upon your knee? She has that air about her when she brings her boy, or comes to fetch him, and asks me how he does. I tell her, truthfully, he is a clever child, and she looks proud, and smiles, and seems less weary, and thanks me from her heart.

She has little enough to thank me for, did she but know it. If none will help him he must be self-taught, for that which I can teach him will not do, when all is said and done. I think there is a rumour in this neighbourhood, and his mother heard it, that my father was a famous man, the most learned in all Christendom! I would he had made me his heir, though but a woman, not for myself, having no wish to be mocked as a learned lady, but to fulfil their expectation, and feed their children's minds, so their bellies be full in after years.

I think on this now, sir, that did not think on it in my youth. How should our children learn, if their mothers cannot read? For we must all be mothers, and help our children prosper in the world. I would not have any son of mine made stupid by too much learning. I beg your pardon, sir, I mean no offence. But, more than the rudiments of reading and arithmetic, this can be a source of both pleasure and profit in later life, and so should be taught more widely, not merely to the rich.

And so, sir, I would have you think on young Barnaby, using your good offices in his favour. It would give me much joy, and his mother also. You are leaving, sir, and will not partake of the pie? I think the coffee house beckons, with more amusing fare than I can offer. No, no, I am not offended. I take it kindly that gentlemen from the great world should think fit to call on me.

Two

THINK YOU I never quarrelled with your father whilst he lived, or thought to go from him, our dispute being yet fresh? Come, child, this is mere foolishness, and well you know it. As we make our bed, so we must lie, and many a woman has greater cause to rue her wedding day than ever you have had. Come, sit by me, and wipe your eyes. I fear you should be abed, and that's the cause of it. No woman in my day would get up so soon. You have told me oft enough there is no help for it, but we should manage well enough a few days more. Think you I came to live under your roof to be a burden merely? I will do what I can, as long as may be.

It is your grief that speaks, else you would not take on so for a trifle. I know this, having lost so many babes in my time. A woman's humour is strange enough at these times, but when the cause is lost, and buried in the churchyard, it can unhinge us quite. I know whereof I speak, daughter, and so, by now, should you, being no stranger to such grief.

Your hands are cold, my dear, and I like not your pallor. Could we not have a fire in this room? The price of coal is high this winter, but I fear for you. Mr Foster would not begrudge it, since you are but lately risen from childbed. Do not protest, I know him to be tender of your welfare, and we can be sparing of other things. I will go cold to bed, and supperless too, if need be. It matters little to me, being old. And perhaps there will be more work this winter. Your brother seems sure of it.

I hope it may be so, else he will be lodging here, unwed, for all his life. I would see him with a good wife before I die, to be a comfort to him. I think the Widow Cutler looks kindly on him, and has her own shop, and lodgings with it, but she is old, and would bear him no children. What think you? That wedlock is no comfort, and a snare?

Come, child, what else would you have in this life? You are peevish, else you would not speak so. Mr Foster is a good man, though he has his faults, as all men do. In marriage we must endeavour to love a man for his defects, it being easy enough to be fond of his virtues. You smile, daughter, and I am right glad of it. Let us have no more speaking of divorce in this family, for it has brought scandal enough, and besmirched my father's name. Besides, divorcing is but for men, and an adulterer's charter, a woman being without independent means. And so she would end a burden on the parish, like any poor soul with child and out of wedlock.

But I hear a knocking at the door. Sit still, and I will answer. I think it must be the professor come to call, from Gresham College. What hour is it? I had quite forgot the time. Is my cap set neatly? It must be him, for his servant carries books, no doubt to try me, stamping his feet from cold. His face quite red with it, and the breath rising from them like steam from a kettle. I am coming, sir.

And no fire neither. I beg your pardon, sir. We keep the hearth unlit during daylight hours, the price of coals being so high. This is my daughter,

Mrs Foster. If you will send your servant to the kitchen, she will see he gets something to warm him.

Oh no, sir, I do not complain. The public has been very generous in coming to my assistance. I would I might even now live by my own industry. Until lately I kept a school at Moorfields, but now my eyesight begins to fail. I am fortunate to have a child yet living, though I would not be a burden to her. She is not well, having but lately risen from childbed, but there is no speaking to her, she will not rest as she should.

I see you have brought books to try me. Greek is it, or Latin? Though my eyes grow dim, I can recite you long passages without looking at the page, having read them out loud so frequently. Would you have Ovid, or Virgil? *Arma virumque cano*, and so forth. There was a gentleman came but lately, did try me on Euripides. I think he could scarce credit what he heard, his eyes as wide as though I had been an automaton, and not a living woman. And so I was, if the truth be told, being used as such, but for my eyes. I know not what I read, and recite but parrot fashion.

Elizabeth, is the servant thawed out in the kitchen? Think on it, the professor has been to Nantwich, and seen my stepmother! She must be a great age now, surely, for she was no spring chicken when she wed my father, being all of twenty-four years old, and hard put to it to find a husband, had he not been blind. No, sir, there has been no correspondence between us for many years, there being so little liking when my father lived. For she was a very termagant, and I had nothing from her but scolding.

To think she yet lives. And has she all her faculties

19

still? I warrant her tongue is as sharp as ever, if she can wag it. She must be wellnigh eighty years old, nay, more, for I was ten when she married my father, and now I am well past my allotted span of three score and ten. They do say nuns live to a great age, and she never bore children. He had more need of a housekeeper than aught else, I think, when he took her to wife. For the price of loving is oft an early death, and both my mother and his second wife did die in childbed.

It was told me some years past that she is now become God-fearing, and a pillar of the Baptist ministry. I am glad of it, for her soul's sake. For if she would see my father in the next life, she has much need of penitence in this. Such double dealing, and a forked tongue, giving him honeyed words and us but vinegar. I have heard she is become a woman of property, from what my father left her. But still the miser, and lives so frugally, the neighbours speak of Mrs Milton's feast, meaning enough but no more. Well, she has feathered her nest, that being her purpose. That like a cuckoo sought to push us out, though not yet hatched and fledged.

It is a shrewd woman marries an old man, with no appetite but for tasty stews and apple pie. I never said she was not shrewd, though a shrew with it. She knew what she was about, when her cousin put her in the way of it. He was doctor to my father, and much in his confidence. And if she would tame us, being thought unruly, she had done better to have sought to do it by loving kindness, and not harsh words.

Pardon me for speaking thus. Christian duty bids us honour our father and mother, and, though I have long since forgiven my dear father for his harshness, she was not my mother. Had she sought to be such, I would have loved her. For truly, I had need of it.

My mother died bringing me into the world, and so I never knew her. It is a hard thing to be thus deprived. A child, being young, must needs have a parent who loves it for itself, a father being remote and stern, loving us rather for our virtues. And I think our father did mislike us, not for our lack of them, but for being our mother's daughters, and this we could not mend.

I would not speak of this, sir, for it pains me. Though I did not know her, she bore me in her womb, and I do not believe her to have been a sinful woman. Foolish perhaps, and worthy of our pity, but no more. She gave her life for mine, and for this I honour her and love her in my heart. Would I might have loved her in her life, I might have looked back to my youth with happier heart, and fonder memories. I honour my father, for he did great things in the world. But no man yet died giving birth to his child, and for this I must love her, for all her frailty.

Daughter, I would not have you think I deem it right that a young wife should leave her husband after but a few weeks of wedlock, visiting her parents, and refusing to return when sent for. She knows whereof I speak, sir, it is between us. I believe matrimony to be a sacred bond, and hope my children will ever think likewise. We are decent people, who live decently, and know our duty. But those were turbulent times, a civil war beginning, and travel hazardous. I have heard my grandam say the roads were perilous betwixt Forest Hill and London, so she and Mr Powell would not have their daughter set forth.

There are two sides to every coin, sir, and the fault was not all with my mother. Though I know it is a wife's duty to obey her husband, she but obeyed her father in marrying a man she scarcely knew, except her father, being in his debt, would have him for his son-in-law to buy him off. So now she but obeyed in failing to return to one thought renegade, and like to lose his head, the war once won.

Besides, I have heard my grandam say her daughter was sent away, my father not liking her conversation, and thinking he had made an ill bargain, the dowry being unpaid, and the girl having nothing but foolishness in her young head, which had captured him with fresh looks and youthful prettiness. And so he thought her an unfit companion for his gravity and serious ambition.

You find some credence in this version of the event, having studied his pamphlets on divorce? I am glad to hear it, sir, for I think my poor mother has been much maligned in this regard. I have ever found it strange, that he should think a meet and happy conversation to be the chief end of matrimony, and yet deny girl children equal education with their brothers. Surely it is a foolish hope that we should converse wisely, if we are kept ignorant? Besides, had he no chance to talk with her before he was betrothed, and so find out if they were like to suit? He married in haste, sir. Indeed, we know this to be so, for he rode out a bachelor to collect a debt, and rode back wedded, a thing not be expected in a man of older years and studious habits, and left his kin astounded.

My father was wont to put upon others a frailty he would not own. I have seen this in him, and have ever thought it his chiefest fault. I must speak frankly, sir. You have not come to the poor streets of Spitalfields to hear me utter falsehoods. If he chose his bride unwisely, was this her fault? He was twice her age and, as the world judges, he had twice her wisdom, and so I think him doubly culpable for any error. He knew this, sir, and so his loathing for her was but doubled.

If he did marry in haste, he had much leisure to repent, they being parted till the war was wellnigh ended. But though many do repent them, they are not minded to write pamphlets on divorce, and so bring scandal on their heads. It is not Christian, sir, and though he might twist and turn the Bible to his ends, and say it meant by this some other thing, being ill translated or interpreted, it would not do. If he was vilified for writing so, I think, sir, he did bring it on himself, for seeking to use women like discarded garments, to be thrown out at pleasure.

The shock nigh killed me – thus my grandam. She was no reading woman but, the scandal being so great, reports of it had reached the countryside. The minister spoke against it in church, to our eternal shame, as she recalled it. My poor dear daughter, so I told your mother, God rest her blessed soul, first throws you out of doors, and now would cast you off entirely, leaving you quite dishonoured, neither maid nor widow nor an honourable wife. For what man will look upon another's leavings, and not despise it? I fear this law which he would have to favour lawless men, licentious libertines, now that these godless renegades have won the war, may yet find favour.

So she advised my hapless mother, who was wont to obey her parents in all things. Though a wife in name, she was yet a child, and childlike. I had this also from our old servant, who was fond of her, and thought her hardly used. She would speak of her as chattering like a magpie, gay as a country thrush that sang about her work, until she heard her master coming out the study, or his voice upon the stair, when she would blench and fall silent. As though she had forgot her married state and liked not to remember, fearing his harshness and authority.

Though I knew her not, I think I know her as I do myself, for I was much in the same case as his daughter. And she might have been his daughter, being so young. You can have no notion, Elizabeth, how it is to live in such a house. Mr Clarke, my late husband and her father, was also my senior by many years but, being no scholar and a simple man, a mere mechanical, a weaver like my son and son-in-law, did not think himself my better, and despised not my understanding. What he read, I could read also, and all things were freely discussed between us. You think yourself ill used upon occasion, daughter, but it is much the same betwixt you and Mr Foster. Though you may disagree from time to time, you have your say, and say it loudly, and after make it up and are friends once more. Think yourself fortunate, and make your peace with him.

I beg your pardon, sir, we speak of private matters. I know it is now the custom that women of the better sort should have some cultivation, to make them fit companions for their husbands, and able to converse in drawing rooms. It was not so in my youth, nor in my mother's time. We were bred for household tasks, hard labour and child-bearing. And if we could read it was but to know our Bible.

I have some pity for my mother's case, whatever the truth of it. She knew her duty, but being so

24

long a daughter and but newly wedded, she was accustomed rather to obey her parents than her husband. And it is a hard thing to be married to a creditor who comes knocking at the door, so as to fob him off. Like so much chattel. I had no dowry, sir, and married a poor man, but I ever knew he took me for myself.

And so, being married on account of an old debt, she incurred but a new and greater in the marrying, her dowry being unpaid. He never forgave it, sir, and oft did speak of it. Let them have their mother's dowry, so he would say in his last years, we being her daughters, and as much unloved, and all the rest to Betty. And so he kept her sweet, his dearest Betty, who pandered to his whims, so she might be a widow who lived at ease. As she now does.

Sir, you are cold. The fire must be lit, I think. Besides, it grows dark, and it will spare us a candle. The night draws in so fast. We shall have snow before morning, the clouds hanging so low. This early dusk speaks of it. I would not have you deem us inhospitable, though we are poor. I am cold myself, and I see how you rub your fingers.

Do not fret, Elizabeth. You are not yet well. I will not have you penny-pinching, and catch your death from it. She is married to a good man, sir, who is as anxious in her behalf as I am. But work has been hard to get this winter, and ill paid. The rent must be found, and so he will preach thrift and stern accounting more than needful. To fall sick from parsimony is no good housekeeping, and I think he would not bury his wife for a few coals.

Had he ridden out himself to fetch her from Forest Hill, it might have been otherwise. I speak now of my father. For if there was some vexation between them, she leaving London so soon after their mar-

riage, and being not back at Michaelmas as promised, she must have thought it high-handed in him
to send a messenger to fetch her home, and not
ride out himself. Such feeling as she might have
had for him, if not quite nipped in the bud by earlier
coldness, must now have been extinguished. Is it
any wonder her parents sent his messenger away,
and did it curtly? Is this the way to woo an errant
wife, if so she was? And if the previous fault was
all upon his side, as my grandmother would ever
have it, he but compounded it.

Though a wife be got much like a mare at market,
yet must she be wooed for easy riding, with coaxing
and tender words. And I doubt not my grandfather,
thinking at the first to have disarmed his creditor
by making him a son-in-law, had changed his mind
since then, the war once started and my father being
of the opposing faction. Why, had the king been
victorious, as they both thought and hoped, their
daughter had been but a youthful widow to the
gallows. Had they been star-crossed lovers, and as
much besotted as Romeo and Juliet, their path had
not been easy. And my father was no Romeo. They
were, as our old servant would have it, as ill-paired
as ox and mare in one yoke.

And yet, sir, as we make our bed, so we must
lie. I fear my father, though old in years when he
married, was but a virgin in the ways of the world,
having seen but little of it, his eyes being ever on
ancient texts, and he scarce leaving his study. As
my uncle would have it, my father was as like to
see the promised dowry of a thousand pounds, and
the loan with interest added, for which he first rode
out to Oxfordshire, as he was to see the sun rise in
the west and gold coins grow on trees. For the
Powells' estate had long since been mortgaged to

the hilt, from easy living and careless ways, and such a man will promise his bed for the morrow so he can but sleep easy tonight.

A like foolishness, coming from too much study, beguiled him when he took my mother to wife so hastily. As you say, he hints of it in writing of divorce – can you recall the words? I would have my daughter hear them. Who have spent their youth chastely, haste too eagerly to light the nuptial torch? And much in the same wise? I have heard him speak so in later years, how bestial necessity will make a man blind, till he wake to bondage with an unfit wife. Indeed, I have heard him say he was glad he had lost his eyes when he took his dear Katharine to wife, since, not being ensnared by her looks, he heard but her conversation and so chose wisely. And though he would not have a young man sow wild oats, this being contrary to virtue, it were better he went to the stews than to find himself chained to a stinking carcass in the marriage bed.

I blush to speak so, sir, but my father did not mince his words upon occasion, as you must know, having read his works. His hate being aroused, he could find more common words of loathing, more abuse, than is thought fit in genteel society, and was not shy to use them. I have been the target, and know whereof I speak. All those not of his opinion, the lower sort, unschooled and ignorant, and females also, great ladies excepted, could rouse his scorn. Like Jove from up on high he cast his thunder on a despised rabble down below. This was the price of his sublimity, as this age now calls it.

Ideals can make us harsh, is it not so? We have all had dreams when young, and had to wake to the real world, and make our peace with it as best we could. So I tell my daughter here, when she is troubled. None had dreams more fanciful, more glowing, than my father. I think you know this, sir, being familiar with his poetry. Yet none had lived as little in the common world, being bookish in his habits. It made him cruel to such lesser mortals as lived in it, and disappointed him. I know this, having been the object of his sarcasm.

Well, there is more to marriage than four bare legs in the bed, as our old servant was wont to warn us in our youth. My sister Mary being apt to speak of wedlock as the means whereby she would escape from out our father's house, and from his tyranny. For my poor sister, bearing our mother's name, and most like to her in feature, was most his enemy, and early grew rebellious. She was oft abused for being too like our mother, having her defects of nature, so he said, and a pert and ready tongue. Such words but made her more unruly. She said she would sooner be like our mother, who was loving and kind, as she remembered her, than like unto her father, being neither. And so their war continued.

It is a hard thing, when the sins of our parents are visited upon us. He had no liking for us, for our mother's sake, though we had no part in the choosing. It was you chose my mother, not I, so my sister would retort. Taking dictation at his behest had given her some edge of learning, despite her sex, and his contempt. God gave us free will, you tell us, to choose for better or for worse, and if you chose for worse, then more fool you. I am not to blame, for Christ died on the Cross so that the sins of the fathers, aye, and of our mothers, first and last, should not be visited upon us. And so I stand absolved.

She had been wiser to have held her tongue, for there was too much truth in her words not to rankle, and to think himself in error was not to my father's liking. Children and fools tell the truth, lacking the wisdom to stay silent before those who rule them. A silent cunning had served her better, and to call him fool was but blowing on the coals so the sparks flew in her face.

And then there was no end to hearing of my mother's unpaid dowry, as though we had been to blame in this likewise. They shall have their mother's dowry, he would say, the rest going to Betty. I doubt not my mother heard him speak of it also, this being her father's default. For such debts as Mr Powell had had before the war were now made desperate, the king's side losing. I have heard my grandam speak of this time, how all was lost, their property being sequestrated. I never thought to live to see the day, she'd say, the shame of it! For the remembrance of it much distressed her in old age. And all for being on the side of rightful monarchy! My husband in poor health, and eleven sons and daughters in the house who must be fed and clothed, the sons made gentlemen, the daughters married! If I have got grey hairs I got them then – for she would boast about her looks when young, how many courted her before she married Mr Powell.

So it was, the Powell fortunes being at their lowest ebb, my father and his bride were reconciled. My grandam would tell us of it with tears in her eyes, though smiling also. Tears for her daughter, long since laid to rest, smiles for us, her offspring, of whom she was most fond. The old, I think, are thus. Dwell in the past and weep for it too readily. I feel it in myself.

As she told it – Mary, so I spoke to your dear mother, we must get us to London. You must fall upon your knees and beg his pardon. I care not whose fault it was, or who spoke first in anger, this is no time for niceties. The war is lost, and we are ruined utterly. I never thought our state would come to this, but it is so. You are Mrs Milton, and must take your rightful place within his home. I have four other daughters who must be got husbands, and you have one already. He loved you once, and will do so again, if you are sweet with him, and do his bidding. I fear we must act speedily, else, being in the victor's camp, his notions on divorce may be made law, and then you are undone. Who will have you then, being cast off by him? It will not help you, the fault being his, or not, it is all one. Being damaged goods, you may sing heigh-ho for a husband.

We must all live in the real world at last, for all our dreams. Is it not so, daughter? Men and women both must do so, if they would live together, and be a help unto each other. I think my mother, in the years between, had grown from scarce more than a child into a woman, and so more sensible. She did her parents' bidding, surprised my father in a neighbour's house, where he was wont to call, and fell upon her knees.

She sought forgiveness, sir, from dire necessity, and he forgave her, as a Christian should. I know not who was most to blame for their parting, but I think my father, being he who forgave, the righteous victor in this civil war, ignored such errors as must fall to him, and so he made her suffer. Her life with him was but one long repentance. I have heard our servant call it so, and I believe her.

To forgive is not enough. He should have loved

her, sir, and raised her up, for to do less is not forgiveness but a mere semblance of it. And so it proved in the event, he despising us for her remembered faults. A woman's lot in wedlock is not easy. I know this, having brought ten children into the world, and losing seven in infancy. But Mr Clarke was ever tender of me, and sought my welfare as he sought his own. My daughter here must say the same of Mr Foster. But my mother, sir, she had but condonation from her husband, and little else. Seven years of wedlock followed from their re-uniting, she dying at my birth, the fourth childbed she endured.

I have much pity for her. For childhood has an end, and we escape from out our father's house into the world, and look to this in youth. But wedlock has no end except in death, and this most likely, being brought to bed. And, though we pray to God in such extremity, it is our husband's fondness gives us comfort here below, our time drawing nigh. It is a deed of love that we must do, in much pain and fear. But where such love is lacking, to lift us up, then 'tis scarce to be endured.

Where are you going, daughter? I will not have you catch your death out of doors. I think, sir, it distresses her to hear us speak of childbed, being scarce out of it, and the child not living. I wish I might have bit off my tongue, rather than speak so. She should be in her bed, but will not rest, seeking rather to find distraction in going about her work. You saw her pallor. Grief has her in its grip. She has wept much this past month, and refused nourishment. I would I knew how to counsel her and give her comfort, but her ears are sealed at present and will not hear. Say too much, and she will but quarrel with those nearest to her.

Is it snowing? I have seen her venture out of doors this past week, and it so cold. I think we shall have snow before nightfall. The clouds look as though they would touch the rooftops. She should be in her bed. Though poor, we are not yet so poor that it should come to this. Did you know, my eldest sister died in childbed likewise, as did our mother? Though born a cripple she yet found a husband, for she was beautiful, a gentle soul who never gainsaid any man. Being defective in her speech, and not able to read aloud with fluency, for she would stammer, she was spared my father's rigours. And she never learnt to write. But I fear she was not apt for wedlock either, her body being infirm. And so her first child brought her to her death, and was buried with her.

It grieved me much to hear of it. I lived in Ireland then, with Mr Clarke. I think, sir, such a loss is doubly felt when we are far off. I have but lately lost my other son, Caleb, who went to live in India many years since. I wish I might have seen him once more, before he died, and spoken with him. But I have seen his son, young Abraham, who came to England from Madras but a few years ago. He looked so like his father when he left these shores, so youthful, strong, and upright in his bearing, I thought that time had played a trick on me, and here he stood, my Caleb, as he was when last I saw him, on the verge of manhood. Though he bears my husband's name – for Mr Clarke was christened Abraham – I saw in him my Caleb come again. He had his eyes, his features, though a little less in height. I wellnigh wept for joy on seeing him. Being well-mannered, he was respectful, but yet I was a stranger to him, though he was not to me, or so I fancied. Doubtless he thought me strange, to be so fond.

Alas, sir, I was deceived, since vanished time can never come again. For it was while young Abraham was here in England, the poor boy heard his father was deceased, and so he must return immediately. But though I mourned for him, I took some comfort in his son, being so like him. Caleb is dead, but something of him yet lives on.

The looms will soon be idle. The work is too poorly paid, this winter, to continue by candlelight. Urban will be back directly, now the light is going. He is a weaver also, and lodges with us here, working elsewhere in Spitalfields, in a French workshop. Such fine silks they weave, their finishings a wonder, yet are many reduced to penury, and find it hard as we do. He is now my sole surviving son, but in good health. I would he might marry before I die, and his wife bear him a son with his features. It would give me joy. But I think he will not.

He has a little of my father in him. About the eyebrows and the forehead. You will see it, if he comes. I fear he is not a reading man, for Mr Clarke put him to work at ten years old. He reads but little, and never willingly. And yet, I think, he most nearly resembles him.

Would you not say so, daughter? That Urban has some look about him of my father? I know you never knew him, but you have seen his portrait. True, he resembles me in feature, more than you do. She is like her father. Mr Addison was pleased to say: Madam, you need no other voucher – your face is a sufficient testimonial whose daughter you are. He was most kind, and was most active in my behalf until his death. It grieved me much to hear of it.

You are leaving us, sir? Will you not wait for my son? But you may see him as you walk down Pelham Street, fair-haired and small of build. Perhaps you are wise to leave before nightfall, for there are pickpockets hereabouts, and ruffians prowl the streets. I trust your servant is a brave fellow. But I see you are armed. You do well to go so, the streets being not safe for decent people now. Do not forget your books.

Three

How quickly it grows dark, and the mending still undone. But I would not shame us by having him see our poor bits and tatters, such a fine gentleman. Did you not think him a fine gentleman? Saw you his buttons? I never saw such in all my life, and he but a commoner, and come from trade, so I surmise. But folk are grown so fine these days, and think it no sin to wear silk and lace a-plenty, and their wives know nothing of patching and mending, but are idle the whole day long, and must have a maid to dress them.

Such wealth, where it comes from I know not, but I would a little might come to those who must labour all the hours God sends, and yet find little comfort. Saw you his buttons? I think the cost would keep us all in good wool cloth this winter. And yet he was courteous, for all his finery, and sought to turn a blind eye to the poor rooms in which we live. Did you remark it, when he left the house, how his eye scarce lingered long enough to take in walls or floor, or rotten plaster? Such is the nature of civility, that would have us all one before God.

What's that you say? You would rather he saw truly, for turning a blind eye will not mend matters? What should he do, daughter, become a martyr to

35

philanthropy? Or cease to walk abroad, for fear of seeing what he cannot mend? Besides, he came not empty-handed, as you will see if you do look upon the mantel, or so I think. He would not have me see him put the money thither, yet I saw well enough. But I can play the lady likewise, having been brought up civilly, and so played his little game as he would have me play it, affecting to see nothing.

How much is it – five whole guineas? You see, I have done better with my clacking tongue than Mr Foster at his clacking loom this day. Do not weep, daughter. 'Tis weariness that weeps in you, and I but spoke in jest. Were it not for my father, I could no more earn such wealth by idle chatter than pluck the sun from out the sky to give you warmth. You know this well enough. 'Tis my father they honour thus, and shame, such as they feel at my distress, is only as his daughter. Else they would let me languish.

Five whole guineas! Now we have money, you must get more help. I insist upon it. For you are up too soon, and so your health will suffer. Do not argue with me, I know whereof I speak. The servant you have now will not suffice. Why, she is but half a servant, being so young. Though she does what she can, poor thing, and costs but little.

And then you must have good nourishment to cheer your spirits. What would you say to a fat capon, and some Lisbon wine? Melancholy after childbirth is a fearful thing, and you are very low. Look up, daughter, and dry your eyes. Though you have lost this babe, you yet have little Liza, to be a comfort to you. I know how it is, my dear – have I not buried seven in infancy? But yet we must trust in the Lord, believing in Him. In sorrow shalt thou bring forth children, so the good Book says, and truly, it is so.

Would I were a man, that labours mightily to bring forth verses in the comfort of his study, without the spilling of a little drop of blood, and pangs but of the spirit! So they grow old, and prosper. Men may seek to change the world, but change not this, and we must suffer it as best we may.

He will come again, he says, and bring another such gentleman, who would hear me speak of bygone times. So we shall have coals this winter. Why, it begins to snow in earnest, did I not say it would? And Urban not yet home. Have no fear, daughter, we shall eat this winter, though the work is scarce, and but poorly paid. Such visitors continuing, it will save us from destitution. And though I would rather some other way could be found to keep us from want, beggars cannot be choosers, and we must be thankful for such charity.

He said I looked much like him. Poor father, it would not please him to hear it. My face has been my fortune, more so now than in my youth. What a topsyturvy world it is, to be sure, that I should earn sovereigns with my wrinkles and white hair! I see you smile at last, and I am glad of it. We must all laugh a little at how the world goes, for crying will not mend it. And thank your stars I am my father's daughter, else might we starve and no one care a jot. As many do this night, born as they were of Master Nobody or common Jack.

To be sure, child, I would rather live out my days in comfort by my own industry. Who would not, pray? I have said as much, in begging for support. Yet what profits it to fulminate in such a manner? You may spare your breath, it will change nothing. We must be thankful for their notice, that they come with their notebooks to question me, till I scarce know if I be in this age or the last. Pride is a luxury for those that can afford shoe leather, and fine buttons to their coats. Such work as we do with our hands, though skilled, will not spare us the humiliation of begging when we are old.

I fear 'tis so, daughter, though you work all the hours God sends, and your little one also, once she is old enough to wind spools and help in the shop. I fear 'tis so, for all our proud talk of making our own way, and thrift and industry. Have I not heard your father speak thus, in our early days? And yet his widow has but a widow's mite. We would be master of our own workshop, thinking thereby to rule our fate, to sink or swim as we be prudent or profligate, work hard or lie abed. But there are forces quite beyond our knowing, to wreck the humblest hopes, like gales and storms at sea which blow small skiffs to shipwreck. I have seen it in my time, child, and know whereof I speak. Your father was no idler, nor I neither, and yet we left you nothing but a poor widow, to sit a burden at your hearth. For which I am right sorry.

So, she lives at Nantwich yet, and is prosperous. That is the way to widowhood. Marry an old man and keep his goods, not bury seven infants in the graveyard. There is but little profit to be got from that, and you survive. Forgive me, daughter. It slipped from me, I know not why. I did not mean to pain you by speaking of such matters. But she is living proof, if proof were needed, that 'tis a lie, that industry and thrift go well rewarded and idleness does not. We are but a nation of hypocrites, I fear, to have thought thus. We were misled, that thought so in my youth – that we are free to rise and free to fall, and need not charity, but only virtue.

It is not so. Those who have a modicum of comfort think themselves virtuous, that are but fortunate, and should thank God for it, and show a little pity for their neighbours that are not so. And yet they hold themselves accountable for their good fortune, and others for the misery they suffer. I fear it is so, daughter. I have heard sermons enough in my time, both in the chapel and out of it.

Had we gone to the New World and not to Ireland, who knows, it might have been another story. They say the life is hard, yet do many prosper there. But for the troubles in King James's time, we had lived out our days in some comfort. And then the Frenchmen come to take our business, and watered silk suddenly all the fashion, so plain silk would not do. Who could have foretold such sudden dislocations? We think ourselves free, and take much pride in owning our own loom, or even two, in being a small master rather than a servant, and yet we are the slaves of chance and fashion. The factor takes the fat, and leaves but little lean for us to thrive on. We but labour for him, when all is said and done. He farms out work and takes the richest harvest.

So much for independence, child. I have had my fill of it, these fifty years. The market is a jungle, and beasts of prey do flourish there. The honest man goes under, like as not.

Five whole guineas! And all for a little gossip. You shall have a wool cloak, daughter, and new shoes to wear on Sunday. And I would have you light a candle to mend by, to spare your eyes. For none will pay such as us when we have lost our sight. You see how it is with me, else I might be

39

teaching school even now. For he would have me up at all hours of the day and night. Dark or light, 'twas all one to him, having no sight. And ever had been, so our old servant said, which was the ruin of his eyes in earlier years. Mine too, I think, for I have had to wear spectacles since eighteen years of age, and from what other cause, I know not.

Such a fine gentleman! Though he use his eyes, he will do so to some purpose, and so he walks abroad with silver buckles on his shoes, and when he reads 'tis not by rushlight, nay, nor tallow neither. I have seen how it is, daughter, those who have thoughts in their heads, and have been to the university, and can read in ancient books and know whereof they read, the world sees them well fed. They do not walk the streets, crying 'for charity'.

Did you not see how easily he parted with his coin just now? And all for a little learning, for going to school, and afterwards to college. 'Tis an investment, like any other, and brings more dividends than buying of a loom will ever do. My grandfather knew what he did, in sending of his sons to Cambridge. For he was but of humble stock, you know, his father being a yeoman. As for stitching and making lace, as I was taught to do, to have me out of doors, 'tis but a certain path to poverty, and industry will not help us. For doing more is doing it for less, as like as not, for what is plentiful is cheap, and there are many willing hands, with starving bellies, who would do the work, and fewer wealthy ladies who will buy.

Let us throw this stocking out, daughter. Why, it is more full of holes than a colander. It will do for a dishclout, but it is not worth the mending. You must have new stockings, if there are more in such a parlous state. Thread this needle for me, for the eye escapes me, and I will do Urban's shirt. Still not home, and the snow falling so thickly, the window is nigh on obscured. Perhaps the Frenchman has more work this night, and keeps him longer. Or he has gone to call upon the widow. What think you?

I hope it is work that keeps him. Besides, I think her too old for him. That he is not such a great catch, I know this, daughter. But she might do worse, I think, being past thirty. Such women, having the means, are apt to look kindly on a youthful bachelor, poverty being of less account in their eyes.

I wish he might have had more schooling in his youth, and so gone further. You say he has no aptitude for scholarship. Think you the sons of gentlemen have aptitude? Why, they must have Latin whipped into them, and most would rather be elsewhere. And then, if he had got the taste for it in youth, he might have grown more studious.

But there, child, what's the use to think on it? If wishes were horses, beggars would ride. We must be thankful for the little we have, not ask for more. You would have more? Alas, daughter, have you not heard your father speak of this? I know he is dead long since, and you but young, and yet he spoke of it so often, how his hopes were dashed, I thought you would have some recollection of it.

He grew up a weaver's son, but with hope of better times to come, and justice here on earth. You must have heard him speak of it. How, when he was a boy, it was customary to gather round the fire on certain nights of the year, singing and playing instruments, to await His coming, and not be caught in slumber when Christ did come again. Having heard sundry prophecies, that all which had been foretold in the Book of Daniel should soon come to

41

pass. Four beasts, he said, four empires had risen and fallen in the course of time, and now the fifth was come, the kingdom given to the saints forever. This being so, he verily believed, justice must reign, the lowlier sort must prosper like their betters, being better only through Adam's sin in Paradise. For some are rich, some poor, not by God's design but as a punishment for eating of the apple, consequent upon our first parents' crime. So now redemption comes, by time and Christ together.

This was their hope, I heard him speak of it in after years, though bitterly. We were betrayed, he said, our leaders, that did call themselves the saints, were but frail men, with all men's frailties. And yet the Book of Daniel, he believed it still, its Christian message. Four beasts, he said, four empires risen and fallen in the course of time, Babylon, Assyria, Greece and Rome. Likewise the Book of Revelation did describe the slaying of the Beast, foul Papacy, and coming in of saints.

Alas, men are but men withal, and prone to err. You think, because you are young, that you can put the world to rights, had you but the means to do it. But your father in his time, and I in my first youth, saw the world turned topsyturvy, and yet no better for it. Why, my father, at the very hub of it, these great events, who thought it right the king should lose his head, yet was like a king within his household, nay, your aunt would have it, more like to a tyrant. Despised us for our sex, and used his manservant most shabbily, so he did leave his service. I fear that property or privilege will ever rule, and so the poor, and women most of all, have naught to hope for from such overturning, and much to dread. Why, I have seen it for myself, child. Men such as my father, who would have those set above them not their betters, would keep those born below them still inferior, to do their will. To feed their purpose, not our bellies, this is their intent. And so it is that men cry liberty, to which we must submit, slavish to their authority.

You have heard me speak, I think, of the lady Merian, she who took me to Ireland as her companion. She it was who spoke her mind upon such issues, and in such a manner as I had never heard before. I fear my father, had he heard her give of her opinions, would not have thought her a fit person to have the care of me, if he had thought at all in my behalf, or cared by then what did become of me, which he did not. I can speak thus, child, she told me, for no man holds the purse strings over me, which is a rare thing indeed. I only speak as many would, if they were free to do so. Necessity doth put a brank upon our tongues, and many think that which they durst not say. So men do fear the axe, or to be thrown in jail for what they speak out loud. But what can we do, that have a censor at our pillow night and day, and hearth and house a prison of our thoughts, if we would live at ease? A sorry tale, she called it, the late history of overturning. I fear, she said, a partial vision doth affect those who would see most clearly, and trump their views out to the world, of mighty reformation, that cry liberty, liberty, yet keep their household slaves.

But 'twill not be forever thus, she said, for thoughts will out, and a door half opened can be opened wide, by those who follow after. It is ever thus, so she was wont to say, that some would ope the door for their own liberty, but slam it shut before the rest can follow. I am born free, they say, but thou, being born to serve me, that is, born a woman, are not so. Or poor, unprivileged, or what you will.

'Tis for such sophistry they'd keep us out of school, so she would tell me, on the long voyage out to Ireland. Being voluble of her opinions, I think she had need of a companion to hear her thoughts, more than to serve her. For they can argue till the cows come home, having their texts to prove them in the right, and cite at every turn. So your father, to be shot of an unfit wife, could write his pamphlets, quoting sundry texts such as an untutored girl had never heard of, that could scarce write her name. What kind of equity is this, she'd argue, when some are ever in the wrong, not from having sinned, but lack of knowledge to defend themselves, being disbarred from pleading?

'Tis property that rules the world, not justice. So she would say. And we are but as chattel. For those who fought and won, if for a while, during the late troubles, fought but for property and not for justice, else had they been levellers all.

She spoke most frankly, early widowhood making her free to speak so, and gold the oil to her tongue. Each cares but for his own interest, so she said. So it was in the late wars, and this was their undoing. He who is without property hath no interest in the kingdom, if he do merely breathe, so said the men of property who led the fight, and so said Cromwell. So merchants said, merchants must have their rights, but not apprentices. Apprentices, meanwhile, would give unto themselves some say, but not to beggars. And as for women, they came last of all, being but sinful daughters of Eve, mother to all our woes. Or so they tell us, they who would not hold themselves culpable for their own ills.

So each sort had their faction, and few could see

beyond their noses, or find a common purpose. 'Tis a rare master gives his servant leave to speak, and the husband that would hear his wife truly speak her mind is not yet born, I think. So fathers rule their children, men their wives, and those with benefit of learning them without, who labour with their hands. Though 'tis nigh on fifty years since last I saw her, I hear her voice yet, so marked the impression she did make upon my youthful mind.

They were heady days for me, escaped from out my father's house, from tedious workshop labour, to see something of the world, and not yet bound in wedlock. And so they stay with me, glowing like distant jewels. And she most rare of all. For I did grow to love her like the mother that I was born without. And she, that did promise my father she would treat me like a daughter, did so, loving me likewise. And did instruct me as she would a daughter, had she but given birth to one.

Her words are with me yet, though she herself, poor lady, has long since turned to dust. She'd say, that in the kingdom of the blind the one-eyed man is king. And so we stumble blindly on, from mire to mire. Those who see further, looking with both their eyes, and not the I of self that looks asquint, of interest only, they are rare indeed, truly the visionaries of our time, unschooled though they may be, and lacking Latin.

She loved to talk so, and would have me listen. Such a spirit as I found in her was strange to me at first, I scarce durst credit it. Women have tongues, and thoughts, but lack the liberty to speak their minds, or lack the education to speak wisely. What had I heard till then? A scolding housewife merely, and an angry sister, both captives to their state. Likewise our old servant, full of ancient superstitions and old saws. Each spoke some partial truth perhaps, but spoke it partially, blinkered by custom. But my lady loved to talk for talking's sake. Such great eyes she had, would sparkle with the joy of argument when the mood was on her. For she found pleasure in the following of her thoughts.

Aye, pleasure, daughter. Have you not seen a skylark dip and swerve, for joy of being alive? Thus was she, on happy days, and thus her thoughts, when she was in the mood to follow them. That there were darks days also, I grant you, for she would swing from high to low. From thinking that which I had thought unthinkable, being answerable to no one but herself, to God and her own con- science, which gave her leave to speak; to black night fears, dark doubts, and melancholy. Then she would pace the floor, and have me walk with her, and speak of death and that which lay beyond, and tremble in her shift, and fall upon her knees, praying to her Saviour. For, so she said, this mood being upon her, we are in the dark, and that which we think conscience may delude us. What Hell must then await us, being wrong, our conscience but a snare to trap us into error, and we forever judged amongst the damned.

To hear her speak thus put the fear of God in me. Indeed, I know not which did fright me more, to hear her speak of Hell and Judgement Day, of being not elect and therefore cursed, or in her sprightlier mood, her daylight self, when she did scoff at long accepted wisdom and called it foolishness, or worse, hypocrisy. For might is right, she said, this you must know, whether in battle or within the house, beside your hearth. So Plato spake, that justice is no more than the interest of the stronger, and Lucan also. I think she said 'twas Lucan. I was much in awe, having been taught that women were unfit for higher learning, being born to serve, not study. Which, when I spoke of it, did make her laugh most heartily. Books are their arsenal, she said, did I not tell you might is right? So they must keep us out of school, else fear for their dominion.

I hear her still. A tinker may see clearer than a king, yet end in jail for saying what he sees. Thus runs the world, she said, and I fear 'twill ever do so, whether the king be born to his estate or put there by the sword. 'Tis all one. For might is right, and those who have it think themselves elect of God, whether they rule in Westminster or a small house at Bunhill, put there by a pair of breeches and little else besides, like a cock in the farmyard crowing lustily by virtue of his comb. So we must flatter, bow and scrape, or take the consequence. Have you not seen how women speak to men, feeding their self-regard? Yes John, no John, if you say so husband. Though men do hate our tongues they hate them only when we speak truth, which they call scolding, being but the repetition of that which they would not hear. When we do oil and flatter they will hear us readily enough, and think us virtuous.

When she spoke thus, it did put me in mind of Mistress Betty, our stepmother. What did she ever do but carry idle tittletattle to his willing ears, and twist and turn the veriest trifle into some monster of iniquity, for her own ends? Which she has got, I think, being well set up in comfort. A man is ever a willing dupe when self-love sits at his elbow.

I spoke of this to my lady, having some bitterness yet in my heart. For I was young, and smarted still from hurts but lately got. It was she who instilled some pardon in my heart. It grieved her, she

47

declared, to see a man so great in stature conduct himself so pettily. As for your unkind stepmother, she said, her state is much like yours, though you think not. What other choice hath she, being born a woman, with neither face nor fortune to her name, but to keep house, and serve, and bide her time, her husband being old? Three previous daughters cannot serve her interest, but to consume her portion, being yet unwed and still within the house. She served her interest, who did but serve her husband, and saw in it but wifely duty, to keep his peace. He who accepts such service, so she said, 'tis he who is at fault.

Shall we not light a candle, being now so wealthy? It grows dark, and Urban not yet home. I think he has gone to the widow, for she keeps a good table, so I hear. A tasty stew would tempt him to sup with her, though her complexion is sallow. And by candlelight it may look well enough. I will stoke the coals, at least, to give us light and heat. Our old servant would say, whilst mending by the fire, if she had but had a farthing for every candle he did burn at nights, she could have lived and died a rich woman. Instead of stitching by a dying hearth, from which is to be got but poor eyes, sore thumbs, and poverty.

He let go the sole right of printing, else you and I might have done without charity to warm us this night. They say there are more copies sold now than ever he burnt candles, but the bookseller will give us nothing for being descended from him. So he grows rich, and we must labour to patch an old shirt. Yet I spoilt my eyes with reading to him, and oft took down the lines now printed in such numbers.

Virtue should be its own reward, I know, and

duty also, yet 'tis a hard principle, with but little justice in it. Even an ass will labour better with carrot than with stick, and we have souls that should be nurtured, that we may grow. My cousins, though they died poor, did yet have opportunity to profit from his learning. But there is little profit to be got from women's work, unless it is six feet of earth.

There, the shirt is done, but will not withstand much washing, so I think, for all my endeavour. 'Tis no wonder that she is miserly, my father's widow. It makes us niggards in our own behalf, if we can but earn by saving another's pence. Look at this poor patched shirt, for all my labour. A prudent wife, we say, meaning one who has a care to keep her husband's pence. Who will make do and mend, and scrimp and save, and call it wealth to have a silken gown and a few baubles to adorn herself. When Adam delved and Eve span, who was then the gentleman? But now our gentlemen have given over digging, being sent to college, and Eve yet sits and spins. This was another jest my lady told, who held that girls should have the like education as their brothers. Which some men of the time did hold, though not my father.

How easily he parted with his coin, that gentleman just now. And yet not born high, I think, but from the middling sort. He carries his wealth in his head, and gets a living by it. See you in him that thrift which should keep us from want? Why, he spends more on garnet buttons for his coat than we get in a year to keep us clothed and fed. He saves no candle ends nor mends a shirt thrice over.

But yet she knew how to manage matters, that shrew, to suit her purpose. For she would coddle his fancy with nice dishes and sweet puddings. Old men and babes are alike in this, that nothing will

49

keep them so content as a tasty morsel. Dear Betty, he would say, as the steaming dish was put upon the table, so he could smell its odour close to him, his blind head alert to such sensation, everything I have goes to you when I die. Sniffing at cinnamon and spice, or a rich gravy, and smiling. It was a jest that ever went between them, she gratifying his appetite with her skill, and though he spoke in jest, in truth he spoke in earnest, reminding us and her, and all who heard him, that nothing was writ down concerning his last will and testament, and so could yet be altered. To hark thus ever on his goods and chattels, by word of mouth, whilst making yet no written testament, what was it but an everlasting bribe, a cajoling from this day to the next, to keep her kind to him? And so, though speaking seemingly in jest, he would remind her who had yet control, for all his age and disability. He kept her at his beck and call like a kite in the wind, having but to tug the string to make her do his bidding.

Though I had no liking for her, being a scolding shrew from first to last, I see how she was caught. Such petty tricks and turns are played when a man marries but to keep his house, and she to keep herself. This is no bonding betwixt like and like, and liking is not in it, nor goodly fellowship. So she is apt to fawn and flatter.

I thank my stars I was not wedded to a husband who could quote me Latin. You and I, though poor, and oft in need, have yet more dignity within our household. We are not thought a lesser being for labouring with our hands, our husbands doing likewise. They need our toil to prosper. But I would not have you wear yourself to a shadow. We shall get by this winter, even though the work is hard to come by.

Your father ever held that laws were writ in Latin but to fox the poor man in the dock. And though the practice ended with our late rebellions, we are as far now from plain language as before, lawyers making it their business to confuse us. For all the blood that was shed. That Rome was banished quite, this did give him some comfort in his latter years, but little else.

Yet my uncle died a Papist, that was the kindest man I ever knew. He held the freedom that was sought by men such as my father was but the liberty to be a tyrant within doors. So my father would have but conscience as his guide in ruling us.

I know nothing of law, daughter. But, as my uncle told it, the law provides that widows must be cared for, and offspring likewise. This your father thought but intermeddling, he said. And so I thought it best (and here his eyes would twinkle in the telling) to humour him, when he did speak of leaving all to Betty, as he would do when I did call on him, betwixt the law courts and returning home to Ipswich, thinking you and your sisters would be better served by doing nothing. And so we got a little when he died, the case coming to court, and probate being refused to Mistress Betty, for all her scheming. We got the portion that was due to us. Being but lately married to your father, though far off in Dublin, it proved a timely marriage portion.

A kind of obstinacy, I think, held him to the last, and would give him no rest. That he, an author and a scrivener's son, besides being elder brother to a lawyer of the Inner Temple, should leave no written will and testament is otherwise so passing strange as to defy all logic. And yet, being sound of mind, such wilfulness is surely nigh to blindness of another sort.

He was kind to us, our uncle Christopher. I hope, for his sake and mine, you will be mindful of his daughters, should they have need of you. Mary and Catherine grow elderly, as I do. Whilst they have each other for company they are content enough in Highgate. But I hope, one dying, you will not leave her sister comfortless and lonely. And they have been kind to you also, when you were a child. Being unmarried and childless, they made much of you, would kiss and fondle you, and give you sweetmeats. Too much, upon occasion, for your stomach.

Though I like not to depend upon charity, it is good to see so much coin together. I would a woman were paid in wages, and not in kind. It gives a kind of lift to the spirit, to hold such coins in the palm of your hand and think how you would spend them. Why, even a servant must be paid in wages. I think our little Liza should get new shoes with this, what think you? She grows apace, and those she has begin to pinch. What would you have, daughter, with these guineas? For they are yours to spend, I will not touch a penny. My needs are few, being old, and such garments as I have will see me out.

If Mr Addison had lived, he would have got me a pension, and I provided for. But the poor gentleman is dead, and there is no help for it. It is not much, is it, daughter, that we must needs cry charity at the end of a hard life with much labour in it? I thank God that you and Urban have been spared me, to be a comfort to me now. For though they call it labour to bring babes into the world, none pays us for it. Yet the world would go ill without us.

But that has ever been the way. You have heard your father speak of it, that nothing changes though it seems to do so. For he lived through those troublous times, and saw his kind deluded. We fought and died, he used to say, beguiled by promises of liberty. But those who led us, and would have us take up arms against the king, were more intent upon their property, on keeping what they had and getting more, and being spared such taxes as they would not pay. For property, they said, did give them rights within the kingdom, and we without had none. Such thanks we get for fighting of their battles, to be sent home unpaid and unrewarded.

I am no politician, daughter, and have but little knowledge of affairs. Yet I cannot think it right the country should belong only to those who have an interest in it, as they say, meaning they presently own much of it, and would have it remain so. So feudal lords would keep us yet in Norman bondage, which none think right. And yet their freeholds give them a voice we lack. So masters would rule their servants, men their wives, and this they call a just state, and democracy? All men are one in this, though in nought else.

Yet have we tongues, and will wag them, give us but half a chance. I have oft heard it spoken of, with pride by women, and with scorn by men, that when the troubles started wives and gentlewomen, and others of the female sex, took it upon themselves to petition the House of Commons, as did likewise such common riffraff as boatmen, porters and apprentices. There was much complaint made of this rabble by those who held discourse within. Go to your kitchens, so the crowd was told, it is not fitting for women to show themselves thus publicly, you have no business here. Yet they made answer, that Christ died to save both sexes, that women are sharers in the common calamities of both Church and state, suffer as much, and were held in Newgate also, for refusing to go against conscience, and so brought about the bishops' downfall.

As for the meaner sort, were they not soldiers in the war, fighting many a grievous battle for their betters, at risk of life and limb, and should they do this without some recompense? That promises were made I doubt not, and if not made, inferred. For who will fight but to maintain another's interest, and then go home unpaid? Our middling sort did not think enough on this, when they summoned up the poor. For men that have no land, nor freehold to their name, may yet find they have a conscience all their own. And being likewise taxed, in shillings, giving quarter, and in blood, will find they are unwilling to be ruled, since they have had no vote.

No, the middling sort did not think on that, when they summoned up their tenants to form troops of horse, and merchants got their servants and apprentices to put up barricades in city streets, aye, and their wives and children too. For when the war was won and the king's army routed, there were the poor, those selfsame soldiers, clamouring about the streets, unwilling to go home unpaid. They were the debtors now, the prosperous gentry grown fat on Church lands, the merchants newly rich, and now victorious. An army must be paid, kings have ever known that, for which they have sought taxes, whether ship money or any other levy. Now the rebels found it out. Soldiers must be paid, if not in coin, then in some other kind. Such promises as will send men into battle with psalms upon their lips are great promises indeed, and must be kept.

Freedom was the watchword, yet would their commanders send them home with empty bellies. Freedom to go without is scarce worth fighting for, but now it seemed that those with property would keep it for themselves, and give no wider share in saying how the kingdom should be governed, for fear of losing it.

Soldiers, being unpaid, did roam the streets, and turned their pistols on their officers, crying 'money, money, money'. Our old servant would speak of those times. Nothing but rumours running through the streets, apprentices rioting either for king or Parliament, and bands of reformadoes, as they were known, disbanded soldiers, roving about the city, intent on mischief. It was a time, she said, when a woman was fearful of her life in the getting of a dozen eggs or a pound of candles, and few sellers coming to the door.

I never heard so much talk as then went on, she'd tell me, as I sat shelling peas or some such task. I liked to help her in the kitchen, more than to do my father's bidding, for she would gossip of old times in such a manner as made them live for me. So much of arguing as went on then, she'd say, on the rights and wrongs of it. Every man was become a lawyer, though he could scarce write his own name, and each woman who could read the Bible for herself a preacher or a prophetess of things unfolding. And some did fear the army, saying this was no rule of law to flout the Commons thus, and others holding that the army did represent the people more than Westminster, it being elected but by very few, the men of property. As for me, she'd say, 'twas all one, being but a woman and a servant, and thus excluded by both factions from having any say. But the price of milk was high, and butter barely to be found.

And then the army marched into the city with sprigs of laurel in their hats, their leaders with them, each riding at the head of his regiment. Though gossip had it that they went but with the tide, having no other choice. The storm being unleashed, they now must ride it, like a straw atop a wave. Cromwell and Fairfax might look proud upon their mounts, yet were they led from behind. For he who would dance must pay the fiddler, or dance a gallow's jig.

Such a pother, she would say, and with nothing to show for it at last. For when all was said and done, one faction was as like to t'other as a pea to its neighbour in the pod. The army, having won the day and taken London, against the wishes of their paymasters, that had no pay to give them, took to debating the future of the kingdom on t'other side the river, as though elected so to do, if not by Magna Carta then by swords and muskets. All shall have a voice they said, in choosing parliament, all but women, servants and beggars. On hearing which I said, bring back our king, but alas, soon his head was off, this course being voted for by force of arms, for all who would say nay were purged from out the House, and kept from entering.

I was but a child during those times, and saw and heard with but little understanding. Yet I recall that all who spoke of it, as afterwards your father, spoke of it as a time of hopes dashed or deferred, of grievous disappointment. From this I do deduce that we must have a care of meddling too much in things politic, for fear of losing that which we would gain, and more besides upon occasion. You speak rashly, as those yet young will do, lacking experience, but desiring justice. Yet it is hard to come by in this world, and blood spilt will scarce get it for us.

And if humility is a Christian virtue, 'tis ever lacking in affairs of state. For men that thought themselves elect of God, and come to perfect grace, were but imperfect, and prone to error. Thus conscience can beguile us, so my uncle said. Take but authority away and all is turmoil: the law must be obeyed or we are lost. My father, on the contrary, despised the rabble, and thought it right that those few men who heard the voice of God should rule by force if need be. Yet who can say that what he hears is God, and not his own voice whispering that which he would hear? And so there will be a mighty babble at the last, and much confusion.

I think my lady Merian spoke but the truth when she did say self-interest ever rules. So landlords feared to lose what they had got, and tradesmen thought themselves but poorly used, for who it is, they said, makes for our country's wealth? Meaning not such as you or I, that do but bring babes into the world, and wash and mend and mind the pot, but those whose industry is paid in coin. So, I think, each faction feared to lose, or not to gain that which they hoped for by their strife. But those with nothing, landless beggars, who did but seek a patch of common ground to grow their crops, so as to fill their empty stomachs, these were turned away and soon sent packing, first by soldiers, then by all who lived nearby.

But our interest, so she opined, is in our fellow men, and women too, that all should have enough. I can but eat so much, sleep in one bed, wear one gown at a time, yet others starve, sleep on the bare ground, and shiver out of doors whilst I enjoy this surfeit. And yet, she'd say, those who have enough, or more than a sufficiency, are wont to speak as though it were a virtue, not their good fortune. As though it were industry alone, and righteousness, that spared them beggary, not privilege of birth, inheritance, or sex or mere rude health. It is not by dint of virtue we are wealthy, nor poor through lack of it. This is but an argument against charity, so those without may beg unheard.

For though the good Book tells us that the slothful will not plough in winter and must beg in summer, it tells us also that he that hath mercy upon the poor lendeth unto the Lord, and the Lord will recompense him that which he hath given. For charity is but a kind of interest, and brings us profit of a greater kind. And though it seems not so, it is self-interest to think not just on self: not to gain reward in Heaven, but here upon this earth. For we must dwell upon this earth together, and whilst my brother and my sister want for food and shelter, we shall not undo the sin of Adam, nor shall there be a Paradise regained upon this earth, nor Second Coming.

It was for this the war was fought, or so the Generalissimo would have them think, that risked their lives for him. And so my father thought, aye, and yours likewise, that what began upon the battlefields of England, God giving victory, should quickly bring about the final transformation through the world. And yet, no sooner was the victory given, and unpaid soldiers seeking their reward, then their officers would have them go home hungry, in body and in soul.

England belongs, declared their chief of men, the General, to men of property. Those who have no interest in it other than to have been born in it, and by virtue of breathing, can have no say in how it shall be governed, for such a course would lead to anarchy, each man desiring what he had not got, and striving for it through the ballot. He that had heard the voice of God in going into battle, in bringing such upheavals to our land, would now cry order order, and go home go home, enough it is enough.

We speak of God, and goodness, so my lady said, but in our hearts is naught but property. And though we pray for the coming of His kingdom, we rather fear to lose that which we have, than get a better world here down below. For those with much know it unjustly got, whilst others go without. Else would we face the judgement of the Lord, his Second Coming, with equanimity. However it may come, whether by stealth and slow democracy, or some miraculous event.

You must have patience here on earth, I fear. 'Tis no use fretting. I hear your father's voice still. We seek but an honest competence, he'd say, yet laws, wars and taxes, unprotected trade and cheap importing do take it from us. How can we prosper if we have no say in how the country is governed?

I fear his life was but a tedious, unavailing search for betterment. First, being a Fifth Monarchist, he sought it here in London, and sought in vain, the Good Old Cause betrayed. Then in Dublin, where trouble but followed us in King James's time, and back to London when King James was ousted. Some would have the cause now won, King Billy coming, but 'tis as unlike the vision your father nursed in youth as our back yard is to Adam's garden.

And so it will remain, I fear. We must take charity where we find it, and not grumble needlessly, that some have garnet buttons and we patch fustian. I was born into a time when great beliefs did flourish, and men saw glorious visions. Such hopes were dashed, and now we think it foolish, a dream of Paradise not to be found this side the grave. You, who come after, know the hope is lost. Though whether 'tis better to be born with hope and lose it, or to come into this world a cynic, and so get what you can, I know not.

Whatever is, is right, is now the current thought. They do betray my father that think so, for all their worship of him. And those who must beg out of doors this cold night know otherwise, though they have no shillings to spend at the bookseller.

And Urban not yet back. I think he must have gone to sup with the widow. Shall we stoke the fire, daughter, or let it die? And what's for supper? Daughter? Are you awake? Poor child, she's fast asleep, and no wonder. She should never have got up so soon after her delivery. But yet she would not hear me, when I told her to stay abed.

Four

Y OUR NAME, SIR? I have no recollection of it, and the professor has not been here for some time. I fear you come at an inopportune moment, my daughter being unwell. She took sick this morning and I have scarce left her side. I would not be inhospitable, but we live in poor circumstances, with an only servant, who is young and clumsy. There is much disorder in the house, and this room not fit for callers.

Will you not return at some more fitting time? You see we are all at sixes and sevens, with the floor not swept. My daughter's pregnancy does not go well with her, and I am anxious. She has lost two babes already, and is very low.

Then pray, take a seat. I hope it is not dusty. The child is slow at her tasks, but today must be excused. Two hands can only do so much, and she has had more than her share this day. I would offer you a dish of tea but there is no one to prepare it, and now I think on it, no tea neither. I find it very dear still, and so we buy it sparingly. My daughter had the last of it an hour ago.

She is in the fourth month, but the sickness will not leave her. I think she is fearful to lose this child also, which makes her fretful. I was in the same case myself as a young woman, losing many children in infancy, so I understand her thoughts. Such fears serving no purpose, we must strive to master them, but 'tis easier said than done. But she has one child living, the prettiest girl you ever did see. She is with a neighbour at present, her mother being sick, else you could see her.

Relics, sir? I can think of none, unless you would call me such, being old, and the only one of his children now living. My poor sisters are both dead this long while, and neither had offspring to survive them. Mary died unwed and Anne in childbed, her infant also.

You see how poorly we live here. Some bits and pieces of household furniture were sent to me in Dublin after his death, but not brought back on our return, since they did not warrant the expense of shipping. My father's silver seal I gave to my daughter on her wedding day. It is hers to dispose of, not mine. I will not trouble her in her condition, else you could ask her yourself, though I know what the answer would be. It has an eagle on it, with two heads and wings spread wide, his family arms.

For other relics, as you call them, you must visit my stepmother. She is yet living, in Nantwich, and I doubt not but has a great horde of such mementoes.

Books, sir? Look around you. You see how sparsely this room is furnished. Does it look like a gentleman's parlour? We have but the bare necessities here, and no room for such luxury, had they been left me. My father gave much space to his books, but here we are packed tight as oysters in a barrel, the house being small, and my son also lodging with us.

No study in this house, nor rows of books. You

have come on a fool's errand if you thought otherwise. Many were sold before his death, my father having no heirs that he would recognise to make good use of them. We were but girls, and thus unfit. And yet I spoilt my eyes in reading to him, and have worn spectacles since I left his house. A paltry inheritance.

But the bookseller has grown rich, I hear, with bringing out his work in new editions, having got the sole right of printing for nought. I would I had a little of those earnings now, to get comforts for my ailing daughter. You see how little he thought on us, to let it go so lightly. Was it not a life's work like any other, and would a man give away house and land, a lifetime's capital, ignoring his children's needs? Had his father done likewise, he might have been apprenticed to labour with his hands, as I was, and died a pauper, as like as not. And so goodbye to study.

Forgive me, sir. You did not come to hear me speak of such matters. I fear I cannot help you, and you must leave with nothing. You come at a bad time, and I am anxious. I have heard there is much profit to be got from autographs, and similar mementoes of famous men. You may have something in my hand if you wish, for, being blind, I wrote at his dictation, but I think this is not to your purpose. A pity, else I might buy new shoes for my daughter's child, and more tea to ease her discomfort.

No, sir, I have told you once already, the seal was given to my daughter as a gift, and I know she would be unwilling to part from it. You would but see it? I left her sleeping, and will not disturb her on such an errand. Now, if you will excuse me, there is much to do within the house. Our sole servant is gone to market, and I must to the kitchen.

But now I think on it, I do have some mementoes of a kind. My cousin Edward, when he died, left me a box of papers belonging to my father. They are of little interest now, else they had long been given away or sold for profit. For despite the learning he received from my father my cousin did not prosper and was oft impoverished. Authorship without good fortune is not a life to choose, I think, and in this my father may have done my cousins some disservice, for all his schoolmastering. Great gifts bring great rewards, mostly in Heaven, but small talents little coin. As for Grub Street, 'tis only fit for worms and insects, so my father said, yet did both his pupils sink to it. My uncle Christopher ever felt they had been better employed learning some honest trade, or going to the university, or to the inns of court to study law, as he did. Such education as your father gave them, he would say, made them unfit for all but that for which they had no gift, and no true calling. He said it kindly, being a kindly man, but meant it in good earnest.

The papers? I cannot at this moment recollect where they are put. My daughter moved the box some time ago, I do recall. We were spring-cleaning at the time. But where she put it I do not recollect. And it is scarce worth hunting for, being of no interest. There is nought in the box but pamphlets, old political stuff no mortal gives a fig for now.

This is your particular passion? Is that so? Then you are rare indeed, for few now value my father for his politics, or study his times. My late husband also was much engaged with such interests, being my senior by many years, and having the hot blood of youth in him during those years of turmoil. But both spoke bitterly at the end, feeling themselves betrayed. He was a weaver, not a poet, you understand, and so his hopes were more particular.

I have heard him many a time in his last illness, musing on early dreams and late despair. For he died poor as he began, for all his industry. We cried for freedom, liberty, he'd say, yet what was it, when all is said and done? But the freedom to bob about like flotsam on the waves, or leaves blown in the wind. Without just government 'tis but the freedom of the wilderness where savages do roam, to kill and pillage as they please. Not a fruitful garden, as God intended, where all is order, all sufficiency. For those who have get more, this being the law of interest, whilst those without stay poor, for all their labour.

The box, sir? I will search for it presently. The rooms are so higgledy-piggledy just now, my daughter being unwell and the servant disorderly on account of her youth, I scarce know where to look. I would tell you what I know of my father's opinions but, being a mere child during those troubled times, I recollect little, and saw all things with a child's eye. So I oft confused his bitterness concerning all that had gone amiss in the great world with his domestic discontents, being more familiar. Was it my mother who had brought about the Fall and troubled times? Was my childish failure to obey his every wish the reason for the turmoil in the streets, and his displeasure? It almost seemed so, for in childhood guilty thoughts do grow like giants, to seize on every trifle.

And yet I heard much talk in the house from my earliest years, of what had been before my birth. That which I recollect may be of use to you. We had a servant, sir, who had been with my father many years and knew him as a boy, having first served his parents. Which fact, she thought, did give her licence to speak her mind on each and every matter, which much displeased my father, who was wont to wax sarcastical on women's tongues. But to me and my sisters, lacking a mother to beguile our ears, her gossip was ever welcome. She told us how, when the war first started, the whole city was rife with talk on future government. I think that she herself must have been infect with those unruly times, for ever after she did blab her thoughts to those that did employ her, whether they would hear them or no.

There were those, she said, who though mere servants, would not wash dishes for conscience's sake upon the Sabbath. This was not my way, she said, since our stomachs rumble as loudly on that day as any other, and infants cry, and ashes smut the hearth. But I will speak my mind when conscience tells me, and none shall shut me up. This was her way, sir, and I did love her for it, though at the last . . .

I will get the pamphlets directly. I think the box is in the back room, by the coals. My daughter had a mind to use them for tinder, but I would not have it. Indeed, it is a wonder so many yet remain, since our old servant roused my father's ire by burning some of them during that first winter of the civil war, there being no coals come in from Newcastle, for the roads were cut off by troops. Having nought else to cook the dinner with, she burned them, and would not be rebuked. To her mind 'twas all hot air, and fit as such only for cooking stews. Besides, she said, what else was there to do? You cannot cook without fire, and fire with neither wood nor coals within the house is hard to come by. Did they not teach you that at your university? You go upstairs and put the world to rights within your study, and leave me to my business in this kitchen. 'Tis hungry work you do, and I doubt you have the stomach for eating raw, like savages. What my father said to this I know not. 'Tis possible the tale got more pert with the telling, as we do oft embroider our little triumphs against authority.

Now, for the box. I hope there are yet some pamphlets remaining. Our servant needs watching, and is apt to follow her own whims. I have seen her use my Bible as a stepping-stone when cleaning shelves. Do not touch it, sir. The lid is smutty and must be wiped. I would not have you dirty your hands.

I must put on spectacles for this. *Tyrannical Government Anatomized* – will you look through it? They are all much in this vein, as I recall. Those who come to visit me of late find such matter tedious and of little moment, so the box has gathered dust. They seek the poet, thinking him sublime, and ignore the rest. But, since you say you have an interest in things political, you will wish to study what yet remains within.

A Discourse Shewing in What State the Three Kingdoms Are in. Printed in sixteen forty-one, almost a hundred years since. How curious it is to look on it. Printed at the sign of the Cock. This was the fashion then in publishing, and few put their names to that which they had written, fearing reprisal. But this you know, how foolish of me to lecture you thus.

A Slingshot Against all Tyrants. And here a few receipts. Two yards of fustian, a pound of candles. A remedy for fever – this is in my sister's hand. She's long since dead. I had not thought to find such things here. Like dry leaves from a vanished season. The ink has changed colour with the years.

What's that you say? That censorship broke down, the war beginning? 'Tis little wonder then, that such a spate of pamphlets issued forth.

My father did welcome such liberty of speaking. But he was not so within doors. My poor sister did suffer much from this, turning rebellious at his dominion. Each protest did but harm her cause, and to endure in silence was not in her nature. I was once companion to a lady who held that men do differ in their public and their private life, cry freedom for themselves, but not their wives and children.

The Nation's Tongue Unleash'd. And it was, from all I have heard. Servants and beggars were as like to clack as any preacher. Printed in Goldsmith's Alley. So much commotion to so little end, think you not? Each title lengthier than the last, like a kite's tail in the wind. Indeed, I have heard our old servant confess that some were used as such by my cousins, and a sore whipping they got for it, which terrified our mother and had sent her running, if nothing else had driven her hence.

She meant my mother, sir, who died at my birth. You have doubtless heard the scandalous gossip of her going home and failing to return when sent for. And then my father's pamphlets on divorce, which brought the greater scandal to our name. I know not if they are here. But they have been thought so notorious that you must be familiar with them. They had unlooked for consequences which my father much misliked, thinking the freedom which he sought himself to be another's licence. It seems a preacher dwelling in Bell Alley abjured her husband, called him unsanctified, and took to living with another man, a preacher also, who had a wife yet living, and many children. So they practised what my father preached, having studied his doctrines.

It seems that others also took my father's word as law and laid aside their spouses to take another, thinking that conscience only was their guide, which was in fact mere lust or lack of liking. This much displeased my father, so my uncle had it. He was a lawyer and outlived my father by many years. For that which he called freedom for himself was not intended for the lower sort, for an unregenerate rabble, nor for women.

My uncle never spoke of it within his hearing, but only after his death. Freedom without responsibility, he'd say, how can this be? If God gave us authority over wives, as doth the law, they are also given in our charge for better or for worse, as children are, and servants. Shall I then put my wife aside because her face mislikes me, or she lacks conversation? Did I marry her for this or, if I did, had I not time enough to chat with her, and try her at my leisure?

Thus spoke my uncle, ever the lawyer. I can hear him still. The law is yet the law, and must be obeyed. He thought it wrong for any man to put himself above it for conscience merely. Else each becomes a law unto himself and chaos follows. These are nice points of philosophy, not easily resolved. I would hear your opinion. What if the law be wrong, must we obey it? Yet, if each man takes his conscience as his guide he is like to become a law unto himself, and conscience often tells us that which we would hear. I know not how to resolve this riddle.

What think you, sir, that have an interest in things political? What is the orthodoxy now? I believe that we must suffer in this world, whether it be the vagaries of fortune, bad harvests, falls in trade, or those failings in a spouse we cannot mend. But I am a mere woman, and have not studied. That the Fall must be redressed, this was widely held during my father's time, and many thought that suffering meekly, and mere virtue, would not do it. The Norman yoke, which took away our freedoms, did so by violence, and so must be violently opposed, if need be. And yet, if each man has his voice, aye, and woman too, to speak his mind and follow it with action, how can ought but disorder follow?

Those who rule, I think, must seek consent, else turmoil will result. Is this not your opinion? Whether it be within the household or the state, 'tis all one. A wife must be wooed with kindness, and he who would have children must be a father. This my uncle understood more nearly than my father, for my cousins loved him dearly, and my aunt also. I never saw strife betwixt them, or serious argument.

He called us unkind daughters at the last, yet got but what he gave, unkindness for unkindness, harsh words for harsh. We give our freedom gladly to those we love, and serve them willingly. This I know, having been both wife and mother. For freedom is but a notion, when all is said and done.

Do not touch the box, sir, you will soil your fingers. If you are in haste it will keep for another occasion. As I told you, there is nothing of value in it, unless it be for curiosity. I would you had come at a more opportune time, and given us warning of your visit. I might then have found the papers of most interest. No, you may not remove them to your lodgings.

Now you have led my thoughts astray. What was I searching for when you distracted me? I know I had it in mind to show you a particular document. Ah yes, here I have it, the ordinance of sixteen forty-three against seditious books and pamphlets, issued by Parliament. It orders that no book, pamphlet or paper shall be printed, bound or put to sale unless first licensed according to the ancient custom. Will you peruse it? As I recall, it speaks of searches to be made for unlicensed printing presses, and for authors and printers of such unlicensed works to be apprehended and brought before the House of Commons.

Rebels turned rulers do mislike freedom of speech as much as those they ousted, for free opinions may be well enough but become a great inconvenience once in government. So my father found to his cost, in turning censor, despite his noble words defending liberty of speaking. For fools will crow as loudly as a prophet, and make a pandemonium in place of order.

I am but a woman, and our tongues must be still whoever rules. What are your views in the matter? I would gladly hear them. My late husband judged the middling sort no better than the rest, in terms of knowing truth. If truth is not in privilege and rank, forever fixed, why should it stop with men of property and leave out all the rest?

He was a weaver and, during those troubled times, a mere apprentice with but little education. And yet, he said, I could read the good Book as well as any man, and understand its meaning right enough. So why should such as I be silenced? Was the war fought for this? But our old servant took an earthy view, and saw in this but chaos, if all would rule and no one obey. A fine thing for the chicken, she'd say, if it could cite Scripture to prove that it should not have its head wrung off for the pot, but a poor prospect for those who would eat their supper. And tell me not to be a silly child, to feel pity for the poor dead bird in her lap, its feathers being plucked.

I think my father was no hypocrite, for all he found himself a licenser at last, that had preached freedom of the presses, and of opinion. You must not think so. He feared to lose that which had been gained at such great cost. Yet progress by oppression is but a poor way forward, and 'tis little wonder many thought themselves betrayed.

Men, when they cry liberty, and would have the freedom of opinion to defend it, mean only to their own kind, and never to their foes. Else had my father given the like freedom to Papists, whom he loathed above all others. Yet he did not so. 'Tis human nature. Men who cry liberty of speech silence their wives and daughters without a thought, and those who serve them.

What's that you say? We cannot give liberty of printing to those who would deprive us of our liberties? I see you have indeed studied my father, for I know this to have been his opinion. Forgive me, sir, for to be frank I had taken you to be something of an impostor, and here for gain. I have made you blush, and I am sorry for it. 'Tis I who should do so, but my cheeks are too old to change colour.

'Tis an argument I would fault. Can mere opinion enslave us, if we be free? Surely our liberties, if they be firm, can withstand some knocks, and suffer little hurt. To stop our ears for fear of hearing seems foolish, since we must know the argument in order to refute it.

Was it not Ulysses who stopped his ears so he should not hear the sirens' song? I think so, though all my learning is but secondhand, and rusty now with lack of use. We live in modern times, now reason rules, not superstitious fear of magic, as it did in times of old. I think we need not fear to be beguiled, and stop our ears with wax, and tie us to the mast to sail a steady course. If we are bound for truth we shall not waver, and God will see us safely into port.

But let us to the box, it is not yet empty. Here it says that every man and woman are by nature equal, and have been so since the time of Adam and Eve. This is a red rag indeed, to set the bull by the horns. None of them having by nature any authority one over another, but merely by mutual agreement or consent. All lawful powers reside in the people, for whose good all government was ordained. Know you this pamphlet? The first page has gone astray. Lilburne, you say? Was he not put in prison by Parliament? 'Tis little wonder. They did not fight the war for this.

I know such sentiments were little to my father's liking. He thought the great mass unregenerate, blind to the merits of godly men, and too easily swayed by evil orators. It is not agreeable, he said, that such persons should ever be free. However much they may brawl about liberty, they are slaves, and deserve not a government of their own choosing, since they will never choose wisely.

Yet God gave us presses so the poor should learn to read, not just the middling sort, and there is no way back from that. Else had He kept His truth locked up in monasteries, and kept us popish to the last. So my husband thought, and many like him. And if we read, we think, and know our minds, there is no way back from that neither, for all their ordinances. Why, once it was forbidden to read the good Book, the very lifeblood of our truth, and source of all we know. And for why? So those who ruled by force of arms should keep us cowed, and ever in subjection.

Freedom can be abused, I doubt not, and partial knowledge is a dangerous thing. Yet who can say he has a hold on truth, and knows in all things better than his neighbour? What is sauce for the goose is sauce for the gander and, if conscience rules, mine is as good as any man's.

I had forgot how much was stored within this box. We live in other times, and such old debates have little meaning now. It makes me sad to think such turmoil of opinion was all in vain. I would not have you think me a friend to anarchy, and yet I see here something we have lost. You are young, belonging to a time more cynical, but I am a child of my time, and recall such hopes I once heard spoken of with some regret still at their passing.

You see how variable these pamphlets are, in voice and in opinion. Liberty should be a garden, so I think, where many flowers do flourish, all shapes, all scents, all hues, but orderly and trim, with no rank weed strangling its fellows. I do not like the age we live in now, finding it hard and unchristian. The wealthy are richer than ever they were in my youth, but with less regard for those who are poor. And love themselves for their good fortune, when they should love God.

Believe me, sir, I have seen much in a long life, and know whereof I speak. At the bottom of the box, as I remember, lie those papers I thought most remarkable. They have a kind of poetry to my ears, however much my father must have despised them. How like you this, if I can read it yet – 'the same spirit that hath lain hid under flesh, like a corn of wheat for an appointed time, under the clods of earth, is now sprung out and begins to grow a fruitful vine, which shall never decay'. And further on – 'This is the kingdom of God within man. This is the grain of mustard-seed, which is little in the beginning, but shall become a mighty tree.' I see you smile, and indeed, I never yet saw a mustard-seed become a tree. 'Tis humble stuff, I grant you, yet if words can move us, these will surely do so, despite reason. Besides, my father, for all his erudition, had greater errors in his work than this, but was readily pardoned for it by those who estimate his vision, despite cosmology.

And here's another by the same hand – 'all places stink with the abomination of self-seeking teachers and rulers. For do not I see that everyone preacheth for money, counsels for money and fights for money, to maintain particular interests? And none of these three, that pretend to give liberty to the creation, do give liberty to the creation; neither can they, for they are enemies to universal liberty; so that the earth stinks with their hypocrisy, covetousness, envy, sottish ignorance and pride.' This forthright tone is much to my liking. 'The common people are filled with good words from pulpits and council tables, but no good deeds; for they wait and wait for good and for deliverances, but none comes . . . Many that have been good housekeepers (as we say) cannot live, but are forced to turn soldiers and so to fight to uphold the curse, or else live in great straits of beggary.'

This was written in sixteen forty-nine, the king being lately dead, and I have little quarrel with it even now. It has the ring of truth to it, and to this day it touches me. A plain truth plainly spoken, and the better for all that. Poor people need no scholars to understand this. 'Tis as plain as a pike-staff, surely, and as purposeful. Yet who now reads Winstanley? I fear, sir, we care more for flourishes and rhyming than honest matter in these days.

We talk of troubled times, but forget the hope that was in them. No man can speak now in this fashion, with daily expectation of a new Paradise on earth, not just in England, but spreading thence across the world in a great reformation. I fear that younger authors now do turn to ancient stories not for truth, as was my father's way, but merely to divert a passing hour for those with too much leisure. So naiads frolic in the grove, and Troy must fall in rhyming couplets to amuse a lady. You see I am yet my father's daughter, and look for meaning.

I was taught that ancient stories, having their roots in truth, are not mere toys to play with, and dress in pretty words. Good and evil, light and dark, are locked in combat from time's beginning to our own, and Satan is as formidable now as ever in the past, and takes seductive forms. Yet who now thinks this way amongst our younger authors? Grown rich with privilege, untouched by war, they pander to a pampered readership, who think that Hector died to give them sport within their drawing rooms.

Reason is now the watchword, and unreason walks in fancy dress, tripping in metric lines. The world is a great clock that strikes the hours, and God has long since vanished, so it can take its course. Now virtue has no grace, and fancy rules where true imagination's long since lost.

I know how it goes amongst fine folks, in the smart quarter of town, although I live here in Spital-fields. You need not gainsay me, or look startled. But alas, the real world in which the poor must struggle rumbles ever on in the same old way, and this man speaks to me most potently with simple words, as a seer should. What is vision, if not the power to see for others, that are blinded by the world, and earthly things? So my father thought, in knowing he had lost his eyes to see more clearly. He doubted not his gift had come from God, to be used seriously, and not for sport.

Now the presses roll merrily enough, without let or hindrance. Yet to give such poets licence is but to despise them, words being mere playthings. They do no harm that seek to do no good, and but line their pockets to amuse.

I can read your thoughts, sir. You think I speak as the old do, ever judging past times better than the present. So Eve spoke, I doubt not, grown old with Adam in the wilderness. But the times grow worse, for all the new-fangled luxuries the wealthy now enjoy. So many carriages rumbling through our streets, yet beggars still a-plenty, the rich growing richer and the poor yet poorer. The advances of mankind are ever in creature comforts, but a new Heaven and a new earth are as far from us as ever they were. Who now thinks to see a Second Coming, to save us from our woes? Or labours for it? Whatever is, is right, is now the cry, and the Devil take the hindmost.

But we must be thankful for such freedoms as we enjoy. You are right to say so. Had it been my youth, I would not be gossiping freely with you, being required to keep silent. Women were much subdued. Is it not fearsome, the ordinance on printing you have in your hand? To have fought a war in the name of liberty of conscience, and then come down to this? That my father had little liking for the suppressing of other men's works I doubt not, you are right in this. Yet did he set his mind to it and lend his name, thinking the ends did justify the means. What think you of this doctrine? It was much in vogue then. I have heard him cite Ovid on the matter. But the end, sir, was not good.

I have heard my uncle say, he would rather be ruled by a hereditary lord than be subject to the rule of saints, the self-elect of God, as he would call them. That it was indeed a dangerous manner of ruling was proved by the outcome. Did not Cromwell kneel and pray before each battle, and see the hand of God in victory? So might was right, and so it followed, as the night the day, we should be ruled but by a single person. For the Lord Protector would shut each parliament almost as soon as he had declared it open, its members not doing that which he would have them do, or not doing it fast enough. For one man in his wisdom can decide in a trice what several hundred will argue on for weeks and months, and then, perhaps, fail to agree. I have been told he tried to rig the outcome of each election in advance, and yet would grow impatient if even these tame ciphers, puppets merely, did not do his bidding with sufficient speed.

How this should differ from what went before – I mean the king – I know not. My father, though uneasy, chose to speak of an unruly mob that must be governed, so the few were not deprived of their just liberty. But the common sort he so despised could see what they had got for their trouble, but a king with another name.

And then, sir, I ask myself – can we be saved despite our choosing? If God thought it fit to give our first parents in Eden free will to choose betwixt good and evil, though they chose the worst, is it meet for men, however good or great in wisdom, to give us less of liberty? I cannot think that this is the way to redemption.

Although I was scarce out of my cradle the first time that Cromwell put an end to Parliament, the manner of it was such, it could not but be part of common gossip ever after. He took with him a party of soldiers and appeared within the House dressed only in a plain black coat and worsted stockings, and though he began by speaking calmly enough he soon became enraged. They say he paced the floor as though he were a madman, kicking the ground and shouting, calling the members whore-masters and drunkards, one man corrupt, another scandalous to the profession of the Gospel. I say you are no Parliament, he shouted, ordering the soldiers to break up the sitting, and fetch the Speaker down from his chair.

Rule by a single person, it was called, who could not rule himself. Is it any wonder there was so much gossip? It seems there was a kind of devilish fury in him, which he said came from God. He called the mace a bauble, one man but a juggler, and told his officers he had not sought to have done this, but, perceiving the spirit of God so strong upon him, could do no other.

Some wag put a note on the door, saying this House was now to let, unfurnished. The city being full of rumours, Cromwell was suddenly sedulous to please all parties, even malignants. He took to visiting churches with a big prayer book under his arm, declaring that the Almighty had inspired him. And he would take umbrage if people did not doff their hats to him in public places, as they had formerly done in the presence of the king.

The Rump having been dispatched in such rude fashion, the Barebones followed, this being no parliament at all, but such men as Cromwell could call upon to vindicate his own authority, including members of his own family, and army officers under him. This was to be the coming together of saints, to bring about Christ's kingdom here on earth. God, he told the assembly thus brought together, doth manifest it to be a day of the power of Christ. They were a chosen body, so he said, at the edge of promises and prophecies. Which was, so gossip had it, but to make him king.

Yet even these saints, handpicked to do his bidding, did not prove sufficiently obedient, and after only a few months were sent packing by his musketeers. Living in state now, at Whitehall and Hampton Court, the Lord Protector would ever after call this assembly a sign of his weakness and folly, which had much teaching in it for the future. But it taught him, not to give a broader voice to the people, but rather to remove it utterly.

All this my father did concur in. You must know this, if you know aught. For, he said, if the greater part of the senate should choose to be slaves, or to expose the government to sale, ought not the lesser number to interpose, and endeavour to retain their liberty, if it be in their power? So he was also for the expelling of rotten members, as he called them, when the House was purged so the king could be voted to his death. But such topsyturvy logic has no merit. If I can see this, so can the common sort. A solo voice sings not in harmony by silencing the rest. And though my father ever thought it lawful that the few should rule the many, if the few had God and wisdom on their side, 'tis a foolish man who thinks himself forever in the right, and all the rest ungodly.

I would I had heard my late husband argue with

my father – there would have been a storm! But they did never meet, my father being deceased before our return to England. He heard only his own voice at last, so said Mr Clarke of the dictator, from listening only to those opinions concurring with his own. He was called His Highness now, that had begun life as plain Oliver, and ambassadors, on entering his chamber, would have to bow three times. But though he thought his own voice came from God, others found in it the voice of Satan, and called him Antichrist. A prophetess saw in him the Little Horn, a horrible excrescence in the head of the Beast, as described in Revelations, just as once his enemies had been revealed in like fashion. So a London apprentice saw in his titles the number of the Beast. And though such seers were thrown in prison, the discontent lived on.

A pretty pass things had come to, that the war should have been fought for this. Is it any wonder so many left these shores? My husband felt betrayed, and lost all hope. The wheel was come full circle when a merchant refused to pay custom duty, it not being authorised by Parliament, and was thrown in prison for it. You must know that the wars had begun in just this fashion, with Cromwell's kin refusing to pay ship money, taxes called for by the king without authority of Parliament. The merchant's lawyers pleaded his case so well that they must needs be thrown into the Tower for language destructive to the government. Whereupon the man pleaded his own case to such effect, the Chief Justice was utterly nonplussed. Delays and chicanery must be employed, else had the whole nation been free of taxes set by the Lord Protector.

I have heard my uncle speak of this case, he

being a lawyer. Many were uneasy, though serving Cromwell. For if an ordinance to levy taxes were not legal, then neither were any other ordinances brought in by the same means, including that for treason.

My uncle told me several judges were dispensed with, including the Chief Justice. He had little taste for what was then afoot, being of the royalist party. I know that judges can be partial in their judgements, like other men. My husband was ever of that opinion, thinking them prejudiced. And yet, sir, we must have some yardstick in our doings, must we not? If the king did wrong in governing without a parliament, I cannot but think the Lord Protector was likewise at fault.

How far can a yardstick bend without breaking? There was a saying in my youth – begin to build a wall crooked, and you must continue it awry till it falls. And use but crooked tools, to say 'tis straight. But two newspapers were permitted at this time, as you must know, both coming from the same pen, at the behest of Cromwell and his Council. They differed not a jot, though coming out on different days of the week. Their author being a turncoat, one who had formerly written for the king. Such crooked tools, sir – could he find no other? Few of his former friends would now defend him, there being but little left worthy to be defended.

A lie hath no legs, so said my uncle, but the Lord Protector would give himself a pair to stand with some authority. So he must needs call another parliament, more tame than those before. On this occasion, before issuing the writs, he locked up, not just royalists, but those of his opponents who had once been his friends. Even this was not enough. Having got them out of harm's way before the election, he had the door guarded by soldiers when the House did meet, admitting only those members with a ticket, so many found themselves excluded by his order, despite election.

To listen to the voices of the rabble was anarchy, my father held. To which my uncle would reply – what is civil war and regicide but anarchy? And I, being little more than a child caught between such contrary opinions, was much bewildered. But uncle, I queried, if the king be a tyrant, that takes away our Christian liberties, must he not be removed? And is every law good, that it must be obeyed? And if it be bad, should we not rebel, by force if need be? As for my father, I knew better than to bandy words with him. He would have taken it unkindly, both for my youth and sex, if I had dared to argue.

I have lived humbly, sir, and know humility, or so I think. We who are little people, leading small lives, do readily confess our faults and try to make amends. But the great men of this world, with great designs and mighty visions, thinking they cannot err, grow obstinate and will not change their course. But the best of men are but men at best, and 'tis our grace to know it.

I doubt not you are better versed in reading of the classics than I could ever be, having but used my eyes to read aloud in parrot fashion, and yet, as I recall, the ancients held it a grievous sin for men to think themselves like unto gods, or greater than they were, for which due punishment would follow. Is this not so? When a hero fell, the fault was in the hero, not in lesser mortals that did surround him and betray his cause. I fear my father, for all his years of study, learnt not this. Whether in things domestic or political, or in his version of the classic mode, he ever put the blame on lesser men and, if he could, on women, these being least of all. Delilah, Eve, or my poor mother, his daughters at the last.

Perfection is in God, not in ourselves, and for this reason Paradise was lost, and for no other. 'Tis but pride to think otherwise, and those most proud will fall the furthest, as the Bible teaches. Those who find perfection in themselves must surely end by condemning all others and, when things do go awry, blame all but themselves.

My religion has taught me this. As for my thoughts upon those times, they come from hearing others speak and thinking on them since. Being but a child my memories are oft childish. So I remember our old servant took a chopping knife to the head of a capon – this for King Noll then, she declared, adding, for he is as like to a king as this silly bird, and deserving to lose his head in the same fashion. Which must have been about the time that Cromwell was offered the kingship, though I had but a confused notion what a king might be, and little understanding of her scorn. So for a long time after I would think a king a crowing cock, his crown a coxcomb, having heard how he did lose his head and seen it for myself, our old servant hold his head aloft and, plucking off his feathers say, fine feathers make fine birds.

You laugh, sir, but a child will think thus, knowing no other way. You must know this for yourself. And what we hear in childhood stays with us forever, image and language both. What is coupled then will not be set asunder, reason how we will. So when I hear of crowns I think of coxcombs, and see the feathers fly within our kitchen, even whilst my reasoning mind knows otherwise.

There was much talk of Cromwell in his latter days, how he did not abjure fine feathers. This stays with me. Though dissuaded from taking of the kingship, he was invested with royal pomp as Lord Protector, robed in purple velvet, with sceptre, sword of state, and coronation chair. And like a cock he thought the sun did rise when he did crow, all other birds being silenced, and the last parliament of fowls dissolved.

So he was cock of the walk at last, crowing lustily, all others stilled, the press acts reinforced. But every cock must to the pot at last, for all his noises, and leave his yard behind. Who would protect them then, those foolish birds, who held that he alone would keep them from the fox and other harms? For he was old, and like to die, and what should follow after, many feared.

Men are but men at best, and cocks but cocks. They think too little on this, who would bear such burdens singly, and transform our world to make a better place. For we must hence, no one knows when, but that we go is sure. And if all our wisdom is pent within one body, what must follow when it dissolves? Without continuity all else is folly and idle turmoil.

I think 'twas for such reasons my uncle, and others like him, did favour the rule of law. Men die, as he would say, the law lives on, likewise the monarchy. A ruler crowned by force hath no just heirs, and force must follow him, if not before his death, then after. And for this reason there was talk of marrying Cromwell's daughter to King Charles's heir. A foolish notion, surely, for who would marry the offspring of their father's murderer? Aye, readily, was my sister's quick retort, but said in a low voice, so my uncle heard it not or, if he did, affected not to hear, being a kind of man who thought it best to be both deaf and blind upon occasion, in the cause of harmony.

Would that my father had been such, seeing his children with a father's eye, and not a judge's. For he would take each barb, each quick retort, at its face value, making no due allowance for those hurts got from his own tongue, which brought them on. A poor freedom, and a rougher justice, that lets a father say what he will, commanding silence and obedience in return. A judge would not pass sentence upon the veriest murderer, his case being unheard. Yet we were not heard, being unjustly accused.

I see you look at me with startled eyes. In my youth 'twas very common for parents to be loathed rather than loved. Some thoughts still rankle. The Bible tells us we must honour them, but dictatorial ways do not breed affection. I tried to rule with fondness as a mother, rather than through fear. Perhaps I went too far, I know not. I only know I have their love yet, those that remain, and am thankful for it. They are good children to me. And better far than this, they are good Christians and good neighbours, who know their duty to themselves and others.

I was not used kindly in my youth. I would not have children spoilt, but hear them out. How oft, a child demanding why a thing should be, do we retort 'because I tell you so', from lack of patience? Yet what avails it, either at home or in the larger state, if children but obey because they must? They should learn to judge betwixt good and evil, or 'twixt lesser ills, else, when they are come to man's estate, how will they live as worthy citizens? Authority must rule, but do it patiently, seeking to guide rather than lead by force. Children will err from time to time, as men do also, and may learn from it, if kindly led. But getting wisdom is no easy matter, and no man has it all, for all occasions.

I question not my father's greater knowledge, only his way of dealing with the lesser sort. He might have made much of us, with more kindness. I doubt not I should have grown under his tutelage, more than his scorn. Why, we had a servant once, simple in his faith and much given to visiting conventicles, where he was told such truths as made my father mock him. He would not stoop to argue with the man in such a way as he might understand, but rather took delight in hearing words he knew to be but foolishness and silly superstition. Whereupon the servant, wounded in his faith, did leave my father's service.

Sir, this is no way to win the lesser sort, either to love us or to bring about a second Paradise. Those with greater learning must seek to raise the ignorant, else we shall never see a better world. But do it tenderly, and not with scorn. I do not say I might have been the equal of my father, but I would he had sought to lift me to his level, for fondness' sake. I might have loved him then, and he got his reward.

I would he had sought to make me his equal, for assuredly we are such before God. Children must err from time to time, but so do all men. Since our first parents were cast out into the wilderness there is no saying, not with certainty, which is the true path, which the false, and 'tis but by trial and error we can say, and having walked this way before, that it leads to the mire.

But, sir, the box is empty, excepting only this last document, and it concerns my father most nearly. It strikes fear in my heart to look on it, but pride also. Our freedoms are but lent to us, and can as readily be taken away. Dated the thirteenth day of August sixteen sixty, and issued by the Court at Whitehall. You must know of this, the royal proclamation for the apprehension of my father and John Goodwin for treasonable writings.

I have some memory of this, for they were days of dread, and fear, though from a source unknown, is felt throughout a household, blowing like cold air through a draughty door. My father, fearing for his life, had left to go into hiding with friends, I know not where, and servants ruled the house. It should have been a time of carefree laughter, my father being absent, but it was not so. Even my sister Mary was thoughtful in her mien, and chided my childish merriment upon occasion. I was much puzzled by it then, she being so unlike herself. It was as though a brooding presence ruled within the house, which all but I could see.

His books to be burned in public by the common hangman, and no man hereafter to print or sell them. This proclamation was put up around the city. So his fame did turn to infamy, the king being restored by general consent, and my father's life was threatened, or so it seemed. Men prize him now for literary merit, but books have higher ends and words more weight than niceties of verse and fancy phrases. In peaceful times as now, when gentlemen of leisure amuse themselves with literary arts and think themselves heroic in composing heroic couplets, 'tis easy to forget that other men, in other times and places, do take such words in earnest and will act upon them.

The Scriptures now are thought mere tales to amuse an idle hour, at best a sort of poetry to instruct us, at worst dismissed as ancient superstition. My father thought not so, nor did he think his task in life was merely to divert his readers. I think this fearsome document does honour him, placarded as it was all over London, and printed in the newspapers of the time. It shows that books are not mere toys, but things of weight and meaning by which we stand or fall, as fortune wills.

Here it speaks of wicked and traitorous principles dispersed in his books. I would not have you think me disobedient to the state, or in favour of forceful overturning of rightful government. No doubt 'twas just, my father should receive some punishment, and see his pamphlets burned. 'Tis but a trifle when others lost their heads. I only mean to say I take some pride in that my father wrote not merely to be crowned with laurel wreaths, commended by his peers and held in honour, but to bring about a better state for men and for the world. If he was mistaken in means, not ends, he stood by what he thought and wrote accordingly.

I know not who preserved this paper amongst these others, but 'tis strange to see it now, a dark reminder of troubled days. A time of terror for those who had thought their freedoms won, not for an interim betwixt oppressions, but for all time. The righteous are apt to think thus.

Yet my father had friends of influence who worked in his behalf. In this he was fortunate. Indeed, I have heard it said that all this placarding about the town to bring him in was but a ruse to get him off the hook and set him free. For all those not named as traitors in the Act of Indemnity, which was debated round about this time, could not thereafter be charged with any offence against the late king or his government. So a false hue and cry was set in motion for his arrest to excuse his name not being listed in the Act which, once made law, the indictment set against him was null and void.

I know not if this be so, and none, I think, can say with certainty. But that fear did stalk his days and nights about this time is sure. For though the immediate peril might be past, yet did my father dread that some fanatic, angered at his escape from execution, might do the deed himself. He lay awake at nights, and kept himself as private as he could, fearing to walk abroad.

It had been easily done, being blind and elderly, though none attempted it. For though the government was politic, wishing more to reconcile than set asunder, the mob is otherwise, its fury terrifying. Of this I have some knowledge, and speak not from hearsay.

About this time we moved to Holborn, and it was down this street, but shortly after, that I saw from our windows how the howling mob did bear the corpses, lately disinterred, of Cromwell, Bradshaw and of Ireton, to be hung at Tyburn. This is a sight, sir, that is with me yet, more so the sounds, for the very walls did seem to shake and tremble. I screamed with terror, and my sisters took me from the windows to a back room, tried to stop my ears, and sang to me some childish songs, so I would cease to hear. But I heard it still, and sobbed with fright, and would not be consoled. Then came our governess and made us pray upon our knees until the noise abated.

My father? He was all this time within his study, and made no sound. He would tap upon the walls, or rap the floor when help was needed, yet we heard him not. 'Tis little wonder, you may say, in such commotion. But our ears were accustomed to hear his least command, sleeping or waking, during night or day. Had he been present, I think I would remember, since every image of that dreadful day is etched upon my mind, and will be till my death.

Our governess did calm us with her words. Pray to God, she told us, not to aid you, but to cast out fear. And praying did so, I think, for hearing our own words spoken out loud in unison did calm our racing hearts and stop our ears to other noises.

I know not who kept this proclamation, but 'tis a dark memento, fearful in its import. I will not let it go from me, though you ask for it. I would have my children look on it, and bear it in their minds. Though they are poor, his blood runs in their veins for all that. If thoughts are free, expression bears a price when authors stray too far from those who read them, or hold them in contempt. Think you not so? My father found this out.

If 'twas he kept this paper, then it was from pride and not contrition, of that you may be sure. Pride in him was strong. It was a dreadful time. But he was privileged, as other men were not, having friends to hide him, and plead his cause amongst the powerful, and see that he came to no harm. He neither lost his life nor fled abroad, as others did, and though he was detained some little time in prison he was soon released, and was greatly honoured in his last years. 'Tis not ever thus, and men of humbler origin, though with as great a vision, have suffered much, with no man to defend them.

Let me close the box. I hope you have got some profit from it, if not in coin. And though you go with empty hands, your head has more in it now than when you came. You are welcome to such homespun thoughts and patchwork recollections as I am mistress of, I can give you little else for your trouble in coming here. We are poor, and but rich in memories. Now I must to my daughter, so pray excuse me.

Five

OUR FATHER WHICH art in Heaven, hallowed be Thy name. Thy kingdom come. Thy will be done, in earth as it is in Heaven. Teach us to know Thy will, Father, so we may follow it, whether to act in righteousness, or suffer meekly if need be, and seek no comfort in this life except in Thee. Teach us to know, Father, when we should be the instruments of Thy commands, and hear Thy voice, and when it is meet for us to bow our heads before the whirlwind of Thy wrath. We are but children, Lord, mere sinners, and many voices speak to us, and seem to come from Thee. Teach us to know Thy will, and know it truly, casting out our own, lest it deceive us, thinking it comes from Thee.

Give us this day our daily bread, and forgive us our trespasses. If I have asked, Lord, more than Thou hast thought fit to give, I humbly beg to be forgiven. There has been bread on the table this night, and for this I thank Thee. It has not been ever thus, and yet Thou hast seen fit to spare me, and bring some comfort to me in this time. Truly the days of miracles are not yet past, that this should be so, and I humbly thank Thee.

Forgive me, Lord, for I confess that fear is ever in my heart. I know the words, Lord – surely goodness and mercy shall follow me all the days of my life.

And yet, Father, I am but a weak vessel. In my youth I had great dread in my heart, that my children should be taken from me. When Thou didst take them to Thyself I grieved and wept. Though our faith teaches us to rejoice, I could not do so. And now, being an old woman, I fear for those children you have left me, those two of the ten I bore in sorrow, Urban and Elizabeth, to be a comfort to me in my old age. Their life is hard, Father, and like to continue so.

I pray, Father, for my son Urban, that he may find a good wife, and prosper at his trade. Also for my daughter Elizabeth, much cast down of late by the death of her newborn child, and in poor health. Bring her to term, and with a living child, and let them prosper, for times are as hard now as they were when my husband yet lived, and uncertain still.

Thy kingdom come. These words Thy son did teach us, to repeat from day to day. In my youth, Father, we thought that day must surely come, and we should live to see it here on earth. I am old now, and my time is spent. Soon I shall be in Thy glory. Yet my offspring suffer, and lack all hope of better days to come. Must it be so, Father? Is it not given to us to bring about a second Paradise in this world, as was hoped for in my father's time, and in my husband's?

It grieves me, Father, to see them live as we did, ever uncertain of their daily bread, for all their industry and skill. My husband was diligent in his workshop, yet got little from it but cares, and left his widow naught but penury. His children scarce fare better. There is talk now of giving up the looms and keeping a grocer's shop, or some such business. Thy will be done. Guide them, Lord, for I fear lest they but exchange one heap of troubles for another.

If Mr Clarke were living now it would give him great sorrow to see such long apprenticeships go for nothing. Is it for this they served, to peddle candles or half pounds of lard? Help Thy servants, Lord, for this earth is yet a wilderness. The market rules, and those with skills so dearly learnt must waste them, if they would eat. Be with them, Father, and keep them in Thy grace. And teach our betters who do govern us to legislate in wisdom, for they do little to protect our livelihoods, and count but cheap those skills so dearly bought, which yet must ever be the rock on which our country's wealth is founded.

Teach us to know Thy ways, for we but wander blindly since our first parents were cast out from Eden. We err as humans will, yet do we love Thee, and would live as Christians should. Keep us in charity, lest hardship makes hard hearts. For though we have but little, and oft dread the day to come, I know full well that many in this land do fare far worse than us.

Thy kingdom come, we pray, the better and the lesser sort alike, as Christians were commanded. Yet do beggars roam our streets, crying 'for charity', and are not heard. Is it enough to mumble with our mouths and yet do nothing, attending passively upon His coming, till time runs out maybe, the Jews converting not? For I was taught that Jesus would not come again to rule His kingdom till the earth was worthy to receive Him, and saints, not sinners, ruled. What must we do, dear Lord, to bring about the Second Coming, His kingdom here on earth? Hear our prayer, and open up the hearts of evil men, who listen not to Thee.

There are those, the younger, fashionable sort,

who think that heavenly revelations now are past, and nature runs its course without Thy meddling. Whatever is, is right, is now the watchword, so peasants lose their little patch of ground and starve in city streets, whilst great lords roam the meadows, all their own, and sheep grow fat, and men and women starve. They fence their parks for sport and recreation, reduce their tenants unto beggary, have town and country houses, lavish wealth on ornaments, fine gowns and carriages, yet turn their labourers out of doors to roam the highways, refusing poor relief to those not born within the parish, when the parish of their birth has made them homeless, destroying their poor hovels and their paltry living. They crowd our cities, Lord, sleep out of doors, and shame us with their plight. Yet those whose shame it is are pitiless, and know no shame. They make their parks a pleasing landscape, remove all things displeasing from their view, and when they go abroad they ride within their carriages, and look not out. Their lofty mansions in the town are guarded well by lackeys, so no importunate beggars cross their path, in seeking alms.

Our Father, who sees into all hearts, unto whom all secrets are known, teach them who but pray to Thee with their lips to open their hearts to Thy will, and do Thy work on earth. For such hypocrisy must offend Thee, as it offends all true believers. Teach them to follow Thy commandments, for they do not, though they may go to church on Sunday, and bow their heads in piety. Thou shalt not steal, we say, yet is the land stolen from those who tilled it formerly to fill their bellies. That common treasury, the earth, is taken from the many by the few, and landlords, whom greed makes greedier, would starve their tenants, and hang the needy who dare poach a rabbit for the cooking pot.

And so it is with all the ten commandments. Who loves his neighbour as himself? We kill, and steal, and covet, and call such sins by other names, to justify our ways. Thou shalt have no other gods before me, this was Thy first commandment, yet wealth and property is now the graven image many worship, that should worship Thee.

They call this freedom, Lord, a land of liberty, to take what you can get and let the Devil take the hindmost. And yet, Lord, when Thou didst vouchsafe us freedom, Thou didst give it not to us so we should plunder, but to choose betwixt good and evil. This was the freedom Thou didst see fit to give us, and I fear we choose but evil.

How shall Thy kingdom come, this being so? Open their hearts, I pray, and let Thy love enter in, that we may yet see a world fit for Christ to reign in.

Father, hear Thy humble servant, for there is no help in us.

Six

Now, CHILDREN, YOU will not be quarrelling
amongst yourselves, I hope. Such a commotion I never did hear. The neighbours will be
round in a trice, fearing there is murder afoot.
Susan, come here this instant, and dry your tears,
Liza. No, I will not have arguing neither, of who's
right, who's wrong, and who began it. 'Tis all one,
and you are both at fault, and must mend your
manners. It is a poor thing if those who think
themselves friends do bicker over some trifle, and
come to blows. For that it was some silly trifle I
have no doubt. So come, both of you, and tell me
what set you scrapping like mongrels in the gutter.

A piece of ribbon? This little scrap of cloth that
will scarce go round your noddle, or tie a bow, or
hold a cap in place? For shame, the both of you, to
quarrel so for such a little thing, and scratch each
other's cheeks, and pull your hair, and ruin your
gowns with tearing. What would your parents say,
to see you now, who have laboured hard and long
to get you fitly clothed? Your stockings torn and
twisted, and, if my eyes mistake not, a seam ripped
open. Is this the way you show your gratitude,
repaying thus their pains?

Bring me my workbox, child, and I will try to
mend matters as best I may, else you will get a

whipping before nightfall, so I think. Now dry your eyes, I'll hear no ifs and buts, who first began it, who did what, and who was most at fault. The blame lies in you both, and both should be ashamed to act so. As for the ribbon, I will keep it now, so neither of you has it, since you cannot come to terms. No argument, I care not for your quarrels, who's right, who's wrong. 'Tis all one to me. I would have quiet, and the household orderly.

Come now, dry your eyes, and sit beside me whilst I try to tidy you. Your hair is disordered, and all in tangles. Ouch, you may well say ouch, who did it, pray? Sit still, else it will only hurt the more. Pulling your head away will not mend matters, the knots must be undone. You should have thought on this before beginning.

Sit still and I will tell you a story, whilst I set you both to rights. But first you must kiss and make up, for I will not have those who should be friends, and love one another, pull each other by the hair and roll around the floor like a pair of wild wolf cubs. What kind of conduct is that, pray? Did not Jesus tell us to love one another, and live in amity, and share that which we have, however small and poor it be, and is this how you follow his commands? Shame on you both, to make such a pother over a mere trifle. You must learn to settle arguments more peaceably than this, or it will go ill with you when you are grown and have greater cause to fall out with one another.

So, now you are quiet I will tell you a tale of quarrelling, and what happens to those who must be ever arguing amongst each other, when they should be making common cause to save themselves. For flocks of sheep should huddle close together, and baah and bleat to keep the wolf at bay, not stray far off from pen and from the herd, where they are easy prey. For there is strength in numbers for the weak, if they but act in concord. But falling out and straying, the wolf will have his dinner sure enough.

Once upon a time, when I was but a little girl like you, there was a mighty shepherd to his flock, who kept the wolf at bay. He had been a soldier, fought in many battles, and could marshal silly sheep for their protection, so they did not stray too far, or fall down cliffs or into gullies, nor were swept away by running water. As for the wolves, he knew them well, and built his fences high, drove them far off with barking dogs, with loud and frightening noises, and ever kept a musket by his side. The leader of the pack, the king of wolves, he had long since shot dead and chopped his head off.

Whilst he lived, his sheep felt mostly safe, though they misliked him. Many felt unfree, for being closely penned and herded up together, they could not wander off at will to taste the tempting grass of sweeter meadows, and pasture as they pleased. Why did you kill the king of wolves, they'd bleat, if now we cannot wander as we please over hill and meadow, without your dogs go snapping at our heels, to round us up? Is this what you call freedom?

Yet this shepherd, who had been a soldier, knew what his sheep did not – that troops must march together to withstand the enemy, and make common cause. And I tell you this, he hated nothing so much in this world as squabbling and petty arguments, and had he seen the two of you just now, he would have knocked your heads together, and sent you supperless to bed. He has done as much to grown men, and sent them packing when they could not be of one mind.

But no man lives for ever, and no thing is done for good and all. Weeds grow in tidy gardens, as they say. The shepherd died at last, as all men must, and left his flock to his son Richard, who was quite another sort of man, kindly but undecided. When his sheep did wander off in all directions he knew not what to do, as some roamed east, and others west, some north, a couple south, and none obeyed his whistles and his shouts. Why should we heed his cries, the sheep did bleat, we fear him not. Besides, the king of wolves is dead, and cannot harm us. So at last we may enjoy the meadows, freely roam, and follow our desires.

But, alas, my children, these were silly sheep, to think thus. For though the old wolf king was dead, yet he had many followers in the pack, who gnashed their teeth with glee at seeing such foolish conduct, both the straying sheep and their weak shepherd, lacking authority and strength of purpose. Why, even his dogs would not obey him, but charged about at will, chasing the sheep hither and thither as the mood took them, thinking themselves the shepherd, that should be but his tool. For dogs are swift of foot, their teeth do bite, yet is their task but to obey, not to take command.

Besides, although the old wolf king was dead, he too had had a cub, now grown large and strong, who prowled beyond the gates, and paced the fences, and bided but his time to gobble up the flock. Indeed, it seemed that even Heaven knew that the old shepherd's passing did bode no good, for on the night he breathed his last a great storm such as the land had not witnessed in living memory blew across the countryside, lifting off roofs and chimneys, felling trees as though with a vast windy axe, knocking down walls and fences, and tumbling poor fishermen from out their tossing boats.

It was such a storm, my children, as none within the kingdom could recall, and indeed, though I was but a child, I yet remember the terror of those hours, how I did tremble beneath the sheets, hearing the windows rattle, shutters bang, and an eerie screech wail round the chimney pots and moan within the house like some unhappy ghost. I clung to my big sister in a fright, so she should comfort me, and hold me tight. And in the morning, going down below, our old servant said she had not slept a wink, and swore it was a sign of great events now ending, or yet to come, and boded ill, being surely Heaven's wrath at sins committed. Which made me wonder much that God should know my little peccadillo of the day before, and make such great commotion in His anger. So guilt will find us out, as you well know, my children, and I had stolen cakes from out the kitchen the previous night.

It was not a day like other days. The streets were empty, but for bits of branches that tossed and tumbled, and no one stirred abroad. And all men knew that Cromwell now was dying, our Lord Protector. I still recall the feelings of those hours, the bolted doors that rattled, and the howling gale about the house. There was an awesome silence within doors, despite the storm, or on account of it. A sense of waiting for it to subside, but fear was in the air, I felt it, for all my youth. I never saw such praying within doors, neither before nor since, except when my first stepmother did die some months before. Thus I knew that death was in the air, though none within our house was sick. Besides, my stepmother had died in quietness, her infant also. This was otherwise. It was as though the whole world was being tossed and turned, and all must suffer.

When the storm subsided I saw our garden wrecked. We had a pretty garden at that time where I could play in summer, and my father sat. Beyond it lay the park, St James's, and there so many trees were felled, their roots up in the air, as though some fearsome giant stalked the earth, destroying as he went. I scarce believed my eyes, to look upon such havoc, and my eyes can see it yet, as clear as yesterday, though I was but a child as you are now, and many, many sights which I have seen since then have left no trace behind.

No sooner was the Lord Protector dead, than those who had been too fearful in his lifetime to argue and to quarrel on how the kingdom should be governed, set to again. Instead of thinking on the enemy without the gates, they sought but enemies within, and therein lay their downfall. Divide and rule, this is an ancient maxim they too easily forgot, and were defeated by it.

Two factions quickly rose, that which would keep the government as it had been but lately constituted, with Richard at its head; and the Army party who, thinking the cause for which they fought now long betrayed, would have all things ordered anew. Like sheepdogs, their old master dying, they turned on his weakling son. We did the shepherd's work for him, they barked, now we shall herd the flock. We know best where they should pasture, and will not heed his whistle.

So all the chief dogs did meet together and decided that they would not have this shepherd Richard for their master. They had feared his father, and obeyed him to the end, but his son was not so fierce, and lacked authority. So when they barked at him, and told him go, he went without a murmur, fearing their teeth, and having little stomach for a fight. Having no will of his own, he saw the will of God in all things, and was much unlike his father in this, who found rather his will to be the Lord's. Whether it is more Christian to be resigned, or fight for Christian virtues, I scarcely know. Either way, I fear, we may end up with the Devil.

Sit quiet, children, you must hear me out. The tale is not yet told. So now, the shepherd's son being chased from out the farmhouse, this pack of dogs, the army officers, could choose to herd their flock as they thought fit. But how? That was the question more readily posed than answered. For each dog had his opinion, and barked as loudly as he could to make it heard. Such a commotion, children, never yet was heard. The birds were frighted off, and left their nests, and hens mislaid their eggs.

You laugh, my dears, to hear me tell it so, but truly, 'twas no laughing matter. For I fear these dogs, like all men of good will the whole world over, are ever more united on that which they would banish, than on those things with which they would replace it. So it was now. Each dog would have his say, and thought himself the best for barking loudest. Since all did bark, none listened, nor could they, for so much noise.

At long last they all grew tired of this confusion, put down their heads between their paws, and slept soundly through the night. Next morning they decided that each should bark in turn, and give their views on governing the sheep. So it was done. The first dog gave it as his opinion, that a council should be held each morning, and a vote taken, as to where the sheep should graze. Another thought that going by rotation, with each dog taking turns to have his day, would be a wiser course. These two proposals resulted in some scrapping between the rival camps. The noise grew loud, until an aged dog, silent until that time, proposed a compromise. Each dog should have his day, but that the common council should have the right of veto. Or, if you prefer, the common council should be held each day, but that two senior dogs should have the right of veto. Either way, a balance would be struck.

These notions much impressed all those who listened, yet could they not decide on which course to follow, the problem being this. Whichever course they chose as being the most just, it must be justly chosen. One vote for each, squeaked out a lively puppy, wagging his tail. But all those present barked out their objections, and drowned him out.

When the uproar had grown less a black dog with a patch of white across one eye proposed that each dog should have as many votes as he had years, thus giving each a voice but also due weight to seniority and wisdom. No fool like an old fool, squeaked the puppy, but was bitten in the ear and withdrew to whimper most piteously. The young one being silenced, and the bitch who bore him told that females have no vote, this method found much favour with the majority.

Now quite tired out with so much hot debate, the sun being set, the dogs all slept again. But the following morning new disputes arose. One had dreamed, for dogs do dream, that the Good Shepherd of ancient lore was come to earth again, and thought they all should hold themselves in readiness for Him, not outlaw single rule. It was time, they all agreed, to vote upon the method of procedure. But the problem now was this: should each dog have one vote to vote upon the voting, or several votes according to his age?

This caused a new commotion, for if they voted each according to his age, then the procedure which they sought to choose, it was already chosen. But if by simple vote, it was not valid, whether passing or defeated. For if defeated, it was by a method neither just nor chosen, if passed, then by a method now rejected.

Besides, said one, a genius at mathematics, there is a bias either way. For if we vote with one voice each, it is but natural that the younger dogs will vote against the other method, it being unfavourable to them. But if each have a vote according to their age, the outcome is foregone. Why, our oldest member is nigh on fifteen years, and can outvote us all, or almost. Sixteen, growled the dog, which began a scuffle, for several said he lied.

Thus passed another day in argument, for none did rightly know how to proceed to reach agreement. To complicate the case no dog could prove his age beyond all doubt, their births being not recorded in a book. Besides, they could not read. A shaggy mongrel limping on three legs proposed that, length of years going with infirmity, those with least teeth and most grey hairs should have most say, these being signs of venerable status. But this found little favour with the pack, since herding sheep requires authority, and barking without bite is little use.

The sun being long since set, they took their rest, and slept most soundly, wearied with their labour. They woke to hear a twittering of birds upon the rooftop, and hens a-cackling in the yard, the cockerel crowing lustily, and all the feathered kind, it seemed, likewise engaged in arguing how nature should be run. A wondrous chorus rose unto the morning sky, a sweet cacophony of sound, heralding freedom's dawn. It was a very parliament of fowls, shrill and disorderly. The cock crowed loudest, boasting how, alone of all the birds, he made the sun to rise, but lesser voices drowned him with their squabbles.

The dogs rose up, and prowled about the yard, but no bird paid them heed. Small sparrows picked the ground afront their paws, then flew aloft at will. Hens left the farmyard, heedless of the rooster, and laid their eggs in hedgerows far from home, whilst fluttering doves cooed round their cote.

The dogs yawned, stretched, and broke their fast, then settled down to work. A thought had come to one of them, which, until then, had not been voiced. He put it forward now as but a thought, with some timidity. Shall we consult the sheep? It being for their welfare that we labour, would it not help us in our work if they ran willingly where we would lead them?

This was a novel notion, and as such must needs be much discussed from each and every angle. It being known that sheep were silly, with but little brain, it was not meet to ask for their opinion unless the outcome was assured. For sheep, 'twas known, would wander into gullies, be swept away by floods, or eat such crops as were not meant for them, and which could do them harm. Left to their own devices, all agreed, the flock will perish, or we lose them every one. This being so, the choice, such as we give them, must be no choice at all.

So, said the eldest dog, what we must do is to put to them but those questions where the answers matter not a jot. We must not ask them whither they would roam, or when move on. These are weighty matters, only fit for us. Ask not whether they would graze upon the upper or the lower meadow, but tell them they must go into the lower meadow, choosing the gate by which they enter, the lefthand or the right. Likewise it matters not to us which sheep goes first, and which shall follow after, provided all go in. Leave to them the order of their going, as being but their democratic right, and they will sheeplike follow our commands, and make our task far easier than till now.

In all this time they quite forgot their sheep. For while they talked and argued, point by point, their flock had wandered off, being long since unattended, and hungry for new pasture. They bleated first, but when none heard their cries one of them found a gate left loose and pushed it open. The whole flock followed, and soon they strayed, this way and that across the hillside, for juicy grass, sweet clover and the like. For sheep must graze or starve, this being nature's way, and stomachs will not wait, as you well know.

At first they wandered idly, following their nose for choicest feeding. But as night drew on the beasts grew fearful, finding their numbers scattered far from home, with neither dog nor shepherd to protect them. Lost now in ones and twos in darkest night, the shadows boded ill, each eerie sound might be a beast of prey stalking the night to kill them. They huddled in their pelts beneath thorn hedges, or in dips and hollows, and prayed for daylight.

When the dawn was come they found but little comfort. Far from home, under a wintry sky, they bleated piteously to find each other, the flock being scattered over hill and dale. Neither did they know the best way to proceed, being used so long to obey their shepherd and his snarling dogs.

And so they strayed, hither and thither, through unknown fields and meadows, knowing not which way to go. Until at last some few of them did find a neighbouring farmhouse, and upon the stoop a sheepdog, fast asleep. They woke him with their cries and pleaded with him to find their fellow sheep. For we are lost, they said, and have no shepherd, and singly we will perish.

This was a wise old dog, who barked but little, and heard them out. Some called him cunning and, if cunning is to bark but little and prick up your ears to hear the sounds around you, he was so. His name was George, and in the farmyard he was oft called Silent George, being seldom heard to bark, a quality but rarely found in dogs.

Being silent, and but wagging of his tail, this dog did hear them out, those silly straying sheep. Please help us, they did bleat, for we have strayed and know not our way home. The flock is scattered, round us up, we pray.

The dog did nod most sagely, heard their pleas, then trotted off abroad, through field and meadow. No path was left untrod, no common ground left unexplored. Little by little he did round them up, the forlorn, bedraggled flock. Some were found huddled in the lea of rocky boulders, others wandering through woods or on the highway. One old sheep was caught in midstream, trying to cross the water, and knew not whither. Their fleeces snagged with burs, some lame of foot, they followed where his snout did usher them, this wily dog. And so they ran before him, glad to be a flock once more, in which they found much comfort. For to be singly straying through the land could do them naught but harm.

And so he brought them home, this wily dog, not to the home they left, but to his master's, who praised him highly and rewarded him with titbits. The sheep cared little who was now their master, being weary and despondent. After such little liberty as they had savoured they feared but anarchy, and would no longer roam unshepherded. To be forever herded in a flock was their delight, and if this master had an appetite for mutton pie, they bore it humbly, hoping the axe would fall upon some other neck than theirs, they going unnoticed in the herd.

Meanwhile the several sheepdogs at the other farm were arguing yet, how best to herd their sheep, when one of them, returning from a walk abroad, informed them that the flock had vanished quite, the pasture empty and the fields around deserted likewise. On hearing which the dogs got in a frenzy and began to search the country all around, scampering about the hillsides in despair.

They found no sheep, and when at last they found a flock with other markings grazing in a field, the boy who watched the herd threw stones at them, then fetched his master, who, to send them off, did fire his musket. One dog was hit and died, the rest ran off, to skulk within the woods like wolves or foxes, fearing the hunt. And so they lived out miserable lives, outcast, in hiding, who had sought to guide the flock, and lead it to green pastures presently, dissension being ended. Had their argument been less they might have kept their sheep, and lived out lives of honour, not contempt.

This, my little ones, was a tale told to me in my childhood, against quarrelling by those that should be friends. Mind it well, such fables come from truth, and should instruct us. Well may you weep, as I shed tears to hear it, as did the teller who first told it me. But wipe your eyes, for tears will not mend matters. Kiss and make up, you two that should be friends, for out of doors are enemies enough, who wish you ill. Now to supper, for it grows late.

Seven

Y OU COME TO a grieving household, sir. I fear
you find us much cast down in spirit. It is but
two days since we buried her, who should have
seen us put into the ground. But eight years old,
and as healthy a child as you could wish to see a
month ago. I can scarce credit it even now, though
I have had much sorrow in my time. I bore ten
infants, to bury seven before they were out the
cradle. Alas, sir, old age takes many pleasures from
us, but not our sorrows. I had not thought to feel
such grief again, but yet I feel it nearly.

Eight years old, sir, and such a child as would
make your heart glad. Pretty as a picture, and as
lively as a cricket but a month since. If you had
heard her then, how she would chatter, and run
laughing down the alley, you would not have
thought it possible. No, sir, pray stay. We must
master what we cannot help. I must ask you to
forgive my woman's frailty, which now overcomes
me. I had not thought to weep in strangers'
company, and beg your pardon.

Have you brought books to try me? I will dry my
eyes, and you may test me. Yet I fear my eyes are
weak now, and I see but poorly. Else I might yet
have earned a little by my teaching, lessening the
burden which I now must be upon my daughter's

household. They have so little that I would not make it less. Yet am I thankful to have a living child to care for me, being old. It is a comfort for which I thank God daily. Else had I died long since, of want, and lack of love. To bury many children is a sorrow which a man can never know, having borne them not, flesh of his flesh, in living anguish. Though his heart may grieve, he finds much comfort in other labours and, if his wife should die in childbed, takes another, to give him living heirs. His grief is milder, and his loss but temporary, finding new rewards on earth, which we must seek in Heaven.

I fear now for my daughter, suffering this loss. She has buried two babes already, that were born sickly. Now this, our little Liza. Who would have thought it, so full of life, and never ailing till now. For eight long years she thrived, and scarcely gave us cause to feel anxiety, though every mother is anxious from time to time, when fever comes, or cold, or babes grow fretful. 'Tis but natural, part of our daily care. This we bear gladly, finding our reward in thriving children who grow strong and tall. But such a loss as this, how can we bear it? She says but little, sir, yet I do fear the grief is deeper for it. I wish she would weep, as I do, and give release to that which burdens her. For to be sparing in our tears is to be heavier yet of heart, carrying the burden longer.

And she carries another burden within her, which grows with every month. They say a woman should not weep when with child, else it will know but sorrow. I would have a son, she told me but yesterday, for I would not have a child of mine, if it should live, feel what I feel this day. This she said to me, her face so stony and her cheeks so pale, you might have thought her dead to all the world. But I know otherwise, for I have been where she dwells now, and my heart breaks for her, a second rupture, doubling my grief. I would I could give her ease, both for herself and for the child that grows within her. We pray both night and morning, but as yet the words rise easier than our hearts.

The Lord giveth and the Lord taketh away, and we must bear our grief as best we may. Truly, we are punished most bitterly for the sin of our first mother, in eating of that tree. Yet I cannot think that, when He takes unto Himself such little ones as our sweet Liza, He does it out of wrath against our fallen race, but rather out of love for such dear innocence. Think you not so?

But you did not come for this. Please do not seek to leave, sir, it is I who am at fault in going on so. What cannot be cured must be endured, as the saying goes, and it may ease my mind to speak of other matters.

So, what would you know of me? Have you brought ancient texts for me to read out loud, in Greek or Hebrew? I will do it gladly, can I but find my spectacles. I have done it oft before, when learned gentlemen did visit me. I think, sir, they would have proved me and my sisters liars, that would calumniate our father out of hate and bitterness. You do protest, but I fear 'tis so, women being oft thought tellers of untruth by very nature, sinning most when telling tales of our most sainted men, whom history reveres. My father now is such, and so they would not think him cruel to his daughters. Come, sir, you came to test me, is it not so? You need not blush, I take it not unkindly, and I will read your Greek for you, if you have it by you, and my eyes fail me not.

But I am no liar, and would I had happier memories of my youth, and fonder tales to tell you. It gives
me naught but grief to speak ill of a father long
since forgiven. Besides, such stories as you hear
come not from me but from my cousin Edward,
who knew our household as did no other man,
loved my father most tenderly, and revered his
work. Would he besmirch his idol, except to honour
truth? It was but lately the great world knew I lived,
a lowly widow, poor and in distress. Since then I
do confirm what has been told, and do it sadly, no
more. I think fondly now of him who fathered me,
pitying his faults. For is it not a matter for great
pity, that a man should find no love within his
heart for offspring given him by God? Had I three
daughters now to comfort me I would thank my
Maker from my heart. Mine He took, all but Elizabeth, as Liza now is taken.

He had a son, sir, taken in infancy. Did you
know this? I think that had he lived, he might have
lavished on him such fondness as he did not show
to us, being but girls. Women are our misfortune,
he would say, and liked to tell me in his mocking
fashion that Eve was Adam's rib, and his misfortune, the word in Hebrew meaning both at once.
Tsela the word is, if my memory serves me right.
You see the limits of my scholarship, a thorn but
meant to goad us. Such academic niceties did much
delight him, for he would use superior scholarship
to humble those beneath him, such as us, not raise
us up.

I have no recollection of this brother, for he died
shortly after my birth, which took my mother. And
yet his little life did haunt our household in later
years, like unto a promise given but not fulfilled. A
nurse was blamed for his untimely death, whilst I,

the newborn infant, thrived. He had borne it better, so I think, if I had been the child to perish, and my brother lived. The nurse, dismissed, had now become an ogress, though our old servant spoke of her as blameless in the matter, and much maligned.

The Lord giveth, and the Lord taketh away, and we must bear such griefs in all humility. To do otherwise is but to prolong our anguish, and blind us to His mercy, which is a mystery we cannot fathom. This is a teaching of our faith which I have clung to, through many such times of loss, and their attendant pain. Yet I fear humility was not my father's forte, or his chiefest virtue, but he must ever blame some faulty woman when things did go awry, despite our best endeavour. I think he thought that God would do his bidding, did he but follow virtue, as he saw it, and so must blame some weaker vessel when misfortune struck. The Book of Job was not for him, there being no woman in the case.

You smile, sir, but indeed it is no smiling matter if born to petticoats. It is no light thing, ever to bear the sins of man upon slight shoulders, shrug them as you may, they drop not off. Christ our Saviour died to take our sins from us, both men and women, yet for my father, in his deepest heart, woman was not redeemed, and bore the sins of Eve, and many since, her nature being more fallible.

I am old now, and think that we must bear that which we cannot alter, nor seek to question it this side the grave. Our little Liza's gone, and there's an end, and no theology will bring her back, nor reasoning restore her. Who then should I blame for this our sorrow, to make it less? What balm is anger to a gaping wound, to close it up? I think, sir, we must rather be as little children are, accepting humbly what we cannot understand, and trusting in His mercy. This was not my father's way, else had he lived a more contented man, instead of pouring scorn on lesser men, whether in skirts or breeches. Harsh words, I know, but I am grown too old to mince matters for a stranger.

So, you have brought no texts for me to read? I confess I am glad of it, my eyesight being so poor. They say I look much like him, and Mr Addison was pleased to say, when I first met him, that I did need no other voucher, my face being testimonial enough of whose daughter I had been. Weak eyes are yet another, one I could rather do without.

His eyesight being gone when I was born, he never saw me. Is this not strange? I thought it so. And nursed the notion, had he but known my face and how like it was to his, he might have loved me better. Yet I fear the wish was father to an idle thought, since he cared little for my sisters, whom he had seen at first. I think he saw our mother in us, and liked us less for it.

Well, sir, we must bear that which we cannot alter. There are those who say that all we suffer is a punishment for sin, and none is without sin. They said this of my father, he being struck blind so soon after the king was executed, and he defending it. I see you look aghast, but these are other times, less superstitious, and more prone to look for natural causes in unusual events. Why, sir, did you know that when General Monck did march from up north to London, there were those who saw in this the prophecy of Daniel come to pass? I jest not, nor did my father jest in having Satan raise his standard in the north. The words go thus – So the king of the north shall come, and cast up a mount, and take the most fenced cities: and the arms of the south shall not withstand, neither his chosen people, neither shall there be any strength to withstand.

Know you the passage? It is not the custom now, I know, to read the Bible as was done formerly, in my youth. It comes from Daniel. A book much favoured at that time for prophecy. Why, sir, when silent George – I mean the General Monck – did march from north to south, the most ignorant apprentice could have told you that passage, and discoursed upon its meaning, and others similar. We knew our Bible, sir, and saw in it a map for past and future, that should guide us on a way that none had trod before. My late husband did read it so, being persuaded in his youth that Daniel told us the Second Coming was at hand.

Do not mock us, sir, for I see something of laughter in your eye. How else should they proceed, but by the Book, in such a wilderness? If you have come here out of reverence for my father, you must not mock, for he, like other men, did think thus. Why, even Cromwell and his officers did halt their counsels for to hear a prophetess who came to speak with them, so think it not confined to lesser men, the meaner sort, unschooled and unrefined. No, we lived by the Book, aye, lived and died for it, most often.

Now I am old I see it otherwise, as do my children, born in another time, with lesser hopes. Indeed, I know that I was born too late to feel the full force of the hope that moved my father's time, and spurred them on. I have but heard the echoes of that epoch, muted by disenchantment, and from persons long since disabused, their faith embittered. You are younger far than I, and cannot know the age of which I speak. Whether you are in this more fortunate, I know not. Is it better in this world to have our hopes deferred, and shattered utterly, or to be born without? For you, sir, being born to wealth, such questions have but little meaning. Indeed, that things should long continue as they are must be your comfort, rather than your pain. For the poor 'tis otherwise.

As for General Monck, he was by some called a wolf in sheep's clothing, that did betray us at the last, and we the helpless flock. I have some recollection of that time, vivid yet, the days being so tumultuous. His name was on all lips, whilst turmoil reigned without upon the streets. What would he do, what not, his troops now drawing near, like to a vengeful messenger of God, or mystery of fate, I know not which. Being but a child, with a child's fancy, his name for me did conjure up some fearful ogre, with the power to blow down chimney stacks at will, and gobble naughty children for his supper.

Fear and excitement both, a sense of awe, and great events in train. This was the feeling as the army marched towards us. All tongues a-wagging, and the streets unruly, wellnigh to anarchy. Groups of apprentices did roam about the town, jeering at soldiers, or pelting them with stones. The military scarce dared show their faces in the city, for fear of angry citizens, and streets chained off, and all men crying for a free parliament, not the ancient Rump but lately re-assembled.

I saw then with the eyes of a child. Now I am grown, I know it was not some all-seeing fate, some instrument of God that marched on London, but a man much like any other, uncertain of his path. Nay, with more humility than those he lately served. An instrument of government, and not of God, was how he saw himself, and rather sought to serve the people than to be their master. He listened much, spoke little, and was nicknamed silent George. He heard the people who petitioned him as he marched southward, all calling for a full and free parliament, heard them out, and kept his own counsel. Even my father, as I think you know, did write to him, though in another manner, wishing to avert, even now, what all men wished for.

I think he was much mocked for publishing a pamphlet at that time, which he did send to the General, in which he put forth a ready and easy way to keep the commonwealth, and stop the monarchy from coming back. Alas, had it been so easy, it should have been accomplished long since, and now it was too late. And yet, sir, though he dreamed still when others long had woken, I find in this a kind of hardiness that makes me love him, though I loved him not when I was at his mercy, and a child. I have heard this spoken of with much derision, as showing him to be not merely blind in body, but blind to simple truth. There was a tract published against him, I know, for my cousin showed it me, called *No Blind Guides*, and with the motto, 'If the blind lead the blind, both shall fall into the ditch'.

I have it not, else I would show it you, but it has stayed with me. For my father, you must know, when many saw his blindness as a punishment from God, saw in it a mark of special favour. For God gave poets, like seers, an inner light to see by, whilst lesser men are blind to vision, so he thought.

I do not know if there be truth in this, though Homer too was blind, or so they say. As a child, and ever since, I have thought it marvellous that he should see such things as Paradise, and Heaven, and beauteous Eve, when I saw puddles in a muddy yard, and chilblained hands, and greasy pots that must be scoured. And yet, sir, whether it be a welcome gift to see such visions, turned blind to common things, I still must doubt. The likes of you and me must live in the world as it is, and make do with what we find. If we can discover a little beauty now and then, in a world long since grown ugly, it must suffice us. For we are fallen too far.

Perhaps we are blinded by the common day, as he would have it. But in common justice it is hard to see so far when we are cold and hungry, and want the wherewithal for living decently. I have heard my children crying, not the angels sing. So the hungry man sees puddings in his dreams, and his visions are all of a little comfort, no more than this. But anarchy brings neither, as my uncle was wont to say, no coals to empty hearths, nor cabbages to market.

My father's brother was a royalist, and thought it mighty strange that, in a last ditch stand against the Restoration, some would rather see a commoner made king than rightful Stuart kings returned. But General Monck declined the offer made to him, not from cunning, or devious designs, as many claimed in after years, but that he would in all things abide by his own precept, that a soldier is but an arm of civil government, obeying its commands, never his own desires.

This is a simple thing to do in settled times, but in a time of anarchy and overturning it is not so. For though the House, being then the only voice of government, did order him to put down riots and disorders in the city, the citizens were of another mind, it being not elected recently, but stale with twenty years, nor full and free, so many members being yet excluded.

I think, sir, this must be the hardest thing of all, to go, not with our inclination, but with the will of

God, and men. We women know this sorrow, when our life's labour, in a little child, is taken from us, and we must not question why, but silently accept it. Men that do labour in the world must see their best endeavours come to nought, and suffer it, and take the consequence. Who knows, sir, what he thought, this General, caught as he was betwixt a running tide and principles held dear for many years? And so he first obeyed the Parliament, and quelled the riots. A deed which stupefied all citizens, as I remember, as posts and chains were taken off, and gates unhinged and smashed. Gossip had it that the very soldiers raged to do such work, being loath to do it.

And then his mind was changed and, changing with it, his orders countermanded. Soldiers and citizens were now as one. The bells rang out, housewives gave food and drink to soldiers standing guard, and many a bonfire burnt its rump upon the street, to mark its ending. The Roasting of the Rump, they called it, and apprentices did dance in triumph. Out of doors, sir, was so much joy, such wild rejoicing as it was rare to see, but within hushed voices, an uneasy stillness reigned, like death. We had heard the cheering crowds, the loud huzzahs, as the troops were marched down Whitehall and the secluded members escorted under guard into the House, and though I was but young I understood that something was afoot the like of which I had not known till then. Nor such feelings of division, uncertainty, where evil was, where good.

This I chiefly now remember, not the cheering crowds, the bonfires, and the like, but my perplexity, at such division, that light was dark, dark light, and grown men living under God were so divided.

It was the earliest inkling to my childish mind that eating from the tree by our first parents, though bringing to us knowledge of both good and evil, brought us not sufficient insight to tell us which was which on all occasions.

The certainty that reigned within our house but fuelled my unease. For if my father, this old, blind man, had purchased truth with loss of sight, with learning, then how could God permit such a vast multitude to be deceived, and hurry to their doom with such rejoicing? For so it seemed, I being made to feel that dark days were upon us, and yet the people cheered out on the streets. Was this some living nightmare or a punishment from God for heinous sins committed, and by whom? I did not know, but only felt the world a fearsome place, mysterious, not fully understood.

This is another age, and men live now by other certainties. The Bible now is like some ancient tale, told to divert the childhood of our race, but put aside since then. For you the world's a clock that ticks and ticks, even though its owner sleeps, a steady pace that nothing will disturb. But in my father's time, aye, in my husband's also, for he in youth did think so, time's truth and man's destiny were thought to be unfolding to some great triumph and perfected end, Christ's kingdom upon earth, and this great truth was spoken of in Scripture, which prophesied all things. Hence it followed that promises unkept must come from sin.

I am old now, sir, and have seen much sorrow. This latest grief is but one of many in a long life. I fear such certainty, of right, of wrong, makes a harsh master, and one unkind to human frailty, and human need. And then I think they were mistaken, for we must seek to find Heaven within us, rather than here on earth. I cannot think the Lord would punish an entire people, any more than He would punish my poor daughter by taking Liza from us.

But in those distant times men thought that great events were brought about by God, either to reward or punish, or to fulfil prophecy. So my father thought, enraged at lesser men who now returned the king, and by their lack of virtue kept our Lord from coming down to earth, to establish His kingdom in this land. Is it right, he said, that we, the few, should now return to slavery, because the many choose not to be free? Despising common sense, and common goals, which lesser men must look to. I fear in this great men are greatly blind upon occasion. Besides, sir, that which I endured, my sisters also, was it not a kind of slavery, and brought about by him that spoke of freedom? I fear the liberty he spoke of was but for an elected few.

Some thought the nightmare ended, some the dream, but either way great changes were afoot. I have since heard tell that politicians did indeed behave as though a dream had passed and now all men awoke. General Monck having marched the members purged from out the House so many years before, and sent them into Parliament protected by his soldiers, to cheering crowds, the members within now proceeded to their business as though it had been December eleven years ago, the king's head yet upon his shoulders, and all things as they once had been, before the overturning. They finished speaking of things broken off long since, as a grandam nodding by the fire will wake up suddenly, and speak as though her children were yet by her side, that are departed. Or like men at midsummer, bewitched by elves and fairies, who vanish with the sunrise.

You would have me say whether the dream was good or ill? Alas, sir, though my father's daughter, he did not seek to make me his heir. I was taught to make lace, and do embroidery for rich men's coats, to read a little in my mother's tongue with understanding, but my father's many tongues without due comprehension. I was not raised to speak of such lofty matters, and would you now have me put my head above the parapet so you may shoot it off?

I think that those who call themselves elect of God are prone to human error, being human. In this they chiefly err, not to confess it. Obstinacy in a lost cause is but foolhardy. We must consider why the cause was lost, not cling to idle dreams.

I think, sir, if there be punishment for sin committed by a nation, if sins there were during those troubled times, such punishment will come in direct consequence of folly, and not from Heaven. And yet many thought that great afflictions, other than those brought about by kings and politicians upon a suffering populace, were sent from God. I mean the dreadful pestilence, and the fire that followed after.

That something should occur, momentous, unexpected, was widely held, sixteen sixty-six being the Year of the Beast, as given to us in Revelations. 'Here is wisdom. Let him that hath understanding count the number of the beast: for it is the number of a man; and his number is six hundred threescore and six.' The words are with me yet, for as the year approached they were oft quoted, with hope or dread, or mingling of the two, since even greatest faith must have its doubts, and though we may surmise God's purpose, as many did, the manner of its unfolding must ever be a mystery.

I heard much of this from my late husband, and from others of his trade. For many in his family, along with other people in this neighbourhood, had kept within their hearts the promise of the Second Coming, whilst others made their peace with circumstance. Indeed, a youthful cousin of his rallied to the standard at Mile End, when a headstrong, foolish few sought to rise up against the might of Cromwell, and bring about the godly kingdom here below, long since betrayed. He was imprisoned for his pains and yet, a few years later, when the king had been returned, took part in just another such rebellion, inspired by readings and by discourses in Coleman Street, a favourite meeting place for Christian sects, and with this rabble rampaged through the streets, demanding that King Jesus reign instead of Charles. This time he met his death in the fighting that ensued, and many judged him and his fellows foolish, to think to overturn the powers that be by simple violence.

Such fighting was abjured, but not the hope. This I know from Mr Clarke, and others like him, though humbler than my father, much like to him in this, for all lived by the Book, and by their common hope of better things to come. In the Bible they sought promises of change, being impotent for ought but waiting.

So when the pestilence came to this city, it did seem a punishment from God, as many were struck down from hour to hour. Some thought that this was the beginning of destroying Antichrist, and that our Lord was doing now what men had failed to do. If you should deem this cruel, to think that such a plague should come from God, how much more cruel were it to suppose it came without a purpose? Which, I fear, it did, since many saints did perish, to be thrown into a common pit with strangers, and when it passed the world was much as it had been before, except more empty, and destroyed by fire.

Alas, sir, we must not question God's purpose, or His wisdom, in bringing such great suffering to His people. As I have told my daughter, we must not ask the why and wherefore for such dreadful loss, but rather seek to find our comfort in the knowledge of His mercy, and find our peace therein. Suffer the little children to come unto me, Jesus told us. And they are angels now, of light, having gone into His grace. I have seen so many go before, but I think this latest grief is the hardest blow of all. Forgive me. I am old now, and tears come easily, to put me to shame.

And yet we were spared, sir, at the time of the great pestilence. For all the talk of God's punishment, it must be said the Lord dealt kindly with my father, and so gainsaid their judgement. Whilst thousands died, he lived. We fled the city, it is true, and so escaped the worst, yet even in the countryside some died, as I recall. And when the Great Fire swept the city our house near Bunhill Fields was not destroyed, though we could see smoke rising less than half a mile away.

The fire came so close, we had begun to move out books and chattels from the house, as did our neighbours. So many as he had, it would have been no easy task to save them all. My sister, being loath to shift them, said they would make a merry bonfire. She had a sharp tongue, did Mary, and had but little liking for our father's studious habits. I think she thought to be rid of them at last, but was in this disappointed.

My poor sister would speak in this fashion when the mood was on her, which was frequent. Speaking of my father's lack of sight, I have heard her call it a blessing, else he would know his new wife, our stepmother, had a face no better than the hind parts of a cow. He had no eyes, she said, because he would not see, and so was blind. My father, for his part, would say that God had punished him with daughters, unkind, undutiful, and what you will. And so the taunts flew back and forth, ever more barbed, like arrows.

Though she bore her mother's name, and was hated for it, I think Mary was more like her father than either would acknowledge. She had his wits, left unattended and so grown wild, untamed by discipline or proper use, and like him could be satiric and unsparing. One tongue, so he would say, is enough for any woman, and in my sister's he found one too many for his liking.

These are ancient quarrels, and I would not trouble you with them. My poor sisters are long since dead, and I too old to harbour grudges. Though is it any wonder great men cannot fashion a better world, where all shall live in harmony, if their own private household be ever in a state of civil war?

My sister thought his blindness made him foolish, but I rather was of the opinion that it bestowed on him some special gift, in seeing wondrous visions denied to sighted men. Being but a child, I thought, if I could but keep my eyes shut long enough, I too would see them. And so I stumbled in the dark, trying not to peep, when daylight beckoned from under screwed-up lids, and marvels did not come.

You smile, sir, but the young have simple notions, and must find the world out for themselves. What I thought came from God, it derived from books, which we must read but could not understand. Have you brought a text for me to read? Though my eyes are weak now, never of the best even when young. A poor inheritance for one who must stitch for her daily bread. It is close work, sir, and harms the eyes.

I would offer you some slight refreshment, but you find us unprepared for visitors. Indeed, we have been so taken up with sorrow this last week, that such civility has quite gone by the board. Pray, forgive us.

Think you that all things are foretold, and cannot be amended by what we do? Many have thought so, but 'tis a fearsome doctrine. And yet, sir, to think otherwise brings terrors also, and guilt with it. I would not have my daughter wracked with it, to add to all her woe. I speak to her of God's will, as I was taught to do, but I fear she but listens with half an ear.

Grief is deaf, as I know from my own experience. Must you go, sir? I would not drive you hence, but it is difficult to speak of past times, the present being so heavy on us, and I have but little heart for it.

Eight

Is THAT YOU, daughter? I must have slept, I think.
You should have woken me ere this. I would not
be idle. The Devil finds work for idle hands, so they
say, but I have ever striven . . . never a moment
. . . shelling peas in the morning sun. Idleness is
the root of all evil, so she said. Stitching till my
fingers were sore with it. Spotting the linen, she
said, for I was forever pricking my fingers, being
clumsy at it. And the tears running down my face,
not with the pain of it, but from vexation. Wishing
for other things, I know not what they were. The
young lack patience. And scolding atop the discomfort, my aching fingers, for the blood spots that
would need soaking, and my stitches too large.
Well, she said, Adam and Eve walked naked in the
garden, having no knowledge of their own shame,
and now for our sin we must sew garments just as
soon as we can thread a needle, and stitch shirts
for our masters. Besides, she said, the weather
has turned cold since then, and climes far more
inclement.

Aurea prima sata est aetas. Those who study Latin
are not required to stitch shirts. *Ante mare et terras
et quod tegit omnia caelum unus erat toto naturae . . .*
how does it go on? A little patience, sir, it will come
back to me. My eyesight is not what it was, and my

memory fails me now and then. And I have been unwell this past fortnight. But if you have brought some ancient text with you, I will endeavour to read it. I would not have you think I told an untruth. I am no liar.

I tell the truth, sir, though you whip me for it. I am no thief. I would I knew the meaning of those books, and so escaped stitching. My brother John, now, had he lived, would have sewn no shirts. It is a poor way to lose your eyesight, bringing little reward. A shirt is but a shirt, when all is said and done. But I would not have you think I told an untruth.

I knew the sounds by their letters, though not the meaning. I wish I had known their meaning, and so got something for my trouble. Something about a golden age, I think, without laws to compel, nor fear of punishment. My lady told me, that took me to Ireland. Else I had never known it.

It grows cold, daughter. What is left to burn, now we have no coals? And winter not yet over. The child must be kept warm, but there has been no work this past fortnight. I like not his pallor, husband. I would we had money to buy coals, this house being damp and draughty. Nothing will ease his coughing. Have you not heard him this night? I have scarce slept, for pacing up and down with him. Honey will not soothe it, nor the linctus. Pray for him.

Is that you, daughter? Take my shawl, I would not have you shiver. I shall be well directly. I would not be a burden. Sir, I said, I would live by my own industry, liking not to exist by charity. But he was very kind. Madam, he said, you need no other voucher for whose daughter you are – your face is sufficient testimonial. He would have got me a pension, had he lived. Such kindness in my old age. I had not thought to see it.

How dark it grows. Get us a candle, so we may have light. I have worn out my eyes with stitching, and working by firelight is not good, neither for sight nor stitching. If I had a penny, so she said, for each and every candle he burnt over his books, I would be a fine lady now, with servants of my own. But she let her tongue run away with her upon occasion, thinking long service gave her licence to speak her thoughts. Alas, I fear it did not. Have I told you of her, how she stood by us at the end? I think I did, surely, she being almost a mother to us, that had none.

I will speak out, she said. You may stop my wages but you cannot stop my mouth. And let out such a flood as none could halt. These girls are innocent of wrongdoing, and I must speak for them, that have no other to take their part. And if they had not been, who could blame them? For they are used, and spurned, and sorely tried both day and night, and I have watched it now too long with aching heart. To see such daughters is to know a servant free.

Aye, free to go, she screeched, and father sat, his blind smile on his face, and saying not a word. To have used her so, that served you since a child, and spoke but from devotion. She was like a mother to us, that had none, in her rough way, though flouting sentiment. And sat up late of nights, when he was but a schoolboy, to make sure he got safe to bed when all the world was sleeping, and he must yet be at his studies. Scarce more than a child herself, and hardly able to keep from dozing off, as she would say.

Unlettered as I be, and this she told him, I still can see what's plain as any pikestaff, and needs no tutoring. If love is blind, self-love is blinder far, and you have lacked in duty to your children, that are forever calling them unkind, undutiful to you. Love begets love, she said, and much else in the same vein, and called his wife a scheming harridan, that sought but to serve herself in serving him, who was too blind to know it.

I fear I weep even now to think on it. Forgive my weakness, but the old are foolish, and tears come easily for ancient hurts, that should not pain us now. But such a storm as broke about our heads that day, I never knew till then. Like to the summer's end, when sultry days explode in thunder after long rumblings, and clouds burst out their contents in a cold downpour. From that time on there was no turning back.

Have I been sleeping? Send little Liza to me, and I will teach her her letters. I think she has the gift for learning readily, and must profit from it. I hear that gentlefolk now send their daughters to school, where they learn French, and other tongues. And read rather for pleasure than profit. I should have liked that, had I been born to it. But I was not, though I think on it sometimes, how it might have been otherwise. But the child must learn all she can, though poor, and use those wits she has, and not neglect them. I would we could have done more for you, but there's no use crying over spilt milk, and times were hard. Send her to me. Why is the house so quiet? Are they all outdoors? If the sun shines, I am glad of it. It will do her good, for I know she has been unwell. Sunshine and good country air will do more for body and soul than any physic. I know this from my youth. Did I not tell you of the time we fled to the country?

If we could but afford more candles. I have worn out my eyes with stitching, and working gold thread for rich men's coats, not a task, he said, fit for his children. What was he thinking of, to let you be apprenticed for such work, contrary to principles of faith and politics? To foster luxury by slavish labour, was this a righteous end? Alas, sir, as I told him, he thought not so, else had he taught us in a manner fitting for his heirs. But he despised us, thinking on us as our mother's offspring, not his own, and would be rid of us as nuisances, being less than dutiful. Mr Addison has been most kind. He would have got me a pension, had he lived. Sir, I told him, all my life I have been industrious, and I would be so now, if the means can be got. To live upon charity is not in my nature, but I fear the means desert me. I have had to wear spectacles since a young woman, and am my father's daughter in this. A little in pride also, I must confess, liking not to live upon charity. But beggars must be no choosers.

I am no thief, madam, no, nor ever have been. That you should call it theft when books have gone astray, calling his children to account, and then his servant, shows how you think on us. You would be rid of us, I know. Time for them to earn their daily bread, if they cannot get husbands, I have heard you say this to him oft enough. What should we do, you shrew? Find some old man and turn his daughters out? Calling them thieves, and telling tales, that lack of sight makes easy? Is this the path of womanly virtue you would have us follow? I thank you, madam, but I scorn to sink so low, and if penury must follow, so be it. Besides, I should be hard put to it to find another such, so full of rancour, and so gullible.

I grow hot. This room lacks air. I would have a window open, and drink a little. Even daughters should inherit, and get their patrimony. This is no theft, I think. So my uncle thought, and he the lawyer. He saw us right in the end, using his lawyer's cunning. I have heard him say, it is not just that heads of households should hold absolute sway, as my father thought. Being of the opposite opinion, and thinking ever that Church and state must overrule domestic tyranny, which some called freedom. Wives may be unloved, and daughters disobedient, so he said, and yet must be protected under law. He did humour him but, in so doing, ensured we should inherit.

My cousin Catherine has spoken of this. He was a kind man, my uncle, and would not blow his own trumpet, thinking discretion the better part of valour, and would have no thanks. But I must thank him even so, as must my sisters, for getting us the little that was our due. He knew, you see, that, as he put it, where there was no will there was no way for his own children to be disinherited, and all left to his wife. And so he let my father babble on, each time he called, and seemed to humour him in his designs, knowing that, if he put not pen to paper, the will would surely fall, as proved the case. The court refused her probate, though she got a spiteful servant, who never knew us, to speak ill of us in court. He being neither sick nor dying at the time, there should have been a written testament. My uncle Christopher, since he was a lawyer, had always known this, and, had he thought it right, could have forestalled the outcome, but did nothing.

It was but little, and yet I must be thankful for it. Your father married me when I had nothing, no dowry to my name. I was glad to bring a little, when it came, to help our early struggles. He sent back my mother, the dowry being unpaid. So my grandam told us. Let them have their mother's dowry, nought else – I hear he spoke thus at the last. Meaning we should have nothing. Poor father, so mean of soul in petty matters, it fits not to his gift, that God did give him. I would speak of him only with reverence, as the world does. And we must be thankful for it, relieving, as it does, our penury. I would speak truth, but speak it kindly. I have long since forgiven.

You had a good father, daughter. He took me when I had nothing, in honest affection, and never sought to reproach me for it in after years. If thou dost bring as much in fondness as I bear for thee, then I am rich indeed. So he spoke. I think I wept, daughter, to hear such words, uttered so kindly. I was not used to it. He was a father to me, then a friend, and such a husband as I trust you have in yours, a helpmate ever.

And yet, I think you have. Is he not a weaver also? Do not marry above your station, for it is a sure way to be contemned. As our old servant used to say, when Adam delved and Eve span, neither could read Latin. We are to be kept ignorant, I think, to keep us in servitude.

But I am my father's daughter for all that. Mr Addison had no doubts in the matter, when first he saw me. Madam, he said, your face is sufficient testimonial. *Aurea prima sata est aetas.* I will recollect how it goes on, if you but give me a moment. My memory, like my eyesight, begins to fail me. It was the lady who took me to Ireland with her who first told me something of the meaning. Before that I would recite but parrot fashion. My poor child, she would say, for, though hired to be her companion, she did ever treat me like a daughter, having promised this to him who should have done so . . . you do but squall like a parrot, that hath no soul, and thus no understanding. But you have both, and so you must endeavour . . . how did she speak to me? . . . and so you must endeavour, against all odds, to seek the understanding men would yet deny you. Such a lady, I never knew her like. She put me on my mettle, as no one else. Are you a silly bird, or are you human? I hear her still. It had to do with that first golden age, as I remember, as ancients saw it.

It grieved me to be despised by him, I do confess. I am no silly bird, sir, no, and pride, I fear, burns in my veins, even though deemed sinful in a woman. I have seen my sister lash out sarcastical as ever he could be, and that without schooling, or benefit of higher learning. Well, blood runs thicker than water, as they say, and we might have given him cause for pride, had he but looked upon us differently.

How a man looks upon his children, now there's a mystery. It is quite otherwise with us women, for we know them to be flesh of our flesh, though opposite in gender. Heir to all our ills, and helpless at the start, like to fall sick, and die, and keep us wakeful with their crying in the night. Which of us has not paced the floor, and kissed his tiny cheeks, and felt our hearts grow cold within us at such fragility? And should we then think them a different breed, for that they have a little tassel dangling betwixt their legs? But they are taken from us, if they live, and must be turned to men. And so turned from us, as I believe.

It is not the custom to speak of such things, but there is none to hear us. Besides, I am old, and I think I am not long for this world. I have felt so strange of late, as though I drift between my former selves and myself as I am now. I thought I spoke to your father but a little time ago, yet I know he is dead long since. I think I will be with him presently, and he but beckons. And I am ready, else I would not hear him. The Lord is merciful, and I shall see my babes again, that caused me so much sorrow.

So will you, daughter, when your time is come. Be sure of it, though you grieve now, and find but little comfort in the thought. I would not have you weep. I heard your father's voice as I was dozing, as clear and strong as though he stood within this room, and he did tell it me. Your babes do live, and you shall know them, as you know me that speaks. Is it not strange? But so it was. I feel such sureness now, as never yet. For I inhabit different times and places, and move as easily as any ghost or spirit, belonging nowhere. And so will you.

Is it night now? I think I must have slept too long. Why did you not wake me? No matter, I will get up presently and do what I can, once this weakness leaves me. I would not be a burden. You have cares enough as it is. I know it. I have lived as you do, and I know how it is. But my mother, dying at my birth, I never saw her. And so I did not tend her when she was old. Think you she will know me, and I her, when all souls are risen from sleep? And yet I have dreamt of her, from time to time, both lately and long ago, and always knew her for who she was. I cannot tell you how she looked, except that she seemed fond, and tender, and quite unlike his last wife. I knew her not by outward shows, which in dreams are oft belied by other forms of knowing, as though the outer form were variable, but not the inner spirit, which shines forth, and so declares itself. How will my babes look, think you? Will they know me in like manner?

A little broth will give me strength. I would teach Liza her letters, she has the aptitude for it. My little Lucy died of the cough, else she might have done well at her books. I never quarrelled with your father, except in this. He thought I set too much value on book learning, he being all for practical matters, and keeping of accounts, and such like skills. Let them help in the shop, he said, and wind quills. And yet you are as poor now as ever I was, being wedded to a weaver. Honesty will not suffice, nor hard work.

Not a man in the family I came from ever laboured with his hands, but was sent to school, and studied, and was turned to a gentleman, that need not bother his head on a falling off in trade, or foreign imports that do take the bread from out our mouths. My father should have gone into the Church, but found another course, despising it. As for my uncle, he did study law. Now that's a way to live and die in comfort. Daughters must have dowries, or else go down in the world.

Or marry an old man with desires no lower than his stomach. That is the way to make old bones. They say she still lives, the termagant, and is as sparing now with her pennies as ever she was. Too mean with her breath to die, as the saying goes. And yet I would not quarrel with her, not now, for all her scolding. A shrew is not born, but made so, and I doubt she was content. I know this now, being old. We are creatures of circumstance, and I have not always been so forbearing as I should have been. I know this and, if I have caused you grief through lack of patience, I ask you to forgive me. It is a sovereign virtue, but hard to practise, though we be women. Confess it, is it not so? I think I should find it easier to wield a sword, show bravery, or any attributes deemed manly, than dull old patience, which is rather seen by what is not, than any presence, positive and sure. And yet we must endeavour to be patient, a quality that by its very nature is measured out in years, not hours. The briefest falling off will smirch our virtue, whilst heroes lie at rest.

I shall be well by and by, do not fret. I need but to get my strength, for nothing ails me. Why do you not send the child to me, and I will instruct her? Besides, I like to have her by me, she prattles so sweetly. Loving women do not make old bones, she would say, when mocked of her long spinster-hood. I speak now of our old servant. And yet she was like a mother to us, that had none, though her rough ways would deny it. She spoke up for us at the last, and so lost her livelihood. For I am honest, so she did declare, and to speak honestly I think you are not so, for you are bent on seeing evil where there is none, this being most oft in the eye of the beholder, as I do think, for you would rob these motherless girls of the little they do have, and so you call them robbers. A book may go astray, and so may pence, without that they be stolen. But a birthright stolen, or honest reputation taken away by idle tittletattle, that's a theft indeed, and you are guilty of it, so I think, in speaking thus.

You should have heard her, banging pots and

pans the while in furious clatter, so all the world could hear it. Such a din from out the nether regions, it reached up to the study, kept silent and secure. Pandemonium, my father called it, delighting in the word, though little else.

I saw her weep that day, though only tears of rage, her face flushed crimson that a servant should speak thus, and flout authority. She never wept otherwise, I think, being too much the shrew for tenderness, or womanly sorrow. Well, loving women do not make old bones, and she must be ancient indeed now, in her long widowhood. I wish her joy of it, these tedious years. I doubt if they be joyous. Coddle your cold bones, aye, your cold heart, by a warm hearth. I must pity rather than hate you now.

We should die having made peace with our enemies, that could not live in friendship with our neighbours. Forgive us our trespasses, as we forgive them that trespass against us. Such a pandemonium, he said, for she flew up to him at once, in outrage. He would have quietness at any price, I think. And so he heard but her voice, which was shrill enough, and heard no other. Buying tranquillity, though dearly bought. No rights but his, no argument but hers, that catered for his needs, a tranquil household.

Else how could he send her from him, letting her be dismissed, that had served him since childhood, though but a child herself, when in his mother's house? And all the years since then. To let her go so. I think she loved us, though she spoke not of it. I know so. I would that I had put my arms about her more often, and told her my affection. As a child I did it, when she gave me sugar plums, or wiped my tears. But she was never one for such displays, and losing infancy we lose the gift of showing our affection, and taking in return the love that's given. Get off with you, she'd say, for I have work to do, and hot air never yet made dumplings. She would give me raisins, my head being little higher than the table, and call me duck, and tell me stories of her father's farm, which she could scarce recall, being so young when put to service. Her skin did smell of onions, I remember, and when I smell them now upon my hands, I think of her.

I have looked upstairs and down, father, but I cannot find it. I think, with so much moving, it must be mislaid. What am I to do, father, will you not hear something else? No, sir, I know a book is not like a pudding, so you may eat rhubarb in place of plums, but it cannot be found. Mary is not in the house, so I cannot ask her. I read from it only last week, at your behest, I know, but now I cannot find it. Has someone other read from it for you? It will be found in time but, though I have searched high and low, I cannot see it. A book having no legs, as you say, it cannot walk out the house by itself. Did you lend it to someone? Then it must be within doors.

No, father, who should have sold it, and for why? She would do no such thing and, besides, she cannot read. No, nor the dunghill women neither. I think you have been speaking with my stepmother, else you would not accuse her of such a deed, nor us. I would buy you another, gladly, but I have no money of my own. Nor have my sisters. Is it then valuable? I thought we were poor, and yet so much for a book, and then so many of them. The house so full, there is scarce room for us.

But I am no thief, sir. You do wrong us.

She says the dust in them brings plague, and will shift them about no more. Besides, since she cannot read, how is she to put them back just so? They are all as Greek to her, even if in Latin or her mother tongue. So though you cry order, order, it is of little use. But a thief, father, how could you think it, after such long service?

So we must be her eyes, and help her to it. Such scheming. But I mean not my sisters, I mean your wife. Who would be rid of us. Like the false cuckoo she is, emptying the nest of fledglings. Though they be honest, and your own. She it is who has been pouring poison in your ear, else you could never suppose such devious plots, and credit such designs within your house. Because we are but women, father, deceitful as Delilah? And yet our step-mother's a woman too. As your honest servant was wont to say: there's none so blind as they who will not see.

I have seen her burn papers for kindling, it is true, but this is no theft, but ignorance. And yet, I think, she had enough wits to make a scholar, were she born your brother. And more than enough homespun wisdom to make a preacher, though you laugh at it. As she would say, you get from a vessel what you put into it, no more.

How cold it grows in this room. We must have coal, else the child will get sick. It was catching cold that took Isaac from us when he was six months old, for all his swaddling. Though, to tell the truth, he was born sickly, and I never knew an hour from his birth that was not fearful and full of dread. Did I tell you of it? I hope you may be spared such sorrow, for I think it is harder far to bear when they live beyond childbed, and look upon your face, and learn to smile, and know your voice. To go through the valley of the shadow, and then be bereft, it requires more fortitude than I am mistress of, and a humbler spirit. Yet I have tried to be a good Christian, thanking God for His mercies.

I pray you may be more fortunate. You have a good husband, though he is poor. Better a dinner of green herbs, where love is, than a stalled ox and hatred with it. I have known both, child, and I know whereof I speak. Yet we must have coals, else the child will take sick.

Is it night, and the child gone to bed? You must keep her at her lessons, for she is bright as the morning star, and quick to learn. I would I had been half so quick, for I might have gone further, and not stumbled. And yet, not so. There are those who are made stupid by education. We have been spared this, being poor, and female besides. Having our arses flogged to quicken sluggish brains, whether we would learn or no. Construing Latin by the hour. Useless lumber, your father called it. For learning is not wisdom, and would have us foolish for speaking merely in our mother tongue. This is the privilege by which they rule.

Aurea prima sata est aetas. Yet I do know a little, if you will hear me. I am no liar, sir. I was compelled to it, as were my sisters. Anne was excused, for she did stammer. *Quae vindice nullo . . .* it will come to me, and others also, if you would hear me. My eyesight now is poor, but memory serves. *Poena metusque aberant . . .* You are very good, sir, to take an interest in my plight.

Let her keep accounts, and do arithmetic. Your father was much in favour of this, as mine was also. A shilling not put down in the book was a shilling

144

stolen, which could be wellnigh a hanging matter. So let her do sums, else there will be discord in her household. Write down, it was spent on flour and candles, so harmony shall reign.

It was spent on flour and candles, father, I will swear to it on the good Book. She knows it, and seeks but to stir the pot. But I would be at peace with you, and settle accounts at last. So much commotion for a mere trifle! I would lie in my bed without strife, and sleep easy.

Think you we shall sleep without dreams, to kiss and make amends in Heaven? We should do so in this world, and so leave it in amity, and quietness. The young may die otherwise, which is their peril, but those who are old should first settle all accounts, and so go peacefully. Such a pother for a shilling gone astray, and the whole house topsyturvy when the book could not be found. But she would blow upon the coals, and it were in Hell.

Well, there are those who think that the old Adam is in every man, aye, and grandmother Eve also, and the story of our first fall but a parable, of greed and suchlike vices. I have read this somewhere in my youth. My husband showed it me. The old Adam is in every man, of greed and tyranny, and Paradise shall come again when the earth is a common treasury, each man taking that which will provide sufficiency, but no more. For property, and buying and selling of land, is the curse upon us. As if the earth were made peculiarly for them, that have got it by violence or cunning, and enforced people to pay them money for what should be a public use. We are a long way now from such thoughts, and yet I think there is some truth in them, and reason also.

Is it morning yet? We must be up before sunrise,

if it is winter, for there is much work to do. Did not the cock crow? To tell the truth, I thought myself wellnigh in Paradise, the year we went into the country to escape the plague. I was never so happy, and would be out of doors before the cock. And see the dawn come up, a wondrous sight for someone from the city, forever in a smother.

Though it was but a few short months in all, it shines forth in my memory of girlhood as though it were wellnigh the better part of it, and counted in years. Is it not ever thus, memory playing strange tricks on us, so the grey years leave not a jot behind, but one day's sunshine suffusing all? The years since Mr Clarke died, and Caleb took ship for India, what has become of them, can you tell me? 'Tis all like a grey fog, and grey in my hair to prove it, each hour like the one before it, much of a muchness. If there are landmarks, they do drift within it, uneasily, having no firm foundation on solid ground. I have lost my husband, and since then much else, as those who grow old must do. And yet some hours shine in the dark like jewels, though half a century lies in between. I think it is God's grace, to comfort us, so we may know the promise that waits for us in Heaven.

If Paradise should be as those green fields of England long ago, and muddy lanes, and rampant hedgerows, twisted apple trees, I should be well content. Our little Liza would soon be well if she could run free in such sweet air. It is not good for infants, the foul stench of our city streets. They thrive like country crops, and so grow strong. And yet, we must earn our livelihood in this plague pit, there's no help for it, though soot besmirch fresh linen before it is dry, and brings on the cough.

I would our little Lizzie might run in the meadows

as I did once, and lie on her back to watch the skylark soar, and clouds float by. When you were sick I told him, Mr Clarke, if we could but get this child some good country air, and herbs still wet with dew of a May morning, then I am certain it would thrive. I thought you would die like the others, if the truth be told.

If wishes were horses, he said, then beggars would ride. Besides, he said, you talk but old wives' gossip, and God's will is done as surely in country as in city, despite our travail. I thank God you lived, and yet I think your Liza would benefit from going out of town.

If it rained, I have no memory of it. We were packed tight as oysters in a barrel, the house being so small, yet out of doors was all the world to roam in. You must accept His will, daughter, and not weep. The child is in God's keeping. But summer must have an end, and winter follow. I thought I should never cease from fretting when we returned, the plague having abated. Not just for the hedge-rows, and the birds singing, no, though that was well enough, but to be free as the wind that blows, heeding no master, no hourly duty, that was a wondrous gift I never knew till then, nor found it since. There being fewer books to try us, fewer tasks, and far more space for refuge.

Well, we must all leave our Eden, is it not so, and be thrust out of Paradise, though the brief taste of it do haunt us ever, and will not leave our thoughts. So sorrow follows joy, and is the deeper for it. This is our trial, I think, to know from whence we came, and find no path by which we may return.

God grant us faith to find it, in this our wilderness. For we have need of Him. I see it yet, the skylark, how it rose in perfect freedom, and hear it singing. I think the Lord allows us such a sign, a memory such as this, so far, and yet so clear, to be for us a beacon in the night when we are lost, glowing on a distant hillside. I would return, and see what I saw then. You shall come with me, and get the wind upon your face. It will cure you fast enough. I like not your colour, no.

Dry your eyes, child, and we will go. There are poppies growing, and the clouds run like sheep in the sky. You will see it, and grow strong, and tall as an oak. Your father knows nothing, no. Gold will not cure it, nor physic, if my soul sickens. It pants for air and light in which to grow. Money will not heal it, nor sternest discipline, though I obey.

I thought I should never be done with grieving, back at Bunhill, and it a plague pit, and walled in, though there were trees enough, and green spaces, and windmills turning merrily. But I had lost that which I had but lately found, and knew myself bereft. To taste such heady fruit and then to be deprived, it wounds the spirit. From that time forth I served unwillingly, forever in a pet, nursing an ill humour at every given task, and longed to run away, as once I could, and hear the silence and my brooding thoughts, and speak with nobody.

It was the Devil that was in me, so she said, our stepmother. Why, she was well enough till now, but takes after her sister, and mimics her, having no better model. Another time she'd say it was my age, I being then fourteen or thereabouts, the mother rising in me, female humours stirring, or some such thing. All but the thing itself, a wild and unschooled spirit which, having tasted freedom, craved for it.

Was it the serpent spoke to me? I know not. If so, then I have had a lifetime to repent, in bitterness and sorrow. I have brought forth children in pain and misery, and buried them again. You know this, as you know how we must serve, changing a father for a husband, and look to him. I have been forgiven, I think, my husband being a kind man, and loving.

Lavender grew by the wall. I would sleep with it under my pillow, to bring sweet dreams. I cannot think it was the Devil, for all her scolding. And yet, I wished her ill. She read it, being no fool, in my black looks, at Bunhill. Such dreams as it brought me, who knows whether for good or ill? Beguiled by fleshly things, and by the spirit. For the scent of new-mown hay I would have done such things, I know not, nor cared, if not found out.

But if God sees all things, I am lost, if joy of such a kind is sinful. And earthly things. To disobey, I know it is a sin, but what of conscience? If God speaks in the skylark, must I not hear him? And hear him in my blood, which likewise speaks? Such confusion as I felt, I feel it yet. Honour thy father and thy mother, this we must surely do. And yet Jesus has spoken otherwise, telling us to leave them.

Is that you, father, knocking on the floor with your stick? How dark it grows, and you in haste. I know not where I put the candle, and cannot find it. I will come as quickly as I can, though my fingers are stiff with the cold in them, so I can scarce hold a pen. And when I heard an owl screech in the night, though it was but an owl, she swore it was poor souls in the plague pit, crying for Christian burial. Being tumbled in like cattle, they could not rest. It is not healthy in this city, I would we had not returned.

We shall have rest at last, I know it, and sleep till

Judgement comes. I could rest now, were it not for the knocking. Will he not sleep in his grave like other men? My children, though they cried in the night often enough, they do not wake me now. This is a strange thing indeed.

And yet, though books may carry contagion, they do not die of it. Not as our children do. And so we are judged. God gave you a great gift indeed, when he took away your eyes, else had you seen much that is ugly. It is we, with our eyes, that are in the dark. And so I must find the candle.

That the fire should spare us also, it was a sign of His favour. So he would have it. For it came within sight and sound of our windows, and marred the hangings. I could smell it long after, though we aired the rooms. But if the air itself be full of soot, washing and hanging out will do no good. As our old servant said, only so much can be done by hard labour and honest housekeeping, and if the air be foul 'tis no use fanning. For which she was called impudent.

Such a commotion I never saw before nor since. And Mistress Betty was for moving our chattels out of the house, as neighbours had begun to do, the wind blowing in our direction. And my father said never mind the few chairs and fewer garments, it was his books we should be stacking out of doors. Aye, said our servant, and there they will make a pretty bonfire, God willing. And madam our stepmother asked her to explain her meaning, knowing how she had but little liking for them. I mean only, she said, that they are as like to burn out of doors as in, if a cart cannot be got to take them further afield. But yet we were spared, and the books likewise.

The booksellers who did remove their wares to

the vaults of St Paul for safekeeping lost all when the church burned. I remember it was much spoken of.

Is it daylight yet? I dreamt I lay in the orchard, hearing the insects hum about me, and the smell of ripe fruit strong in my nostrils, and thought myself in Heaven. I was filled with such sweet content, and yet so airy light, I knew I dreamt. Think you it will be so, and we shall find our dearest moments in eternity? I could wish it. And yet we have fustian thoughts, and lack vision. Our eyes are too much on stitching, and scouring pots, to know the Holy City.

But I have thought, upon occasion, that both are with us daily. The best and worst, both Heaven and Hell, if you will. I have no learning, but I think we may hope for quietness, and rest, since God is mercy.

Come closer, daughter, I would see your face. You are much like my sister, who died long ago. You never knew her, else you would have loved her gentle spirit. I shall see her, I think, but whole, and no more crippled. An end to pain is a good end, and should suffice us, if the Heavenly City be long in coming, to open up its gates. Have no fear, child, for God is merciful, and will deal more kindly with you at the Judgement-seat than ever men will do upon this earth.

It comforts me to have you near. I would I had known my mother. I ever tried to be a loving parent, thinking the world harsh enough when we are grown. It was no uncommon thing in my youth to hate a parent, being roughly used. But I would rather my little ones should know what it is to be cherished, than to learn in a hard school, and be made hardy for the life that follows. To have known a little joy in youth, and loving comfort, this is a lantern to us all our days, and brings light on a winter's night.

For the young are innocent, I think. Though we are all born in sin, and must bear the fault that comes from our first parents, there is a kind of goodness, a purity, that should not be marred. I doubt that beatings and harsh words will make of them good Christians. Such a comely child you were, with your blonde locks. It was a miracle to me that you lived, having lost so many. I am thankful to God you were spared, to show me some kindness in my old age. A mother dotes, as you know full well, tied by the bond of flesh, and every little fever makes her fearful. I thought I should lose you once. Your face hectic, and coughing through the night. A father, being less bound, can be more stern, and mete out punishment like the God of the Israelites that Moses knew.

Still no daylight? I could drink a little now. But this is tea – have we then come into riches? Or did Caleb send it us? I should like to have seen him once more, but they tell me he is dead, and buried far off. The world is changing, that we drink tea now. I am used to small beer, and not much else, though I care not for it.

Let me sip a little more, for my mouth is dry. Our little Liza is dead, is she not? I thought as much. There is a kind of silence in the house, that speaks of it. I see you weep. You must not do so, for she is now with God, and in His love. And yet it is hard, I know, for a woman to think so. Men speak such comfort easily enough, having not endured the pangs that we must suffer. Yet when their schemes do founder they are not resigned. Chimeras, dreams, these are their hard-born children, that they would not see die, but rather fight and suffer. Though half the world must suffer with them, they will on. But we must be resigned, and bear our sorrow, it being the will of God. Child, His wisdom is a mystery that cannot now be fathomed. But at the last all will be made light, as we enter into His glory.

It is nearly morning, and I will get up soon. I feel easier now. Put back the shutters. I did hear the cock crow in Bedfordshire. You must dry your eyes. It will pass, this present pain, believe me. I have been where you are now, and know this to be so. Time is a great physician, as they say, and cures all ills. It is a harsh school, this life of ours, is it not? And when we have done learning, our time is run. I would we could learn it from books, and pass *cum laude* as our betters think to do.

And yet they fool themselves, that think so. For we are all born ignorant, and must learn by our errors, that is the pity of it. I think, though they speak of two, that the tree of knowledge and the tree of life are but one and the same, and in eating the fruit of one we must taste the other. If this be heresy, I plead guilty.

Will you not get my gown? I feel refreshed, and would wash my face. I thought I knew it once, in a country orchard, all that God would have us know. But no doubt I was foolish, being a young girl. And yet, if conscience is our yardstick, then I heard His voice, and knew His wisdom. Such a stillness, child, I never knew till then, nor found it since. In which the trees did whisper, as in awe, feeling the breath of God upon them. So I thought. And listened to His Word. I heard the insects hum, and mine own heart within me. He told me, peace.

Hearing no more, I knew He told me this. I would I might have stood thus for all eternity, and nothing alter.

How long ago was this? I was but thirteen years of age, and now I am old. And yet I see it clear as though it were yesterday. Is this not strange? And so it has no end, though time did pass, and all things alter with it. The sun shines up above, and I am young. The apple tastes sweet in my mouth, I taste it still, and hear the bees hum. It is a sign, I know, of how our souls will fare, within His mercy.

Now it is morning I must go about my business. I have spoken of this to no one, in all these years. For to see such a vision, and speak of it, is to invite mockery. Or unwelcome fame. Though I am my father's daughter, I must keep silent. He would not wish me to speak thus, it being thought unfitting. Say nothing of it to him, I beg of you. I dread his scornful tongue. And I would not have her know where I go. I shall be scolded for idleness. And yet I do what is necessary, no task undone. But some other will always be found, if I stay. This is the way of it, being ever at their beck and call. And so I hid in the orchard, to find myself at last. Finding Him also, so I think, but durst not tell of it.

I feel light of spirit now, all my pain is gone. *Aurea prima* . . . they say there was a golden age once, before men fell from grace. Could we but return . . . But, I think, there was never living without struggle, else had we been feeble, and not fit.

Blow out the candle, daughter. It is morning. I would not have us waste the hours. Such a long night as this has been, but now I see daylight. Give me your hand, and I will take you with me to the orchard. You will taste the fruit.

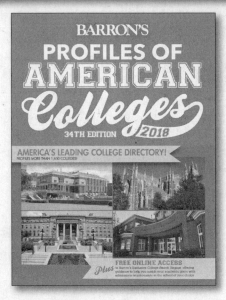

Contents

1

An Introduction to the SAT

WHAT THE SAT IS AND HOW *SAT EXPRESS* CAN HELP

In the eighteenth and nineteenth centuries, very few Americans went to college. Those who did usually went to elite prep schools for high school. So colleges were familiar with their applicants' schools. Admissions officers for colleges knew from experience what the grades from each school meant. These admissions officers based their decision making on students' grades alone.

By the twentieth century, the emerging middle class was sending more and more Americans to college. Admissions officers had an increasingly difficult time deciding on which applicants to admit. Now students from hundreds or even thousands of high schools were applying instead of the students from the usual prep schools.

In 1901, the College Board started giving tests to high school juniors and seniors. These tests took days to complete. The College Board then offered the scores to any college that wanted them as another piece of information to help decide whether or not to admit a student. The first SAT was given to about 8,000 students in 1926, and it has grown to be a bigger and bigger part of college admissions to the present day.

The SAT has changed over the years, but it has always focused on skills deemed important to college success. Those skills can be learned and strengthened. Therefore, using this book will help you get the best score possible.

SAT Express will guide you through the concepts and strategies that will give you the most success on the SAT in the shortest period of time. The concepts and strategies are clearly presented so that you can prepare for the test as quickly and efficiently as possible.

THE PARTS OF THE SAT

The SAT is split into two parts, English and Math.

The English Test has two components: the Reading Test and the Writing and Language Test. The Reading Test covers comprehension, interpreting data from graphics and charts, and vocabulary through context. The Writing and Language Test covers grammar, graph analysis, and revising skills. The Reading score is combined with the Writing and Language score to get the English score. There is an optional essay on the SAT, but that is not part of the English score.

The Math Test has two main parts: calculator and noncalculator. Both parts of the Math Test cover the same topics—algebra, geometry, data analysis, and trigonometry skills. They are just presented in slightly different fashion in the two parts.

Reading Test

The Reading Test is the first section you will take when you sit for the test. You will have 65 minutes to answer 52 questions. There are 5 reading passages or pairs of passages (2 passages about the same subject but with one set of questions). Each passage or set of passages has 10 or 11 questions. The reading passages can be pieces of literature, important historical documents or great speeches, essays about the social sciences (like economics, psychology, or sociology), and/or articles about the physical sciences (like biology, chemistry, or physics).

Tables, charts, and graphs accompany some of the passages. Questions about these graphics test your abilities to interpret data. However, these questions do not require math.

Writing Test

The Writing Test is the second section of the SAT. It has 44 questions, and you will have 35 minutes to complete it.

The questions are inserted into nonfiction passages. They are not standalone questions in individual sentences. There are 4 passages, so each passage has 11 questions. The Writing Test has two types of questions. The first type includes sentence-level grammar, usage, or mechanics questions. The second type includes paragraph or whole-passage questions, so you cannot simply read each question in isolation and then answer it. You must read the passage.

Math Test

The Math Test consists of two sections. Remember these details about the first section:

- No calculator permitted
- 25 minutes
- 15 multiple-choice questions
- 5 grid-in questions
- 20 questions total

Remember these details about the second section:

- Calculator permitted
- 55 minutes
- 30 multiple-choice questions
- 8 grid-in questions
- 38 questions total

There are 58 questions altogether in the Math Test. Since you are permitted 80 minutes to take the entire Math Test, you should complete each question in 1–2 minutes.

Questions in the Math Test focus on three major areas:

- The Heart of Algebra
- Data Analysis and Problem Solving
- Passport to Advanced Mathematics

Part Three of this book focuses on each of these areas. You will find tactics that will prepare you to succeed on the Math Test.

Essay (Optional)

The SAT includes an optional essay. Since the essay is not required, it is the last section of the test. Those who are not taking this section can leave, and those who are taking it can stay.

For the essay section, you will be presented with an article and given prompts that ask you to analyze the author's argument. You will have to read the article carefully. In addition, you will have to understand not only what the article says but also how the author persuades the reader. Your essay will be scored based on your understanding of the reading, your analysis of the argument, and your writing mechanics.

You must remember that all of the English in the optional essay revolves around your ability to *understand* what you read. Having just a surface-level understanding (like "Who was the main character?") will not suffice. Instead, you will have to read for understanding of both the content and the form of the passage. In the essay section, the SAT focuses all the testing of English skills on reading. For this reason, it is important to carefully read every section of the article and of the essay prompts.

HOW THE SAT IS SCORED

The SAT is not scored like a regular school test, in which the top score is 100 and the lowest is 0. Instead, students earn raw points based on the number of questions that they answer correctly. Students never see their raw point scores. Instead, those raw points are converted to a scale ranging from 200 to 800. Since there are two parts to the test, English and Math, and since scores for each of those parts range from 200 to 800, students can score between 400 and 1600 on the entire SAT.

The SAT also has an optional essay. It is evaluated and given three separate scores: reading interpretation, analysis, and writing skill. Each one of those areas is evaluated by two different scorers on a scale between 1 and 4. So students can score between 6 and 24 on the optional essay.

Knowing when the test is given is important as you make your study and testing plans. You should plan on taking the test more than once because doing so will help your chances of getting accepted into more colleges. Why?

First, the SAT offers something called Score Choice. Basically, if you don't like your scores from a certain sitting of the test, you can hide them from colleges. So if you have a bad day, there is no problem; you can toss out the scores.

More important, you should understand the way most colleges look at SAT scores. Most schools combine the best English and Math scores across different sittings of the test (also known as "superscoring"). For example, let's say these are your scores from two different sittings of the test:

Month	English Score	Math Score	Total Score
March	580	500	1080
June	490	540	1030

Most colleges will take a composite score from your two tests:

English Score	Math Score	Total Score
580	540	1120

So you can see that it's in your best interest to take the test at least twice. Some students will take it a third or even a fourth time. Usually, taking the SAT two or three times is plenty.

Plan on taking the test as soon as you complete *SAT Express*. You will get your scores back about three weeks later. Look at those scores, and see if there's an area where you want to focus. For example, you might decide you're happy with your English score. You would then put your effort into the Math Test the second time to try to raise that score. Even if you're generally happy with your first scores, take the test as soon as possible after you get your scores.

The SAT is like training for a sport or learning a musical instrument. When you learn it and practice it, you do better than when you stop practicing. So if you take the test in March, plan on taking it again in May with June as a possible third time. You will be done with the test before the end of the school year and can concentrate on college applications and enjoying summer!

The worst thing you can do is take the SAT in March and then decide to wait until October before taking it again. Your SAT skills will have slipped in the long time between tests, and you'll have to work much harder to get your scores where you want them to be.

So remember that the SAT is a process, not a single test. Take it, get your scores back, and take it again.

BIG STRATEGY #3

Don't Get Competitive with Scores

Remember what the SAT is—a test that colleges use to help decide who to accept. Once your scores are in the range you need to get accepted to a college, you've reached your goal.

Students often lose sight of that. When you hear friends talking about their SAT scores at the lunch table, don't start thinking of your scores versus theirs. Their scores are theirs; yours are yours. Getting into a bragging match about SAT scores is worthless and pointless.

Your only goal with the SAT is to do the best you can to give you the most opportunities with college. Once you've earned the scores you need to get into the college you hope to go to, you've met your goal.

HOW TO WORK THROUGH THIS BOOK

Think of each chapter as a lesson. Give yourself about a half an hour to an hour, depending on the subject and on your reading speed, to complete a chapter. That means that you will have all the lessons completed in somewhere between 8 and 16 hours. The Practice Test is your chance to put the lessons to use. Complete it in one sitting. The SAT takes 4 hours. So figure on spending between 12 to 20 hours to complete this book and prepare for the test.

Your study schedule depends on when you start preparing for the SAT using *SAT Express*. Here are some options for preparing based on how much time you have until test day.

Two months before the test:

- Complete two chapters of *SAT Express* per week for the first month and then three chapters per week for the second month.
- Take the Practice Test the weekend before the SAT.

One month before the test:

- Complete a chapter of *SAT Express* every other day during the week and one per day on the weekend (for a total of five chapters per week) for three weeks.
- Take the Practice Test four or five days before the test.

Two weeks before the test:

- Complete two chapters of *SAT Express* per day.
- Take the Practice Test four or five days before the test.

One week before the test:

- Complete five chapters of *SAT Express* per day on the weekend before the SAT and then three per day the Monday and Tuesday before the SAT.
- Take the Practice Test three days before the test.

Obviously, having more time before the test to prepare is better than leaving your studying for the last minute. No matter how much time you have, though, you can be prepared for the SAT if you work at it!

Chapter Overview

The SAT is split into an English Test and a Math Test. Each portion can earn you

> **Key Tips** have been included throughout the book. You'll find these **Key Tips** set in shaded boxes.

200 to 800 points, for a total SAT score between 400 and 1600. If you take the optional essay, it is scored separately on a scale of 6 to 24. Plan on taking the test as soon as you have completed this book. Then take the SAT again as soon as possible. Don't put it off! In the coming chapters, we will break down the English and Math concepts to show you what the test is asking of you and how to approach each concept. No matter how much time you have, if you focus on the lessons in this book, you will feel confident when you take the SAT!

PART ONE: WRITING AND LANGUAGE TEST

On the Writing and Language Test, you will be asked to revise and edit different types of writing by making changes to words, phrases, and sentences. The Writing and Language Test is combined with the Reading Test into a single English Test for a possible score of 800.

Components of the Writing and Language Test

- The test is 35 minutes long and has 4 passages.
- Each passage has 11 questions.
- Each passage is between 400–450 words long.
- The passages are based on 4 possible topics: careers, humanities, sciences, and social studies. Careers includes topics such as health care, business, or technology. Humanities includes topics such as art, dance, poetry, or music. Sciences includes topics such as physics, biology, or chemistry. Social studies includes topics such as history, politics, geography, law, or education.
- There are 44 questions altogether.
- Each passage and its 11 questions should be completed in 8–9 minutes.

The Writing and Language Test is half of the English score. Remember that grammar and writing skills appear on every test. This means that you can raise your score on the Writing and Language Test if you learn or refresh your knowledge of the rules of grammar and style as well as general writing skills. We will work on those skills in the next four chapters.

2

English Is Balanced

The SAT may ask anything from English grammar, usage, and mechanics. However, it tends to focus on certain topics and skills. If you can practice and get used to these topics and skills, you will be able to spot the errors consistently as you read the passages. Let's take a look at each of the main grammar topics below. First, though, let's learn a BIG Strategy.

BIG STRATEGY #4

Read the Passage!

Read the whole passage. You can't skim the passage on the Writing Test.

Remember, these passages are short, only 400–450 words. Since you will be asked to perform several different editing and revising tasks, it's important to have a sense of the overall main point of each reading passage. You cannot just read the questions and look at the sentences in isolation. Also, you might be asked questions that deal with the whole paragraph or the whole passage.

So read a paragraph. Then stop and answer the questions in that paragraph. Once you get to questions in the next paragraph, keep reading. As you read, think about the main idea, its support or examples, and errors you see in the passage. That way when you get to the questions, you will already be thinking about the answers. The Writing and Language Test is an editing test. Without reading the passage carefully, you will struggle with questions that are specifically designed to punish students who do not read the passage or who do not understand the main idea of the paragraphs and of the passage.

PARALLELISM

Picture a butterfly. You see a pair of perfectly matched wings with the butterfly's body in the middle. The way in which one set of wings mirrors the other is a good example of symmetry. Humans love symmetry, not only in nature but also

in words. When something is not parallel in a sentence, we find it unappealing. The idea is simple—make one side of the sentence match the other. The SAT can present this in several different ways. Try this problem.

1. My goals for the day are <u>running, swimming, and to lift weights.</u>

Before you look at the choices, ask yourself, "What does not match?" *Running* and *swimming* both end in -ing, but *to lift* does not. Now look at the choices.

(A) NO CHANGE
(B) swimming, to lift weights, and running
(C) to lift weights, swim, and run
(D) running, swimming, and lifting weights

The only choice that makes all parts of the list match is choice D. That choice makes the sentence parallel.

Of course, this is a simplified sentence. On the SAT, a problem like this would be disguised by a longer list. A question on the actual SAT might look something like this.

2. My goals for the day are <u>running five miles through the park in the morning, swimming fifty laps in the afternoon, and to lift two hundred pounds of weights in the evening.</u>

Notice how the problem seems more complicated? The extra words disguise the parallelism issue. If you see a list like this on the test, identify the main words in the list (in this case, *running, swimming,* and *to lift*).

3. A good barista knows how to make a cappuccino and <u>keeping the orders straight.</u>

When you see a sentence like this in which there are either two choices or two things being compared, be very careful! Here is another case where our brains will autocorrect and miss something. The conjunction is the wall separating the two things. Let's circle the two things the barista knows.

> Force yourself to see two choices or the two terms of a comparison by circling the two choices or the two things being compared.

3. A good barista knows (how to make a cappuccino) and (keeping the orders straight).

Now look at your choices.

    (A) NO CHANGE
    (B) keep the orders straight
    (C) to keep the orders straight
    (D) how to keep the orders straight

See what the test is hoping that you'll miss? Since your have *to make* and *keeping*, you'll immediately correct *keeping* to either *keep* or *to keep*. Then there's choice B and choice C, both of which look good; however, notice that they are missing the word *how*. See how the test puts these incorrect answers before the correct choice, choice D, which includes the missing word *how*?

When you circle the two things being compared or two choices, you'll recognize whether there's a parallelism problem. Remember that you are looking for the problem, not listening for it. Circling makes the problem visual. Let's try it again.

4. The number of bike paths in Philadelphia is greater than <u>any other city on the East Coast</u>.

    (A) NO CHANGE
    (B) all the cities on the East Coast
    (C) the number in any other city on the East Coast
    (D) every other city on the East Coast

What's better, twenty-six or Seattle? That's a ridiculous question, of course. You can't compare a number to a city. If you circled the two sides of the question, you saw that you can't compare *the number of bike paths in Philadelphia* to *any other city on the East Coast*. You have to compare *the number* to another number. The only choice that does this is choice C.

SUBJECT-VERB AGREEMENT

English is a very simple language; we are the ones who make it complicated. When you make a noun plural in English, you add the letter *s*. There are very few exceptions to this rule (like man, woman, child, and deer).

Look at the sentence again and the choices. The variations all center on the word *they*. That word has been removed in choice B, has been changed in choice C, and has been reiterated in choice D. Ask what *they* refers to, and you'll see it's the word *team*. How many is *team*? Does it end with an *s*? Since *team* doesn't end with an *s*, it's singular. If *team* is one thing, its corresponding pronoun is also singular—*it*. Therefore, choice C is correct. Try again.

11.   If any one of your friends needs a ride, they can come with us.

    (A) NO CHANGE
    (B) he can come with us
    (C) they will ride along with us
    (D) the friends can come with us

The word *they* does not refer to *friends*! Look carefully at the sentence. If it helps, cross out the prepositional phrase *of your friends*. The word *they* refers back to *any one*, and *one* is a he or she. That makes choice B correct.

12.   If you are worried about a specific cause, then one can always volunteer to help the campaign.

    (A) NO CHANGE
    (B) then you can always volunteer to help the campaign
    (C) than one can always volunteer to help the campaign
    (D) then one volunteers to help the campaign

> **Remember: You'll find Key Tips set in shaded boxes throughout the book.**

This is a slightly different question. However, you are still matching a pronoun to another pronoun. In the underlined part, *one* refers back to the word *you*. *One* is third person (e.g., he, she, it), while *you* is second person. So the pronouns don't match. This is called a "pronoun shift." Of course, the name of this grammar feature doesn't matter on the SAT. What matters is that you can spot a pronoun shift. The only choice that has *you* match the first part of the sentence is choice B, making choice B the correct answer.

VERB TENSE

You learned about the different tenses of verbs (past, present, future, simple, continuous, and perfect) in grade school. However, you probably haven't studied them in years. Now they're on the SAT!

Don't worry. The key thing here is balance. You have to match one verb to another. Try this problem.

13. As the wind intensified, some of the smoke drifted over the houses and then <u>had fallen</u> as particles onto the roofs and lawns.

    (A) NO CHANGE
    (B) will fall
    (C) falls
    (D) fell

Each of the answer choices contains a different verb tense. Knowing the tenses does not matter. Remember that English is balanced. So look at the other verbs in the sentence. If you don't recall, a verb shows an action (run, talk, play) or a state of being. (We will discuss state of being verbs when we discuss linking verbs in Chapter 3.) Just remember that verbs are the engines of the sentence.

Read the sentence again. You can see that *intensified* and *drifted* are the other verbs. Now look at the verb choices. *Had fallen* is the past perfect tense. *Will fall* is the future tense. *Falls* is the present tense. However, the terms or names for the verbs don't matter! Only choice D, *fell*, matches the past tense verbs in the sentence.

In other words, *drifted* matches *fell* and keeps the sentence in balance. Try another.

14. Technology is changing the way people communicate. In former times, people relied on wired telephones to call each other. Now people can pick up a cellular phone and call someone across the world. No longer are we tied to wires to communicate; we now <u>carried</u> a device that connects with the whole world in our pocket.

    (A) NO CHANGE
    (B) will carry
    (C) carry
    (D) had carried

Look to balance the verbs not just in the sentence but in the paragraph as well. The first sentence is in present tense. The second uses past tense to remind the reader of the way things were before going back to the present tense. Look most specifically at the part of the sentence where *carried* appears. See the verb *connects*? That's the strongest clue that the *carried* should also be present tense or the sentence wouldn't be balanced. Also, the word *now* precedes the verb, which is another indicator of present tense. So choice C, *carry*, is the answer to the problem.

When you are given a list of verbs as answer choices, look to balance the verbs in the sentences and paragraphs. Since English is balanced, the verbs must be balanced as well.

PUNCTUATION

Like verb tenses, it has probably been a long time since you studied punctuation in English class. However, punctuation is tested on the SAT. Fear not. Just like verb balance, look for punctuation balance in the sentences instead of just memorizing the punctuation rules.

Of course, you should have a basic understanding of the marks of punctuation and their functions. Although the list below is not a complete list of English punctuation rules, it includes all of the rules seen most frequently on the SAT.

→ A **period** (.) ends a statement.

→ An **exclamation mark** (!) shows excitement or emotion.

→ A **question mark** (?) ends a question.

→ A **comma** (,) has many functions.

1. A comma splits up items in a series.

   I like <u>cake</u>, <u>pie</u>, and <u>ice cream</u>.

2. A comma is used before a conjunction (for, and, nor, but, or, yet, so) to combine two sentences.

   He likes cake, <u>but</u> she likes ice cream.

3. A comma is used to set off introductions.

   <u>While running to the exit</u>, he tripped and fell.

4. A comma is used to set off appositives or parenthetical expressions.

   Juan, <u>my brother</u>, is coming home next week.

5. A comma sets off a phrase that expresses contrast.

   Some say the world will end in ice, <u>not</u> fire.

➜ A **semicolon** (;) combines two related, complete sentences without using a conjunction.

> **Call me tomorrow; I'll have my answer by then.**

Note: If you used a conjunction in the previous sentence, you would need a comma instead.

> **Call me tomorrow, and I'll have my answer by then.**

➜ A **colon** (:) has several functions.

1. A colon is used to introduce a list if there is a pause before the list starts. Usually, the words *as follows* or *the following* are cause for a pause.

   > **Please bring the following to class: a pen, a pencil, and a notebook.**

2. A colon also may be used instead of a semicolon between two combined sentences or between a sentence and an example when the second part of the sentence illustrates the first part.

   > **Larissa achieved what she had worked so hard for: she was named captain of the swim team.**

➜ An **apostrophe** (') has a few rules that are stressed on the SAT.

1. An apostrophe shows possession. If the person or thing that possesses something is singular, it is always apostrophe and then *s*.

   > **I found Tianna's keys.**

   If the person or thing that possesses something is plural, the placement of the apostrophe depends on whether or not the plural person or thing ends with *s*. If it ends with *s*, the apostrophe goes after the *s*. If the plural person or thing does not end with *s*, use apostrophe and then *s*.

   > **The bats' cave is dark.**
   > **The sheep's pen smells.**

2. An apostrophe forms contractions.

   > **Don't you have to leave?**

3. With personal pronouns, an apostrophe is always a contraction. This is a **key rule**!

it's = it is
its = belonging to it

you're = you are
your = belonging to you

If you are ever stuck, think of another personal possessive pronoun like *his* or *hers*. Since there is no apostrophe in those words, there is none in *its* or in *your* when you are making a possessive. These are the most common mistakes in written English, so expect to see them tested on the SAT!

4. Remember—the apostrophe is a useful piece of punctuation. However, it can also cause confusion, especially with pronouns. As a quick review, remember that an apostrophe can either show possession or show a contraction when dealing with nouns.

Jim's pencil is sharp.
(The pencil belongs to Jim.)

Bob's going with us.
(Bob is going with us.)

However, for the core personal pronouns (*I, you, he, she, it, we, you, they*), an apostrophe shows only a contraction.

You're my best friend.
(You are my best friend.)

Your dog is in my yard.
(The dog belongs to you.)

If you cannot remember the rule, try this: change the person to a pronoun.

Jim's pencil is sharp.
Does it become *his pencil* or *hi's pencil*?

Of course, it is not *hi's pencil*! So follow that thinking if you're stuck. Try this problem.

15. <u>The police officer said its time to go because your visiting time is up.</u>

    (A) NO CHANGE
    (B) The police officer said its time to go because you're visiting time is up.
    (C) The police officer said it's time to go because you're visiting time is up.
    (D) The police officer said it's time to go because your visiting time is up.

Answering this question is simple now that we know that an apostrophe with the common subject pronouns is always a contraction. To check these answer choices, simply say the sentence with the contractions split apart, like this:

The police officer said it is time to go because you are visiting time is up.

Seeing the contractions split apart makes it easy to see that *it's* is correct and that *your* is correct. Therefore, choice D is the best choice.

Moving on to the next mark of punctuation . . . .

→ A pair of **em dashes** (—) is used much like a pair of commas to set off a parenthetical expression. However, unlike a comma, an em dash shows an interruption or a change in thought.

I was going to buy you—I've always wanted to see one of these—a pet iguana.

Note that an em dash is different than commas, which set off a parenthetical expression.

Mrs. Scott, my lawyer, will be in her office in an hour.

In the sentence above that contains the commas, there is no break in thought. Instead, extra information is given about Mrs. Scott.

These punctuation rules lead us to the main point about punctuation problems on the SAT. Just as in questions involving parallelism, agreement, and verb tense, look for balance in the sentences. Try the following examples that demonstrate balance in punctuation.

16. <u>Modernism a philosophical movement that began in the late nineteenth and early twentieth centuries,</u> sprung from those who felt traditional forms of art and literature were outdated in the new social and economic order.

(A) NO CHANGE
(B) Modernism, a philosophical movement that began in the late nineteenth and early twentieth centuries,
(C) Modernism—a philosophical movement that began in the late nineteenth and early twentieth centuries,
(D) Modernism, a philosophical movement that began in the late nineteenth and early twentieth centuries—

The key here is to look for balance. It is obvious from the punctuation choices given that a phrase is being set off from the rest of the sentence. So choice A cannot be correct because it is not balanced; a comma is only at the end. Now look at the other three choices. Which one has balance?

Choice B is balanced because it has commas on both sides of the phrase. Choices C and D are not balanced because they have a comma on one end and an em dash on the other. If there were a choice with em dashes on both sides of the phrase, that choice could also be correct.

17. Because natural gas produces less greenhouse gas when <u>burned, it therefore has helped</u> the United States reduce its overall greenhouse gas emissions as it has increased the use of natural gas and reduced the use of coal.

(A) NO CHANGE
(B) burned, it has helped
(C) burned, so it therefore has helped
(D) burned; it has helped

Again, think of balance. The key to this sentence is the first word, *because*. It starts an introductory phrase, and introductory phrases end with a comma. So which choice is the right answer? Here's where you can use what the test offers as choices to help you find the answer. Choice D has a semicolon, which is used in compound sentences. That can't be right because an introductory phrase is not its own sentence. Since choice D is wrong, choice C is also wrong because it also is trying to form a compound sentence with a comma and a conjunction. So between choice A and choice B, the one that keeps the balance of the

sentence is choice B. Choice A is unbalanced because *therefore* is unnecessary since the sentence already has *because*. So the balanced sentence is choice B.

18. <u>Dr. Ross even offers a solution to the problem; economic</u> stimulus from a broad tax on consumer goods.

    (A) NO CHANGE
    (B) Dr. Ross, even offers a solution to the problem; economic
    (C) Dr. Ross even offers a solution to the problem: economic
    (D) Dr. Ross even offers, a solution to the problem economic

In this sentence, the rule that is stressed is a colon for clarification, choice C. However, if you do not know that rule, you should be able to remove two other answer choices based on balance. Choice B and choice D have commas that throw off the balance of the sentence by interrupting the sentence at the wrong point. Those pauses cause the sentence to hit the brakes when there is no need, ruining the balance.

Chapter Overview

The grammar topics in this chapter are half of the main grammar points on the SAT. Remember that the SAT may ask anything from English grammar, but it tends to focus on certain topics and rules. English grammar is about one item matching another and is also about simplicity. English is a logical language. You can use that driving idea to help you find answers more easily. We will take a look at other grammar topics in the next chapter.

3

English Is Logical

English is a logical language. It makes sense. With very few exceptions, English follows patterns. If you know that English is logical and follows patterns, you can use what you know and apply it to other grammar problems. Keep this in mind as you work on the grammar part of the SAT.

DANGLING AND MISPLACED MODIFIERS

How often do you use proper English when you speak?

If you're like most people, the answer is probably very little. However, if most people don't use proper English when speaking, then how do we understand each other?

Perhaps the best way to answer this question is to look at texting. When you are texting and forget to capitalize the pronoun *I*, your phone or tablet does it for you. Autocorrect is the same thing your brain does when someone is talking to you. Otherwise, we would have no idea what other people are telling us.

Although autocorrect is great when engaging in conversation, it can work against you. When you read something and it's incorrect, your brain will often autocorrect it to tell you the message.

Look at the question below.

1. At the age of five, my grandfather taught me how to fish.

If your brain is autocorrecting, it has told you the basic message of the sentence. You're probably picturing a little boy and an old man fishing on the water. However, the autocorrect has caused you to miss something horribly wrong!

Circle the phrase *at the age of five*. This is a modifying expression. In English, a modifier describes the noun closest to it. What noun is closest to this phrase?

The *grandfather* is closest! If your grandfather is five years old, then something is wrong with your family. Obviously, this is not what the author meant.

So now that we've identified the problem, how do we fix it? Look at the sentence again. Ask yourself, "Who is five years old?" In the sentence, *me* is five. So cut the phrase *at the age of five* and paste it to the end of the sentence. Now read it through. *Me* is five, grandfather is old, and all is right with the world.

Here are the choices.

1. At the age of five, my grandfather taught me how to fish.

   (A) NO CHANGE
   (B) At the age of five, I taught my grandfather how to fish.
   (C) At the age of five; my grandfather taught me how to fish.
   (D) My grandfather taught me how to fish at the age of five.

Choice D is correct since it moves the modifier close to the noun that the modifier describes. Choice B is grammatically correct, but the meaning of the sentence is completely changed. Choice C makes the problem even worse by adding a semicolon.

Let's try some others. First, cover the answer explanation and attempt the problem on your own. Then check your answer and the explanation. These examples are variations of how modifiers can be placed in the wrong place on the test.

2. The teacher gave Mika a pass who was asking to go to the bathroom.

   (A) NO CHANGE
   (B) a pass to Mika, who was asking to go to the bathroom.
   (C) Mika a pass so that he asked to go to the bathroom.
   (D) Mika a pass that was asking to go to the bathroom.

Choice B is correct. The problem in the original sentence is that *who was asking to go to the bathroom* is closest to the word *pass*. A pass cannot ask for anything, much less ask to go the bathroom. Choice B fixes the problem by moving what should be modified, the word *Mika*, closest to the modifying phrase. Choice C is incorrect because it changes the meaning and is awkward too. Choice D replaces the word *who* with the word *that*, which is fine, but it does not solve the problem of the misplaced modifier.

Here is another important note! Sometimes one problem causes another. Look at the original sentence again. Do you see the words *pass who* next to each other? In English:

> *Who* modifies only people.
> *Which* modifies only things.
> *That* modifies either people or things.

So *pass who was asking to go to the bathroom* does not make sense because *pass* is not a person. Speaking of *who*, it is time to address one of the most confusing things in English.

WHO AND WHOM

Most people know *whom* is a word, but they are unsure when to use it. Many people think of it as a fancy *who* and imagine that it is used in England when visiting the queen.

Who and *whom* used to be used correctly all the time. Slowly over the past century, *who* has replaced *whom* in informal speech, which means people grow up hearing only *who*. Since that's all people hear, they have trouble knowing when to use *whom*.

Whom does follow a pattern that all other pronouns use.

Think of another set of common pronouns, *he* and *him*.

> *He* ends with a vowel and is a subject pronoun, just like *who*.
> *Him* ends with *m* and is an object pronoun, just like *whom*.

So when you see *who* versus *whom* on the SAT, just plug in *he* and *him*. If *he* sounds right, you need the pronoun that ends with the vowel (*who*). If *him* sounds right, you need the pronoun that ends with *m*.

Look at the question below.

3. <u>Babe Ruth, a baseball Hall of Famer</u> played for the Yankees.

    (A) NO CHANGE
    (B) Babe Ruth, who was a baseball Hall of Famer,
    (C) Babe Ruth was a baseball Hall of Famer
    (D) Babe Ruth, whom was a baseball Hall of Famer,

For your choices, you should be able to see that choice C creates a run-on, so that's easy to eliminate. Choice A could be correct, but the phrase *a baseball*

Hall of Famer needs to be separated from the rest of the sentence with commas. Since there is only a comma after *Ruth*, choice A is incorrect.

So you have to choose between choice B and choice D. By looking at the two choices, you can see that they are essentially the same with one difference. Choice B has *who*, and choice D has *whom*. Plug *he* and *him* into the phrase to see which pronoun is correct.

(B) *he* was a baseball Hall of Famer,

(D) *him* was a baseball Hall of Famer,

Since *he* sounds correct, *who* is the pronoun that should be used here. Choice B is the correct answer. Try another.

4. <u>Who's parked the car in the loading zone</u> needs to move it before it gets towed.

(A) NO CHANGE
(B) Whoever parked the car in the loading zone
(C) Whomever parked the car in the loading zone
(D) Whoever's parked car in the loading zone

Whoever and *whomever* are subject and object pronouns, too. So follow the *he* and *him* tip. Is it *he parked the car in the loading zone* or *him parked the car in the loading zone* correct?

Since *he* sounds right, *whoever* must be right. Therefore, choice B is correct.

5. Rachel bought a box of chocolates for her grandfather, <u>who</u> she adores.

(A) NO CHANGE
(B) whoever
(C) whom
(D) which

Again, use *he* and *him* to help you find the answer. Flip the phrase around. Is it *she adores he* or *she adores him*? Since *him* sounds correct, we know that *whom* is correct since both *him* and *whom* end with *m*. So choice C is the answer.

Who and *whom* are not mysterious at all! They follow the pattern of English. Simply replace *who* and *whom* with other pronouns that serve the same function. Using *he* and *him* makes it easy because one ends with a vowel and one

ends with *m*, just like *who* and *whom*. Plugging in *he* and *him* for *who* and *whom* will help you find the right answer.

OTHER PRONOUN PROBLEMS

Pronouns are shortcuts. We get tired of constantly naming someone or something, so instead we use pronouns. Pronouns are like substitutes. When the game starts, the pronouns are on the bench. As the game goes on, though, the pronouns go in when the nouns are tired. Pronouns can, however, cause many problems in English. Let's take a look at some common problems with pronouns.

6.   Police suspected that the robber <u>was her.</u>

   (A) NO CHANGE
   (B) had been her.
   (C) would be her.
   (D) was she.

To figure this out, let's look at a math problem: $2 + 2 = 4$. If you were to say this as a sentence, you would say:

Two plus two is four.

What you've done is made a sentence with a linking verb, *is*. Remember, not every sentence has an action verb. The *is* in the above sentence is the same as an equals sign.

Recall this from your algebraic proofs:

If $2 + 2 = 4$, then $4 = 2 + 2$.

So apply both of these thoughts back to the problem. In the sentence, *was* is the linking verb or the equals sign. So flip the sentence over:

Her was the robber the police suspected.

The logic behind English makes this easy! The sentence obviously should contain *she*, not *her*. So choice D is the correct answer. Remember that this is true when the sentence has a linking verb, not an action verb. Let's try another.

7. <u>My brother and they</u> are great friends.

    (A) NO CHANGE
    (B) My brother and them
    (C) My brother and all of them
    (D) Them and my brother

On problems like these, the SAT is trying to get you fooled by throwing a pronoun after a noun. If you read them to yourself, they both sound right. This brings us to our next BIG Strategy.

———— BIG STRATEGY #5 ————

Don't Listen for the Answer; Look for It!

Don't go with the answer that "sounds" best. Most people who take the test will do this. The College Board test makers know that is what most people will do. The test will often have a question choice that sounds great but is wrong, or it will have a question choice that sounds wrong but is right. So don't *listen* for the answer; *look* for it!

Take a look at the problem again. There are two subjects joined by *and*. These two subjects are *my brother* and *they*. Again, use the logic of English to help get the answer. In English, if it works for two, it works for one. If it works for one, it works for two. In other words, cover up the noun *my brother* and see what you have left. (Since you're eliminating one of the subjects, you don't need the conjunction *and* either.)

~~My brother and~~ they are great friends.

So *they* is correct. Whenever you get a noun and a pronoun together like that, simply cover up the noun. You'll immediately see what's right. In this problem, since *they* is correct, choice A is the answer.

REPETITION, REDUNDANCY, AND WORDINESS

Good writing should be straightforward and to the point. When it's not, it is confusing or boring. If your writing is either of those things, people will stop reading it. So on the SAT, when a sentence is wordy (has too many words), it's usually wrong. You should look for ways to streamline the sentence. Try one.

8. She quit the band <u>on account of the fact that it was necessary for her to help her mom with her younger sister.</u>

Before we look at the answers, think about what information in the sentence is essential. The sentence shouldn't seem long-winded, going on unnecessarily. So how do you fix it? Ask yourself first, "What is the sentence about?"

In this case, the sentence is about her (*she*).

Then ask yourself, "What did she do? Why?"

In this case, she *quit the band*. Why did she quit? She quit *to help her mom with her younger sister.*

Those words are essential; everything else is not. So now look at the choices.

8. She quit the band <u>on account of the fact that it was necessary for her to help her mom with her younger sister.</u>

   (A) NO CHANGE
   (B) because she had to help her mom with her younger sister.
   (C) since it was necessary for her to help her mom with her younger sister.
   (D) to help her mom with her younger sister.

Choice B and choice C both improve the sentence by making it less wordy. They use *because* and *since* to replace *on account of the fact*. However, choice D cuts the sentence to its essential parts, making choice D the best answer choice. Note that the shortest choice was the correct one. Of course, this is not always true. However, if you are guessing between two grammar answers, the shorter answer is the better guess. Of course, this does not mean that you should just choose the shortest answer. However, if you have narrowed the choices down to two and cannot decide between them, the better guess would be the shorter one.

Try another example.

9. Nate loved to play video <u>games, of which he found *Call of Duty* the best.</u>

   (A) NO CHANGE
   (B) games; he found *Call of Duty* the best.
   (C) games, the best was *Call of Duty*.
   (D) games, and it was *Call of Duty* that he found to be the best.

There are two thoughts in the sentence. The first is not underlined, so it is correct. In the second part, the words *of which* are unnecessary. Look at the choices. Choice C is shortest, but it creates a comma splice. Choice D is wordier

than choice B, and choice D makes the second sentence about *it* instead of about *he*. So choice B is the best answer.

10. Perhaps nowhere in this timeless classic do we see how Victorian Christmas was both similar and different from our modern Christmas than in the three spirits who visit Scrooge. In the three spirits, we see in the Spirit of Christmas Present a jolly, fat, bearded presence that is full of celebration. He is undoubtedly an early version of Santa Claus.

   (A) NO CHANGE
   (B) Here
   (C) In this classic story from Charles Dickens
   (D) Therefore

Read the sentence before the underlined portion. Do you see how the story is described as a classic and that there are three spirits? To mention the spirits again would not be logical and, in fact, would simply be repeating what has already been said. Choice A leaves in the repetition of three spirits, so it is not correct. Choice C mentions that it's a classic story again, so this choice is also incorrect. Choice D, the word *therefore*, does not make sense as a transition. So choice B is the best answer.

TONE

If you are angry, your words show your anger. If you are happy, your words show your happiness. Consider this simple logic when confronted with a question like the following on the SAT.

11. The rapid increase in the production and use of natural gas has forced those involved in the business to address its detrimental effects on the environment. But given that natural gas produces half the carbon dioxide that coal does, proponents of natural gas claim that the advantages of natural gas outdo the drawbacks of it.

   (A) NO CHANGE
   (B) outweigh
   (C) destroy
   (D) outperform

The key here is the tone. After reading the sentences, it is clear that this is a scientific text. The passage is not about war or sports; it is not competitive in

tone. Strong words that would be used with sports or other competitions do not logically fit here. So *outdo*, *destroy*, and *outperform* are all the wrong tone. Only choice B, *outweigh*, logically fits with what is being said.

12. Fiber makes you feel full right away, and fat works with your hormones to tell the body to stop eating. Protein makes you feel <u>satiated</u> for longer periods of time, so it is good to have all three in each meal.

   (A) NO CHANGE
   (B) fulfilled
   (C) complacent
   (D) sufficient

In this case, the sentences are about making the body feel full from eating. This tone must follow for the underlined word. *Fulfilled* has more of meaning of "doing what is required." *Complacent* means "satisfied" but in terms of how things are, not in terms of food. The word *sufficient* means "enough" to meet the needs of a situation. Although all of these are in the ballpark for meaning, only *satiated* matches the tone of feeling full from food.

Small differences in words occur not just in tone but in meaning, too.

WORD CHOICE

English probably has more words than any other language on the planet. This enables English to create subtleties in expressions and meanings that may be harder to express in other languages. Of course, when words sound alike, they can lead to confusion. The makers of the SAT will test you on some of these.

It is impossible to cover every set of confused words. However, the following is a list of very common ones. Try to think of a logical way to remember these. A hint is included for each word on the list.

→ *affect, effect:* The main difference is part of speech. *Affect* is a verb, and *effect* is a noun.

   Her words don't *affect* me.
   The black lights created a creepy *effect*.

→ *accept, except:* To *accept* is to receive, and to *except* is to leave out. Think *exception*, and you'll keep these straight!

   She *accepted* her second Academy Award.
   Children under ten are *excepted* from the contest.

→ *allusion, illusion:* An *allusion* is a reference to something, and an *illusion* is something that gives a false impression.

> Samantha made an *allusion* to President Abraham Lincoln's speech in her essay.
>
> It looked like an oasis in the desert, but it was an *illusion*.

→ *complement, compliment:* I say nice things, so I give *compliments*. A *complement* is something that goes along with something else and completes that something else.

> When she told him he was smart, his smile showed how much he liked the *compliment*.
>
> I brought ice cream because I thought it would *complement* your apple pie for dessert.

→ *elicit, illicit:* To *elicit* means "to bring out" or "evoke," and *illicit* means "unlawful." *Illicit* has the same beginning as *illegal*!

> Her uncle could not *elicit* a response from Tommy.
>
> Trespassing on that property is *illicit* behavior.

→ *emigrate, immigrate:* To *emigrate* is to leave a country, and to *immigrate* is to enter a country. Think *E* for exit. Think *I* for in.

> Their family *emigrated* from Russia and *immigrated* to the United States.

→ *imply, infer:* To *imply* is to give a hint, and to *infer* is to take a hint. Look at *infer*. When you **in**fer, you take **in** a hint.

> She *implied* that R.J. shouldn't go to the party, but he missed the hint.
>
> Reggie *inferred* that his SAT score would increase if he worked on his writing skills.

→ *lay, lie:* These are the most confusing verbs in English! To *lie* means "to rest," and to *lay* means "to put down."

> I'm sleepy; I think I'll *lie* down for a nap.
>
> *Lay* down your pencils. The quiz is over.

Note: The past tense of these verbs is even more confusing! The past tense of *lay* is *laid*. The past tense of *lie* is *lay*! People say this incorrectly all the time, so most people think that the past tense of *lie* is *laid*. It's not!

> I *laid* down my keys, and now I can't find them.
>
> I was sleepy, so I *lay* down early last night.

→ *set, sit:* To *set* is to put down something, and to *sit* is to seat yourself.

> *Set* out the dishes on the table.
>
> *Sit* down until the bell rings.

→ *than, then: Than* is used to compare, and *then* is used with time or conclusions. *Then* rhymes with and answers *when*!

She is taller *than* I am.
We'll go out for lunch and *then* meet you at the movies.

Try a couple of problems with these words that sound alike. Use the logic of knowing one word to help to know them both.

13. The flower bouquet <u>complimented her prom dress better then</u> a single rose would have, I think.

   (A) NO CHANGE
   (B) complemented her prom dress better than
   (C) complimented her prom dress better than
   (D) complemented her prom dress better then

When you are working on problems where you see two changes in the choices, go to the one you're more sure of first. Let's say you're one hundred percent positive about *than* and *then*. Since *than* makes a comparison, that's the word we need. So choices A and D are eliminated quickly, getting us down to a 1-in-2 chance of getting the question right. Remember, a *compliment* is something nice to say, not what this sentence is saying. That eliminates choice C, so the answer is choice B.

14. The kitten that <u>lay on my neighbor's windowsill all day long affected</u> my decision to adopt one of my own from the animal shelter.

   (A) NO CHANGE
   (B) lay on my neighbor's windowsill all day long effected
   (C) laid on my neighbor's windowsill all day long effected
   (D) laid on my neighbor's windowsill all day long affected

Again, start with the set of words you're stronger with and use that logic to narrow your choices. Let's say you are positive that *affect* is the verb and that *effect* is the noun. Since the word in this sentence is an action, we can eliminate choices B and C. Now work on the tough one! Remember, most people say *laid* for the past tense of *lie*, but they are incorrect. The past tense of *lie* is *lay*, which eliminates choice D. Choice A is correct.

Chapter Overview

Even though we might not think it, English is ruled by logic. It must make sense in order for us to make sense to other people when speaking or writing. Apply that logic to the SAT to help you figure out the correct answer. Since English is logical, you can figure out the answers! It is not a matter of memorizing endless rules. Instead, think the problem through. That way, you'll be in a position to get every Writing and Language Test question correct!

4

It's All in the Details

▰▰ ▰▰ ▰▰ ▰▰ ▰▰ ▰▰ ▰▰ ▰▰ ▰▰ ▰

W hy do we bother to write down words? Even when we are texting, details have a purpose. Whether it is to express ourselves, entertain others, or pass along information, we need details in our writing to make it worth reading. The SAT will test your understanding of placing the right details, moving or changing details, and transitioning from one detail to another.

PLACING DETAILS

When a detail is out of order, it throws off the message being stated. When you are taking the SAT, read each paragraph, ask yourself what the main idea is, and then keep asking yourself if the information is coming to you in the right order. After reading a sentence, have you ever paused and said, "Wait a second; something's missing"? Have you then found that missing something a sentence or two later? If you've answered these questions "yes," then you found a misplaced detail.

Like the dangling modifiers discussed in the previous chapter, a misplaced detail needs to be moved to where it makes sense.

Read the paragraphs on the next page, think of the main idea, and then read the questions that follow.

In the decades after World War II, the use of modern plastics expanded, and today, plastics are in most of the things or in the packaging of the things we buy. Then, people have used plastics, materials that are designed to last indefinitely, just once and then have thrown them away. It is estimated that Americans only recycle one-quarter of the plastic that is produced each year.

[1] While much of the remaining plastic ends up in landfills, other garbage is carried by rain into streams, then rivers, and then the oceans. [2] ❶ The largest dump for plastic in the world is a stretch of the Pacific Ocean known as the Great Pacific Garbage Patch. [3] Because of the ocean currents, discarded plastic accumulates in an area north of Hawaii about the size of Texas. [4] Each year, the Patch only grows larger as people use and discard more and more plastic. [5] Even worse, the plastic does not biodegrade; it photodegrades, which means the sun breaks it into smaller and smaller pieces of plastic. [6] By the middle of this century, if nothing is done, there might be more plastic in the ocean than fish. [7] The world fish harvest has been in a decline from ninety-four million tons in 1996. [8] So long as some scientists are working on ideas to clean the plastic from the ocean, the easier solution is to reduce our use of plastics. [9] This in turn means that fish and other creatures ingest the small bits of plastic as they swim, harming sea creatures. ❷

1. To make this paragraph make the most sense, sentence 2 should be placed

   (A) where it is now.
   (B) after sentence 3.
   (C) after sentence 4.
   (D) after sentence 5.

2. To make this paragraph make the most sense, sentence 9 should be placed

   (A) where it is now.
   (B) after sentence 4.
   (C) after sentence 5.
   (D) after sentence 6.

The main idea of the second paragraph is that plastics end up in the ocean. One of the details that supports this is the information about the Great Pacific Garbage Patch. For the plastic to get to the Garbage Patch, it must be carried out to sea and then make its way to the area of water north of Hawaii. As you read the paragraph, did it seem odd that the Patch was named and then the next sentence (sentence 3) finishes describing its origins? Sentence 2 should be placed after sentence 3, not the other way around. So the answer to the first question is choice B.

Let's try some others. First cover the answer explanation and attempt the problem. Then check your answer and the explanation. There are various ways in which a modifier may show up in the wrong place in a passage.

Read the beginning of sentence 9 again. The first word is *this*. What does *this* refer back to? Based on where the sentence is currently placed, *this* refers to reducing our use of plastics. Why would reducing our use of plastics cause fish to ingest more plastic? So the sentence is in the wrong place. Eliminate choice A from the second question. Now think about what *this* must refer to, and go to each sentence to find it. In sentence 4, the patch grows larger because people throw away more plastic. Could that cause fish to ingest more plastic? It is possibly correct. However, there seems to be a link missing. Leave choice B for now. If nothing better comes along, come back to it.

Sentence 5 mentions the plastic getting broken down into smaller and smaller bits, which is a strong link to ingesting small bits of plastic. So that strong connection means that sentence 9 should be placed after sentence 5, which is choice C.

ADDING DETAILS

Another type of detail problem on the SAT involves adding details. This is not about moving a detail that has already been written but is in the wrong place. Instead, this type of problem has you consider what is written and then decide whether a new detail would improve the text.

Read the passage below, think about the main idea, and then read the questions that follow.

In the decades after World War II, the use of modern plastics expanded, and today, plastics are in most of the things or in the packaging of the things we buy. Then, people have used plastics, materials that are designed to last indefinitely, just once and then have thrown them away. ❸ It is estimated that Americans only recycle one-quarter of the plastic that is produced each year.

While much of the remaining plastic ends up in landfills, other garbage is carried by rain into streams, then rivers, and then the oceans. Because of the ocean currents, discarded plastic accumulates in an area north of Hawaii about the size of Texas.

3. Which choice most effectively sets up the preceding information?

(A) Therefore, plastic must be thrown away immediately after use.

(B) People recognized this one-time use problem and set up recycling programs for plastics, but that did not completely solve the problem.

(C) However, despite its ability to last a long time, it is not very useful as a material for making consumer products.

(D) The irony is that plastic was designed for one-time use.

The largest dump for plastic in the world is a stretch of the Pacific Ocean known as the Great Pacific Garbage Patch. ❹ Each year, the Patch only grows larger as people use and discard more and more plastic. Even worse, the plastic does not biodegrade; it photodegrades, which means the sun breaks it into smaller and smaller pieces of plastic. This in turn means that fish and other creatures ingest the small bits of plastic as they swim, harming sea creatures. By the middle of this century, if nothing is done, there might be more plastic in the ocean than fish. The world fish harvest has been in a decline from ninety-four million tons in 1996. So long as some scientists are working on ideas to clean the plastic from the ocean, the easier solution is to reduce our use of plastics.

4. The writer is considering adding the following sentence.

And Texas, as anyone who has studied geography knows, is second only to Alaska in terms of state size.

Should the writer make this addition here?

(A) Yes, because it reinforces the paragraph's main point about the size of the Patch.
(B) Yes, because it gives additional detail about Texas and therefore the Patch.
(C) No, because it blurs the paragraph's focus by introducing a new idea that goes unexplained.
(D) No, because it undermines the passage's claim about plastic pollution.

The main idea of the first paragraph in the third question is that the use of plastics has expanded, but people discard the durable material. The sentence before ❸ says that people have used plastics once and then have thrown them away. The sentence after ❸ says that Americans recycle only a quarter of their plastic. Now think of what detail could bridge the two sentences. There is a leap of thought from throwing away plastic to recycling only a fraction of it. What there needs to be is a detail sentence that brings up the idea of recycling. Now look at the answer choices, and look for mention of recycling. Only choice B brings up the idea of recycling, so the answer is B.

Before attempting an answer for the fourth question, do just as we did before. Think about the main idea of the paragraph (the Great Pacific Garbage Patch), and then look at the sentence before and after ❹. The sentence before states that the plastic accumulates in the Pacific. The sentence after names the accumulation as the Great Pacific Garbage Patch. Now look at what you are asked to consider adding: *And Texas, as anyone who has studied geography knows, is second only to Alaska in terms of state size.* Does this add a relevant detail? How does the fact that Texas is the second biggest state help strengthen the main idea about the Garbage Patch? This addition doesn't really mention the Patch; instead, it veers off into a geography fact. Since it does not help the writer's case, eliminate choices A and B. Note that with this kind of problem, doing this first step will cut out half the choices at once! This will quickly put you in a strong position to gain points on the test.

Now look at choice C. Yes, it does introduce a new idea that is not developed or even mentioned again elsewhere in the paragraph. So leave choice C for now and look at choice D. How does Texas being the second largest state undermine the claim about plastic pollution? Since it does not, eliminate it. You are then left with the correct answer, choice C.

DELETING DETAILS

The other major type of detail problem on the SAT asks you to delete details. Like adding details problems, deleting details problems ask the reader to look at a sentence that is in the passage and consider deleting it. Like adding and placing details, deleting problems are all about details.

> You are not asked to delete sentences for style or grammar!

Read the paragraph on page 43, consider the main idea, and then read the questions that follow.

5 In the decades after World War II, the use of modern plastics expanded, and today, plastics are in most of the things we buy or in the packaging of the things we buy. Then, people have used plastics, materials that are designed to last indefinitely, just once and then have thrown them away. It is estimated that Americans only recycle one-quarter of the plastic that is produced each year.

While much of the remaining plastic ends up in landfills, other garbage is carried by rain into streams, then rivers, and then the oceans. Because of the ocean currents, discarded plastic accumulates in an area north of Hawaii about the size of Texas. The largest dump for plastic in the world is a stretch of the Pacific Ocean known as the Great Pacific Garbage Patch. Each year, the Patch only grows larger as people use and discard more and more plastic. Even worse, the plastic does not biodegrade; it photodegrades, which means the sun breaks it into smaller and smaller pieces of plastic. This in turn means that fish and other creatures ingest the small bits of plastic as they swim, harming sea creatures. By the middle of this century, if nothing is done, there might be more plastic in the ocean than fish. **6** The world fish harvest has been in a decline from ninety-four million tons in 1996. So long as some scientists are working on ideas to clean the plastic from the ocean, the easier solution is to reduce our use of plastics.

5. The writer is considering deleting the underlined sentence. Should the writer do this?

(A) Yes, because it does not mention the Great Pacific Garbage Patch.
(B) Yes, because it fails to introduce the main idea of the paragraph.
(C) No, because it uses World War II in the introduction.
(D) No, because it sets up the idea in the paragraph about the increased use of plastics.

6. The writer is considering deleting the underlined sentence. Should the sentence be kept or deleted?

(A) Kept, because it provides a detail that supports the main topic of the paragraph.
(B) Kept, because it refers back to a detail in the previous paragraph.
(C) Deleted, because it blurs the paragraph's main focus with a loosely related detail.
(D) Deleted, because it repeats information that has been provided earlier in the paragraph.

Think of the main idea of the first paragraph in question 5—that the use of plastics has expanded but that people discard the durable material. Now look at that first sentence. Does it work as an introduction? Since the underlined sentence states that the use of plastics has expanded, yes, the first sentence is an effective introductory detail. Eliminate choice A and choice B. Like adding details, note that with this kind of question, you can eliminate half the choices quickly, which gives you a strong chance of gaining points!

Now that you have narrowed your choices, look at choice C. Does using World War II make a good detail? In all likelihood, no, so look at choice D. Yes, the mention of increased use of plastics does set up the paragraph, so choice D is the answer. This brings up a BIG Strategy.

BIG STRATEGY #6

Eliminate Like a Coach Making Cuts

The SAT is mostly a multiple-choice test. Use that to your advantage. On some (and hopefully most) questions, you will know the answer. However, there will be other questions where you're not sure or have no idea. What should you do then?

There is no penalty for choosing wrong answers, so answer every question. To get a higher score, pretend you're a coach making cuts before the season. Coaches don't simply make one cut and then form the roster. They make first cuts, eliminating those who don't know on which hand to put the mitt. Then the coaches take a look again and make second cuts, eliminating those who are close but not quite right.

If you can eliminate any answer choices, you increase your chances of getting the question correct and increasing your score. For example, say you take a wild guess on 10 questions on the English portion of the SAT. Each question has 4 choices. If you eliminate none of the answer choices, you have a 1-in-4 chance of getting each question correct. Over 10 questions, that means you probably get 2 or maybe 3 correct, raising your score by 20 to 30 points.

If you eliminate one bad choice from each of those questions, you now have a 1-in-3 chance of getting each of those questions right. Now you probably answer 3 or possibly 4 correct, boosting your score by 30 to 40 points.

If you eliminate two choices, you now have a 50-50 chance of getting those 10 questions correct. So you probably answer 5 questions correctly, which boosts your score by 50 points.

Instead of adding up to 20 points to your score by taking wild guesses, you can raise your score by up to 50 points simply by eliminating answer choices.

Eliminating choices before guessing can add up to a big increase in your score!

Now let's move on to question 6.

At first, it might seem difficult to know why to keep or delete a detail. Remember, think of the main idea first and cut half the choices! The main idea of that paragraph is how Great Pacific Garbage Patch is harmful to the planet. Does the fish catch in 1996 support that? Even though it mentions a decline from a peak, the fish harvest is making the paragraph veer off topic, so eliminate choices A and B.

Now look at the other choices. Again, think of the main idea. Choice C does describe what the fish harvest statistic does for the paragraph, blurring the focus. If you are not sure, though, look at choice D. Does the author mention the fish harvest earlier in the paragraph? Since the author does not, choice C must be the answer.

In all cases of placing, adding, or deleting details, the most important thing to know is the main idea of both the passage and the paragraph. That will be your starting point to getting the right answer. Thinking of the main idea as you read will make answering these detail questions easier.

TRANSITIONS

Ideas and details need transitions to make them flow. Transitions can show similarity, contradiction, cause, effect, example, time, space, or conclusion. Transitions can take a reader from one paragraph to another, from one sentence to another, or even from one part of a sentence to another.

The key thing to understand with transitions is that they connect ideas to make a writer's message clear. When you are asked to choose the right transition on the SAT, you must understand both the main idea of the passage and the details that are being connected.

Read the paragraphs on page 46, think of the main idea, and then read the questions that follow.

In the decades after World War II, the use of modern plastics expanded, and today, plastics are in most of the things or in the packaging of the things we buy. **❼** <u>Then,</u> people have used plastics, materials that are designed to last indefinitely, just once and then have thrown them away. It is estimated that Americans only recycle one-quarter of the plastic that is produced each year.

❽ <u>While</u> much of the remaining plastic ends up in landfills, other garbage is carried by rain into streams, then rivers, and then the oceans. Because of the ocean currents, discarded plastic accumulates in an area north of Hawaii about the size of Texas. The largest dump for plastic in the world is a stretch of the Pacific Ocean known as the Great Pacific Garbage Patch. Each year, the Patch only grows larger as people use and discard more and more plastic. Even worse, the plastic does not biodegrade; it photodegrades, which means the sun breaks it into smaller and smaller pieces of plastic. This in turn means that fish and other creatures ingest the small bits of plastic as they swim, harming sea creatures. By the middle of this century, if nothing is done, there might be more plastic in the ocean than fish. The world fish harvest has been in a decline from ninety-four million tons in 1996. **❾** <u>So long as</u> some scientists are working on ideas to clean the plastic from the ocean, the easier solution is to reduce our use of plastics.

7. (A) NO CHANGE
    (B) For decades,
    (C) Formerly,
    (D) Forthwith,

8. (A) NO CHANGE
    (B) After all,
    (C) Besides
    (D) However,

9. (A) NO CHANGE
    (B) For instance,
    (C) Even though
    (D) Therefore,

Think of the main idea as you move from sentence to sentence through the paragraph. Since this paragraph is about the increased use of plastics, the transition needs to be one that reflects time. The first sentence mentions *after World War II*. The word *then* doesn't do a good job connecting the idea that plastic use increased and people used and discarded plastic for all those years. So eliminate choice A from question 7. Choice B mentions *decades*, which indicates a long time. So choice B does show the idea that people have thrown away plastics for years. Leave it and look at choices C and D. Choice C goes backward in time, so it is no good. Since *forthwith* means "immediately," it does not work either. Choice B is the right transition and therefore the right answer.

Let's now look at question 8.

The first paragraph is about the increased use of plastics and the fact that plastics are mostly thrown away. The second paragraph explains that much of the plastic that has been discarded over the years has ended up in the middle of the ocean, resulting in an environmental disaster. The first paragraph ends with the fact that Americans recycle only a fraction of the plastic produced. The next sentence, which starts the second paragraph, states that some plastic goes to landfills and that other plastic is washed away and ends up in the ocean. So we need a transition between the two paragraphs that shows cause. Choice A, *while*, does just that. It shows that *while* some plastic is put into landfills, other plastic winds up in the ocean. Leave choice A and see if there is anything better. Look at choices B and D. With their commas and their phrasing, they create another problem in the sentence. Since they do not make the first part of the sentence an adverbial clause, they make the sentence a comma splice (two sentences smashed together). That makes them bad choices.

> If a choice creates another writing problem, like grammar or tone, eliminate it!

Choice C, *besides*, means "in addition," and that does not show cause. So choice A is the best answer.

BIG STRATEGY #7

Don't Be Afraid to Choose "NO CHANGE"

Remember that the SAT is not like a test made by teachers. When teachers write tests, choices like "None of the above" or "All of the above" are rarely correct. The SAT carefully balances its choices, though. So there is as good a chance that the correct answer is choice A ("NO CHANGE") as it is choice D. Remember to answer every question. Leave no answer spaces blank. After all, there's no penalty for guessing!

Let's work on one more transition problem.

Think of the ideas that end that second paragraph in question 9. The problem of plastic pollution is presented. Then the paragraph ends with possible strategies for addressing the problem. The technical solution that scientists are working on is presented as an option, and reduction of the use of plastic is presented as an easier option. So we need a transition that shows a contradiction between the technical solution's inadequacy and the relative ease of the reduced use of plastic. Choice A does not show a contrast between those ideas because it indicates a transition of time. Eliminate it. Choice B gives a transition for an example, so eliminate that choice, too. Choice C shows the contrast that *even though* scientists are looking for an answer, we can simply reduce our use of plastics. Leave choice C and look at choice D. *Therefore* shows an effect or a result. That is not the kind of transition we need, either. Choice C is the best choice.

Chapter Overview

For our ideas to make sense, they must be relevant to the topic, and the text must flow from one idea to the next. On the SAT, you will be asked to add, delete, move, and transition ideas. To do all of these, you must read the passage, find the main idea of the passage as a whole, and identify the main idea of each paragraph. To answer questions about details, you must first understand what is being said and what those details are. Only then can you attack the questions. Even though it is called the Writing and Language Test, to do well you must read carefully and understand what you are reading!

5

Graphics

Charts and graphs are often included in the things we read and write. They help convey the main point or certain details more effectively than just words. Since graphics are such a common part of reading and writing, the SAT has graphics questions on both the Writing and Language Test and the Reading Test. The question types you will see on the Writing and Language Test are slightly different from the question types that you will see on the Reading Test.

WHY ARE GRAPHICS IN BOTH SECTIONS?

Since graphics are a large part of the information we receive and consume, they are part of both the Writing and Language Test and the Reading Test. The thinking is that since the SAT measures college readiness and since graphics are part of the materials that college students read, graphics should therefore be part of the test.

WRITING AND LANGUAGE QUESTION TYPES

What do you do when you see a graphics question? As we learned in the last chapter, the key tip (also see page 54) is to read and try to determine the main idea of the text. This makes perfect sense. After all, graphics are a way to support visually the ideas found in the text itself. In order to answer questions about graphics, you have to understand the text. Once you've done that, the rest is straightforward.

Read the passage on pages 50–52, try to determine the main idea, and then read the questions that follow.

Principal Wars of Conflicts in Which the United States Participated:

U.S. Military Casualties, 1775–1900

War or Conflict	Branch of Service	Total Deaths	Total Battle Deaths	Wounds Not Mortal
Revolutionary War	Army	4,044	4,044	6,044
	Navy	342	342	114
	Marines	49	49	70
War of 1812	Army	1,950	1,950	4,000
	Navy	265	265	439
	Marines	45	45	66
Mexican War	Army	13,271	1,721	4,102
	Navy	1	1	3
	Marines	11	11	47
Civil War (Union Forces Only)*	Army	359,528	138,154	280,040
	Navy	4,523	2,112	1,710
	Marines	460	148	131
Spanish-American War	Army	2,430	369	1,594
	Navy	10	10	47
	Marines	6	6	21

*Authoritative statistics for the Confederate forces are not available. The final report of the Provost Marshal General, 1863–1866, indicated 133,821 Confederate deaths (74,524 battle and 59,297 other) based upon incomplete returns. In addition, an estimated 26,000 to 31,000 Confederate personnel died in Union prisons.

From The Congressional Research Service. "American War and Military Operations Casualties: Lists and Statistics," January 2, 2015. *http://fas.org/sgp/crs/natsec/RL32492.pdf*

The United States has had its share of wars. Students learn that Americans have fought and died in wars throughout the country's history. Students learn about generals and battles, and they see paintings and pictures of the bravery and savagery of warfare.

What is generally not understood by both teachers and students, however, is the actual number of casualties of those wars. Many

people are surprised to learn the specific number of casualties that the United States suffered in each war. Comparing the casualties suffered in one war to those suffered in another can be an eye-opening experience. The Revolutionary War, for example, is portrayed as a long and bloody struggle. The numbers, however, paint a different picture. Just over four thousand Americans died in that war, and the War of 1812 also produced a surprisingly low number of casualties. The wars that established the United States did not have casualties anywhere near the casualties of those that followed.

The Civil War is by far the bloodiest war the United States has ever fought. ❶ The surprising thing about the wars that followed is not just the large number of casualties in the Civil War. Since we live in an age of advanced medical care, it is hard for us to understand that the number of battlefield casualties pales in comparison to the number that died from disease during warfare. In the Civil War, ❷ over 359,000 Army casualties occurred off the battlefield. Of course, there are not many paintings of troops suffering from dysentery. And the number of wounded was also astronomical compared to previous wars. The number of Army wounded outnumbered the total killed in battle, and the Navy's number of wounded was close to the number killed in battle.

1. At this point, the writer wants to add specific information that supports the main topic of the paragraph. Which choice best completes the sentence with relevant and accurate information based on the table?

(A) The number of Civil War casualties is slightly higher than the casualties from the Revolutionary War.
(B) The casualties from the Revolutionary War, the War of 1812, and the Mexican War combined equal the casualties from the Civil War.
(C) The casualties from all the other wars before 1900 are in the low thousands, but Civil War casualties run in the hundreds of thousands.
(D) The Civil War's 359,528 casualties from the Army were ten percent of the U.S. population at the time.

2. Which choice most accurately and effectively represents the information in the table?

(A) NO CHANGE
(B) 138,154 of the 359,528 casualties died off the battlefield.
(C) 280,040 casualties occurred off the battlefield.
(D) Only 138,154 of the 359,528 Army casualties occurred during battle.

But these casualty numbers of Army, Navy, and Marines from the Civil War do not even come close to portraying the shocking number of deaths from that war. In truth, the 138,154 Army, the 2,112 Navy, and the 148 Marines killed in battle represent only about **3** <u>one-third</u> of the number of Americans killed in battle in the Civil War. In the Civil War, no matter who was killed, it was an American. The Confederate casualties are not counted as official United States military personnel killed because, at the time, the Confederates were in open rebellion and had broken away from the United States.

The United States was made by war, and it continued to be shaped by it. However, our ideas about those early wars do not match the actual numbers from those wars. American wars became bloodier and bloodier as time progressed, perhaps as a result of changing tactics on the battlefield and of the growing size of the country.

3. Which choice most accurately and effectively represents the information in the table?

(A) NO CHANGE
(B) one-tenth
(C) one-half
(D) two-thirds

The overall concept of the passage is American war casualties. The main idea of the third paragraph is about how bloody the Civil War was and how many troops did not die in battle. Now that we know this, we can approach the question.

First, understand that this is a graphics question from the Writing and Language Test. You are being asked to add details using information from the table. So you should take the same approach as we did in the last chapter. Think of the main idea, and then match the detail that backs it up. Second, you should understand that this is a detail question, not a grammar question. The choices are correct in terms of grammar and usage. Third, inspect the table or graph. Look at the title, key, data, and units. In other words, you will not need a calculator for these questions.

> Even though you are looking at numbers on a table or graph, the math itself is not difficult!

With this strategy in mind, look at choice A. There are two things wrong with it. First, it says that Civil War casualties were *slightly* higher than those of the other wars. Again, you do not need a calculator to see that the casualties from the Civil War eclipsed those of the Revolutionary War. The second thing wrong with choice A is really in the question itself. The question says the writer wants to add *specific information* to the text. There is nothing specific about that answer. For both of these reasons, eliminate choice A.

Choice B does require some very basic math. What are the combined casualties from the Revolutionary War, the War of 1812, and the Mexican War? The casualty numbers are about 4,500, about 2,000, and about 13,000, respectively, for a total of just under 20,000. Now look at the Civil War. In the Army alone, the casualties were over 359,000. Notice that advanced math skills are not necessary for these problems. It's easy to cross off choice B.

Choice C requires you to look again at the casualties from all the wars. Are the casualty numbers for all wars except the Civil War in the low thousands? Yes, they are. Are the casualties from the Civil War in the hundreds of thousands? Again, yes. So leave choice C and see if choice D is any better.

Choice D does have some specific information since it mentions the exact number of Army dead, but where does the table give the total U.S. population at the time? That information is not on the table. So this answer cannot be correct. Remember that the question asks you to include information from the table. So if the information is not found in the table, the answer choice is wrong.

The answer then must be choice C.

One of the question types for graphics on the Writing and Language Test is to add a detail or details using the information from the table or graph. It is really not much different from any other adding a detail question. Try another question.

> If two choices are very similar, more often than not, one of them is the answer.

Question 2 (page 51) again revolves around knowing what the main idea is and being able to read the table. Look at choice A and then at the table. There were over 359,000 Army casualties. However, that is the total number, not the number of deaths that "occurred off the battlefield." So eliminate choice A.

Look carefully at your other options. Do you notice anything about choices B and D? Do you see how similar they are? Before we analyze them, check choice C. If you look at the table column title that corresponds to 280,040, you will see that the number represents the soldiers who were wounded but not killed. Although choice C is a correct statistic, it does not match the idea that many deaths in the Civil War occurred off the battlefield. So eliminate choice C.

Now look at choice B. It states that 138,154 Army soldiers were killed off the battlefield. Look at the table column title; that number is the number killed on the battlefield. So choice B is incorrect, which makes choice D correct.

Now look again at choices B and D. Do you see that their wording is slightly different? Did you notice that choice B, the incorrect answer, is given first? This

> Always read the paragraph through to help understand the main idea and all the details!

is a good example of the SAT trying to grab your attention with the right numbers but the wrong wording. Read the choices carefully! Now let's look at question 3 (see page 52).

The key is to finish reading the paragraph. If you read only up to the end of the sentence, you could very well miss the big hint. The end of the third paragraph states that the numbers are not accurate because the Confederate Americans killed are not taken into account.

Now that you understand that the Confederate casualties are part of the author's argument, you have to find the number of Confederate casualties if you are going to figure out the correct fraction. Read the footnote at the bottom of the table. The number of Confederate casualties is listed. The footnote states 133,821 Confederates were killed in the war.

> The information that is in footnotes can be important!

Remember that the table and graph questions do not require any advanced math or the use of a calculator! Go back to the sentence and reread it. It says that *in truth, the 138,154 Army, the 2,112 Navy, and the 148 Marines represent only about*

❸ *one-third of the number of Americans killed in the Civil War.* Notice that the word *about* occurs before the fraction. That means that we are rounding off here.

If you roughly add up the Union casualties in that sentence, you have about 140,000. The Confederate casualties are about 75,000. That means that there were about 215,000 casualties total. Make a fraction. The approximately 140,000 Union casualties divided by the approximately 215,000 total casualties rounds to about 140 over 215, which is about 14 over 21. This reduces to two-thirds. The Union casualties are about two-thirds of the casualties in the war. So the answer is choice D.

READING TEST QUESTIONS

Let's try another kind of question. This is where we start to transition from Writing and Language Test questions to Reading Test questions. Remember, there are two parts to the English Test, but graphics and tables are in both parts. You will see that graphics questions test the same essential skills in both sections but in a different way. Give the question a try (see page 57). It is based on the passage from pages 50–52.

The United States has had its share of wars. Students learn that Americans have fought and died in wars throughout the country's history. Students learn about generals and battles, and they see paintings and pic-
Line tures of the bravery and savagery of warfare.
(5)   What is generally not understood by both teachers and students, however, is the actual number of casualties of those wars. Many people are surprised to learn the specific number of casualties that the United States suffered in each war. Comparing the casualties suffered in one war to those suffered in another can be an eye-opening experience. The Revolutionary
(10) War, for example, is portrayed as a long and bloody struggle. The numbers, however, paint a different picture. Just over four thousand Americans died in that war, and the War of 1812 also produced a surprisingly low number of casualties. The wars that established the United States did not have casualties anywhere near the casualties of those that followed.
(15)   The Civil War is by far the bloodiest war the United States has ever fought. The surprising thing about the wars that followed is not just the large number of casualties in the Civil War. Since we live in an age of advanced medical care, it is hard for us to understand that the number of battlefield casualties pales in comparison to the number that died
(20) from disease during warfare. In the Civil War, over 359,000 Army casualties occurred off the battlefield. Of course, there are not many paintings of troops suffering from dysentery. And the number of wounded was also astronomical compared to previous wars. The number of Army wounded

outnumbered the total killed in battle, and the Navy's number of wounded
(25) was close to the number killed in battle.

But these casualty numbers of Army, Navy, and Marines from the Civil
War do not even come close to portraying the shocking number of deaths
from that war. In truth, the 138,154 Army, the 2,112 Navy, and the 148 Marines
killed in battle represent only about one-third of the number of Americans
(30) killed in battle in the Civil War. In the Civil War, no matter who was killed,
it was an American. The Confederate casualties are not counted as official
United States military personnel killed because, at the time, the Confederates
were in open rebellion and had broken away from the United States.

The United States was made by war, and it continued to be shaped
(35) by it. However, our ideas about those early wars do not match the actual
numbers from those wars. American wars became bloodier and bloodier
as time progressed, perhaps as a result of changing tactics on the battlefield and of the growing size of the country.

Principal Wars of Conflicts in Which the United States Participated: U.S. Military Casualties, 1775–1900

War or Conflict	Branch of Service	Total Deaths	Total Battle Deaths	Wounds Not Mortal
Revolutionary War	Army	4,044	4,044	6,044
	Navy	342	342	114
	Marines	49	49	70
War of 1812	Army	1,950	1,950	4,000
	Navy	265	265	439
	Marines	45	45	66
Mexican War	Army	13,271	1,721	4,102
	Navy	1	1	3
	Marines	11	11	47
Civil War (Union Forces Only)*	Army	359,528	138,154	280,040
	Navy	4,523	2,112	1,710
	Marines	460	148	131
Spanish-American War	Army	2,430	369	1,594
	Navy	10	10	47
	Marines	6	6	21

*Authoritative statistics for the Confederate forces are not available. The final report of the Provost Marshal General, 1863–1866, indicated 133,821 Confederate deaths (74,524 battle and 59,297 other) based upon incomplete returns. In addition, an estimated 26,000 to 31,000 Confederate personnel died in Union prisons.

From The Congressional Research Service. "American War and Military Operations Casualties: Lists and Statistics," January 2, 2015. http://fas.org/sgp/crs/natsec/RL32492.pdf

1. The table following the passage offers evidence that Marines had the best chance to survive American wars from 1775–1900 based on

   (A) the number of "Wounds Not Mortal" column.
   (B) the total number of Marine casualties in each war compared with the casualties in the Army and Navy.
   (C) the number of Marines killed in the Spanish-American War.
   (D) the number of Navy casualties compared with the number of Marine casualties in each war.

Here you are not being asked to change the writing; you are being asked to analyze the writing. We are not adding, deleting, or moving a thing. Instead, we are looking at what is written and how it is written. However, we must still understand the main idea and the details. Then we can look back to the table and answer the question.

The question says that the information implies that the Marines had the best chance of not getting killed. We know the main idea of the whole passage was about American war casualties. Start with the Revolutionary War. Find the row that says "Marines" and see how many casualties occurred. Now look at how many "Army" and "Navy" casualties occurred for that same war. Do the same for each war listed in the table. In every war, which of the three branches of service had the lowest number of casualties? In each case, it was the Marines. So the Marines had the best chance of surviving based on those numbers. Now if you're about to say that the Marines are the smallest service and the Army the biggest so the percentages might be different from the total, consider this BIG Strategy.

BIG STRATEGY #8

Don't Overthink the Questions!

Often, juniors and seniors use the same process while taking the SAT as they use in English class every day. In class, their teachers say, "OK, here's what the author said in chapter 12. But what did he *really* say?" Those students then have to take what they've read and apply it to another idea to create a new thought. In other words, the teachers try to get students to use higher-level thinking skills to create ideas. That's great, of course. However, the SAT doesn't do that! When the SAT asks what the author said, it is simply referring to what the author said. Do not take an inch and make it a foot. Do not add information that you know from somewhere else. You are being asked only about what you just read and nothing more. The test questions do not run very deep. This does not mean that the Reading Test is easy! It just means that the Reading Test questions are asking only about what is on the page and not about anything beyond it.

With this in mind, the table shows that the lowest casualties in each war were the Marine casualties. From there, it's easy to eliminate choice A and choice C. Since choice D says to compare Marine casualties only to Navy casualties, it incorrectly leaves out the Army numbers. So choice B is the answer.

Try another type of question.

2. Based on the table and passage, which choice gives the correct number of Navy service members wounded in the Civil War?

    (A) 4,523
    (B) 2,112
    (C) 1,710
    (D) 280,040

There are a couple of things to note here. First, note that the question says the answer is *based on the table and the passage*. Therefore, it is not simply a matter of looking back at the table. You must first go back to the third paragraph, which is about the Civil War. Look for anything about the Navy. You will see that the paragraph ends with the phrase *the Navy's number of wounded was close to the number killed in battle*. So we have our first clue.

Now look at the table. Notice that every number in the answer choices relates to the Civil War. To get this answer correct, you have to focus on the key word. What number are they asking for about the Navy in the Civil War? The question asks for the number of wounded. So we have to go to the columns at the top and read the titles. The column to the far right says "Wounds Not Mortal." Follow that column down until you get to the row for the Navy in the Civil War. Since that number is 1,710, the answer is choice C.

Try a two-part question next.

3. Do the data in the table support the author's view that American wars became bloodier as time progressed?

   (A) Yes, because the Revolutionary War, the War of 1812, and the Mexican War all had far fewer casualties than the Civil War, and since the Civil War came after them, American wars must be progressively bloodier.

   (B) Yes, because the number of wounded in the Revolutionary War, the War of 1812, and the Mexican War all had far fewer wounded than the Civil War, which came after, and therefore, the wars must be progressively bloodier.

   (C) No, because the Civil War number of killed and wounded is not complete without the Confederate killed and wounded included, and since the data do not show the total number of Americans killed and wounded in that war, the author cannot support his claim.

   (D) No, because even though the number of killed and wounded is lower in the wars before the Civil War, the Spanish-American War, which was after the Civil War, is also lower in casualty numbers.

First, reread the sentence that corresponds to the question. It says that *American wars became bloodier and bloodier as time progressed, perhaps as a result of changing tactics on the battlefield and of the growing size of the country*. Is that true? We must look at the table to see. The table title says, in part, "U.S. Military Casualties, 1775–1900." Since the first war listed is the Revolutionary War and the second is the War of 1812, it is easy to see that the wars are in the order in which they happened.

Now look at the numbers of killed and wounded for each war. Yes, the Revolutionary War, the War of 1812, and the Mexican War all had casualty numbers far lower than those of the Civil War, so it is tempting to pick choice A. However, those numbers are incomplete. After the Civil War, the Spanish-American War is listed. The total killed in the Spanish-American War was less than 2,500. Therefore, based on the table, American wars were not progressively bloodier. Eliminate choices A and B.

Now look at choice C. Although the number of Confederate Americans is not included in the table, those numbers are available in the footnote. With or without those numbers, the numbers from the Spanish-American War show that the author's viewpoint is wrong. Therefore, choice C is incorrect, making choice D the answer. Choosing D leads us to our next BIG Strategy.

Now let's look at the follow-up to question 3. Follow-up questions will immediately follow the primary question.

4. According to the table, which of the following data provide evidence in support of the answer to the previous question?

    (A) Civil War 359,528 killed; Spanish-American War 2,430 killed
    (B) Civil War 359,528 killed; Mexican War 13,271 killed
    (C) Civil War 359,528 killed; Revolutionary War 4,044 killed
    (D) Civil War 359,528 killed; War of 1812 1,950 killed

Follow-up questions will ask for the data that proves the previous answer. So look back at the previous question and its answer. That question asked whether the author was correct in stating that American wars grew progressively bloodier over time. We chose choice D, which said no, they did not. We know from the data provided in the table that the Spanish-American War came after the Civil War and the number of casualties from the Spanish-American War was far lower than those of the Civil War.

Now we are asked for those numbers. Look at the table again. Find the numbers for the Civil War and for the Spanish-American War. Now find those numbers in the answer choices. The only possible answer is choice A. When you are presented with this type of question, know that you are being asked to use the graphic to confirm your answer.

Chapter Overview

Graphics and tables are in both parts of the SAT English Test. Even though the Writing and Language Test and the Reading Test are asking different questions, the approach to questions containing graphics is the same. You must first understand the main idea of the passage or paragraph. Then you must look at the graphics to see what the question wants you to consider changing in the Writing and Language Test and what it wants you to analyze in the Reading Test. Once you have the main idea and have read the question, find the evidence in the graphics to support the correct answer.

PART TWO:
READING TEST

On the Reading Test section of the SAT, you will read passages and answer different kinds of questions that require reading analysis. The Reading Test is the second half of the English score. Its score ranges from 100 to 400 points.

The Components of the Reading Test

- The Reading Test is 65 minutes long and has 5 reading passages.
- Each passage has 10–11 questions.
- Each passage is between 500 and 750 words long.
- The passages are based on various topics: literature, social studies, science, and one important historical document.
- The social studies passage and one of the science passages will have an accompanying graph.
- There is one section with two passages on the same topic. These paired passages might also include a graphic.
- There are 52 questions in total.
- Based on the time available and the number of questions, you should complete each passage and its 10–11 questions in 12–13 minutes.

The Reading Test takes work. Even though you will quickly learn the question types, the fact that they are always applied to a new reading passage makes the test difficult. With the Reading Test, the more you practice, the better you will do. First, though, you need to learn the question types and the skills necessary for conquering them. We will work on these skills in the next four chapters.

6

Vocabulary Words That You Won't Study

For decades, students taking the SAT dreaded the vocabulary questions. The words tended to be obscure. For years, the questions were analogies (for example, cat is to dog as mouse is to _____). For students to do well on the vocabulary section, they had to study lists of vocabulary words for hours upon hours, trying to cram those obscure words and their definitions into their heads and hoping the words would stay there for test day. Fortunately, one of the best features of the current test is a move away from all of that. The test no longer rewards those who study flash cards for hours. Instead, the SAT rewards resourceful students who can read and use context clues to figure out a word's meaning. In other words, the vocabulary is now based on skill, not on rote memorization.

So how do you avoid memorizing definitions?

BIG STRATEGY #10

Come Up with Your Own Answer

Think of the answer before you look at the answer choices. The Reading Test will try to trick you into choosing wrong answers. To avoid this trap, you have to decide what the answer is before you look at the choices offered by the test. Imagine going to a restaurant wanting a steak. Then you read the menu and, after getting caught up in the description of a dish, you order the chicken. As you are eating the chicken, you realize that your meal has been ruined because you did not get what you wanted. This is how the SAT Reading Test is designed. The only way to avoid choosing the wrong answer is to decide what you want first and then search for it. Remember: that applies to every question, not just the vocabulary questions.

MAKE YOUR OWN WORDS

Read the following sentence, and then write your own word in the blank. If your mind comes up with a phrase, that's fine! Your answer doesn't have to be a single word.

1. The inspector found the evidence lacking, but he _____ with the case.

What did you come up with? Did you write something like *continue, carry on, persist,* or *go on*? If so, you're right there! Look at the answer choices:

(A) premiered
(B) predicted
(C) persevered
(D) permeated

If you see the synonym for *continue* and for *carry on,* great. Choose it. Let's say, though, that you don't see the synonym. Here's how to work through the answers.

ELIMINATE . . . ELIMINATE

Start by eliminating the answer choices that are obviously wrong. In this question, there are two that are easy to discard. The prefix *pre-* means *before.* Since this has nothing to do with what the inspector is doing (that is, it does not

> Use prefixes to eliminate choices.

match our solutions of *continue* or *carry on*), we can eliminate choices A and B. Just like that, we have narrowed down our chance of answering the question correctly to 50-50!

Now that we've gotten it down to two choices, read each and see if one matches either *continue* or *carry on.* You probably see the answer now, but let's suppose you don't see it. What would you do? Plug in the remaining choices one at a time. Decide which one works. Yes, this is guessing, but there is logic to this procedure.

First, remember, the vocabulary on this test is high school level, not college level or beyond. You may not know the definition of every word. However, there is a good chance that you have read the word in a sentence at some time previously, even if you have done only half of the reading assigned for school. You are also not being asked to define any words; you are being asked to recog-

nize which word fits in a sentence. Second, words tend to be used in similar contexts. So you might recognize the correct word by reading it in a sentence.

When you have it down to two choices and do not see the right one, plug in each answer and read it in the sentence. Then choose whichever answer seems better.

Whether you use prefixes to narrow down choices or plug the answer choices into the question, you are using effective strategies. Both are better than simply guessing the answer randomly. So let's try this plugging-in strategy with the two choices left.

> The inspector found the evidence lacking, but he <u>persevered</u> with the case.
> The inspector found the evidence lacking, but he <u>permeated</u> with the case.

Which seems better when you read it, or which sounds like it doesn't fit or make sense? If you are unsure, read them again and try to eliminate one.

The second sentence does not fit in this case (*permeate* means "to spread throughout"). So *persevered* (meaning "to carry on"), choice C, is the correct answer.

CROSS OUT THE WORD(S)

Now that you see the basic approach to coming up with your own answer, the next step is to see how the SAT presents the words and the answer choices. You are not given a sentence with a blank in it, as you saw in question 1. Instead, you will see a word in a paragraph as part of what you read. Then you will be asked what the word means **in that sentence**.

Cross out the word in the passage.

You have done this for years. With every vocabulary unit, you have been asked to choose the right word to fit the blank. By crossing out the word in the passage, your brain will see the blank and kick into vocabulary unit mode. Read the short passage from "What to the Slave Is the Fourth of July?" by Frederick Douglass below, and then read the accompanying question.

> He who could address this audience without a quailing sensation, has stronger nerves than I have. I do not remember ever to have **appeared** as a speaker before any assembly more shrinkingly, nor with greater
> *Line* distrust of my ability, than I do this day. A **feeling** has crept over me,
> (5) quite unfavorable to the exercise of my limited powers of speech.
> The task before me is one which requires much previous thought and

study for its proper performance. I know that apologies of this sort are generally considered flat and unmeaning. I trust, however, that mine will not be so considered. Should I seem at ease, my appearance would

(10) much misrepresent me. The little experience I have had in addressing public meetings, in country schoolhouses, avails me nothing on the present occasion.

2. As used in line 2, "appeared" means

   (A) materialized.
   (B) arrived.
   (C) published.
   (D) performed.

> **Do not look at the answer choices! In fact, cover them with your hand or with the answer sheet.**

Go back to the line and cross out the word *appeared*. The word is shown in bold in the passage to make it easy for you to find. Be aware that on the SAT, the word will not be bolded.

Develop the good habit of covering the answer choices when reading the question. Now read the sentence again and come up with your own word. Since the sentence refers to being in front of an audience, the blank should be something like *getting up in front of people.* Remember that you don't have to fill in the blank with a single word. If you think of a phrase instead of a word, that's great. Use the phrase.

The next step is to look at the choices and eliminate any that don't match your predetermined answer. Do you notice anything about the answer choices? If you went to the dictionary and looked up the word *appeared*, you would find every one of the choices as definitions. The SAT is designed to test your vocabulary through context reading skills, not your ability to memorize. It does not matter that the definition is in the dictionary. What matters is what the word means **in that sentence.**

> Studying—or memorizing—definitions will not help much if you are only a few weeks away from taking the SAT. (If you are months away from taking the SAT, memorizing prefixes, suffixes, common roots, and definitions will help increase your word recognition and make the vocabulary questions easier.)

This should be great news! This means that studying word definitions is not the best way to prepare for the SAT if the test is quickly approaching. If you are close to the testing date and want to do better on vocabulary questions on the SAT, practice sample problems instead of trying to cram the meanings of words into your brain.

Let's get back to the problem at hand. We know that the word means something like *getting up in front of people*. Look again at the four choices. Cross off the ones that in no way mean that. You should be able to eliminate choice A and choice C. Now look again at what is left. Choice B, *arrived*, is close. However, choice D, *performed*, is better. You can plug it back into the sentence to be certain: "I do not remember ever to have *performed* as a speaker before any assembly more shrinkingly, nor with greater distrust of my ability, than I do this day." Yes, *performed* fits well. Choice D is the answer.

SEARCHING FOR CLUES

Let's try another question from the same passage and use a different method to find the answer.

3. As used in line 4, "feeling" means

    (A) love.
    (B) pride.
    (C) idea.
    (D) opinion.

Cover the choices, go back to the sentence, and cross out the word *feeling*. The sentence before the one in which *feeling* is mentioned states that he has great distrust in his ability to give a good speech. The sentence after the sentence in which *feeling* is mentioned states that much thought and study should go into preparing for a performance like this. These clues from the other sentences suggest, with regard to the sentence in which *feeling* is used, that *a thought* has crept over him about his fear of making a good speech.

> Rereading the sentence before and after the one that contains the word often helps you get the full meaning of the word.

By looking at the choices, we can quickly eliminate choices A and B. From what is left, we see that *opinion* is close but that *idea* is much closer to *thought*. Choice C is the best answer.

Remember that many words in English can be used as more than one part of speech. *Feeling*, for example, is often used as a verb.

> The word choices will always be the same part of speech as the key word in the passage. In other words, if the word is used as a noun in the sentence, all the answer choices will also be nouns. So you can eliminate based on only definition, not part of speech.

— BIG STRATEGY #11 —

If You Are Asked Something You Already Know, Be Careful!

Remember, the SAT is a test of your reading skills, not of your knowledge. Often, the test will have questions that seem to be common knowledge. If you read carefully, though, the information is actually different from what you learned in school. This is most true on vocabulary, where a word you studied may not be used with the definition you studied.

Let's get some more practice. Read the passage below from a letter to John Adams from Abigail Adams dated March 31, 1776. Then answer the questions that follow.

The town in general is left in a better state than we expected; more owing to a precipitate **flight** than any regard to the inhabitants; though some individuals discovered a sense of honor and justice, and have
Line left the rent of the houses in which they were, for the owners, and the
(5) furniture unhurt, or, if damaged, sufficient to make it good. Others have committed abominable ravages. The mansion house of your President is safe, and the furniture unhurt while the house and furniture of the Solicitor General have fallen a **prey** to their own merciless **party**. Surely the very fiends feel a **reverential** awe for virtue and patriotism, whilst
(10) they detest the parricide and traitor.

4. As used in line 2, "flight" means

   (A) aeronautics.
   (B) escape.
   (C) flock.
   (D) staircase.

If you cover up the choices, cross out the word, and read through the passage, you should get a sense that the owners of the houses are gone and that the houses were taken over by others. So *flight* must mean something like *going*

away. Once again, the choices are all various definitions of the word *flight*. So do not worry about memorizing what the word means beforehand from a vocabulary list. Instead, cross out any meaning that is not related to *going away*. In this case, you can easily cross out choices A and D. Now take a closer look at what is left. *Flock* is close but refers more often to birds than to people. *Escape* fits exactly, so choice B is the best answer. Try another from the same passage.

5. As used in line 8, "party" means

    (A) celebration.
    (B) individual.
    (C) caucus.
    (D) group.

Again, cover up the answer choices and cross out the word in the sentence. Since the passage describes others taking over people's homes, we get a sense that it is a *large group of people*. (Notice the words *fiends* in the sentence that follows the word.) Look at the choices. You should easily cross out choices A and B. Now look more closely at the two choices that remain. Choices C and D are close. If you are not sure which one is correct, put each one back into the sentence and read the sentence again.

In this case, *caucus* has a political meaning but *group* does not. There is nothing that hints that a political group is involved. So choice D, *group*, is the best answer.

Now that you have the answer, look at the choices again. Many people who take the test will not bother to look back at the passage and will instead just forge ahead with their idea of what the word means. This is a great example of that. What is the first thing that comes to mind when someone says the word *party*? That's right, most people think of a *celebration*. See how *celebration* is placed right up front as choice A? However, the answer is not choice A.

> Beware of eye candy, items that look good but aren't good for you! Think very carefully about every choice. Do not jump at what might seem to be an obvious answer.

6. As used in line 9, "prey" means

    (A) quarry.
    (B) plunder.
    (C) target.
    (D) prize.

If you cross out the word and cover up the answer choices, you should have a sense that the house was a *victim* of sorts. Look at the choices. You'll notice that choices B and D are almost synonyms. How is it possible for one of those to be the answer if they are so close in meaning? Eliminate them. Between choices A and C, choice C is the better choice. *Quarry* has more to do with hunting and killing an animal. *Target* is closest to *victim*, so choice C is the correct answer.

Try one more question from the same passage.

7. As used in line 9, "reverential" means

   (A) respectful.
   (B) bowing.
   (C) religious.
   (D) mocking.

Once again, cover up the answer choices and cross out the word in the sentence. In order to understand the context, read the previous sentence and then the sentence with *reverential* in it. When Abigail Adams wrote the letter, she made the two sentences parallel to each other. The sentence that precedes the one in which the word *reverential* appears states that the house of the President is safe while the house of the Solicitor General has been damaged. The next sentence says that the fiends are in awe of patriotism but that they detest a traitor. This must mean that they *respect* the President and his house while they detest the Solicitor General and his house. So choice A, *respectful*, is the correct answer.

Chapter Overview

Vocabulary is a big part of the Reading Test but not in the way most people think. Cramming definitions into your head is not the best way to prepare for this test if the SAT is fast approaching. If you do have adequate time to prepare before the test, flash cards can help. However, if the test is just a few weeks away, using them is not the best use of your preparation time. Instead, determining the meanings of words depends entirely on using the context, which is a definite skill that can be refined and improved upon. To do your best on vocabulary questions, start by covering up the answer choices the test gives you, crossing out the word in the sentence, and then reading the sentence again. When you have your own sense of what the word means, uncover the choices, eliminate the answer choices that clearly do not match your predetermined answer, and then take a second look at the remaining answer choices. If you still cannot decide, insert the remaining choices into the sentence and choose whichever sounds best. If you follow this procedure, you will maximize your score on the vocabulary questions!

7

Details, Details, Details

In Chapter 4, we saw that the Writing and Language Test puts an emphasis on details in writing. On the Reading Test, we find much of the same thing. In college, you will need to know not only how to read but also how to understand the details of what you are reading. Since you will need this skill in college and since the SAT is a measure of your readiness for college, detail questions are on the SAT. Before we get to detail questions, though, you need to know how to read the passages.

BIG STRATEGY #12

Read One Paragraph at a Time

Most people who take the SAT feel that the reading selection is very difficult to focus on and to understand. The test wants you to read the whole passage at once. When you do, though, staying focused is difficult because you are reading a random page from the middle of a book you have probably not read. Who reads like this? Since this is a completely unnatural way of reading, the material is, by its very nature, difficult to absorb all at once. To make the reading selection easier, you should read one paragraph at a time and answer whatever questions you can. Then read another paragraph and answer more questions.

READ ONE PARAGRAPH AT A TIME

By reading one paragraph and stopping to see what questions you can answer, you are narrowing your focus and thus making the test easier. The best part is that, in general, the questions go in order through the passage. In other words, the first question is about the beginning of the passage and the last question is about the end of the passage. Sometimes the first question is a main idea question. A main idea question tries to make you think that you have to read the entire passage first. Of course, this is not true. If you see this type of question,

skip it and then come back to it after you answer all the other questions for that passage.

By breaking the passage into smaller parts, you will be able to focus and understand what you are reading much better. Consequently, you will score better on the test.

The first question in connection with a passage is usually a main idea question. Answer it last, after you have read through the entire passage. Start by answering the detail questions. After you have read the entire passage and can look at the big picture, you will see the answer to the main idea question better.

> **Answer the detail questions first.**

Read each paragraph and see what detail questions you can answer. Once you get to questions that you cannot answer, it is time to move on and read another paragraph.

So let's try some detail questions, which will be based on Abigail Adams' letter to John Adams dated March 31, 1776. Instead of presenting the entire passage at once and asking you to read only the first paragraph, it will instead be presented one paragraph at a time with the questions following in order to accustom you to the approach to reading these passages.

The following is from a letter to John Adams written by his wife, Abigail Adams, on March 31, 1776.

I wish you would ever write me a letter half as long as I write you, and tell me, if you may, where your fleet are gone; what sort of defense Virginia can make against our common enemy; whether it is so situated
Line as to make an able defense. Are not the gentry lords, and the common
(5) people vassals? Are they not like the uncivilized vassals Britain represents us to be? I hope their riflemen, who have shown themselves very savage and even blood-thirsty, are not a specimen of the generality of the people. I am willing to allow the colony great merit for having produced a Washington—but they have been shamefully duped by a
(10) Dunmore.

1. The author refers to Washington (line 9) in order to

   (A) concede a point.
   (B) introduce an argument.
   (C) question a motive.
   (D) support a conclusion.

For this question, notice that there are two parts to each answer. First, there is the function word (*concede, introduce, question,* and *support*). Then there is the statement word (*point, argument, motive,* and *conclusion*). When an

> **When given two main words in an answer choice, split them up!**

answer choice has two main words, split the words. Think of the math of doing so. If you consider both main words together, you have only four choices and you have to eliminate three of the four. If you split the words, you have eight clues to use to eliminate three answer choices. This greatly increases your odds!

Look at only the first word in each answer choice and eliminate what you are sure is incorrect. If you are not sure, leave the answer! Let's try it. Of *give, introduce, question,* and *support,* which does the use of Washington definitely not do? You should see that Washington is not being used to question anything. Since the author uses the words *I am willing to allow* in the sentence where Washington is mentioned, she is not making an introduction, either. So just from the first words, you can eliminate choices B and C.

Now look at the second words for choices A and D. (We don't need to look at the second words for choices B and C since we have already eliminated them as choices!) We have the words *point* and *conclusion.* Again, from Abigail Adams' words *I am willing to allow,* you can see that she is not making a conclusion. So eliminate choice D, leaving you with the correct answer, choice A, *concede a point.* See how splitting the words makes solving the question easier?

Now that you have answered that question, you would go to the next one. If that question still relates to the first paragraph, you would answer it, too. If not, move on to the second paragraph. In this case, you will now read the next paragraph.

> I have sometimes been ready to think that the passion for liberty
> cannot be equally strong in the breasts of those who have been
> accustomed to deprive their fellow-creatures of theirs. Of this I am
> certain, that it is not founded upon that generous and Christian
> (15) principle of doing to others as we would that others should do unto us.

2. Adams asserts in lines 11–15 that the love of freedom harbored by people who persecute others is _____.

Before you look at the answer choices, take another look at the paragraph. Note the words *the passion for liberty cannot be equally strong* in the sentence about those who deprive others of their liberty. So we have the idea that Adams thinks they cannot love liberty as much as those who don't take away the liberty of others. Do you see how you now have your idea of the answer before you look at the answer?

So with an idea of the answer in your mind, now take a look at the question again, this time with the answer choices.

2. Adams asserts in lines 11–15 that the love of freedom harbored by people who persecute others is

   (A) substantiated.
   (B) inconsistent.
   (C) equal.
   (D) sincere.

Do you notice anything about three of the four choices? Think positive and negative. Do you see how three are positive and only one, *inconsistent*, is negative? Remember that by first reading the question without the choices, you could see the answer was something like *unequal*. The only negative word in the choices is *inconsistent*. It also most closely matches *unequal*. So choice B is the answer. By looking back at the passage, coming up with your own answer, and then eliminating the answer choices that are obviously incorrect, you can quickly and accurately get to the correct answer.

Before moving on, look again at the other answer choices to see how the test writers try to trick you into choosing incorrectly. Choice C, *equal*, is there to grab the attention of people who look back but only to scan for words. Adams uses the word *equally* in the paragraph. Of course, the word *not* precedes it. However, people who are merely scanning for words will probably miss that and confidently choose an incorrect answer. Choice D, *sincere*, is there to draw people who noted the words *of this I am certain* and thought that they indicated sincerity. Again, the test writers will place a trail of breadcrumbs leading to wrong answer choices. If you come up with your own answer first, though, you will not be lead down those false paths.

Read the next paragraph in the passage.

Do not you want to see Boston? I am fearful of the small-pox, or I
should have been in before this time. I got Mr. Crane to go to our house
and see what state it was in. I find it has been occupied by one of the
doctors of a regiment; very dirty, but no other damage has been done to
(20) it. The few things which were left in it are all gone. I look upon it as a new
acquisition of property—a property which one month ago I did not value
at a single shilling, and would with pleasure have seen it in flames.

(Here there are no corresponding questions, so move on to the next paragraph.)

The town in general is left in a better state than we expected; more
owing to a precipitate flight than any regard to the inhabitants; though
(25) some individuals discovered a sense of honor and justice, and have
left the rent of the houses in which they were, for the owners, and the
furniture unhurt, or, if damaged, sufficient to make it good. Others have
committed abominable ravages. The mansion house of your President
is safe, and the furniture unhurt while the house and furniture of the
(30) Solicitor General have fallen a prey to their own merciless party. Surely
the very fiends feel a reverential awe for virtue and patriotism, whilst
they detest the parricide and traitor.

3. The passage indicates that the conditions of the homes occupied by the
    enemy were mainly due to

    (A) having to leave suddenly.
    (B) jealousy of the homeowners.
    (C) scorn for the Adams family.
    (D) respect for the homeowners.

Again, do not look at the choices. Think of the question. As you look back at
the passage, search for the answer. The key to this question is to reread carefully.
The paragraph does state that *some individuals discovered a sense of honor
and justice.* The paragraph also says that *others have committed abominable
ravages.* The first excerpt is hinting to you that choice D, *respect for the
homeowners,* is correct, while the second is trying to trick you into choosing
choices B or C.

However, a close reading of the first sentence of the paragraph reveals that the conditions of the homes were *more owing to a precipitate flight than any regard to the inhabitants*. Even if you are unsure of the meaning of the word *precipitate*, taking it away reveals that the conditions were *more owing to a flight than any regard to the inhabitants*. So fleeing was the main reason, and that is what we are being asked for. Choice A is correct.

WORK BACKWARD FOR PAIRED QUESTIONS

Now read the next two paragraphs.

I feel very differently at the approach of spring from what I did a month ago. We knew not then whether we could plant or sow with safety,
(35) whether where we had tilled we could reap the fruits of our own industry, whether we could rest in our own cottages or whether we should be driven from the seacoast to seek shelter in the wilderness but now we feel a temporary peace, and the poor fugitives are returning to their deserted habitations.
(40) Though we felicitate ourselves, we sympathize with those who are trembling lest the lot of Boston should be theirs. But they cannot be in similar circumstances unless pusillanimity and cowardice should take possession of them. They have time and warning given them to see the evil and shun it.

4. The passage indicates that the change in thought about the beginning of spring is caused by

    (A) the weather.
    (B) more certainty.
    (C) tolerance for the enemy.
    (D) victory in war.

Before you go to the answer, take a look at the next question.

5. Which choice provides the best evidence for the answer to the previous question?

    (A) Lines 34–39 ("We knew . . . habitations")
    (B) Lines 40–41 ("Though we . . . theirs")
    (C) Lines 41–43 ("But they . . . them")
    (D) Lines 43–44 ("They have . . . it")

These are called paired questions. Question 5 is a follow-up to question 4. You are being asked to answer a question and then to provide the evidence that supports your answer. These follow-up questions appear in every reading passage.

This might seem intimidating at first. If you approach them in the right way, though, you will see that they can actually be much easier than you think. You can use two different approaches to answer paired questions. For this question, you will answer the question with the usual approach.

Look again at question 4. You are being asked to identify the reason for the change in thought about the coming of spring. Reread the paragraph. Do you see the mention of feeling different about the coming of spring than a month ago? The second sentence goes on to say that they were unsure if they could plant their crops and live in their homes safely, but now they *feel a temporary peace*. A month ago they had been uncertain; they were now more certain. If you look at the choices for question 4, you see that choice B is the answer.

Now move on to question 5. Where did we see the evidence? It was in the long sentence starting on line 34. So choice A is the answer.

This example shows one way to approach these paired questions. Now read the last two paragraphs of the passage and attempt the next questions.

(45)   I long to hear that you have declared an independency. And, by the way, in the new code of laws which I suppose it will be necessary for you to make, I desire you would remember the ladies and be more generous and favorable to them than your ancestors. Do not put such unlimited power into the hands of the husbands. Remember, all men

(50) would be tyrants if they could. If particular care and attention is not paid to the ladies, we are determined to foment a rebellion, and will not hold ourselves bound by any laws in which we have no voice or representation.

That your sex are naturally tyrannical is a truth so thoroughly

(55) established as to admit of no dispute; but such of you as wish to be happy willingly give up the harsh title of master for the more tender and endearing one of friend. Why, then, not put it out of the power of the vicious and the lawless to use us with cruelty and indignity with impunity? Men of sense in all ages abhor those customs which treat

(60) us only as the vassals of your sex; regard us then as beings placed by Providence under your protection, and in imitation of the Supreme Being make use of that power only for our happiness.

6. It can be inferred that Abigail Adams believed that women should

    (A) be fully independent of men.

    (B) have the right to vote, hold office, and own property in the new country.

    (C) be given more protection and independence from their husbands under the law.

    (D) be kept completely dependent upon their husbands with no say in domestic or political matters.

7. Which choice provides the best evidence for the answer to the previous question?

    (A) Lines 45–48 ("And, by . . . ancestors")

    (B) Lines 49–53 ("Remember, all . . . representation")

    (C) Lines 54–57 ("That your . . . friend")

    (D) Lines 57–59 ("Why, then . . . impunity?")

For this set of paired questions, try a new approach. Let's say that you have reread the passage and don't see the answer to question 6. In that case, skip ahead and read question 7. One of those pieces of evidence must show or match one of the choices from question 6. Professional poker players talk of looking for another player's "tell," the sign that shows what cards the opponent has. The evidence question, which always is the second of the paired questions, does just that.

Go to question 7. Look at choice A. Does the sentence *And, by the way, in the new code of laws which I suppose it will be necessary for you to make, I desire you would remember the ladies and be more generous and favorable to them than your ancestors* show that women should be independent of men, have the right to vote, be given more protection, or be kept completely dependent on men? No, it provides no evidence of any of those. So eliminate it.

> For paired questions, if you don't see the answer, go to the question asking for evidence and work backward.

Now go to choice B in question 7 and do the same thing. Do the words *remember, all men would be tyrants if they could. If particular care and attention is not paid to the ladies, we are determined to foment a rebellion, and will not hold ourselves bound by any laws in which we have no voice or representation* show any of the choices for question 6? It might imply that women should have the right to vote, but that would be a bit of a stretch. It is probably not the answer. If you find

nothing better, though, you will choose choice B in both questions 6 and 7 and then move on.

Go to choice C in question 7. Does the sentence support any of the choices for question 6? No, it doesn't. Eliminate it.

Now go to choice D. Think of the words *why, then, not put it out of the power of the vicious and the lawless to use us with cruelty and indignity with impunity?* Does that show that women should be independent? No, that's too much. The same goes for holding the right to vote. However, choice C for question 6 says that women should have more protection and independence from their husbands. The words *put it out of the power of the vicious . . . to use us with cruelty* supports that statement.

So we have found both answers. Question 6 is choice C, and question 7 is choice D. By working backward, you use the evidence the test provides you with to help you find the answer to paired questions!

Chapter Overview

The Reading Test is filled with detail questions. They come in different types, but the approach is always the same. First, read the passages one paragraph at a time to stay focused. When you read the question, do not look at the answer choices. Instead, go back and reread to find your own answer. Then match your answer to the correct answer choice. Last, for paired questions, you can either answer the question first and then answer the evidence question, or you can use the evidence choices to match and find the original question's answer. Answering detail questions takes work. If you follow this game plan, though, you will get a great score!

8

Special Question Types

In the last couple of chapters, you learned how to approach vocabulary and detail questions on the Reading Test. Even though these make up the majority of the questions, there are other types of questions on the Reading Test. This chapter will show you special types of questions and teach you how to approach them. Before you focus on the types of questions, learn the next BIG Strategy.

BIG STRATEGY #13

Always Look Back on the Reading Test

The SAT is the best kind of test: open book! You are not being asked to immediately memorize what you have read. You are also not being asked to be an expert on what you just read. Instead, you are being asked some questions that pertain only to the text on the page when the page is still right in front of you. If you do not look back to search for or confirm your answer, you are giving away your biggest advantage! If you neglect to look back at the passage for your answer, you are reducing the number of questions you will get correct. Use the passage to find the answers!

ATTITUDE OR TONE QUESTIONS

The first type of special questions deals with either the author's attitude or the passage's tone. You will be asked to choose the author's feelings about the topic. Be careful! Find descriptive words and phrases in the passage. Circle them. Base your answer on those words and phrases. If you do not go back and identify words that show emotion or description, you can easily be pulled into an incorrect answer.

> When deciding the author's attitude or tone, always go back and find descriptive words or phrases. Circle any you see, and then decide based on that evidence.

For example, suppose the passage you are reading was intended to be funny when it was written a hundred years ago. Do people today have the same sense of humor as people did a century ago? Of course we don't. So you may not see the humor in the passage, even though the author wrote it to be funny.

What's more, you will be up early on a Saturday morning to take this test. So will you be in any mood for laughs when you take the SAT? Of course you won't.

For these reasons, people who do not look back at the passage are often pulled into choosing wrong answers. Don't let it be you! Let's try a question.

The following is from a letter to John Adams written by his wife, Abigail Adams, dated March 31, 1776.

I wish you would ever write me a letter half as long as I write you, and tell me, if you may, where your fleet are gone; what sort of defense Virginia can make against our common enemy; whether it is so situated
Line as to make an able defense. Are not the gentry lords, and the common
(5) people vassals? Are they not like the uncivilized vassals Britain represents us to be? I hope their riflemen, who have shown themselves very savage and even blood-thirsty, are not a specimen of the generality of the people. I am willing to allow the colony great merit for having produced a Washington—but they have been shamefully duped by
(10) a Dunmore.

I have sometimes been ready to think that the passion for liberty cannot be equally strong in the breasts of those who have been accustomed to deprive their fellow-creatures of theirs. Of this I am certain, that it is not founded upon that generous and Christian
(15) principle of doing to others as we would that others should do unto us.

1. The author's attitude toward Virginians is best described as one of

   (A) apprehension.
   (B) appreciation.
   (C) dislike.
   (D) patriotism.

Before you answer, go back to the passage and underline or circle any words or phrases that stand out. Here is an example:

> I wish you would ever write me a letter half as long as I write you,
> and tell me, if you may, where your fleet are gone; <u>what sort of defense</u>
> <u>Virginia can make against our common enemy;</u> whether it is so situated
> Line   as to make an able defense. Are not the <u>gentry lords</u>, and the <u>common</u>
> (5)   <u>people vassals</u>? <u>Are they not like the uncivilized vassals Britain</u>
> <u>represents us to be</u>? I hope their <u>riflemen</u>, who have shown themselves
> <u>very savage and even blood-thirsty</u>, are not a specimen of the generality
> of the people. I am willing to <u>allow the colony great merit for having</u>
> <u>produced a Washington</u>—but they have been shamefully duped by
> (10) a Dunmore.
>   I have sometimes been ready to think that the <u>passion for liberty</u>
> <u>cannot be equally strong in the breasts of those who have been</u>
> <u>accustomed to deprive their fellow-creatures of theirs</u>. Of this I am
> certain, that it is not founded upon that generous and Christian
> (15) principle of doing to others as we would that others should do unto us.

Now that we have identified phrases Abigail Adams wrote about Virginians, we can look at them and come up with our answer. First, note that she questions whether Virginians can defend themselves. Then she questions whether they are more like the British in that they have rulers (*gentry lords*) and the ruled (*common people, vassals*). She wonders if the savagery of Virginians when fighting reflects on the people as a whole. She does concede that Virginia did produce George Washington. Then she questions if Virginians can have the same feelings about liberty if they take away the liberty of others (slaves).

> First get rid of the positives if you are looking for a negative answer, or first get rid of the negatives if you are looking for a positive answer.

So Adams has many questions and some bad feelings about Virginians. She has some fears and anxiety about them. Now that we have our answer idea, look at the choices.

We know we are looking for something negative, so eliminate the positive answer choices. We can easily eliminate choice B, *appreciation*, and choice D, *patriotism*. We already have our choice down to a coin flip!

Now look at the two remaining answer choices. Think again of our idea of fear and anxiety. *Dislike* is too strong a word for fear and anxiety, so we can

eliminate choice C. This leaves us with the answer, choice A. *Apprehension* means a sense of fear and anxiety.

When answering questions about the tone of the passage or the attitude of the author, treat those questions like you would any other. Go back to the passage, find the evidence, and then form your answer.

INFERENCE QUESTIONS

The next type of special question is implied or inferred questions. First, remember that *to imply* is "to give a hint" and *to infer* is "to take a hint." They are two ends of the same candle; it is all in how the question is phrased.

> On implied and inferred questions, gather hints before forming your answer.

You have answered these types of questions since grade school. You have to read between the lines to find the answer. You approach these questions in exactly the same way you do other types: go back to the passage and find the answer. Just be careful!

Read from the same passage by Abigail Adams and then move on to the question on the following page.

I wish you would ever write me a letter half as long as I write you, and tell me, if you may, where your fleet are gone; what sort of defense Virginia can make against our common enemy; whether it is so situated
Line as to make an able defense. Are not the gentry lords, and the common
(5) people vassals? Are they not like the uncivilized vassals Britain represents us to be? I hope their riflemen, who have shown themselves very savage and even blood-thirsty, are not a specimen of the generality of the people. I am willing to allow the colony great merit for having produced a Washington—but they have been shamefully duped by
(10) a Dunmore.

I have sometimes been ready to think that the passion for liberty cannot be equally strong in the breasts of those who have been accustomed to deprive their fellow-creatures of theirs. Of this I am certain, that it is not founded upon that generous and Christian
(15) principle of doing to others as we would that others should do unto us.

2. It can most reasonably be inferred from the passage that Adams views slavery as

   (A) inconsistent with the idea of freedom.
   (B) generally helpful to those in Virginia who want to bring freedom to the United States.
   (C) irrelevant to the current revolution against Great Britain.
   (D) largely acceptable if those in the colony support it.

Go back and look for evidence. Adams calls the *gentry lords and the common people vassals*. However, common people are not slaves. Still, you can get a sense of a ruling class and an underclass. In the second paragraph, Adams says *the passion for liberty cannot be equally strong in the breasts of those who have been accustomed to deprive their fellow-creatures of theirs*. Here is the implication. Who have been deprived of their liberty in Virginia? Slaves. So *those who have deprived their fellow-creatures* of their liberty must, then, be the slave owners.

Now we have the answer. Adams does not see how people who take other people's freedom can resolutely want freedom themselves. After looking at the choices, we can easily get rid of the two choices that are positive, choices B and D. Of the two remaining answer choices, choice A is closest to what we found. It is the correct answer.

PAIRED PASSAGE QUESTIONS

The next special question type appears when you are given two passages about the same topic. In the last chapter, you saw paired questions in which one question was dependent on another. Paired passages are similar in that they follow one another, but they are slightly different in approach.

Paired passages address the same topic. However, they usually have different viewpoints and are written by different authors. The detail questions focus on the first passage and then on the second. At the end of the group of questions, you will find at least one question about both passages that asks how the passages relate to each other. In other words, the questions that ask you to compare and contrast the two passages are last.

> When working on paired passages, read one paragraph at a time as always and answer the questions in order. Do not read both passages at once!

If you read both passages at once, the authors and their viewpoints will be scrambled in your mind. You might choose an answer that is based on Passage 2 when you are actually asked about Passage 1 and vice versa. So follow the game plan of reading one paragraph at a time and answering as many questions about that paragraph as possible.

In order to practice how to answer paired passages, you will first read Abigail Adams' letter to John Adams and then will read his reply.

Passage 1 is from Abigail Adams' letter to John Adams, dated March 31, 1776.
Passage 2 is from John Adams' reply to her letter, dated April 14, 1776.

Passage 1

I long to hear that you have declared an independency. And, by the way, in the new code of laws which I suppose it will be necessary for you to make, I desire you would remember the ladies and be more
Line generous and favorable to them than your ancestors. Do not put such
(5) unlimited power into the hands of the husbands. Remember, all men would be tyrants if they could. If particular care and attention is not paid to the ladies, we are determined to foment a rebellion, and will not hold ourselves bound by any laws in which we have no voice or representation.
(10)   That your sex are naturally tyrannical is a truth so thoroughly established as to admit of no dispute; but such of you as wish to be happy willingly give up the harsh title of master for the more tender and endearing one of friend. Why, then, not put it out of the power of the vicious and the lawless to use us with cruelty and indignity with
(15) impunity? Men of sense in all ages abhor those customs which treat us only as the vassals of your sex; regard us then as beings placed by Providence under your protection, and in imitation of the Supreme Being make use of that power only for our happiness.

Passage 2

As to Declarations of Independency, be patient. Read our Privateering
(20) Laws, and our Commercial Laws. What signifies a Word.
    As to your extraordinary Code of Laws, I cannot but laugh. We have been told that our struggle has loosened the bands of government everywhere. That children and apprentices were disobedient—that schools and colleges were grown turbulent—that Indians slighted their
(25) guardians and negroes grew insolent to their masters. But your letter

was the first intimation that another tribe more numerous and powerfull than all the rest were grown discontented. This is rather too coarse a compliment but you are so saucy, I won't blot it out.

Depend upon it, we know better than to repeal our masculine
(30) systems. Although they are in full force, you know they are little more than theory. We dare not exert our power in its full latitude. We are obliged to go fair, and softly, and in practice you know we are the subjects. We have only the name of masters, and rather than give up this, which would completely subject us to the despotism of the petticoat, I
(35) hope General Washington, and all our brave Heroes would fight.

3. What choice best states the relationship between the two passages?

    (A) Passage 2 provides further evidence to support an idea in Passage 1.
    (B) Passage 2 exemplifies an attitude promoted in Passage 1.
    (C) Passage 2 challenges the point of view in Passage 1.
    (D) Passage 2 restates in different terms the argument presented in Passage 1.

This type of paired passage question requires you to think about both Passage 1 and Passage 2 and then determine how they compare or contrast. You cannot answer this type of question until you have read both passages. Ask yourself whether the passages agree or disagree with each other. Then work backward, eliminating answer choices as you go.

> When asked to describe the overall relationship between two passages, ask yourself whether the passages agree or disagree.

A cursory reading of the two passages suggests that they disagree. Abigail Adams suggests to her husband that new laws need to be instituted to reduce the amount of control husbands have over wives, and he rejects this idea. Now that you have determined that they disagree, look at the answer choices. Choice A says that Passage 2 gives further evidence, which would mean that the two are in agreement. Eliminate choice A. Choice B states that Passage 2 exemplifies an attitude from Passage 1, which also means that they are in agreement. Eliminate choice B. Choice C states that Passage 2 challenges Passage 1. So leave choice C because it indicates disagreement. Choice D states that Passage 2 restates the argument of Passage 1. So choice D indicates agreement. Eliminate it too, leaving choice C as the correct answer.

Now try a different kind of paired passage question.

4. Which choice best describes how Abigail Adams would have reacted to John Adams' remarks in the final paragraph of Passage 2?

    (A) With approval, because men do not fully exert their control over women
    (B) With resignation, because men will never resign their authority
    (C) With skepticism, because Adams does not substantiate his claim with examples of women really being in charge
    (D) With disapproval, because if women were really the true masters, they would be writing the laws of the new nation, not the men

In this question, you are being asked to pretend you are the author of Passage 1 and then to react to Passage 2. It might seem like a more difficult question. However, if you follow the **Key Tip** (see page 89), you will see that it is not. Consider again whether the two passages are in basic agreement or disagreement.

These passages are in basic disagreement. Now look at the beginning of each answer choice (the first two words). Choice A, *with approval*, is easy to eliminate. Choice B, *with resignation*, means in basic agreement. So eliminate that answer as well. By following that **Key Tip**, you are down to two answer choices.

Choices C and D both indicate disagreement. It is now a measure of degrees. Would Abigail Adams lightly or strongly disagree with John Adams' remarks? Look back at her words. In her last paragraph, she says that men are *tyrannical* and treat women as *vassals*. Would she then be skeptical or disagree with John Adams' assertion that women are really in charge?

Based on her words, she would surely disagree with what John Adams said. Therefore, choice D is the best answer.

There is one more type of paired passage question. Try the following question.

5. The main purpose of both passages is to

    (A) suggest a way to resolve a particular political struggle.
    (B) discuss the relationship between men and women.
    (C) evaluate the consequences of rapid political change.
    (D) describe the duties that men have to women.

This type of question asks what the two passages have in common. You know these passages are in disagreement. Since that is the case, over what do

they disagree? (If the passages were in agreement, you would ask yourself about what they agree.) In these two passages, both Abigail and John discussed the place of men and women in society. While Abigail asked for more authority for women, John stated that women were already really in charge. Although they disagreed, they both wrote about what role men played and what role women played.

Now look at the choices. Since you know what you are looking for, go through the choices. Based on the other passage questions, choices A and C are not in the ballpark of the answer. Now look at choices B and D, which are close in meaning. Think about both. Choice B seems right on the mark. Choice D is only about men's duties to women. That is only one aspect of what both passages said. In other words, it is too specific or narrow. Choice B is correct.

Chapter Overview

The Reading Test does have some unique question types. All require the same basic strategy of reading the question, looking back at the passage, and then forming your own answer before attempting to choose one of the answer choices. In attitude or author's tone questions, identify descriptive words, phrases, and anything that shows emotion before answering. Inference questions are the question types with the most depth on the test because they ask you to read between the lines to form your answer choice. On every Reading Test, there will be one passage that is paired with a second passage. On these, answer the questions in order. There will be questions at the end of the passages that ask you to compare and contrast the two passages. First decide whether the two passages are in agreement or disagreement. That should help you quickly narrow down the possible answer choices. Then, look back at both passages for clues to make your final choice.

9

The Big Picture

N ow that you have learned how to approach the vocabulary and detail questions on the Reading Test, it is time to look at whole-passage questions. You can see from the last three chapters that you should focus on the smaller questions first before attempting the big-picture questions. Before tackling the big-picture questions, understand this BIG Strategy first.

BIG STRATEGY #14

You Won't Completely Understand the Passage

When reading a passage, know that you will not 100% "get it." Accept that fact! You are reading random information. For this reason, the passage won't make perfect sense to you. However, this does not matter because all of the questions are based on information right there on the page. The answers do not extend beyond the passage. So relax. Even though you won't understand the passage completely, you will be able to answer the questions.

You know that you should answer the detail questions first. That will require skipping global/general questions and coming back to them before moving on to the next passage. Do not answer all whole-passage questions for the entire Reading

> Star any whole-passage questions and answer them last, before moving on to the next passage.

Test at once. You will lose your focus on the first passage by the time you have reached the last one. Think of each passage and its questions as its own little test. Complete each little test before moving on to the next one.

Now look at the different kinds of big-picture questions. First start with the letter by Abigail Adams.

The following is from a letter to John Adams written by his wife, Abigail Adams, dated March 31, 1776.

I wish you would ever write me a letter half as long as I write you, and tell me, if you may, where your fleet are gone; what sort of defense Virginia can make against our common enemy; whether it is so situated
Line as to make an able defense. Are not the gentry lords, and the common
(5) people vassals? Are they not like the uncivilized vassals Britain represents us to be? I hope their riflemen, who have shown themselves very savage and even blood-thirsty, are not a specimen of the generality of the people. I am willing to allow the colony great merit for having produced a Washington—but they have been shamefully duped by a Dunmore.
(10) I have sometimes been ready to think that the passion for liberty cannot be equally strong in the breasts of those who have been accustomed to deprive their fellow-creatures of theirs. Of this I am certain, that it is not founded upon that generous and Christian principle of doing to others as we would that others should do unto us.
(15) Do not you want to see Boston? I am fearful of the small-pox, or I should have been in before this time. I got Mr. Crane to go to our house and see what state it was in. I find it has been occupied by one of the doctors of a regiment; very dirty, but no other damage has been done to it. The few things which were left in it are all gone. . . . I look upon it as a
(20) new acquisition of property—a property which one month ago I did not value at a single shilling, and would with pleasure have seen it in flames.
The town in general is left in a better state than we expected; more owing to a precipitate flight than any regard to the inhabitants; though some individuals discovered a sense of honor and justice, and have
(25) left the rent of the houses in which they were, for the owners, and the furniture unhurt, or, if damaged, sufficient to make it good. Others have committed abominable ravages. The mansion house of your President is safe, and the furniture unhurt while the house and furniture of the Solicitor General have fallen a prey to their own merciless party. Surely
(30) the very fiends feel a reverential awe for virtue and patriotism, whilst they detest the parricide and traitor.
I feel very differently at the approach of spring from what I did a month ago. We knew not then whether we could plant or sow with safety, whether where we had tilled we could reap the fruits of our own industry,
(35) whether we could rest in our own cottages or whether we should be driven from the seacoast to seek shelter in the wilderness but now we

feel a temporary peace, and the poor fugitives are returning to their deserted habitations.

(40) Though we felicitate ourselves, we sympathize with those who are trembling lest the lot of Boston should be theirs. But they cannot be in similar circumstances unless pusillanimity and cowardice should take possession of them. They have time and warning given them to see the evil and shun it.

(45) I long to hear that you have declared an independency. And, by the way, in the new code of laws which I suppose it will be necessary for you to make, I desire you would remember the ladies and be more generous and favorable to them than your ancestors. Do not put such unlimited power into the hands of the husbands. Remember, all men would be tyrants if they could. If particular care and attention is not

(50) paid to the ladies, we are determined to foment a rebellion, and will not hold ourselves bound by any laws in which we have no voice or representation.

That your sex are naturally tyrannical is a truth so thoroughly established as to admit of no dispute; but such of you as wish to be

(55) happy willingly give up the harsh title of master for the more tender and endearing one of friend. Why, then, not put it out of the power of the vicious and the lawless to use us with cruelty and indignity with impunity? Men of sense in all ages abhor those customs which treat us only as the vassals of your sex; regard us then as beings placed by

(60) Providence under your protection, and in imitation of the Supreme Being make use of that power only for our happiness.

AUTHOR'S ATTITUDE OR AUTHOR'S FOCUS QUESTIONS

The first whole-passage question type you might see asks how the author's attitude or focus shifts during the passage. Try a question.

1. Over the course of the passage, the narrator's focus shifts from

    (A) fear about Virginians and the state of occupied homes to a demand for women's rights.
    (B) doubt about the war's outcome to excitement about it.
    (C) uncertainty of the motives of Virginians to recognition of men's control over women.
    (D) disdain for the British to appreciation of their laws.

For this question type, you are asked to look back at the whole passage and analyze the shift in the main idea. Each answer choice has two portions to it. To start, look at only the first part of the passage and then look at only the first part of each answer choice. Eliminate any answer choice where the first portion does not agree with the passage. Then do the same with the second part of the passage and the second part of each remaining answer choice.

> Like other SAT questions, divide these answer choices in two and eliminate.

Go back and look at the beginning of the letter. Abigail Adams first wrote about her concerns over Virginians and their ideas of liberty. Then she wrote about the British who had occupied their homes. Now look at the first part of each answer choice. Choices A and C mention fear or uncertainty of Virginians, so leave them. The first part of both choices B and D are about the war and the British, so eliminate them. You are already down to two choices, and you did not even read the whole answer choice!

Now look at the second part of the passage. Adams wrote about remembering women and their freedom when crafting the laws of the new nation. Look now only at the second part of choices A and C. Choice C says the second part of the passage focuses on *recognition of men's control over women*, which is not true. Therefore, choice A is the correct answer.

In whole-passage questions that ask about the author's attitude or focus, split the passage in two and then split each answer choice in two. By breaking down the work into smaller parts, you will be able to see more easily through the fog of the test and choose the correct answer.

SUMMARY QUESTIONS

The second kind of whole-passage question is a summary question. Try one based on Abigail Adams' letter.

2. Which choice best summarizes the passage?

    (A) A woman demands a better position for women in the new country while she has fears of a British victory.
    (B) A woman considers her fellow countrymen and the British occupiers before asking for more rights for women in the new country.
    (C) A wife asks for the protection of her husband and her regret for not having stayed in her home.
    (D) A woman experiences optimism for the war, then frustration, and finally despair that it will be for nothing if women do not get to vote.

Remember to attempt whole-passage questions after you have answered the detail questions. That way, you will have read the entire passage and be better prepared to answer whole-passage questions. You may want to jot down a word or a phrase that describes each paragraph. Write each one in the margin next to the particular paragraph. Then look at all your notes. You will now have a good idea of the whole passage.

> You must still look back at the passage before you attempt to answer whole-passage questions. When you look back, read each paragraph and ask yourself what it is about.

In question 2, again look back and break up the choices. Choice A mentions demanding the rights of women, and choice B mentions considering other countrymen and the British occupiers. So leave both of those choices for a second look. Adams never asks for protection, nor does she have optimism, frustration, and fear about the war. So eliminate choices C and D.

Again, by looking back and making your own summary before answering, you are able to narrow down the answer choices quickly. Now look at the second part of choices A and B. The second part of choice A is about fear of a British victory. The second part of choice B is about the rights of women. Adams never mentioned any fear of losing the war, so eliminate choice A. Choice B is correct.

Saving the whole-passage questions for the end of the passage, looking back and summarizing, and then breaking up the long choices make these questions much easier to handle. Before trying again, read a new passage.

This passage is adapted from Linda Haugen's "How to Identify and Manage Dutch Elm Disease." From the U.S. Department of Agriculture.

Introduction

At one time, the American elm was considered to be an ideal street tree because it was graceful, long-lived, fast growing, and tolerant of compacted soils and air pollution. Then Dutch elm disease (DED)
Line was introduced and began devastating the elm population. Estimates
(5) of DED losses of elm in communities and woodlands across the U.S. are staggering. Because elm is so well-suited to urban environments, it continues to be a valued component of the urban forest despite the losses from DED. The challenge before us is to reduce the loss of remaining elms and to choose suitable replacement trees for the ones

(10)   we cannot save. This guide provides an update for urban foresters
and tree care specialists with the latest information and management
options available for Dutch elm disease.

Symptoms
   Foliage symptoms: Symptoms of DED begin as wilting of leaves
and proceed to yellowing and browning. The pattern of symptom
(15)   progression within the crown varies depending on where the fungus is
introduced to the tree. If the fungus enters the tree through roots grafted
to infected trees (see disease cycle section), the symptoms may begin
in the lower crown on the side nearest the graft and the entire crown
may be affected very rapidly. If infection begins in the upper crown,
(20)   symptoms often first appear at the end of an individual branch (called
"flagging") and progress downward in the crown.
   Multiple branches may be individually infected, resulting in symptom
development at several locations in the crown. Symptoms begin in late
spring or any time later during the growing season. However, if the tree
(25)   was infected the previous year (and not detected), symptoms may first
be observed in early spring. Symptoms may progress throughout the
whole tree in a single season, or may take two or more years.
   Vascular symptoms: Branches and stems of elms infected by the
DED fungus typically develop dark streaks of discoloration. To detect
(30)   discoloration, cut through and peel off the bark of a dying branch to
expose the outer rings of wood. In newly infected branches, brown
streaks characteristically appear in the sapwood of the current year. It
is important to cut deeply into the wood or look at the branch in cross
section for two reasons: (1) As the season progresses, the staining may be
(35)   overlaid by unstained wood, and (2) if infection occurred in the previous
year, the current sapwood may not be discolored.

3.   Which choice best summarizes the passage?

(A) Dutch elm disease devastates the tree, and it is characterized by
yellowing leaves and streaked branches.
(B) Dutch elm disease is a manageable problem, which causes trees to
drop leaves and branches when infected.
(C) Dutch elm disease is hard to identify but easy to treat.
(D) The American elm can be infected by a fast-spreading disease that
is distinguished by always starting in the upper crown.

For this question, again go back and ask yourself what each paragraph is about. Now cut the answer choices in two and examine each of them. Choices B and C are incorrect because the passage does not state that the disease is manageable or that it is hard to identify.

Now look at the second part of choices A and D. If they both seem true, look back at the paragraphs about the characteristics of the disease. The second paragraph says that the disease can start in the roots or in either the lower or upper crown. That makes choice D incorrect, leaving you with the answer, choice A.

PURPOSE QUESTIONS

The last type of whole-passage question is a purpose question. This type of question does not ask what the passage is about; it asks why the passage was written. A purpose question is a variation of the summary question. Try a purpose question based on the passage about Dutch elm disease.

4. The primary purpose of the passage is to

(A) present the background of a scientific breakthrough.
(B) summarize the background and symptoms of a disease.
(C) evaluate the signs of a disease that affects many trees.
(D) explain a branch of scientific study.

Once again, look back at the passage. Make your own summary by asking yourself what each paragraph is about. Then look at the main word in each answer choice. Eliminate those answer choices that have an incorrect main word. For question 4, the main word is the first word of each answer choice: *present, summarize, evaluate,* and *explain.* From these words, we can eliminate choice C; the passage clearly does not include an evaluation.

> Look at the main word in each choice and eliminate.

Now look at choices A, B, and D more carefully. Was there a *scientific breakthrough*? No, so eliminate choice A. *Background and symptoms* were mentioned, so leave choice B. Was the passage about a *branch of scientific study*? No, that would be too broad. It was about only one particular disease. Eliminate choice D. Choice B is correct.

Try one more purpose question. This question is about the first passage in the chapter, the letter written by Abigail Adams on page 94.

5. The primary purpose of the passage (written by Abigail Adams to John Adams) is to

(A) explain why the family home has been occupied and why women have no power in society.
(B) describe the current state of the war in Boston and Virginia.
(C) describe other colonists, the occupation of their homes, and how men rule over women.
(D) evaluate liberty in another colony, in their newly freed homes, and in the rights of women.

Once again, look back at the passage and make your own summary. Now look at the main word for each answer choice. Adams describes the state of only the homes left by the British occupiers. So choices B and C describe details, not the primary (main) purpose of the passage. Eliminate them.

Now look at choice A. Adams does explain that the family home has been occupied, but she does not explain *why* the family home has been occupied. That makes choice A incorrect and leaves choice D, the correct answer.

Chapter Overview

Whole-passage questions are the last questions you should answer for each passage. For any of the whole-passage question types, always go back and make your own summary by asking yourself what each paragraph is about. Then break the answer choices down because answer choices for whole-passage questions tend to be long. If the answer choice has two or more parts, read one part at a time, eliminating as you go. If an answer choice has only one part, focus on the main word. This usually cuts down the answer choices quickly. Then, when making a final choice, look back again to confirm your answer.

10

The Essay

The SAT Essay is a separate part of the test. Like the Writing and Language Test and the Reading Test, the essay requires both reading and writing skills (not writing skills alone). For the essay, you will read a persuasive text. You will then respond to the prompt. The prompt is always the same: how did the author persuade the audience about the subject of the text? You are given 50 minutes to read the text and write the essay.

SHOULD YOU TAKE THE SAT ESSAY?

Unlike the Reading, Writing and Language, and Math Tests, the essay is optional. Since it is optional, it is scored separately from the rest of the test. In other words, the SAT Essay has no impact on your overall English Test score.

Since the SAT Essay is optional, should you take it?

Unfortunately, there is no easy answer to this question. Basically, it depends on the colleges that you are applying to and whether or not they require it. To get a current list of colleges and their SAT Essay requirements, go to

https://collegereadiness.collegeboard.org/sat/register/college-essay-policies

The list provides the state, the college, and the college's requirements. There are three levels:

- Require: You must take the essay as part of your SAT.
- Recommend: The essay is not required, but it is recommended that you take it.
- Neither Require nor Recommend: The college does not need your essay score.

Here is a small sample from the list:

California (CA)

SAT Essay Policies			
State	College Board Code	College or University	Essay Policy
CA	4596	Azusa Pacific University	Neither Require nor Recommend
CA	4123	California Christian College	Recommend
CA	4031	California College of the Arts	Neither Require nor Recommend
CA	4034	California Institute of Technology	Require

Before you register for the SAT, take a look at the list and find the colleges you are considering. You will find that the majority of colleges "Neither Require nor Recommend" the essay. So if all of the schools you are considering are listed this way, you can skip the essay. If any schools "Require" or "Recommend" the essay, you should take the SAT Essay at least once.

If you are uncertain, take the essay. That way, you will have an SAT Essay score just in case you decide to apply to a college that does require it.

HOW THE ESSAY IS SCORED

The essay is scored completely differently than the rest of the SAT. The Math and English Tests are scored by computer, but the essay is scored by two different human scorers.

Each scorer gives the essay three different scores which are then totaled. Each of these scores is for a different category:

- Reading: How well you were able to understand the text.
- Analysis: Your breakdown of the text's argument.
- Writing: Everything from your spelling to sentence and paragraph skills.

Each scorer grades on a scale of 1 to 4 for each category. You can think of the scoring using a simple method:

- 4 = A
- 3 = B
- 2 = C
- 1 = D or F

Since each scorer grades between 1 and 4 for the three categories, the total score ranges between 3 and 12 for each scorer. When the two scorer's grades are combined, the overall score is between 6 and 24.

WRITE AN ESSAY

Below is a sample text and essay prompt. Read the text, and then follow the essay prompt. Once you have written your essay, move on with the chapter, which takes the same text and breaks it down to build an essay.

Directions: This assignment will allow you to demonstrate your ability to read skillfully and understand a source text and to write a response analyzing the source. In your response, you should show that you have understood the source, give proficient analysis, and use the English language effectively. If your essay is off topic, it will not be scored. You will be given 50 minutes to complete the assignment, including reading the source text and writing your response.

Read the following passage and think about how the author uses:

- Evidence, such as applicable examples, to justify the argument
- Reasoning to show logical connections among thought and facts
- Rhetoric, like sensory language and emotional appeals, to give weight to the argument

The following is from a speech by Susan B. Anthony, a co-founder of the National Woman Suffrage Association. In 1872, Anthony voted in a presidential election. Since women did not have the right to vote, she was arrested and fined $100. She refused to pay and gave this speech in 1873.

1   Friends and fellow citizens: I stand before you tonight under indictment for the alleged crime of having voted at the last presidential election, without having a lawful right to vote. It shall be my work this evening to prove to you that in thus voting, I not only committed no crime, but, instead, simply exercised my citizen's rights, guaranteed to me and all United States citizens by the National Constitution, beyond the power of any state to deny.

2   The preamble of the Federal Constitution says: "We, the people of the United States, in order to form a more perfect union, establish justice,

insure domestic tranquillity, provide for the common defense, promote the general welfare, and secure the blessings of liberty to ourselves and our posterity, do ordain and establish this Constitution for the United States of America."

3   It was we, the people; not we, the white male citizens; nor yet we, the male citizens; but we, the whole people, who formed the Union. And we formed it, not to give the blessings of liberty, but to secure them; not to the half of ourselves and the half of our posterity, but to the whole people—women as well as men. And it is a downright mockery to talk to women of their enjoyment of the blessings of liberty while they are denied the use of the only means of securing them provided by this democratic-republican government—the ballot.

4   For any state to make sex a qualification that must ever result in the disfranchisement of one entire half of the people, is to pass a bill of attainder, or, an ex post facto law, and is therefore a violation of the supreme law of the land. By it the blessings of liberty are forever withheld from women and their female posterity.

5   To them this government has no just powers derived from the consent of the governed. To them this government is not a democracy. It is not a republic. It is an odious aristocracy; a hateful oligarchy of sex; the most hateful aristocracy ever established on the face of the globe; an oligarchy of wealth, where the rich govern the poor. An oligarchy of learning, where the educated govern the ignorant, or even an oligarchy of race, where the Saxon rules the African, might be endured; but this oligarchy of sex, which makes father, brothers, husband, sons, the oligarchs over the mother and sisters, the wife and daughters, of every household—which ordains all men sovereigns, all women subjects, carries dissension, discord, and rebellion into every home of the nation.

6   Webster, Worcester, and Bouvier all define a citizen to be a person in the United States, entitled to vote and hold office.

7   The only question left to be settled now is: Are women persons? And I hardly believe any of our opponents will have the hardihood to say they are not. Being persons, then, women are citizens; and no state has a right to make any law, or to enforce any old law, that shall abridge their privileges or immunities. Hence, every discrimination against women in the constitutions and laws of the several states is today null and void, precisely as is every one against Negroes.

Prompt: Write an essay in which you explain how Susan B. Anthony builds an argument to persuade her audience that women should be allowed to vote. In your essay, analyze how Anthony uses one or more of the following: evidence to support claims, reasoning to develop ideas and connect claims and evidence, stylistic or persuasive elements, such as word choice or appeals to emotion, and/or features of your own choice. Be sure your analysis focuses on the most relevant features of the passage.

Your essay should not explain whether you agree with Anthony's claims but, rather, explain how Anthony builds an argument to persuade her audience.

The Approach

In both the Writing and Language Test and the Reading Test, you have learned that the main strategy is to read a paragraph and stop. The SAT Essay is no different. Read one paragraph of the text, stop, and mark up that paragraph before moving on to the next one. This marking will become your prewriting, and it will help you form your outline.

The Prompt

The single biggest mistake that people make when they approach the essay is to not read the prompt carefully. However, the prompt is always the same. It wants you to explain *how* the author persuades the audience about the topic. Some students will write about the topic itself, or they will write that they agree or disagree with the passage. Their essays might be well written. Since they did not respond to the topic, though, they earn low scores. Make sure you respond to the topic!

> The prompt always asks you to write about how the author builds an argument to persuade his or her audience about the passage's topic.

BIG STRATEGY #15

Look for the Argument

The biggest advantage on the essay is that the prompt will always be the same: How did the author persuade the audience? So look for elements of persuasion as you read the text and underline those elements. Then jot a note in the margin once you've read the paragraph about what kind of persuasive writing it was.

This process will save you an enormous amount of time and effort from having to go back and search for how the author persuaded the audience. It will also keep you focused on the topic of your essay. By finding and underlining specifics, you will also be finding specific evidence to include in your supporting paragraphs. The work you do before you write the first word of the essay is the key to getting a good score!

The passage for the essay will be a persuasive text, often taken from what the College Board calls "The Great Global Conversation." The example text below is split by paragraphs. For this example, the student underlines the persuasive writing he or she sees while reading the text. Then the student makes notes after the paragraph but before moving on to the next paragraph. Read the text below and learn what to do to prepare for the essay.

The following is from a speech by Susan B. Anthony, a co-founder of the National Woman Suffrage Association. In 1872, Anthony voted in a presidential election. Since women did not have the right to vote, she was arrested and fined $100. She refused to pay and gave this speech in 1873.

1   Friends and fellow citizens: I stand before you tonight under indictment for the <u>alleged crime of having voted</u> at the last presidential election, without having a lawful right to vote. It shall be <u>my work this evening to prove</u> to you that <u>in thus voting,</u> <u>I not only committed no crime, but, instead, simply exercised my citizen's rights, guaranteed to me and all United States citizens by the National Constitution</u>, beyond the power of any state to deny.

In the margin, the student notes: **Alleged crime** and **rights as a citizen**. The student also notes: **intros charges but no crime** and **voting = no crime** and **citizens' rights—Americans get upset when rights are taken away (used to win over audience)**. Alleged crime is an appeal to **pathos (emotions and values)**.

2   The preamble of the Federal Constitution says: "We, the people of the United States, in order to form a more perfect union, establish justice, insure domestic tranquillity, provide for the common defense, promote the general welfare, and secure the blessings of liberty to ourselves and our posterity, do ordain and establish this Constitution for the United States of America."

In the margin, the student notes: **Cites Preamble to the Constitution. She uses it as a source to make her claim**. This is the persuasive technique **ethos (appeal to the authority of the speaker)**.

3   It was we, the people; not we, the white male citizens; nor yet we, the male citizens; but we, the whole people, who formed the Union. And we formed it, not to give the blessings of liberty, but to secure them; not to the half of ourselves and the half of our posterity, but to the whole people—women as well as men. And it is a downright mockery to talk to women of their enjoyment of the blessings of liberty while they are denied the use of the only means of securing them provided by this democratic-republican government—the ballot.

Here the student notes: **Uses Constitution to make argument** and **states mockery that women are denied the ballot. Establishes central claim and mockery is an appeal to pathos (emotions of the audience).**

4   For any state to make sex a qualification that must ever result in the disfranchisement of one entire half of the people, is to pass a bill of attainder, or, an ex post facto law, and is therefore a violation of the supreme law of the land. By it the blessings of liberty are forever withheld from women and their female posterity.

The student notes: **Reason—disfranchises half the people** and **violation of the supreme law (Constitution). This is logos (logical appeal) by using facts.**

5   To them this government has no just powers derived from the consent of the governed. To them this government is not a democracy. It is not a republic. It is an odious aristocracy; a hateful oligarchy of sex; the most hateful aristocracy ever established on the face of the globe; an oligarchy of wealth, where the rich govern the poor. An oligarchy of learning, where the educated govern the ignorant, or even an oligarchy of race,

where the Saxon rules the African, might be endured; but this oligarchy of sex, which makes father, brothers, husband, sons, the oligarchs over the mother and sisters, the wife and daughters, of every household—which ordains all men sovereigns, all women subjects, carries dissension, discord, and rebellion into every home of the nation.

Here the student notes: **Government no powers from consent**, **instead aristocracy of men over women**, and **will have dissension and rebellion**. **Appeals to pathos (emotions) of audience by trying to get them angry.**

6   Webster, Worcester, and Bouvier all define a citizen to be a person in the United States, entitled to vote and hold office.

The student notes: **Cites authorities defining citizens as having right to vote (citing authorities is an example of ethos).**

7   The only question left to be settled now is: Are women persons? And I hardly believe any of our opponents will have the hardihood to say they are not. Being persons, then, women are citizens; and no state has a right to make any law, or to enforce any old law, that shall abridge their privileges or immunities. Hence, every discrimination against women in the constitutions and laws of the several states is today null and void, precisely as is every one against Negroes.

The student notes: **Builds argument**, **uses a rhetorical question**, and **makes connection: women = people = citizens = right to vote = all laws against are void. Likens women to blacks from before Civil War (and they had gotten the vote since).** Again an example of **logos**.

Outline

Organize your notes into an outline. The big advantage to marking up the text as you read is that when you are done, you can look back and put together your outline. Since you have already gathered your evidence and made notes, you can look back at them and group them together into what will be your paragraphs and your citations. Citations are your evidence for your argument; they show what you are trying to say. Plus, using evidence actually makes the writing easier. State your main idea, provide the evidence, explain what the evidence shows, and then wrap up the paragraph. Not using the evidence you have already gathered is foolish!

Here are the key points to this essay:

Use citations in the supporting paragraphs of your essay.

- Ethos (appeal to credibility)
- Pathos (appeal to emotions)
- Logos (appeal to logic)
- Rhetorical question
- Claim: connection of women are people to people are citizens, therefore must be able to vote

Now arrange the paragraphs in order. The passage requires that you write five paragraphs: an introduction, three supporting paragraphs, and a conclusion. Choose your strongest three points. Of those three, write about the weakest point in the first supporting paragraph. Write about the middle point in the second supporting paragraph. Obviously, write about the strongest point in the third supporting paragraph. Build your argument so it keeps getting better. The following is a fast outline.

Choose your three strongest points, and make them your three supporting paragraphs.

Note that the main purpose is to get your ideas and evidence in order. Note that you most likely will not have time to write out the citations in the outline. You might have time to write only the main point of the paragraph and the first couple of supporting words. The outline below has the full citations so that you can see the argument and evidence in full.

I. Introduction: Susan B. Anthony arrested for voting.

    A. Refused to pay.

    B. Made speech.

    C. Argued women are people and people can vote, so women should be able to vote.

II. Speech uses ethos (building credibility).

    A. Paragraph 6 cites authorities: "Webster, Worcester, and Bouvier all define a citizen to be a person in the United States, entitled to vote and hold office."

    B. Paragraph 2 mentions Constitution, and paragraph 3 cites the Preamble. It says "We the people."

    C. Paragraph 3 uses the preamble: "It was we, the people; not we, the white male citizens."

D. Paragraph 4 cites the Declaration of Independence: "By it the blessings of liberty are forever withheld from women and their female posterity."

III. Speech uses logos (logical appeal).

    A. Paragraph 4: "To make sex a qualification that must ever result in the disfranchisement of one entire half of the people, is . . . a violation of the supreme law of the land."

    B. Paragraph 7: "Being persons, then, women are citizens" and "No state has a right to make any law . . . that shall abridge their privileges or immunities. Hence, every discrimination against women in the constitutions and laws of the several states is today null and void."

IV. Speech uses pathos (emotional appeal).

    A. Paragraph 1: "Alleged crime of having voted" and "Simply exercised my citizen's rights, guaranteed to me and all United States citizens by the National Constitution."

    B. Paragraph 3: "It was we, the people; not we, the white male citizens" and "Downright mockery to talk to women of their enjoyment of the blessings of liberty . . . denied the use of . . . the ballot."

    C. Paragraph 5: "Aristocracy; a hateful oligarchy of sex" and "All men sovereigns, all women subjects, carries dissension, discord, and rebellion."

V. Conclusion.

    A. Use of ethos, logos, and pathos appeals to every kind of person.

    B. Uses ethos to build the logos and pathos.

    C. The credibility of the founding documents are the foundation Anthony uses to build her case.

    D. It is no wonder she helped women secure the right to vote.

USE YOUR EVIDENCE

As you read the text, you gathered evidence. Now is the time to use what you found as you write your essay. When you write, follow your outline. Explain your main points, and use your evidence. Here is the essay built from this student's evidence and outline.

> Follow your outline! All the prewriting effort, from gathering evidence to making the outline, is the hardest part of the essay.

Houston Public Library
Check Out Summary

Title: Barron's AP United States history
Call number: 973.076 R434 3ED
Item ID: 33477485723994
Date due: 11/13/2018,23:59

Title: Barron's new PSAT/NMSQT
Call number: 378.1662 G798 18ED
Item ID: 33477485846290
Date due: 11/13/2018,23:59

Title: Barron's SAT express
Call number: 378.1662 H353
Item ID: 33477485573851
Date due: 11/13/2018,23:59

Susan B. Anthony fervently believed that women deserved the right to vote in the United States. Her argument was based on the principle that if people were guaranteed the right to vote in America, women were people who could vote. She was arrested for trying to vote and refused to pay her fine. Anthony made an impassioned speech clearly stating her beliefs.

Anthony's speech was filled with facts and examples rather than opinion. The foundation of her argument built upon our Constitution, which begins with "We the people." She stresses that women were not excluded from that statement, and the term people is not limited to white males. The Declaration of Independence also identifies the undeniable rights and liberty of women. She reminded her listeners that "it was we, the people; not we, the white male citizens." Anthony also identified that throughout history, statesmen define citizens by their right to vote and hold office. "Webster, Worcester, and Bouvier all define a citizen to be a person in the United States, entitled to vote and hold office." She argues that women clearly qualify to vote.

Anthony continued to base her logic in the beliefs of our Founding Fathers. "Being persons, then, women are citizens" and "no state has a right to make any law . . . that shall abridge their privileges or immunities. Hence, every discrimination against women and the constitutions and laws of the several states is today null and void." Women were never explicitly excluded; therefore, Anthony believed, women must be included. "To make sex a qualification that must ever result in the disenfranchisement of one entire half the people, is . . . a violation of the supreme law of the land."

Anthony also identified the flaws of believing her act of voting was a crime. She argued that she "simply exercised my citizen's rights, guaranteed to me and all United States citizens by the National Constitution." To deny her the right to vote would negate the premise of our government. She declared it was "downright mockery to talk to women of their enjoyment of the blessings of liberty . . . denied the use of . . . the ballot." While stressing

the rights of democracy, Anthony compared her situation to one in an aristocracy or "a hateful oligarchy of sex." She reminded her audience that this circumstance leaves "all men sovereigns, all women subjects, carries dissension, discord, and rebellion."

In making her argument to support the right of women to vote, Susan B. Anthony used ethos, pathos, and logos to appeal to all people. Her rationale was the foundation to support her logical and emotional appeal for equality at the voting booth. Anthony used the Constitution and our code of law to build her argument rather than simple emotion or opinion. Using her knowledge, rationale, and passion, Susan B. Anthony made a strong, concise argument for women to exercise the right to vote.

SCORING THE SAMPLE ESSAY

Before discussing how this essay is scored, remember that there are three categories—Reading, Analysis, and Writing—and that each category is scored on a scale of 1 to 4 for a total of between 3 and 12. (Since the essay is scored by two different people, the total possible score ranges from 6 to 24.) Let's see how this essay scores in each category.

READING: 4

This essay demonstrates a thorough comprehension of Susan B. Anthony's speech. It shows an understanding of the relationship between the central idea and the important details of the speech. The writer paraphrases Anthony's central claim ("Her argument was based on the principle that if people were guaranteed the right to vote in America, women were people who could vote"). The writer then further breaks down the central claim in the supporting paragraphs. The writer's evidence ties the central claim to details from the speech (the cited quotes in the supporting paragraphs). This shows an understanding of not only the central claim but also of the details of the speech. This essay shows advanced reading comprehension.

ANALYSIS: 3

This essay demonstrates a good analysis of the speech. The writer breaks the speech into three elements—ethos, pathos, and logos—and then shows how each helps build Susan B. Anthony's argument. The strength of the analysis is

in the quotes from the speech, which shows how Anthony's argument builds. For example, to show the logic in the speech, the writer says, "'Being persons, then, women are citizens' and 'no state has a right to make any law . . . that shall abridge their privileges or immunities.'" The strength of the analysis is the evidence. However, the supporting paragraphs lack thoroughly detailed responses. In fact, some quotes are not fully explained. Those weaknesses keep this essay from scoring higher in this category.

WRITING: 4

This essay demonstrates an effective use of language. First, there are no major or minor flaws in grammar, usage, or mechanics, which would hurt this score. Second, the essay is structured properly, and it flows well. There are good transitions between sentences and between paragraphs. For example, at the beginning of the fourth paragraph, the writer says, "Anthony also identified the flaws . . . ." The writer also structures the essay to build the analysis of the speech in a coherent way. Last, the sentences are varied and effective. There are no awkward sentences or imprecise word choices that detract from the essay. The essay shows advanced writing.

OVERALL SCORE

Reading: 4
Analysis: 3
Writing: 4
Total: 11 out of 12 (Remember, the essay is scored twice. So this essay would actually score 22 out of 24.)

Chapter Overview

The essay is completely separate from the rest of the SAT. Before you start preparing for the essay, investigate if the schools you are considering require it. The essay has nothing to do with the maximum score of 1600 on the rest of the SAT. Instead, the SAT Essay is scored twice, for a total score between 6 and 24. Remember the major strategies. First, always look for how the author makes his or her argument. Second, underline the information as you read. Third, jot down notes in the margin of each paragraph. Next, group together what evidence you have found. Then write your outline and include the evidence. Finally, write your essay, following your plan and including the evidence (quotes) from the text to demonstrate your understanding. Following this plan will lead you to a solid score for the SAT Essay.

PART THREE: MATH TEST

O n the Math Test, the questions are divided into two different sections. The first section is short and does not allow use of a calculator. The second section is longer and allows you to use a calculator. Both sections have multiple-choice and grid-in answers.

Components of the Math Test

The Math Test consists of two sections. These are details about the first section:

- No calculator permitted
- 25 minutes
- 15 multiple-choice questions
- 5 grid-in questions
- 20 questions total

Here are the details about the second section:

- Calculator permitted
- 55 minutes
- 30 multiple-choice questions
- 8 grid-in questions
- 38 questions total

In both sections combined, there are a total of 58 questions that need to be completed in a total of 1 hour and 20 minutes. Consequently, you should complete each question in 1–2 minutes.

The Math Test focuses on three major areas:

- The Heart of Algebra
- Data Analysis and Problem Solving
- Passport to Advanced Mathematics

In each of the following chapters, you will find tactics that will prepare you for success in all of the math portions of the test, but especially in those three major areas. The first area—the Heart of Algebra—refers to the core concepts within which Algebra in general is rooted. In the Heart of Algebra, the concepts

are broken down into three major categories: the Core of Algebra, the Linear Realm, and Exponential Functions and Quadratic Equations.

We begin by focusing on the Core of Algebra in Chapter 11. That chapter highlights items ranging from basic algebraic functions to utilizing the quadratic formula. Chapter 12 is devoted to the Linear Realm. It refines your understanding of linear equations, linear inequalities, and functions. Chapter 13 has an in-depth study of exponential functions and quadratic equations. The tactics in that chapter will help you gain an overall understanding of what many consider to be the most difficult algebraic concepts.

Chapters 14 and 15 revolve around the next major area: Data Analysis and Problem Solving. They address ratios, percentages, and proportional reasoning to solve problems in real-world situations. These chapters also treat the concept of relationships in graphical analysis and the analysis of statistical data. Interpreting graphs, charts, and tables is a real-world skill that the writers of the SAT have chosen to emphasize.

The final major area in our exploration of SAT Math is called a Passport to Advanced Mathematics. Chapter 16 concentrates on the concepts used in math and science careers and in college-level Math courses. The main focus is on the STEM areas of study: Science, Technology, Engineering, and Math. You will need to be more familiar with functions and complex equations, which will prepare you for calculus in college. There is a brief section on additional topics such as geometry, trigonometry, and complex numbers.

The important thing to remember is that the SAT Math requires a robust understanding of a relatively small number of topics that will be relevant for your future. We will break down the topics to essential tactics. If you master these and become as familiar as possible with problems clustered around these areas, success will be yours!

11

The Core of Algebra

The SAT Math Test is strongly rooted in algebra. That does not always mean that writing an equation and solving it is always the best way to answer a question on the test. If you can familiarize yourself with the types of questions and the best way to answer them, you will get a higher score. Before starting the main algebra topics, look at a BIG Strategy.

BIG STRATEGY #16

Work Faster at the Beginning of the Math Test So You'll Have More Time for the Harder Questions at the End

The math questions become increasingly harder as you work through each section. In other words, the questions at the end of each Math Test section are more difficult than those at the beginning. (More specifically, the math questions go from easy to hard on the multiple-choice questions, and then they reset back to easy on the grid-in questions.) To use this to your advantage, work at a faster pace at the beginning of both math sections so that you have a little more time for each of the harder questions at the end. If you simply give each question equal time, you will have trouble conceptualizing and solving the more difficult questions in the time remaining. Working a little faster on the questions you know are easier will buy you more time to answer those tougher questions toward the end of the test. Only the math questions are presented in order of increasing difficulty, not the English questions. So make this a Math Test strategy approach.

READ QUESTIONS CAREFULLY AND ORGANIZE IMPORTANT FACTS

The algebra problems on the SAT can be complex or hard to conceptualize. Keep in mind that all the math problems on the test are designed to be completed in 1 or 2 minutes. If any problems were designed to take 5 minutes to solve,

students would not be able to finish the test in time. If you keep this in mind, you will realize that it is vital to make every problem as simple as possible.

You can take definite steps to simplify the problems on the Math Test. The SAT Math problems in general are pretty wordy. First and foremost, don't let the wordiness of the problems scare or intimidate you! Know that you may have to read a problem three times before you really understand what the question is asking you to do. That is OK! Once you understand what the question is asking for, gathering the important facts and data you need to solve the problem will be much easier.

Remember: do not let the length of each problem upset you or push you toward skipping it. In most cases, if you work methodically through the problem, a light will appear at the end of the tunnel. Persevere through these problems. If you remind yourself from the beginning that you are going see some long problems, then you won't be upset when they appear.

Let's look at a few examples. Remember that you must practice a variety of questions in different contexts in order to make sure you're ready for the questions you will come across on test day. Give each question a try in the space provided before you read the solution.

1. To edit a manuscript, Danny charges \$70 for the first 2 hours and then \$50 for all additional hours of work. Which of the following expresses the dollars, d, Danny charges if it takes him x hours to edit a manuscript, where $x > 2$?

   (A) $d = 50x - 30$
   (B) $d = 50x + 10$
   (C) $d = 50x + 20$
   (D) $d = 50x + 70$

This is a tricky question. If it helps, read the question again. Ask yourself, "What do they want?"

After looking at the question again, you see that the problem is asking for the formula Danny charges for his business. Now gather and organize the important facts:

- The first two hours are \$70.
- He charges \$50 an hour for every additional hour.
- x = the number of hours.
- x is greater than 2.

Use the gathered information, as seen on page 118, to separate those first 2 hours from the subsequent hours. Do this since the first 2 hours are being charged at a different rate than the remaining hours.

Since you know that the charge is $50 for each additional hour after the first 2 hours, you have to multiply $(x-2)$ times 50. Because Danny has already charged $70 for those first 2 hours, you must add that amount to the formula.

Thus, his charge, d, is written as $d = 70 + 50(x - 2)$. Multiplying 50 by $(x-2)$ results in $70 + 50x - 100$. Then simplify by subtracting 100 from 70 to get $50x - 30$. Choice A is correct.

You might need to read this question at least twice to see that the answer is not as simple as $50x + 70$. Look at the answers again. Choice D would be the one most commonly selected, but of course it is not correct. Without organizing the facts, you may easily forget to subtract those first 2 hours from x and use 50 times x. To avoid falling for such traps, be sure to organize the facts of each problem to determine what the question wants. Do not get lost in the fog of the question. The best way to fight through it is to organize the facts!

Try another similar question. This time, start to think of the facts as you read.

2. A construction company will place y tiles of the same size and shape in a building using a specific brand of tiles. The charge by the painter can be calculated by the expression $xkat$, where x is the number of rooms, k is a constant with units of dollars per square foot, a is the area of each room in square feet, and t is the thickness of the tile. If the customer requests a more expensive tile, which factor in the expression would change?

   (A) t
   (B) a
   (C) k
   (D) x

This is another typical question that tries to trip you over all the variables. However, a close reading (and rereading) will simplify it.

Again, you need to ask yourself what the important facts are. Here are the key facts and the key to the answer:

- x = number of rooms
- k = cost per square foot
- a = area of the room
- t = thickness of the tile

If we read over the problem multiple times, we see that the number of rooms (x), the area of the rooms (a), and thickness of the tiles (t) will not change with changes in costs of the tile. No matter how large the room is or how many rooms there are, the cost of the tile will not change. That is, the cost of the tile will not change based on the size of the room.

So what *will* change is the cost of units of dollars per square foot. The tile is part of the constant cost. Every box of tile will be the same price, the constant. Therefore, choice C is correct. Identifying and interpreting the key facts got us that answer.

3. The owner of a company awarded a total of $6,000 in bonuses to the most productive people in the company. The bonuses were awarded in the amounts of $500 and $1,500. If at least 2 of each bonus amount were awarded, what is one possible number of $1,500 bonuses?

When gathering the important information, the first thing to note is that on this problem, the answer is grid-in. This means you will fill in the number and not choose a number from a list. The problem says "one possible number," which means there may be more than one answer to this question! Now gather the important facts:

- $6,000 is the total bonus money.
- $500 is the least amount given as a bonus.
- $1,500 is the largest amount given as a bonus.
- At least 2 of each bonus were awarded.

This is now not a difficult question. First, note how much is already given in bonuses:

$$2 \times \$500 = \$1,000$$
$$2 \times \$1,500 = \$3,000$$
$$\$1,000 + \$3,000 = \$4,000$$

There is an initial total of $4,000 spent. How do you break up the remaining $2,000?

After viewing the listed information, you'll see the easiest way to find a solution. You have $2,000 left, so an easy combination of money left is $500 + $1,500.

Be careful! The question is not asking for the total number of all bonuses. It is asking for the total number of $1,500 bonuses. Since there are already two $1,500 bonuses and you added one more, you now have a total of three $1,500 bonuses. So one possible solution is 3.

If you instead make the last $2,000 entirely $500 bonuses, you will have:

$$6 \times \$500 = \$3,000$$
$$2 \times \$1,500 = \$3,000$$

When added together, that's $6,000. This means the other total number of $1,500 bonuses is 2. For this grid-in question, you would fill in 2 in any of the boxes and then fill in the corresponding number below it.

When gathering information, you sometimes must convert sentences into formulas. Always be careful and gather everything the problem asks for. When you organize the facts, you are simplifying the problem for yourself. You are also giving yourself a kick start to attack the problem.

REPLACE VARIABLES WITH SIMPLE NUMBERS

What is better when working on a math problem: working with variables or working with simple numbers? Of course, simple numbers are better. Look at the following problem.

4. If x is equal to y multiplied by z, find the equivalent of $\frac{z}{y}$.

(A) $\dfrac{x}{yz}$

(B) $\dfrac{xy}{z}$

(C) $\dfrac{z^2}{x}$

(D) $\dfrac{x}{yz^2}$

> Focus on strategies that will save you time and increase your accuracy.

The best way to approach a problem like this is to replace the variables with simple numbers. When choosing a mathematical strategy, time and accuracy are most important. One way of saving time and increasing accuracy is plugging in simple whole numbers for given

variables. In this example, as in many problems you will face, choosing a simple whole-number value for x will save you time and increase your accuracy.

Organize the important facts first, which in this case is writing the formula:

- $x = yz$

> Avoid replacing variables with 0 and 1 because these numbers have special properties. Also, make sure to assign each variable a different number.

Now replace the variables y and z with simple numbers. Remember: do not use either 0 or 1. For this problem, try using 2 for y and 3 for z. That results in:

- $y = 2$
- $z = 3$
- $x = (2)(3)$
- $x = 6$

The problem asks to find z divided by y. Again use the numbers to find the value of $\frac{z}{y}$:

$$\frac{z}{y} = \frac{3}{2}$$

Now take the same numbers and plug them into the four choices to find a match. You will find a match in choice C:

$$\frac{z^2}{x} = \frac{3^2}{6} = \frac{9}{6} = \frac{3}{2}$$

> Always be sure to reduce when inserting your own simple values for variables. You don't want to be led astray by not reducing the answers that you get.

5. The expression $\frac{4x - 3}{x - 2}$ is equivalent to which of the following?

(A) $\dfrac{4x^2 + 5x - 5}{4x^2 + 4x + 4}$

(B) $\dfrac{13}{2x} - 6$

(C) $7 - \dfrac{7}{x^2}$

(D) $\dfrac{12x - 9}{3x - 6}$

Choosing the value of $x = 3$ will yield an initial answer of 9 when placed into your given expression:

$$\frac{4(3) - 3}{3 - 2} = \frac{12 - 3}{1} = \frac{9}{1} = 9$$

(Note that plugging in $x = 2$ results in the denominator equaling 0, which makes the fraction/expression undefined. If something like that happens, try another number.)

Plug in the same value you initially chose into the answer choices, $x = 3$. Doing this will allow you to evaluate the choices. Choice B and choice C give you values that are drastically different, so they don't work. That leaves choice A and choice D. If you plug $x = 3$ into the remaining choices, you should find the correct answer. Look at the two expressions. Since choice A is more difficult or time consuming, start with choice D.

$$\frac{12x - 9}{3x - 6} = \frac{12(3) - 9}{3(3) - 6} = \frac{36 - 9}{9 - 6} = \frac{27}{3} = 9$$

Since choice D is equal to 9 when $x = 3$, it is the correct answer. What's more, there is no need to bother with the most difficult mathematical expression in the answer choices. Always look for simple ways to save time when taking the test.

6. The line $y = kx + 5$, where k is a constant, is graphed in the xy-plane. If the line contains the point (a, b), where $a \neq 0$ and $b \neq 0$, what is the slope of the line in terms of a and b?

(A) $\dfrac{b - 5}{a}$

(B) $\dfrac{a - 5}{b}$

(C) $\dfrac{5 - b}{a}$

(D) $\dfrac{5 - a}{b}$

The path to this solution is a twist on the concept of replacing variables with simple numbers. Use the solutions to guide your work. Notice how every answer choice includes both a and b? So instead of plugging numbers into the equation, plug in a for x and b for y:

$$b = ka + 5$$

Now solve for the slope, k:

$$b - 5 = ka$$
$$\frac{b - 5}{a} = k$$

Choice A is correct. More important, replacing the variables x and y with a and b, respectively, instead of trying to formulate numbers that will work for the equation is the fastest and easiest way to get to the answer. Use what the test shows in the answers to your advantage! Often, replacing variables with numbers is the fastest way to an answer. Sometimes, though, replacing the variables with things that the solutions reveal can be the fastest way. Be on the lookout for both situations on the test.

MAKE SURE YOU ANSWERED THE QUESTION

The SAT Math Test questions are almost all multistep questions. They start by requiring you to solve an initial step. Then to get the answer, they require you to solve another step or series of steps. The test will tempt students by dangling answer choices that are only partially correct. It is therefore imperative to identify not only the important facts but also exactly what the problem wants answered. Students who fail to do this get questions incorrect that they would have had no trouble getting right! Try a problem.

7. When 4 times the number x is added to 18, the result is 4. What number results when 2 times x is added to 9?

   (A) −9
   (B) −3.5
   (C) −1
   (D) 2

Read the question, and then decide what to do. Gather the key facts. The question here really wants to see if you can convert a sentence into a mathematical expression. Then it asks you to find the result and, with it, form and solve a second equation.

First the question says, "When 4 times the number x is added to 18, the result is 4." Remember, *times* means "multiply" and *is* means "an equals sign." So converting that sentence gives: $4x + 18 = 4$. Now you have your key facts and can start working on the problem.

Next solve the initial equation $4x + 18 = 4$. Subtracting 18 and then dividing both sides by 4 yields a value of −3.5:

$$4x + 18 = 4$$
$$-18 = -18$$
$$4x = -14$$
$$\frac{4x}{x} = -\frac{14}{4}$$
$$x = -3.5$$

Be very careful here! Choice C is tempting because it solves the initial question. What did the problem ask, though?

> The SAT tempts students who do not gather the key facts before starting. It gives answer choices that trick those who have not fully completed a problem.

Go back and look at the problem. The second sentence says, "What number results when 2 times x is added to 9?"

To get the final answer, you have to plug −3.5 into a new expression. So convert that second sentence into a formula. You have what number, y, results (or equals) when 2 is multiplied by x and then added to 9? So the new formula should look like this:

$$y = 2x + 9$$

Now plug in −3.5 for x:

$$y = 2(-3.5) + 9$$
$$y = -7 + 9$$
$$y = 2$$

Plugging in −3.5 gives a final answer of 2, which is choice D. Students who jump into a problem will get the wrong answer. This does not occur because they do not know how to solve the problem. Rather, it happens because they only partially solve the problem. Now try another.

8. If $f(x) = 6x + 4$ and $g(x) = x^3$, find the value of $f(g(-2))$.

   (A) −44
   (B) −8
   (C) 16
   (D) 52

This is where your understanding of the Core of Algebra really gets tested. If you work step by step, you shouldn't have any problems.

Remember that most problems on the SAT require multiple steps. So to solve $f(g(-2))$, you have to start not with the first equation but with the second. Where you should start is $g(x) = x^3$. Simply plugging -2 into the first equation will get you to -8, which is the wrong answer.

Plug in -2 for x and be sure to raise the -2 to the exponent of 3. This will give you -8:

$$g(-2) = -2^3 = (-2)(-2)(-2)$$
$$g(-2) = -8$$

Again, notice that -8 is an answer choice, but it is not the right answer.

Now that you have $g(-2)$, replace x in the function $f(x) = 6x + 4$ with the -8 that you just calculated:

$$f(-8) = 6(-8) + 4$$
$$f(-8) = -48 + 4$$
$$f(-8) = -44$$

The final answer is -44, which is choice A.

Remember that the majority of questions on the SAT Math Test require multiple steps. The test will tempt you with answer choices that are the results of the intermediate steps to the problem. Knowing and checking what the problem wants will improve your score. Whenever you solve for a variable, ask yourself, "Now that I know the value of x, what is the question asking for?" Try one more problem.

9. What are the values of x if $f(x) = x^2 - 5x + 4 = 0$?

    (A) 0, 4
    (B) −1, −4
    (C) −2, 3
    (D) 1, 4

When faced with a problem like this, many students will be left thinking, "What is the question asking me for?"

In order to solve this problem, you first will need to factor the given function. Remember that factoring involves multiplying the First, Outside, Inside, and Last variables and numbers together to produce the original function (FOIL). For the Math SAT, many questions will require you to factor as a core algebraic

skill. Recall that factoring an equation requires splitting it apart into pieces set in parentheses to figure what numbers multiplied together produce the function in question. Sometimes you need to take a few tries to find the numbers that correctly produce the function. For this problem, start by factoring:

$$f(x) = x^2 - 5x + 4$$
$$f(x) = (x - 4)(x - 1)$$

After factoring, you will be left with the binomials $(x - 4)$ and $(x - 1)$. Once you reach this step, you have almost found your answer. Just remember that you must set each binomial equal to 0 and solve in order to find all values of x. If you fail to do this, you will be tempted with choice B. However, if you remember that almost every problem requires multiple steps, you will know you have more work to do:

$$f(x) = (x - 4)(x - 1)$$
$$x - 4 = 0 \text{ and } x - 1 = 0$$
$$x = 4 \text{ and } x = 1$$

Choice D is the correct answer. Knowing that the problems will very often require multiple steps and that the test will tempt you with answer choices based on intermediate steps will help keep you focused on finding what the problem asks.

Chapter Overview

The first step to answering a Math Test question is to read the question carefully and then organize the important facts. You have to understand the question in order to answer it. You also need to have the right numbers and facts to manipulate in order to answer the question. Often the quickest and most accurate path to finding the right answer is to plug in simple numbers for variables. Learning to recognize when using this strategy is an important skill for this test. Always focus on what the problem wants, because the test will punish those who do not. Although this chapter focuses on core algebra problems, keep in mind that the strategies described can apply to all SAT Math question types. No matter what the math skill, you always want to find the fastest and easiest route to the correct answer!

12

The Linear Realm

In this chapter, we review linear equations, use linear systems, and solve inequalities that contain multiple variables. Linear equations are the building-blocks of all higher-level mathematics. Solving systems of equations is one of the foundations of algebra. Since using linear equations and solving systems of equations are skills frequently required in the real world, the SAT stresses those kinds of questions. This chapter discusses how to solve common questions about linear equations, linear systems, and inequalities.

The SAT Math Test is rooted in the Heart of Algebra. This concept refers to the importance of solving equations, systems, and inequalities. It is extremely important that you have a solid foundation in common algebraic concepts. The more you see the SAT Math problems, the more you will know what to do with these questions and how to answer them correctly. As a result, you will get better scores on the math sections. So practice as much as possible.

> Simply practice, practice, practice.

BIG STRATEGY #17

Use Your Calculator Whenever Possible

One of your biggest enemies while testing is time. So do not waste your most valuable resource doing calculations by hand, which is time consuming. In the section that permits it, use your calculator! Do all but the most basic of calculations using your calculator. You are given that resource for an important reason; take advantage of it!

CHOOSE THE BEST MATHEMATICAL STRATEGY FOR LINEAR EQUATIONS

Many algebraic equations can be solved multiple ways. This is especially true on the SAT. Remember that no matter how difficult the question is, it can be solved in minimal time. There are no 5-minute questions on the test. They

should all take between 1 and 2 minutes each to solve. Therefore, you have to pick the mathematical strategy that you feel most comfortable with and that can solve the problem most quickly. Try this problem.

1. Which of the following is equivalent to the equation below?

$$-3(2x + 4)(3x - 1)$$

(A) $18x^2 + 12$

(B) $-18x^2 + 14x + 12$

(C) $-18x^2 - 30x + 12$

(D) $-9x^2 - 12$

How do you begin a problem like this? Do not get intimidated by the leading coefficient of –3. Here the problem can be solved using either of two ways. It is up to you to use the method with which you feel most comfortable. The first option is to distribute the –3 into the first binomial and then multiply by FOIL (First-Outside-Inside-Last). The second option it to multiply the binomials using FOIL and then distribute the –3. (On the SAT, you will have problems that require you to use FOIL.)

$-3(2x + 4)(3x - 1)$	OR	$-3(2x + 4)(3x - 1)$
becomes $(-6x - 12)(3x - 1)$		becomes $-3(6x^2 + 10x - 4)$

If you used the option on the left, now use the FOIL method. If you chose the method on the right, distribute the –3 into the trinomial to find the final answer.

$(-6x - 12)(3x - 1)$	OR	$-3(6x^2 + 10x - 4)$
becomes $-18x^2 - 30x + 12$		becomes $-18x^2 - 30x + 12$

You will notice that no matter which method you chose, the final answer is $-18x^2 - 30x + 12$. So choice C is the correct answer. Either way works; use the method that helps you get the answer quicker and more easily. Try another problem.

2. If f satisfies $f(3) = 5$ and $f(5) = 12$, and if g satisfies $g(6) = 5$ and $g(7) = 11$, what is the value of $f(g(6))$?

At first glance, this problem may look a bit overwhelming, and it is understandably so. However, if you examine the problem for exactly what it is asking you to do, the path to the answer becomes much clearer. In other words, keeping what the test asks for in mind can actually help you work backward and see the path to the answer.

Since you are being asked for the value of $f(g(6))$, start with the inside figure. What's the value of $g(6)$? Refer to the problem. You will see that it is simply a given value: $g(6)$ is equal to 5.

Now see that you are really being asked for the value of $f(5)$. Again refer back to the problem. See that $f(5)$ is actually already a known value of 12. This makes the final answer the given value of 12. Usually, you will use all the information given to solve a problem. On rare occasions like this one, not all the information provided is needed. Let's look at another question.

3. In the figure below, the hypotenuses of both triangles are parallel. What is the value of y?

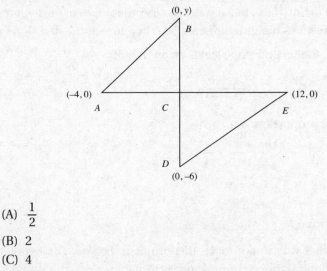

(A) $\dfrac{1}{2}$

(B) 2

(C) 4

(D) 8

The problem asks for the value of y. The drawing shows parallel lines made by the hypotenuses of the two triangles, which then means that the two triangles are similar.

You can approach this problem in two ways. First, you can set up a proportion and solve it using the slope of the given points: (0, –6) and (12, 0) for one

hypotenuse and (–4, 0) and (0, y) for the other hypotenuse. Here is the formula for the slope of a line or line segment:

$$m = \frac{y_2 - y_1}{x_2 - x_1}$$

Next, plug in the numbers:

$$\frac{-6 - 0}{0 - 12} = \frac{-6}{-12} = \frac{1}{2}$$

> Almost every math problem on the SAT requires multiple steps to solve it.

Again, take a quick look at the answer choices. See choice A? Remember that you will be tempted with answers that are only partially complete!

There is a slight possibility that the first few questions on a section may require only one step. However, the majority, if not all, of the questions require multiple steps. So if you have completed only one step, in all likelihood, you are not done!

Use the slope to find the value of y. In this case, the slopes of the hypotenuses must be equal because the lines are parallel. Therefore, if the first slope yields an answer of $\frac{1}{2}$, the second slope yields an answer of:

$$\frac{y - 0}{0 - (-4)} = \frac{1}{2}$$

Now solve the proportion:

$$\frac{y}{4} = \frac{1}{2}$$
$$4 = 2y$$
$$y = 2$$

Choice B is correct.

There is another way to approach this problem. Look at the hypotenuses again. Now also look at the horizontal and vertical lines along the x- and y-axes. Do you see two triangles in the diagram?

The distance from (–4, 0) to the origin in the triangle on the left is 4. The distance from (12, 0) to the origin in the triangle on the right is 3 times that distance, which is 12. Therefore, if the distance from (0, –6) to the origin is 6, then the distance from (0, y) to the origin must be $\frac{1}{3}$ of that, which is 2. So choice B is correct.

Many mathematical concepts are at work here. No matter which method you use to attack the problem, always keep your target in mind. Just choose the method with which you are most comfortable. Here is another problem.

4. If $3r + 6 = -12$ and $5s - 1 = 4$, what is the value of $\dfrac{2s}{3r}$?

   (A) -6

   (B) $-\dfrac{1}{9}$

   (C) $\dfrac{1}{9}$

   (D) 1

On the surface, this problem seems very easy. However, it is easy to get lost in the work leading up to the actual question. The first thing that you need to do for this problem is to find $3r$:

$$3r + 6 = -12$$
$$3r = -18$$

Now find s:

$$5s - 1 = 4$$
$$5s = 5$$
$$s = 1$$

Now plug in $3r$ and s:

$$\frac{2s}{3r} = \frac{(2)(1)}{-18} = \frac{2}{-18} = -\frac{1}{9}$$

So $\dfrac{2s}{3r}$ is $-\dfrac{1}{9}$, which makes the answer choice B.

LINEAR EQUATIONS WITHIN GEOMETRY QUESTIONS

Linear equations can be contained within a geometry question. Try the following problem.

5. The equation of a circle in the xy-plane is shown below. What is the radius of the circle?

$$x^2 + y^2 + 2x - 6y = -3$$

   (A) -3

   (B) 1

   (C) $\sqrt{7}$

   (D) 7

This is a much more difficult problem and one that requires knowing the general formula for the equation of a circle:

$$(x - h)^2 + (y - k)^2 = r^2$$

This equation is not given in the reference section at the beginning of the Math Test. In the equation, the center of the circle is at point (h, k), and r is the radius. You should memorize this equation!

Next, rearrange the equation given in the problem so it is in the same form as the general formula shown above. The general formula is in perfect square trinomial form. Start by moving the x-terms together and then moving the y-terms together:

$$x^2 + 2x + y^2 - 6y = -3$$

Now write the x-terms as a squared binomial and write the y-terms as a squared binomial:

$$x^2 + 2x + ? \quad \text{and} \quad y^2 - 6y + ?$$

The next step is to find the numbers that make each binomial into a perfect square:

$$x^2 + 2x + \mathbf{1} \quad \text{and} \quad y^2 - 6y + \mathbf{9}$$
$$(x + 1)^2 \quad \text{and} \quad (y - 3)^2$$

To make the equation for a circle into a perfect square trinomial, do not forget the right side of the equals sign. Whatever you alter on the left side, you must also alter on the right side. Since 1 and 9 were added to x and y on the left side of the equation, add 1 and 9 to -3 on the right:

$$(x + 1)^2 + (y - 3)^2 = -3 + 1 + 9$$

Before moving on, look again at the answer choices. Notice that choice A is -3 and that choice B is 1. That's not by accident. The test is tempting students who have only partially solved the problem with two numbers that are right in front of them. Remember the question that was asked! The problem asks for the radius, so keep working on the problem.

Look back at the equation for a circle. The number on the right side of the equals sign is the radius squared. So 7 is our equivalent to r^2:

$$(x + 1)^2 + (y - 3)^2 = 7$$

Go back to the answer choices. Do you see that choice D is 7? It's tempting to choose D and move on, but remember the initial problem that was asked.

From the equation for a circle, we see that 7 represents the radius squared, not the radius:

$$r^2 = 7$$

To get the radius, take the square root of each side, which yields the answer:

$$r = \sqrt{7}$$

The final answer is $\sqrt{7}$, which is choice C.

Question 5 is a difficult problem. If you can remember the formula and carefully check that you answered what was originally being asked, you'll get it! Try another problem.

6. What value of k would make the two lines below parallel?

$$2x + ky = -12 \text{ and } y - 12 = -\frac{2}{3}x$$

To solve a problem like this, you must first determine exactly what the question is asking. For this question, you are being asked what value of k would make the two lines parallel. The real question, though, is what information about the two lines must be true in order to have parallel lines. The answer to that is the slope of the lines must be equal.

In order to do this, you must first put the equation that does not include k into slope-intercept form. Add 12 to both sides of the equation. This leaves you with the following equation:

$$y - 12 = -\frac{2}{3}x$$

$$y = -\frac{2}{3}x + 12$$

Once you find out this information, you know that both equations must have a slope of $-\frac{2}{3}$ in order for them to be parallel. This becomes very important when trying to answer the real question: what value of k will leave you with a slope of $-\frac{2}{3}$?

The final step is to put the equation containing k into slope-intercept form. When you do this, you end up with the following equation:

$$2x + ky = -12$$
$$ky = -2x - 12$$
$$y = \frac{-2}{k} - \frac{12}{k}$$

You can now see that in order for the two linear functions to be parallel, the value for k must be equal to 3, which is your solution. In other words, since the slope of the first line is $-\frac{2}{3}$ and the slope of the second line is $\frac{-2}{k}$, then k must equal 3:

$$\frac{-2}{k} = \frac{-2}{3}$$

Cross multiply:

$$(-2)(3) = -2k$$
$$k = 3$$

For this grid-in question, you would enter 3 in one of the four spaces provided.

Note that it doesn't matter that k is the denominator under 12. Remember, we needed only the slope to match. So $\frac{12}{k}$, which is the y-intercept, doesn't make any difference regarding the answer. If it did, the y-intercept would simplify to $\frac{12}{3} = 4$. However, the y-intercept is irrelevant to the solution. On the SAT, finding the answer and getting as many points as possible are the only things that matter.

LINEAR SYSTEMS OF EQUATIONS

Since the SAT is rooted in the Heart of Algebra and since systems of equations are such a crucial component of algebra, you should expect to see many variations of problems like the one presented here.

> Be sure you spend extra time before test day preparing for questions about linear systems of equations.

7. Find the sum of x and y using the system of equations below:

$$9x + y = 16$$
$$3x - 6y = 18$$

Begin the process by taking notice of the form in which the equations are currently presented. Since both equations are already in standard form, this system should be solved using the elimination method. In this case, the elimination method is faster than the substitution method. Elimination requires you to create one variable with equal coefficients but opposite signs. With the given problem, do the following:

$$9x + y = 16$$
$$3x - 6y = 18$$

Multiply the second equation by -3. This makes the leading coefficients have the same value but opposite signs:

$$9x + y = 16$$
$$(-3)(3x - 6y = 18)$$

$$9x + y = 16$$
$$\underline{-9x + 18y = -54}$$
$$19y = -38$$

At this point, add both equations vertically: $9x + -9x = 0$ and drops out of the problem, leaving the following:

$$19y = -38$$
$$y = -2$$

> To find the second value, substitute the first value you find into the equation that is easier to manipulate.

The y-value can then be substituted into either equation to solve for x. Substitute the value into whichever equation will help you solve the problem faster and more easily. In this case, that choice would be the top equation to eliminate the need for the negative values in the calculations:

$$9x + y = 16$$
$$9x + (-2) = 16$$
$$9x - 2 = 16$$
$$9x = 18$$
$$x = 2$$

After finding the x- and y-values, **reread what the problem is actually asking**. (Do you see how the tactics overlap?) Since you are being asked for the sum of x and y, you have one last step. You have to add 2 and -2, giving a final answer of 0. For this grid-in question, you would enter 0 as the answer. Try another problem.

8. In the system of equations below, k is a constant and x and y are variables. For what value of k will the system have no solutions?

$$kx - 4y = 4$$
$$4x - 5y = 7$$

This is challenging, but it can be simplified by keeping a few key items in mind. To begin, remember that linear systems can have three different types of solutions. They can have one solution, which is the most common case. They can have no solutions. They can have infinite solutions. For a system to have no solutions, you must manipulate the coefficients of the variables in such a way that the variables drop out, leaving constants that are not equal.

To begin with, focus on the y-terms. Make them opposite values so that when you add the equations together, the y-values cancel out each other. If you multiply the first equation by 5 and the second equation by -4, you will come up with a new, but equivalent, system of equations. Just remember to multiply both sides of the first equation by 5 and both sides of the second by -4:

$$5(kx - 4y = 4) \longrightarrow 5kx - 20y = 20$$
$$-4(4x - 5y = 7) \longrightarrow -16x + 20y = -28$$

When the new equations are combined using the elimination method, the y-terms cancel:

$$
\begin{array}{r}
5kx - \mathbf{20y} = 20 \\
+ \quad -16x + \mathbf{20y} = -28 \\
\hline
5kx - 16x = -8
\end{array}
$$

All that is left is to cancel the x-terms. Again use the tactic that will give you what you are being asked for. Since you are looking only for a value of k that will yield exactly zero solutions, calculate the equation expression set equal to 0:

$$5kx + -16x = 0$$
$$5kx = 16x$$
$$kx = \frac{16}{5}x$$
$$k = \frac{16}{5}$$

An alternative (and faster) solution is the following. For the system to have no solutions, the lines can never intersect and must therefore be parallel. Since the lines must be parallel, the ratios of the coefficients of x and y must be equal to each other:

$$\frac{k}{-4} = \frac{4}{-5}$$

Then cross multiply:

$$-5k = -16$$
$$k = \frac{16}{5}$$

That's it! The x-values and y-values will cancel out only if k is equal to $\frac{16}{5}$.
If you plug $\frac{16}{5}$ in for k in the original system of equations and then simplify, you will have 0 on the left side and -8 on the right. This makes no logical sense, giving you no solution!

On your answer sheet, enter $\frac{16}{5}$ on the grid. Try another question.

9. Jessica takes on two summer jobs while on break from school. One job is baby-sitting, and the other is working as a lifeguard. She can work no more than 40 hours per week. Jessica earns $9.50 per hour for baby-sitting and $12.00 per hour as a lifeguard. If she must earn $400 per week to pay for tuition, which system of inequalities accurately represents Jessica's situation?

(A) $x + y < 40$
$9.5x + 12y > 400$

(B) $x + y \leq 40$
$9.5x + 12y \geq 400$

(C) $y - x < 40$
$9.5x + 400 < 12y$

(D) $x + y \leq 40$
$12y \geq 9.5x + 400$

The secret to problems like this is to identify each part of the problem separately and then combine the two parts to find your answer.

Remember the tactic of identifying the important information in the problem? This is essential no matter what the problem is! Start by noticing the description of Jessica's work hours: *She can work no more than 40 hours per week.* From this line, you know that the combined hours worked while baby-sitting and for her lifeguard duties must be 40 hours or less. In equation form, represent baby-sitting as x and lifeguard duties as y. So the inequality can be represented as $x + y \leq 40$. Just knowing this reduces the possible choices down to choices B and D by eliminating choices A and C. By taking this one simple step, you have raised the odds of getting the question right from 25% to 50%!

Remember that even if you don't know the answer, keep working to figure out what is *not* the answer and then take your best guess. Doing this will raise your score!

Now create a second equation that focuses on pay. Use the following lines from the problem: *Jessica earns $9.50 per hour baby-sitting and $12.00 per hour as a lifeguard. If she must earn $400 per week to pay for tuition . . . .* Based on those lines and by using the same variables as in the first inequality, the money earned from baby-sitting can be represented by $9.5x$ and the money earned from lifeguard duties can be represented by $12y$. To make enough to pay for tuition, the total money earned must be at least $400. By putting all of that information together, create the equation $9.5x + 12y \geq 400$.

From the inequalities formed, you will see that choice B is the correct answer. Try one more problem.

10. The sum of three numbers is 450. The largest number is 2 times the middle number. The middle number is 50 added to the smallest number. What is the largest of these three numbers?

   (A) 75
   (B) 125
   (C) 250
   (D) 450

At first glance, many students will use guess and check with this problem. This method may or may not get you to the correct answer. You will also use much more time with guess and check than if you use a system of equations. When you see a set of relationships that could be represented by using multiple variables, you should immediately start thinking about using a system of equations to solve the problem. The system for this problem starts out quite simple. The sum of the largest (L), middle (M) and smallest (S) numbers is equal to 450. This equation shows the relationship $L + M + S = 450$.

Finding the second equation is a bit more complex, and doing so will require some critical thinking. When writing a system of equations, you should always be trying to write the equations using as few variables as possible. The ultimate goal is, if possible, to write the system using only one variable.

> When using systems of equations, always try to rewrite your equations using only one variable if possible.

From the information given, you can create three equations, one for each number value. Start with the largest. The largest value is 2 times the middle value, so that means $L = 2M$.

For the smallest value, create the equation $S + 50 = M$. Now manipulate this equation to $S = M - 50$. Now all three equations are in terms of M.

Substitute to get to the answer. By substituting $2M$ for L and $M - 50$ for S, you get the following result:

$$L + M + S = 450$$
$$(2M) + (M) + (M - 50) = 450$$
$$4M - 50 = 450$$
$$4M = 500$$
$$M = 125$$

Be careful! As always, check to see what you are being asked for in the question. The question asks for the largest value. So if the middle number is 125 and the largest number is 2 times the middle number, the largest number is 250. Choice C is the correct answer.

Chapter Overview

When you are working on a math problem, think of your math strengths and weaknesses. Choose a strategy that will get you to the answer in the fastest and easiest possible way. Always do whatever you can to make the test as simple as possible for yourself! You must also understand and be able to solve linear equations, systems of equations, and inequalities. These question types are common on the SAT, so you should familiarize or refamiliarize yourself with them before taking the test. When manipulating equations, work with the equation that is the easiest to manipulate. Try to rewrite equations with one variable if possible. Know that most math problems require multiple steps. If you do not see the answer, try to eliminate the choices you know are incorrect in order to increase the odds of getting the question right when guessing. The main takeaway from all this is to simplify the problems as much as possible to make them easier to solve.

13

Solving Quadratic Equations and Exponential Functions

The use and manipulation of quadratic equations and exponential functions are an important part of the Math Test. Just like other math concepts on the SAT, familiarize yourself with the question types and with the strategies to get you to the answer efficiently.

BIG STRATEGY #18

Never Do More Work than Necessary

Once you have eliminated three of the four choices as possible answers, choose the remaining answer. You should not complete the rest of your work to be sure the last-remaining answer choice is correct. Remember that time can be either your friend or your enemy. If you have an extra minute at the end of test that you need to complete a hard problem, you will be grateful that you saved 20 seconds on one problem and 30 seconds on another by not doing unnecessary work on earlier problems. Do what you can to conserve the valuable resource of time so that you can give every question the time and effort it needs.

GRASPING ALL FORMS OF QUADRATIC EQUATIONS

A quadratic equation can be quickly identified by its squared term. $5x^2 + 8x + 1 = 0$ is an example of a quadratic equation. What should jump off the page to you is the exponent of 2 (from $5x^2 + 8x + 1 = 0$) that goes along with the first term of this equation. When you see an equation with an exponent of 2, you should immediately think about either factoring or using the quadratic formula. These two techniques should be at the ready when that flashing neon sign of the leading squared term pops up during your work.

Remember to try every problem before reading the solution below it.

1. What is the sum of all values of m that satisfies $4m^2 - 2m - 6 = 0$?

(A) -1

(B) $-\dfrac{1}{2}$

(C) $\dfrac{1}{2}$

(D) $\dfrac{3}{2}$

> **The only method that works for all quadratic equations is the quadratic formula:**
>
> $$\dfrac{-b \pm \sqrt{b^2 - 4ac}}{2a}$$

How do you proceed with a quadratic equation? There are multiple strategies of attack when encountering any quadratic equation. You can factor, complete the square, or use the quadratic formula.

If you are unsure of how to approach a quadratic formula question, you should know and use the quadratic formula. If you see that another method will work, by all means, use it, but if factoring or completing the square does not work, go to the quadratic formula.

For this particular problem, begin by gathering the facts. In this case, look back at the equation to get the values to plug into the quadratic formula. Remember, in order to use the quadratic formula, you must be sure the equation is in standard form, which is $ax^2 + bx + c = 0$.

From the equation in the question, you can gather the following:

- $a = 4$
- $b = -2$
- $c = -6$

Insert these values into the formula:

$$\frac{-(-2) \pm \sqrt{(-2)^2 - 4(4)(-6)}}{2(4)} = \frac{2 \pm \sqrt{100}}{8} = \frac{2 \pm 10}{8}$$

You must further simplify this equation by dividing by 8 to get:

$$\frac{12}{8} \text{ and } -\frac{8}{8}$$

$$\frac{3}{2} \text{ and } -1$$

The difficult twist at the end of this specific problem is the request for the sum of the two values of m. The sum of $\frac{3}{2}$ and -1 is:

$$\frac{3}{2} - 1 = \frac{1}{2}$$

So the sum is $\frac{1}{2}$, which is choice C.

So when you see a quadratic equation and are unsure how to proceed, use the quadratic formula. Know that the other methods can work and can be faster, though. As you see more problems, you will get a better idea of when to use the formula and when factoring, completing the square, or a different method will work better. Try another problem.

2. In the xy-plane, the point (2, 4) lies on the graph of the function $y = 2x^2 + bx + 6$. What is the value of b?

(A) −5
(B) 3
(C) 5
(D) 6

When encountering a problem such as this one, many students will start to panic and quickly go down the wrong path. Worse yet, some will skip the problem altogether. First, relax and know that you can figure out this problem. Then take a step back and examine the question a bit more closely. What are you given? You have a point and an equation with a coefficient that needs to be calculated.

The key to this problem is remembering that a point is still in terms of x and y. Plug the given x- and y-values into the equation:

$$4 = 2(2)^2 + b(2) + 6$$

Then simplify it:

$$4 = 8 + 2b + 6$$
$$4 = 14 + 2b$$
$$-10 = 2b$$
$$-5 = b$$

Your final answer is −5, which is choice A.

3. If the expression below is written in the form $ax^2 + bx + c$, where a, b, and c are constants, what is the value of b?

$$(-2x^2 + x - 6) - 4(x^2 + 2x - 4)$$

(A) -8

(B) -7

(C) 6

(D) 7

This is another intentionally intimidating problem that might leave some students scratching their heads or just skipping the problem. When you approach the question step by step, the answer becomes quite clear.

The first thing you should do is to distribute the -4 throughout the second trinomial. This will leave you with one long expression:

$$-2x^2 + x - 6 - 4x^2 - 8x + 16$$

From here, the expression must be simplified by combining like terms:

$$-6x^2 - 7x + 10$$

Finally, evaluate the simplified answer to find the answer to the problem being asked. Since the value of b is requested and b is the coefficient of the variable with the exponent of 1 in our equation, then we need the number next to x.

Again, be careful! The number is not 7; it is -7, which is choice B.

BIG STRATEGY #19

Work Backward from Answer Choices

Take your time reading a problem. If you can generally grasp what is being asked, you might want to look at the answer choices and work backward. Many times, this method can get you to the correct solution quickly. The answer choices will often reveal either the solution itself or the path to the answer. Sometimes plugging in the answer choices to see which one works is the fastest way to finding the solution.

Remember time is not your friend in the math sections. Students usually admit to needing more time. So if you can get to a solution more quickly by working backward and plugging in answer choices, do it!

You want to work accurately but also quickly. Sometimes working backward is the quickest way to solve a problem. For the easier problems that come earlier in the math sections, use whatever method will help you save time. That way you will have time available to complete the more complex problems later in the test. Take a look at some samples and practice them.

4. Which of the following is equivalent to the expression shown below?

$$9x^2 + 12xy + 4y^2$$

(A) $(3x + 2y)^2$
(B) $(3x + 2y)^4$
(C) $(9x^2 + 4y^2)^2$
(D) $(9x + 4y)^4$

This is not a difficult problem. It can be solved using factoring if you remember how to factor out a perfect square trinomial. What if you forget? What if you just don't want to take a lot of time? Instead, look at the solutions and see which one will work and which ones will not work. You can see from the problem that the first number is a 9. So in the answer, the first number must be equal to 9 when squared or when taken to the 4th power. When you go through each choice, it is clear that choices C and D cannot be the answer. In choice C, the first term is $9^2 = 81$. In choice D, the first term is $9^4 = 6,561$. Eliminate those choices. You have already gone from a 25% chance of getting this question correct to a 50% chance!

(A) $(3x + 2y)^2$
(B) $(3x + 2y)^4$
(C) ~~$(9x^2 + 4y^2)^2$~~
(D) ~~$(9x + 4y)^4$~~

Now look more closely at the 3 in choices A and B. In choice A, $3^2 = 9$. In choice B, $3^4 = 81$. Eliminate choice B.

(A) $(3x + 2y)^2$
(B) ~~$(3x + 2y)^4$~~

We are left with choice A, which does make complete sense if multiplied out. By using the answer choices as a tool, you can save time for the more complex problems that will appear later in the section.

5. The equation below represents a parabola in the xy-plane. Of the following equivalent forms of the equation, which displays the x-intercepts of the parabola as constants or coefficients?

$$y = x^2 - 7x - 8$$

(A) $y + 8 = x^2 - 7x$
(B) $y + 7x = x^2 - 8$
(C) $y = x(x - 7) - 8$
(D) $y = (x - 8)(x + 1)$

This looks like a very tricky problem. However, if you simply go through the answer choices and work backward, it is not hard to see that the only choice where the equation is factored into its two intercepts is choice D. The others may be equivalent but really make no sense. Even if you forgot here what factored forms look like, you should be able to see that if x is either 8 or –1, the equation will equal 0 for y. This means the equation will be crossing the x-axis at –1 or 8, which are our x-intercepts.

If that is confusing, then factor the equation:

$$y = x^2 - 7x - 8$$
$$y = (x - 8)(x + 1)$$

Look at the solutions again. You should be able to see that D is the only choice that makes sense.

THE LOOK OF AN EXPONENTIAL FUNCTION

An exponential function should stand out to you at first sight. The standard format that you will encounter will be in the form of a^x, where a is a constant and x is a variable. This type of equation tends to appear when you encounter growth or decay problems that take place over a period of time. The half-life of radioactive material could be a situation where you may encounter an exponential function. Try the problem below.

6. The population of a certain tree species in a rain forest is decreasing by 15% every 10 years. If there are currently 25,000 trees in the forest, which of the following represents the tree population after x years?

(A) $25,000(0.15)^x$

(B) $10t + (25,000)^{(0.15x)}$

(C) $25,000(0.85)^{\frac{x}{10}}$

(D) $25,000(1.15)^{\frac{x}{10}}$

When students encounter exponential functions in word problems, panic mode often sets in. The students then tend to guess randomly at the answer. Fortunately, you will not be experiencing that panic after reading this section.

So what do you do first when encountering a question like this? Extract and organize all of the given information so that you can begin working with what you know:

- Decreasing 15%
- Duration of time = 10 years
- Starting population = 25,000 trees
- What you want to know = the population after x years

Now that you have all of this information organized and have a clear focus in mind, you can use your understanding of exponents to start eliminating choices. The exponential portion of this function is derived from the time period for the population to decrease by 15%. In this case, that time period is 10 years. You do not know the exact number of years. So represent those years by x. Your exponent then becomes the number of years divided by 10, or $\frac{x}{10}$. That one step brings you to either choice C or choice D as the possible answer.

The final component is identifying the question as either growth or decay. Since the size of the forest is decreasing in size every 10 years, this is a decay question. Since this is decay, you start with 100% (or 1.00) and subtract the 15% (or 0.15), giving you a decay rate of 85% (or 0.85). By putting all of this information together, you can now create an expression to best represent the situation being described:

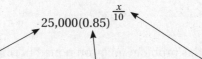

$$25,000(0.85)^{\frac{x}{10}}$$

Starting population   Percentage of decay   Number of years/period of decay

After you have put together all of your information, you will find that your answer matches choice C. Choice D adds 15% to the total, making it 115%. Since that takes the number in the wrong direction, you can eliminate it. Here is another problem.

7. In the equation below, $x > 1$. What is the value of y?

$$\frac{x^3}{x^y} \cdot \frac{x^2}{x^{2y}} = \frac{1}{x}$$

You can solve this problem using your understanding of exponents. First, you must multiply the left side of the equation. Remember that when multiplying exponents with the same base, you must add the exponents together. After multiplying the left side of the equation, you should have the following equation:

$$\frac{x^5}{x^{3y}} = \frac{1}{x}$$

Now cross multiply to get:

$$x = \frac{x^{3y}}{x^5}$$

The last step of this problem relies on remembering that dividing exponential functions with like coefficients and the same base requires you to subtract the exponents. Since the left side of the equation is just x, remember that it has an exponent of 1. Since the right side of the equation is a division problem with exponents with equal bases, the exponents can be subtracted. In other words:

$$x^1 = x^{3y-5}$$

Since the bases are the same, set the exponents equal to each other:

$$1 = 3y - 5$$

Now solve for y:

$$6 = 3y$$
$$y = 2$$

The value of y is 2.

ROOTS OF EQUATIONS AND HOW THEY ARE SOLVED

A basic understanding of the properties of exponents will help you solve root of equation problems. The better you become with transitioning back and forth from radicals to rational expressions, the more comfortable you will become with problems involving roots and fractional exponents.

> When working with fractional exponents, the numerator stays inside the radical and the denominator becomes the index of the root.

Once you try the following problem, the Key Tip above will become clear.

8. Which is equivalent to the expression $x^{\frac{3}{5}}$?

   (A) $\sqrt{x^5}$

   (B) $\sqrt[5]{x^3}$

   (C) $\sqrt[3]{x^5}$

   (D) $\sqrt[5]{x}^{\frac{3}{}}$

This problem is fairly straightforward when done in one of two ways. The first method is simply remembering that when encountering a fractional exponent, the numerator becomes the power inside the radical and the denominator becomes the index of the root. By using this technique, you'll quickly find that choice B is the answer. What happens, though, if this method slips your mind?

You can also use the tactic of replacing variables with simple numbers and using your calculator to compare. You can choose any value for x. For this example, try $x = 32$. If you plug 32 into your calculator and raise it to the $\frac{3}{5}$ power, you will receive an answer of 8. Once you have that information, you can plug $x = 32$ into all of your answer choices and see which choice returns an answer of 8. The matching and correct answer here is choice B.

When encountering problems with variables, especially multiple variables, always insert simple values in place of those variables. This will make your answers more concrete. When used in combination with other tactics, this will lead to you finding many more correct answers. This method can be just as effective when solving quadratic equations as it is solving linear equations. Look at the next question.

9. If $2^a = 4^b$, what is the value of b in terms of a?

(A) $8a$

(B) $2a$

(C) $\dfrac{1}{4}a$

(D) $\dfrac{1}{2}a$

This is not a difficult problem once you realize that 4 is a power of 2. On problems like this one, look for a way to make the base numbers the same. When the base numbers are the same, the exponents are equal to each other.

In this case, you can simplify 4 to 2^2 so that your new equation is now:

$$2^a = 2^{2b}$$

Now that you have common bases, you can say that $a = 2b$. Fantastic! You are almost done. However, when looking back at the problem, your answer is requested as b in terms of a. So you must isolate b.

$$a = 2b$$

$$b = \frac{1}{2}a$$

So b is equal to $\dfrac{1}{2}a$, making your final answer choice D. Try one more.

10. Using the roots provided, what is the value of x?

$$\sqrt[4]{16} + \sqrt[3]{8} = \sqrt{x}$$

(A) 2

(B) 4

(C) 8

(D) 16

This would be a typical roots of equations problem that could appear in the noncalculator section of the SAT. If you evaluate each radical separately, this problem becomes much easier.

Taking the 4th root of 16 gives you 2. If you have trouble, try a factor tree:

$$16 = 2 \times 2 \times 2 \times 2$$

Using the same process for the 3rd root of 8 also gives 2. Now rewrite the equation. It looks like this:

$$2 + 2 = \sqrt{x}$$

Be careful here! Since this is a multiple-choice question, you are guaranteed to find 4 as one of your choices. In fact, that is choice B. However, 4 is not the correct answer. You still have one final step to complete, which is to isolate x.

Remember, to reverse a square root, you must square both sides of the equation:

$$4 = \sqrt{x}$$
$$4^2 = \left(\sqrt{x}\right)^2$$
$$16 = x$$

This gives you $4^2 = x$. So x is 16, making your final answer choice D.

Chapter Overview

In this section, you have learned about the application of quadratic equations and exponential functions. You have also learned about the roots of equations. In order to achieve your highest potential score for the problems found in this section, be sure to review the properties of exponents as well as the quadratic formula. Having a fluid understanding of these major concepts will make your experience taking the SAT test a less stressful one and give you the confidence to do well on the test.

14

Interpreting Graphs and Charts

U sing graphs and charts is so essential to learning that the College Board placed them into every part of the test. The Reading, Writing and Language, and Math Tests all have questions centered on graphs and charts. In the English Test, the math in the graph and chart questions is simple. In the Math Test, the emphasis is obviously on the math. This chapter focuses on visualizing and interpreting graphs and charts to make them simpler and therefore easier to attack.

BIG STRATEGY #20

Make a Quick Sketch

Say that you have a problem that mentions a triangle, but there is no triangle on the page. You must sketch it! Making a sketch will help you see the problem. As you have heard your teachers tell you for years, don't try to do the problem in your head! Sketching will make the problem easier to see and therefore easier to solve. You do not have to be an artist to make a useful sketch that will help you solve a problem. In many cases, adding a visual component to a problem that doesn't originally include one can be the difference between finding a correct answer quickly and wasting your most valuable resource—time. Your sketches need to be accurate. At the same time, they must be done quickly. This is not the time to create a masterpiece. You are simply putting the image onto the page to help you see what the problem is asking and what it wants you to solve.

VISUALIZE THE GRAPH

Graph and chart problems will be presented in two forms: one where the problem includes the graph and/or chart and one where it is not included. Let's get started by discussing the problems where you are not given the graph or chart. The term *visualize* can be interpreted and used in two different ways for problems such as these. You can visualize the problem in your head to help you to find a correct answer. This method may work, or it may not. You can also visualize a problem by creating a quick sketch. This will help free your mind to focus on the question being asked of you, so make a sketch when it is not presented. Remember, as always, to try the problem in the space provided before moving to the solution.

1. If $f(x) = |x|$ and $g(x) = |x - 3| + 4$, then $g(x)$ is a shift of $f(x)$

    (A) 4 left and 3 down.

    (B) 3 right and 4 up.

    (C) 3 right and 4 down.

    (D) 3 left and 4 up.

At first glance, this may seem extremely complicated. However, understanding the absolute value function will let you know what directions the constants are shifting the graph.

Start by graphing $f(x) = |x|$. It doesn't have to be a work of art, but it should be as accurate as possible. Just plotting a few points and then drawing it is usually enough. Here is a visual of what $f(x) = |x|$ looks like:

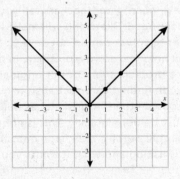

Now look at the equation for $g(x)$. Focus on the + 4 outside of the absolute value bar. This + 4 is referring to the movement of the graph up or down the y-axis. Since the graph has shifted up 4 units, eliminate choices A and C.

Continue to look at the equation for $g(x)$. This time, turn your attention inside the absolute value bars to the $x - 3$. Many students will see the $- 3$ and interpret that as a shift left. However, you must remember that you are not looking for $x - 3$. You are looking for when $x - 3 = 0$. In this case, if you set $x - 3$ equal to 0, you will see that the x-value is actually $+3$. Plot $g(x)$ and sketch a new graph. You will see the answer to the question:

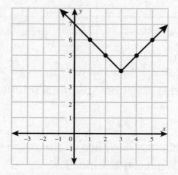

So the original graph moved 4 up and 3 to the right, making choice B the right answer. The graphs show the answer, but you have to draw them. Try another.

2. Some values of x and $f(x)$ are given in the table below. Based on the information provided, if $x = -1$, what is the value of $f(x)$?

x	$f(x)$
0	0
1	1
3	9
5	25

(A) -1
(B) 0
(C) 1
(D) 2

When first looking at this problem, many students might immediately choose choice A, -1, based on a quick look at the pattern in the given chart. Do not fall into this trap! Be sure you have examined the chart and extracted all of the information that has been provided to you. In order to solve this problem accurately, you must realize that the pattern established in the chart is x^2. For this problem, the key is to add your own values to the chart. Follow the pattern. Put -1 in for x and then the value for $f(x)$. Look beyond the initial numbers of

(0, 0) and (1, 1). Go to the last sets: (3, 9) and (5, 25). Do you see that $9 = 3^2$ and that $25 = 5^2$?

x	$f(x)$
0	0
1	1
3	9
5	25
−1	1

Now take −1 and square it. When $x = -1$, $f(x) = (-1)^2 = 1$. Since you are dealing with a squared term in this situation, your final solution is 1, choice C. Try this next problem.

3. In the xy-plane, the point (2, 4) lies on the graph of the function
    $f(x) = 2x^2 - ax + 6$. What is the value of a?

This problem can be done a few different ways. The first and most common method is to attempt to factor the function that you were given. This can be a long and tedious process where you are doing little more than guess and check.

The more effective process is to visualize the value that would satisfy the function. Replace x with 2 and $f(x)$ with 4. Now you can see what the value of a should be for this function. Graph the function on the calculator. It should look like this:

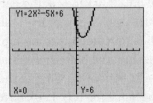

In this case, a should be equal to 5. So on the grid, pencil in 5 and fill in the corresponding bubble below it.

UNDERSTAND WHAT THE QUESTION IS ASKING

The statement "understand what the question is asking" may seem like an obvious piece of advice. However, it may be the most valuable advice you get for the entire Math Test. More mistakes are made by not identifying what the problem is actually asking than any other area. Be sure that no matter what type of question you are encountering, you are answering the question that you are being asked, not a question you may be inferring. Try the problem below.

4. Using the given pie chart below, what percentage of students who only took Precalculus would have to move to having No Calculus in order for the percentage of No Calculus students to be equal to the percentage of students taking Calculus I?

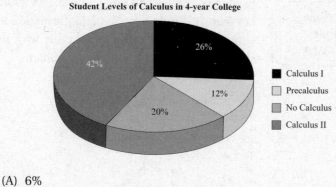

Student Levels of Calculus in 4-year College

26%
42%
12%
20%

■ Calculus I
□ Precalculus
■ No Calculus
■ Calculus II

(A) 6%
(B) 12%
(C) 50%
(D) 100%

At first glance this problem may seem confusing, especially with the constant use of the word *Calculus*. This is the perfect reason why you must identify what the problem is actually asking you to do before starting work with the problem. The key word in this problem is *percentage*. The question is asking you what percentage of students would have to move from Precalculus to No Calculus for the percentage of students taking Calculus I and No Calculus to be equal.

After reading the question, many students may quickly give an answer of 6%, which is the difference between No Calculus and Calculus I. However, you will not fall for this trap. You will read the question carefully and determine

what the problem is actually asking. The problem is asking what percentage of students would have to move from Precalculus to No Calculus. It is not asking what percentage the No Calculus had to increase. You do need to increase the No Calculus students by 6%, and the Precalculus students make up only 12% of the population. So in order in move 6% of students from Precalculus to No Calculus, you would need half of the 12% of the Precalculus students to move. Half of anything is 50%. To put it mathematically,

$$\frac{6}{12} = 0.50 = 50\%$$

This makes your final answer 50%, which is choice C.

USE THE VISUAL PROVIDED TO SOLVE THE PROBLEM

Throughout your SAT testing experience, you will be faced with a variety of different visuals. Remember that those visuals are there for you! They are not decoration or just visual stimulation. The visuals are useful tools that must be

> Do not overthink a problem that contains a visual.

used in your answer. Look at the visual, identify its key features, and then use that information to help you. Do not infer anything else other than what is shown in the visual. Try the next problem.

+ = number of cell phones

5. A class of 20 students was asked how many cell phones were used in their homes. The chart above shows the results of the poll. What is the mean number of the data?

(A) 3
(B) 3.5
(C) 4
(D) 4.5

The visual you are given here contains all of the information needed to solve this problem. First, you need to remember that *mean* is referring to the average of the data. You can then transform the data chart into a series of values that will allow you to calculate the average easily.

Take the data and list it out. Your series becomes

$$\{1, 1, 1, 2, 2, 2, 2, 3, 3, 3, 3, 3, 4, 4, 5, 5, 6, 6, 7, 7\}$$

Add these numbers; you get a total of 70. Now divide by the number of data points, which is 20:

$$\frac{70}{20} = 3.5$$

The mean is 3.5. So your answer is choice B. Try another problem that contains a graphic.

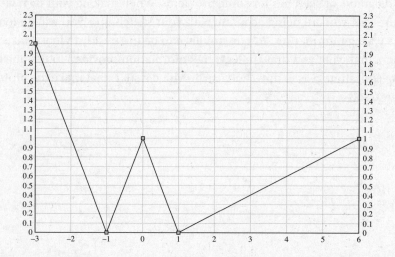

6. The graph of function f is shown above. Which of the following are equal to 0?

    I. $f(-1)$
    II. $f(6)$
    III. $f(1)$

(A) I only
(B) I and II only
(C) I and III only
(D) I, II, and III

Questions like this can become overly complicated. However, if you remember just one simple piece of information, these problems will become significantly easier. You must remember that $f(x)$ is the same as y.

If you remember that $f(x)$ is the same as y, you can recognize that all that this question is asking is where on the graph are your y-values equal to 0. If you refer back to the graph, you can see that $y = 0$ at $x = -1$ and at $x = 1$. Since option I and option III are equal to 0, the correct answer is choice C.

Chapter Overview

In this section, you have learned about the use of visuals, whether they are in front of you or if you have to sketch them. You must use the visuals that are provided for you. Remember that the visuals are given to you for a reason. Use that information to your benefit. You also found that it is important to produce your own diagrams or sketches for some problems. When making your own visuals, be sure that you are being accurate with your sketches or you will be looking at the wrong information. You do not have to be the next Da Vinci. Make sure, though, that what you draw reflects the information provided in the question. The overall strategy is to draw and use provided visuals that make the problems easier to solve.

15

Concepts of Geometry and Trigonometry

This chapter focuses on the geometry and trigonometry concepts tested on the SAT. The terms *geometry* and *trigonometry* can send chills down the spines of some students. Once you learn a few important techniques, though, you will find that geometry and trigonometry are not scary at all. Once you understand this BIG Strategy, you'll be on your way to a higher score!

BIG STRATEGY #21

Focus on the Basics

To excel in geometry and trigonometry on the SAT, you do not have to be a master mathematician. Instead, focus on being a master of the basics, such as the Pythagorean theorem; sine, cosine, and tangent properties; and the basic attributes of geometric shapes (area, perimeter, and volume). Mastering these topics will help you succeed with these types of problems on test day.

KNOW THE MAJOR GEOMETRY FACTS

The best place to start is with what you are given. At the beginning of every Math Test section is a reference box that includes a multitude of formulas and example diagrams. Roughly 85% of the geometry-based problems are derived from the information given to you at the beginning of the section. Use that information! You do not have to memorize the formulas provided in the reference box. Remember that the SAT is a test of your skills, not your knowledge. So when the test gives you information, use it!

Just like in the previous chapters, try each problem in the space provided before looking at the explanation.

1. If in $\triangle abc$ the sine of $\angle c$ is $\frac{3}{5}$, what is the sine of $\angle a$?

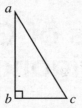

(A) $\frac{2}{5}$

(B) $\frac{3}{5}$

(C) $\frac{4}{5}$

(D) 1

The first thing to think about when encountering a geometry problem is to remember the two big concepts of geometry and trigonometry: the Pythagorean theorem and SOH-CAH-TOA. These two concepts should be your go-to methods for solving geometry and trigonometry problems. Most of these problems that you will encounter on the SAT will involve one or both of these concepts. This problem, for example, requires both SOH-CAH-TOA and the Pythagorean theorem.

> **Know the Pythagorean theorem and how to use it.**

The Pythagorean theorem states that in a right triangle, the square of the hypotenuse is equal to the sum of the squares of the two legs. It is written as $a^2 + b^2 = c^2$, where c is the hypotenuse and both a and b are legs. By using this formula, you can always find the length of a side of a right triangle if you have the length of the other two sides. For example, if the hypotenuse's length is 13 and another side is 12, you can find the length of the third side by plugging in the numbers:

$$a^2 + 12^2 = 13^2$$
$$a^2 + 144 = 169$$
$$a^2 = 169 - 144$$
$$a^2 = 25$$
$$a = 5$$

Sine (sin), cosine (cos), and tangent (tan) are based on right triangles. The side next to an acute angle is the adjacent side. The side across from an acute

Know SOH-CAH-TOA for SAT trigonometry questions.

angle is the opposite side. The hypotenuse is the side across from the right angle. SOH-CAH-TOA is an easy way to remember these functions:

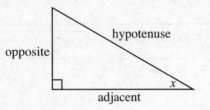

- SOH: sine = $\dfrac{\text{opposite}}{\text{hypotenuse}}$

- CAH: cos = $\dfrac{\text{adjacent}}{\text{hypotenuse}}$

- TOA: tan = $\dfrac{\text{opposite}}{\text{adjacent}}$

With these trigonometry functions, you can find the third side of a right triangle if you know the other two. During the calculator section, use a calculator that has the trigonometry functions on it instead of a simple calculator.

In question 1, start with the sine of $\angle c$ is $\dfrac{3}{5}$, which tells you that the side opposite $\angle c$ is equal to 3 and that the hypotenuse is equal to 5. From this point, you will need to apply the Pythagorean theorem to find the last side of the triangle. By using the theorem, you will find the final side has a value of 4:

$$a^2 + 3^2 = 5^2$$
$$a^2 + 9 = 25$$
$$a^2 = 25 - 9$$
$$a^2 = 16$$
$$a = 4$$

Once you have all three sides, the final step is to look again at what the test is asking. Since it wants the sine of $\angle a$, apply the SOH component of the trigonometry function. Place the opposite side of $\angle a$, which is 4, divided by the hypotenuse, which is 5. This makes the final answer $\dfrac{4}{5}$. Choice C is the correct answer. Try another one.

2. The angles below are acute angles, and $\sin(x°) = \cos(y°)$. If $x = 6a - 19$ and if $y = 4a - 11$, what is x?

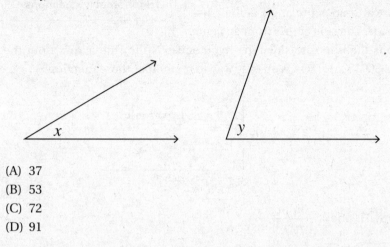

(A) 37
(B) 53
(C) 72
(D) 91

On the surface, this may seem like a very difficult problem. If you take advantage of the clue that is given to you in the problem, though, it becomes much easier. Since you are told that $\sin(x°) = \cos(y°)$, you can take advantage of the complementary angles property of sines and cosines: $x + y = 90$. (Look at the images and trust them. If you add together those two angles in the images, you would have a right angle.)

From here, you can do the following by adding the two formulas together and setting them equal to 90:

$$(6a - 19) + (4a - 11) = 90$$
$$10a - 30 = 90$$
$$10a = 120$$
$$a = 12$$

Now that you have calculated the value of a, insert that value back into the equation given for a to find the value of x:

$$x = 6(12) - 19$$
$$x = 72 - 19$$
$$x = 53$$

This makes choice B the correct answer.

BASIC TRIGONOMETRIC PROPERTIES

Trigonometric properties can send some students into a tailspin. Memorizing every theorem and postulate along with diagram after diagram is not what will help you on the SAT. What will instead raise your score is mastering the most common trigonometric properties for the SAT. If you focus on the major ideas of the Pythagorean theorem, SOH-CAH-TOA, and the applications of 30-60-90 triangles, you will find yourself in a very strong position to do well on these SAT questions. Try one.

3. In a right triangle, one angle measures $x°$. If sine $x° = \dfrac{4}{5}$, what is $\cos(90° - x°)$?

    (A) 0.2
    (B) 0.6
    (C) 0.8
    (D) 1.2

This problem can seem a bit confusing or seem lacking in information at first. However, with a little organization, the answer is essentially given to you. As with most trigonometry-based problems, drawing a quick sketch can never really hurt. In this case, a sketch will allow you to see exactly what is being asked of you. By using your understanding of the properties of sine and cosine, you can extract a tremendous amount of information from the small amount given.

Since the sine of an angle is equal to the opposite side length divided by the hypotenuse (SOH), you can mark the angle location with an x. This would make the side opposite the marked angle equal to 4 and the hypotenuse equal to 5. At this point, the sketch should look something like this:

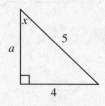

From this point, you can calculate the missing side by using the Pythagorean theorem like this:

$$a^2 + 4^2 = 5^2$$
$$a^2 + 16 = 25$$
$$a^2 = 25 - 16$$
$$a^2 = 9$$
$$a = 3$$

Knowing the length of the missing side adds the following information to the sketch:

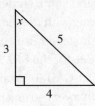

Now you have all of the information you need to solve the problem that is being asked of you, "What is $\cos(90° - x°)$?"

The final key to this problem is to realize that since this is a right triangle, when you are being directed to find $\cos(90° - x°)$, the question is really asking for the cosine of the other angle (that is, the angle opposite from x). Just remember SOH-CAH-TOA and $\cos = \dfrac{\text{adjacent}}{\text{hypotenuse}}$. All you need to do now is divide the value of the side adjacent to that angle (4) by the length of the hypotenuse (5), making your final answer $\dfrac{4}{5}$. Since $\dfrac{4}{5} = 0.8$, the correct answer is choice C. Here is another question.

4. In the figure below, what is $\cos Y$?

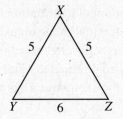

(A) $\dfrac{2}{5}$

(B) $\dfrac{3}{5}$

(C) $\dfrac{4}{5}$

(D) $\dfrac{6}{5}$

When you first encounter this problem, the hardest part will be to decide where to begin. The most important fact that you must remember is that in order to use sine, cosine, and tangent in their most basic forms, you must be working with a right triangle. Your first step must be to make a right triangle like you see below:

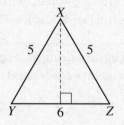

Once you have created two right triangles from the original diagram, you should realize that you created a perpendicular bisector from angle X. Since you did this, your base (side YZ) can be split into two parts of equal length (3).

Your diagram now includes the new lengths of your base components. You can focus your attention exclusively on the left triangle in your sketch.

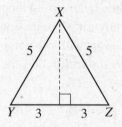

From this point, you can use the Pythagorean theorem to find the height of the triangle, which is 4:

$$3^2 + b^2 = 5^2$$
$$9 + b^2 = 25$$
$$b^2 = 25 - 9$$
$$b^2 = 16$$
$$b = 4$$

You now have all sides of the newly created triangle. Calculate the cosine of Y by dividing the adjacent side length (3) by the hypotenuse length (5). The final answer is $\frac{3}{5}$, which is choice B.

SKETCH A VISUAL

This has been mentioned a few times before, but it needs to be repeated. In geometry problems, more than in any other type of question, you will significantly decrease the difficulty by making a sketch. Unlike other areas of mathematics, geometry is almost entirely visual. Because of this, be sure to sketch what you are being asked to visualize. It is a visual problem, so make it visual!

5. A rectangle was altered by increasing its length by 20% and by decreasing its width by x%. If these changes decreased the area of the rectangle by 40%, what is x?

    (A) 1
    (B) 2
    (C) 50
    (D) 80

This problem may seem overwhelming at first because of its wording. However, organizing yourself makes this problem much easier. First, create a sketch that you can manipulate by inserting length and width measurements. These measurements can be anything, but be smart with your selections. Try to choose values that will work easily with the percentages you are working with, like 10 for the length and 2 for the width. Be sure to include the area since you will be working with that value as well.

$$2 \quad \boxed{\text{Area} = 20}$$
$$10$$

After you have created the first sketch, you need to apply the information in the question to create a second sketch. First, increase the length by 20%. The new length will be 12 ($10 \times 0.20 = 2$ and $10 + 2 = 12$). You then have to decrease your area by 40%. The new area is 12 ($20 \times 0.40 = 8$ and $20 - 8 = 12$). Now that you have both of those values, calculate the width of the missing side that will satisfy the new values.

$$? \quad \boxed{\text{Area} = 12}$$
$$12$$

For the new rectangle to have an area of 12, the new width must be 1:

$$A = lw$$
$$12 = 12w$$
$$w = 1$$

Be sure not to stop here! Many students will stop here and not reread the problem. They do not realize that you are asked for the value of x, which is the percentage decrease of the length of the rectangle. The final step is to calculate the percentage decrease. This is done by dividing the original length by the new length:

New length: 1

Original length: 2

$$\frac{\text{New length}}{\text{Old length}} = \frac{1}{2}$$

Now change that fraction into a percentage:

$$\frac{1}{2} = 0.50 = 50\%$$

This makes the final answer $x = 50$, which is choice C.

CIRCLES AND SOLID GEOMETRY

The SAT Math Test always includes one question about circles and one question about solid geometry. For both types of questions, use the formulas given to you in the reference box. So when you come to geometry questions on the test, flip back to the reference box. Try the following problem.

6. In the circle below, $\overline{XY}$ is a diameter. If the length of $\overarc{XRY}$ is 9π, what is the length of the radius of the circle?

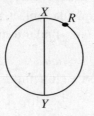

(A) 6

(B) 9

(C) 9π

(D) 18π

If you approach this problem systematically, the answer can become very clear. First, you must realize that $\overset{\frown}{XRY}$ is the length of half of the circle. You need the circumference to solve this problem. So if half of the circumference is 9π, the entire circumference is 18π.

Now that you have the circumference, you can find the length of the radius. Divide the circumference by 2π since the formula for circumference is $C = 2\pi r$. (You can find this formula in the reference box.) Plug in the numbers, and solve for the radius:

$$C = 2\pi r$$
$$18\pi = 2\pi r$$
$$r = 9$$

Be careful! The length of the radius does not include π. Choice B is the correct answer. Try one more question.

7. How many cubes with sides of 2 cm will fit inside the rectangular box pictured below?

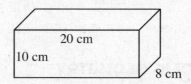

20 cm

10 cm

8 cm

(A) 100
(B) 150
(C) 200
(D) 800

In order to break down this solid geometry problem effectively, you must attack it from one of two ways. The first way is the more standard method: use the volume formula. For a rectangular object, volume equals the length times width times height, or $V = lwh$. First, find the volume of the rectangular object.

$$V = lwh$$
$$V = (20)(10)(8)$$
$$V = 1,600$$

Next, find the volume of a cube with a side of 2 cm:

$$V = lwh$$
$$V = (2)(2)(2)$$
$$V = 8$$

Since the volume of the rectangular object is 1,600 and the volume of each cube is 8, simply divide 1,600 by 8 to get the answer: 200, which is choice C.

You can also determine the number of cubes that will fit inside each edge of the box. Along the length of the box, you can fit 10 cubes since $20 \div 2 = 10$. The width of the box can fit 5 cubes since $10 \div 2 = 5$. The depth can fit 4 cubes since $8 \div 2 = 4$.

Once you have determined these values, think about volume again by multiplying together the number of cubes that fit along the three sides:

$$10 \times 5 \times 4 = 200$$

Again, the correct answer is C. Either method will get you to the correct answer. However, you need to know the volume formula for both to find the answer.

Chapter Overview

This chapter focused on the most important principles in geometry and trigonometry. By mastering topics such as the Pythagorean theorem and the properties of sine, cosine, and tangent, you will be using your study time very efficiently. When the test presents a question that has no visual, sketch it. Geometry is visual. You must make a geometry problem visual if you are not given an image. Make sure you refer back to the reference box when you come to a geometry problem. It can often jar your mind into seeing the path to the answer. By following these tips, geometry and trigonometry problems will be something that you will look forward to seeing on the test!

16

Mathematical Logic

This chapter focuses on real-world problems that you will encounter throughout both sections of the Math Test. Most of these problems will revolve around basic, real-world experiences. They will also test your abilities to apply mathematical logic in order to solve the problems correctly. To do well on questions involving mathematical logic, you simply need to use common sense.

BIG STRATEGY #22

Use Common Sense to Break Down Mathematical Logic

When encountering problems rooted in the real world, break them down into simpler problems. How can you do this? Just use your common sense. Real-world problems require you to draw on personal experiences to understand fully what the question is asking and to find the correct answer in the easiest way possible. Making complicated problems into much simpler problems is the key to success when tackling real-world problems.

BREAK DOWN MATHEMATICAL LOGIC

The best way to solve a problem involving mathematical logic is simply to break it down. Complex logic problems can usually be made simpler if you use one of two strategies.

For the first strategy, you can work backward. By working backward and using the answer choices to guide your work, the answer will essentially fall into your lap in many situations.

> To solve a logic problem, either work backward or break it into simpler parts.

For the second strategy, break down and simplify the problem that is being posed to you. The better you understand what the question is actually asking you, the better chance you have of finding the correct answer.

As always, try the problem yourself in the space provided before going on to the explanation.

1. Travis walks 52 meters in 36 seconds. If his rate stays constant, which of the following is closest to the distance he walks in 8 minutes?

   (A) 690 m
   (B) 693 m
   (C) 1,155 m
   (D) 1,380 m

The trick to this problem is realizing that using a simple proportion will help you arrive at the final answer. Just remember to convert the 8 minutes to 480 seconds. This way, the units will match up. (Since 1 minute = 60 seconds, then $60 \times 8 = 480$.) Once you have made that conversion, you can set up the problem:

$$\frac{52}{36} = \frac{x}{480}$$

Cross multiplying will get you to this equation:

$$36x = 24{,}960$$

Divide both sides of the equation by 36:

$$x = 693.33$$

Your final answer is 693 meters, which is choice B. Try another logic problem.

2. The sum of three numbers is 855. One of the numbers, x, is 50% more than the sum of the other two. What is the value of x?

   (A) 155
   (B) 214
   (C) 513
   (D) 570

This is actually a very difficult problem if you use a system of equations. You would have to create three equations with three unknowns and then slowly isolate each variable. However, you know better. There has to be an easier way—a way that uses mathematical logic.

You can plug in each answer choice to see which one works. Before deciding which choice to start with, follow the BIG Strategy and use your common sense. If x is 50% larger than the sum of the other two numbers and if the three

numbers combined equal 855, x obviously has to be a large number. By simply using this common sense, you can immediately eliminate choices A and B.

How do you finish solving this problem? Create an equation based on the information given in the problem. First, if x is 50% larger than the sum of the other two numbers, y and z, you can create the following equation:

$$x = 1.5(y + z)$$

This equation can be set equal to $(y + z)$ by dividing by 1.5 on both sides.

$$\frac{x}{1.5} = (y + z)$$

Since the sum of the three numbers is 855, we have a second equation:

$$x + y + z = 855$$

Substituting $\frac{x}{1.5}$ for $y + z$ in the second equation gives you the following:

$$x + \frac{x}{1.5} = 855$$

Multiply both sides of the equation by 1.5 to get rid of the fraction in the equation:

$$1.5x + x = 855(1.5)$$

Combine like terms on the left side of the equation:

$$2.5x = 855(1.5)$$
$$2.5x = 1{,}282.5$$

Solve for x by dividing both sides of the equation by 2.5:

$$x = 513$$

The answer is choice C, which is 513. Here's another problem.

3. Let x and y be numbers such that $x + y > 1$ and $x - y < -1$. Which of the following must be true?

    I. $x > y$
    II. $x < y$
    III. $|y| > x$

  (A) I and II only
  (B) II only
  (C) II and III only
  (D) I, II, and III

First break down this problem into its given components. Then answer the question being asked. In other words, make the problem simpler.

You are being asked which of three options *must be true*. For an option to be true, it must always make both inequalities true. Choose values for x and y that satisfy an option. Then plug those values into both inequalities. If those values always work in both inequalities, the option is true. To eliminate an option, though, you simply need to find one counterexample. A counterexample is just an example that is not true.

Test option I:

$$x > y$$
$$3 > 1$$

Now plug $x = 3$ and $y = 1$ into both inequalities:

$$x + y > 1$$
$$3 + 1 > 1 \quad \textbf{True!}$$

$$x - y < -1$$
$$3 - 1 < -1 \quad \textbf{False!}$$

Since we found one counterexample for option I, that option is not true. Eliminate choices A and D since they both include option I.

Before checking option II, look at the two remaining answer choices. Again apply common sense. If choice B is "II only" and choice C is "II and III only," then choice II must be true since option II is in both choices. So there is no need to check option II. Instead, check option III:

$$|y| > x$$
$$|3| > 1$$

Now plug $x = 1$ and $y = 3$ into both inequalities:

$$x + y > 1$$
$$1 + 3 > 1 \quad \textbf{True!}$$

$$x - y < -1$$
$$1 - 3 > -1 \quad \textbf{True!}$$

So both options II and III are correct, making the answer choice C.

MATH IN THE REAL WORLD

A major component of the redesigned SAT is to bring real-world situations into the test. You will encounter situations that you could experience in your everyday life. The idea is to take the real-world situations, break them down into exactly what you are being asked, and then solve. Do not get caught up in the everyday situation and miss exactly what you are being asked. Instead, stay focused on the math problem in the given situation. Try the next problem.

> Do not get caught up in the real-world scenario described in the question. Remember that your goal is to solve the problem quickly, efficiently, and correctly.

4. At Washington High School, approximately 4% of seniors and 9% of juniors passed the AP Chemistry exam. If there are 712 seniors and 694 juniors enrolled in the school, which of the following is closest to the number of juniors and seniors who passed the AP Chemistry exam?

   (A) 90
   (B) 91
   (C) 93
   (D) 105

For this problem, stay away from the everyday situation. Forget your high school and the juniors and seniors taking AP courses. Instead, realize that the problem is asking you to find the combination of subsets of two different groups.

First calculate 4% of seniors:

$$(712)(0.04) = 28.48$$

Next calculate 9% of juniors:

$$(694)(0.09) = 62.46$$

Combine the two groups:

$$28.48 + 62.46 = 90.94$$

If 90.94 students does not make sense, look again at the wording of the question. Notice that it says *approximately 4% of seniors and 9% of juniors*. Since the percentages shown are not exact, the numbers calculated are not exact, so round 90.94 to 91, which makes choice B the correct answer. Try another one.

5. Tickets for the school Art Show cost $7 for students and $10 for adults. If Marie spent more than $21 but not more than $41 on 3 student tickets and x adult tickets, what is one possible number of adult tickets she purchased?

When encountering a problem such as this, the first thing to be aware of is that there will be more than one answer. However, you need to find only one. That is very important. You will not need to write all possibilities, just one that will solve the problem.

Some grid-in questions have several possible solutions. You have to write just one to earn credit for the problem.

To find one solution for this problem, first organize the information that you are given. You know that student tickets cost $7 each and adult tickets cost $10 each. You also know that Marie spent between $21 and $41. Finally, you know that Marie purchased 3 student tickets. Here's what you should write down:

Students: $7 \times 3 = \$21$
Adults: $10
Total: $41

Subtract the $21 for student tickets from the maximum amount spent, $41. So Marie had $20 to spend on adult tickets:

$$\$41 - \$21 = \$20$$

Divide that $20 by the cost of an adult ticket. Marie could have purchased 2 adult tickets and remained within her budget:

$$\$20 \div \$10 = 2$$

On the answer sheet, grid in 2 and the bubble below it.

Another possible answer could have been 1 since the total would be $31, which is within her budget. Remember, though, you need to find only one possible answer for this type of problem. Try one more logic problem.

6. Last week, Travis worked 13 more hours than Tina. If they worked a combined total of 61 hours, how many hours did Tina work?

    (A) 13
    (B) 24
    (C) 37
    (D) 48

This is another problem that could be done in two ways. You can use algebra. However, the easier and faster way is to plug in values from the answer choices to find the solution.

Start with answer choice C since it is one of the middle values. If Tina worked 37 hours, Travis worked 24 hours since the two of them worked a total of 61 hours:

$$61 - 37 = 24$$

However, make sure that you pay attention to the question and identify who is working more hours. Using choice C, Tina worked 13 more hours than Travis since $37 - 24 = 13$. So choice C cannot be the answer.

Now use some common sense! By checking choice C, you learned that if Travis worked 24 hours, Tina worked 13 more hours than he did—37 hours. That means the correct answer must be the reverse. Tina must have worked 24 hours, and Travis must have worked 37 hours. Choice B is correct.

Chapter Overview

In this chapter, SAT Mathematics was brought into the real world. You were introduced to the types of real-world problems that you could encounter—both during the test and possibly in your everyday life. You also learned how to attack mathematical logic problems. You can now break down and solve even the most confusing logic problems. Putting all of these skills into practice will make your SAT score soar!

PART FOUR:
PUTTING IT
ALL TOGETHER

Practice Test

OVERVIEW

You have learned numerous tactics and skills to succeed on the Reading, Writing and Language, and Math Tests on the SAT. Now is the time to put together all that information and sit through a sample test. Take the same amount of time to complete the practice test as you will have to take the actual SAT—4 hours with the essay, 3 hours without it. This will help prepare you for the actual exam.

Set aside the necessary time. Then get a timer, a pencil, and a calculator. Take a few-minute break between sections. However, you should take the entire practice test in one sitting if at all possible. You should try to mimic the actual test conditions, which include the time limitation. Part of the SAT is that it is a grind; students need to develop the mental stamina required to score well. Taking a full practice test allows students to get used to the marathon of the exam.

One more thing: when taking the practice test, turn off the TV and put your devices on airplane mode. Stopping for interruptions is not really practicing under actual test conditions! After all, on test day, you will not be allowed to have any electronic devices with you (other than your calculator). Find a quiet spot so that you can concentrate, and then let nothing interrupt you.

> Take the practice test all at once in a 4-hour sitting.

Directions

The practice test is set up just like the SAT. You will see the Reading Test followed by the Writing and Language Test. The Math Test follows, with the no calculator section first and the calculator section second. The last part is the essay.

Each section has its own directions and then the test itself. The time and the number of questions are listed above the directions.

> Since you know what to do on each part of the test, never read any directions on the SAT. Reading the directions takes precious time that you could better spend answering the questions.

ANSWER SHEET
Practice Test

Section 1: Reading Test

1. Ⓐ Ⓑ Ⓒ Ⓓ
2. Ⓐ Ⓑ Ⓒ Ⓓ
3. Ⓐ Ⓑ Ⓒ Ⓓ
4. Ⓐ Ⓑ Ⓒ Ⓓ
5. Ⓐ Ⓑ Ⓒ Ⓓ
6. Ⓐ Ⓑ Ⓒ Ⓓ
7. Ⓐ Ⓑ Ⓒ Ⓓ
8. Ⓐ Ⓑ Ⓒ Ⓓ
9. Ⓐ Ⓑ Ⓒ Ⓓ
10. Ⓐ Ⓑ Ⓒ Ⓓ
11. Ⓐ Ⓑ Ⓒ Ⓓ
12. Ⓐ Ⓑ Ⓒ Ⓓ
13. Ⓐ Ⓑ Ⓒ Ⓓ
14. Ⓐ Ⓑ Ⓒ Ⓓ
15. Ⓐ Ⓑ Ⓒ Ⓓ
16. Ⓐ Ⓑ Ⓒ Ⓓ
17. Ⓐ Ⓑ Ⓒ Ⓓ
18. Ⓐ Ⓑ Ⓒ Ⓓ

19. Ⓐ Ⓑ Ⓒ Ⓓ
20. Ⓐ Ⓑ Ⓒ Ⓓ
21. Ⓐ Ⓑ Ⓒ Ⓓ
22. Ⓐ Ⓑ Ⓒ Ⓓ
23. Ⓐ Ⓑ Ⓒ Ⓓ
24. Ⓐ Ⓑ Ⓒ Ⓓ
25. Ⓐ Ⓑ Ⓒ Ⓓ
26. Ⓐ Ⓑ Ⓒ Ⓓ
27. Ⓐ Ⓑ Ⓒ Ⓓ
28. Ⓐ Ⓑ Ⓒ Ⓓ
29. Ⓐ Ⓑ Ⓒ Ⓓ
30. Ⓐ Ⓑ Ⓒ Ⓓ
31. Ⓐ Ⓑ Ⓒ Ⓓ
32. Ⓐ Ⓑ Ⓒ Ⓓ
33. Ⓐ Ⓑ Ⓒ Ⓓ
34. Ⓐ Ⓑ Ⓒ Ⓓ
35. Ⓐ Ⓑ Ⓒ Ⓓ
36. Ⓐ Ⓑ Ⓒ Ⓓ

37. Ⓐ Ⓑ Ⓒ Ⓓ
38. Ⓐ Ⓑ Ⓒ Ⓓ
39. Ⓐ Ⓑ Ⓒ Ⓓ
40. Ⓐ Ⓑ Ⓒ Ⓓ
41. Ⓐ Ⓑ Ⓒ Ⓓ
42. Ⓐ Ⓑ Ⓒ Ⓓ
43. Ⓐ Ⓑ Ⓒ Ⓓ
44. Ⓐ Ⓑ Ⓒ Ⓓ
45. Ⓐ Ⓑ Ⓒ Ⓓ
46. Ⓐ Ⓑ Ⓒ Ⓓ
47. Ⓐ Ⓑ Ⓒ Ⓓ
48. Ⓐ Ⓑ Ⓒ Ⓓ
49. Ⓐ Ⓑ Ⓒ Ⓓ
50. Ⓐ Ⓑ Ⓒ Ⓓ
51. Ⓐ Ⓑ Ⓒ Ⓓ
52. Ⓐ Ⓑ Ⓒ Ⓓ

ANSWER SHEET
Practice Test

Section 2: Writing and Language Test

1. Ⓐ Ⓑ Ⓒ Ⓓ
2. Ⓐ Ⓑ Ⓒ Ⓓ
3. Ⓐ Ⓑ Ⓒ Ⓓ
4. Ⓐ Ⓑ Ⓒ Ⓓ
5. Ⓐ Ⓑ Ⓒ Ⓓ
6. Ⓐ Ⓑ Ⓒ Ⓓ
7. Ⓐ Ⓑ Ⓒ Ⓓ
8. Ⓐ Ⓑ Ⓒ Ⓓ
9. Ⓐ Ⓑ Ⓒ Ⓓ
10. Ⓐ Ⓑ Ⓒ Ⓓ
11. Ⓐ Ⓑ Ⓒ Ⓓ
12. Ⓐ Ⓑ Ⓒ Ⓓ
13. Ⓐ Ⓑ Ⓒ Ⓓ
14. Ⓐ Ⓑ Ⓒ Ⓓ
15. Ⓐ Ⓑ Ⓒ Ⓓ

16. Ⓐ Ⓑ Ⓒ Ⓓ
17. Ⓐ Ⓑ Ⓒ Ⓓ
18. Ⓐ Ⓑ Ⓒ Ⓓ
19. Ⓐ Ⓑ Ⓒ Ⓓ
20. Ⓐ Ⓑ Ⓒ Ⓓ
21. Ⓐ Ⓑ Ⓒ Ⓓ
22. Ⓐ Ⓑ Ⓒ Ⓓ
23. Ⓐ Ⓑ Ⓒ Ⓓ
24. Ⓐ Ⓑ Ⓒ Ⓓ
25. Ⓐ Ⓑ Ⓒ Ⓓ
26. Ⓐ Ⓑ Ⓒ Ⓓ
27. Ⓐ Ⓑ Ⓒ Ⓓ
28. Ⓐ Ⓑ Ⓒ Ⓓ
29. Ⓐ Ⓑ Ⓒ Ⓓ
30. Ⓐ Ⓑ Ⓒ Ⓓ

31. Ⓐ Ⓑ Ⓒ Ⓓ
32. Ⓐ Ⓑ Ⓒ Ⓓ
33. Ⓐ Ⓑ Ⓒ Ⓓ
34. Ⓐ Ⓑ Ⓒ Ⓓ
35. Ⓐ Ⓑ Ⓒ Ⓓ
36. Ⓐ Ⓑ Ⓒ Ⓓ
37. Ⓐ Ⓑ Ⓒ Ⓓ
38. Ⓐ Ⓑ Ⓒ Ⓓ
39. Ⓐ Ⓑ Ⓒ Ⓓ
40. Ⓐ Ⓑ Ⓒ Ⓓ
41. Ⓐ Ⓑ Ⓒ Ⓓ
42. Ⓐ Ⓑ Ⓒ Ⓓ
43. Ⓐ Ⓑ Ⓒ Ⓓ
44. Ⓐ Ⓑ Ⓒ Ⓓ

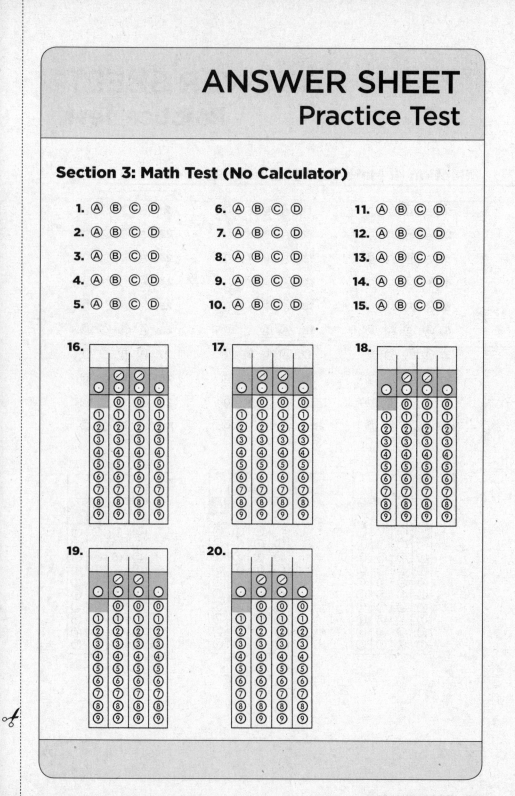

ANSWER SHEET
Practice Test

Section 3: Math Test (No Calculator)

1. Ⓐ Ⓑ Ⓒ Ⓓ
2. Ⓐ Ⓑ Ⓒ Ⓓ
3. Ⓐ Ⓑ Ⓒ Ⓓ
4. Ⓐ Ⓑ Ⓒ Ⓓ
5. Ⓐ Ⓑ Ⓒ Ⓓ

6. Ⓐ Ⓑ Ⓒ Ⓓ
7. Ⓐ Ⓑ Ⓒ Ⓓ
8. Ⓐ Ⓑ Ⓒ Ⓓ
9. Ⓐ Ⓑ Ⓒ Ⓓ
10. Ⓐ Ⓑ Ⓒ Ⓓ

11. Ⓐ Ⓑ Ⓒ Ⓓ
12. Ⓐ Ⓑ Ⓒ Ⓓ
13. Ⓐ Ⓑ Ⓒ Ⓓ
14. Ⓐ Ⓑ Ⓒ Ⓓ
15. Ⓐ Ⓑ Ⓒ Ⓓ

16.
17.
18.
19.
20.

ANSWER SHEET
Practice Test

Section 4: Math Test (Calculator)

1. Ⓐ Ⓑ Ⓒ Ⓓ   11. Ⓐ Ⓑ Ⓒ Ⓓ   21. Ⓐ Ⓑ Ⓒ Ⓓ

2. Ⓐ Ⓑ Ⓒ Ⓓ   12. Ⓐ Ⓑ Ⓒ Ⓓ   22. Ⓐ Ⓑ Ⓒ Ⓓ

3. Ⓐ Ⓑ Ⓒ Ⓓ   13. Ⓐ Ⓑ Ⓒ Ⓓ   23. Ⓐ Ⓑ Ⓒ Ⓓ

4. Ⓐ Ⓑ Ⓒ Ⓓ   14. Ⓐ Ⓑ Ⓒ Ⓓ   24. Ⓐ Ⓑ Ⓒ Ⓓ

5. Ⓐ Ⓑ Ⓒ Ⓓ   15. Ⓐ Ⓑ Ⓒ Ⓓ   25. Ⓐ Ⓑ Ⓒ Ⓓ

6. Ⓐ Ⓑ Ⓒ Ⓓ   16. Ⓐ Ⓑ Ⓒ Ⓓ   26. Ⓐ Ⓑ Ⓒ Ⓓ

7. Ⓐ Ⓑ Ⓒ Ⓓ   17. Ⓐ Ⓑ Ⓒ Ⓓ   27. Ⓐ Ⓑ Ⓒ Ⓓ

8. Ⓐ Ⓑ Ⓒ Ⓓ   18. Ⓐ Ⓑ Ⓒ Ⓓ   28. Ⓐ Ⓑ Ⓒ Ⓓ

9. Ⓐ Ⓑ Ⓒ Ⓓ   19. Ⓐ Ⓑ Ⓒ Ⓓ   29. Ⓐ Ⓑ Ⓒ Ⓓ

10. Ⓐ Ⓑ Ⓒ Ⓓ   20. Ⓐ Ⓑ Ⓒ Ⓓ   30. Ⓐ Ⓑ Ⓒ Ⓓ

31.   32.   33.

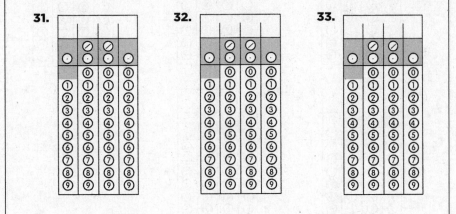

ANSWER SHEET
Practice Test

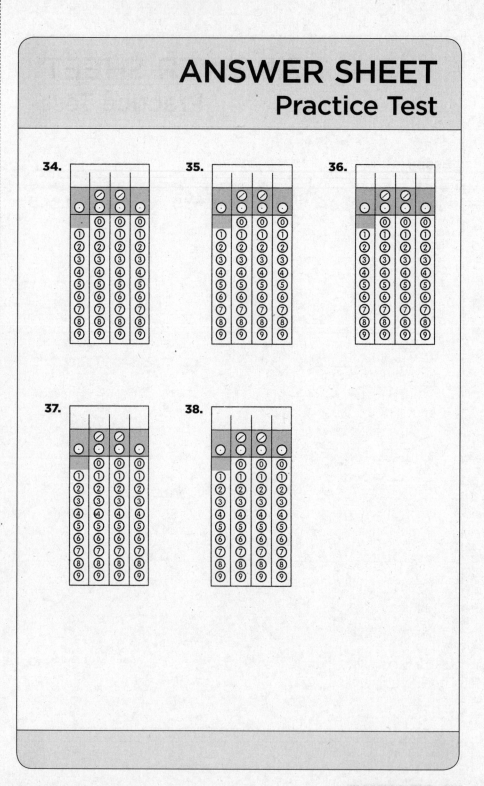

34.

35.

36.

37.

38.

ANSWER SHEET
Practice Test

Essay

ANSWER SHEET
Practice Test

START YOUR ESSAY HERE

ANSWER SHEET
Practice Test

ANSWER SHEET
Practice Test

ANSWER SHEET
Practice Test

READING TEST

65 MINUTES, 52 QUESTIONS

Turn to Section 1 of your answer sheet to answer the questions in this section.

> **Directions:** Each passage or pair of passages below is followed by questions. After reading each passage or pair of passages, choose the best answer to each question based on what you read or inferred in the passage or pair of passages and in any accompanying graphics (such as a table or a graph).

Questions 1–10 are based on the following passage.

This passage is from *Great Expectations* by Charles Dickens. At a lonely cemetery in the marsh country outside London, young Pip has a frightening encounter.

Ours was the marsh country, down by the river, within, as the
river wound, twenty miles of the sea. My first most vivid and broad
impression of the identity of things seems to me to have been gained
Line on a memorable raw afternoon towards evening. At such a time I
(5) found out for certain that this bleak place overgrown with nettles was
the churchyard; and that Philip Pirrip, late of this parish, and also
Georgiana wife of the above, were dead and buried; and that Alexander,
Bartholomew, Abraham, Tobias, and Roger, infant children of the
aforesaid, were also dead and buried; and that the dark flat wilderness
(10) beyond the churchyard, intersected with dikes and mounds and gates,
with scattered cattle feeding on it, was the marshes; and that the low
leaden line beyond was the river; and that the distant savage lair from
which the wind was rushing was the sea; and that the small bundle of
shivers growing afraid of it all and beginning to cry, was Pip.
(15)   "Hold your noise!" cried a terrible voice, as a man started up from
among the graves at the side of the church porch. "Keep still, you little
devil, or I'll cut your throat!"
A fearful man, all in coarse gray, with a great iron on his leg. A man
with no hat, and with broken shoes, and with an old rag tied round his
(20) head. A man who had been soaked in water, and smothered in mud,
and lamed by stones, and cut by flints, and stung by nettles, and torn by

briars; who limped, and shivered, and glared, and growled; and whose teeth chattered in his head as he seized me by the chin.

"Oh! Don't cut my throat, sir," I pleaded in terror. "Pray don't do it, sir."

(25) "Tell us your name!" said the man. "Quick!"

"Pip, sir."

"Once more," said the man, staring at me. "Give it mouth!"

"Pip. Pip, sir."

"Show us where you live," said the man. "Pint out the place!"

(30) I pointed to where our village lay, on the flat in-shore among the alder-trees and pollards, a mile or more from the church.

The man, after looking at me for a moment, turned me upside down, and emptied my pockets. There was nothing in them but a piece of bread. When the church came to itself,—for he was so sudden and strong

(35) that he made it go head over heels before me, and I saw the steeple under my feet,—when the church came to itself, I say, I was seated on a high tombstone, trembling while he ate the bread ravenously.

"You young dog," said the man, licking his lips, "what fat cheeks you ha' got."

(40) I believe they were fat, though I was at that time undersized for my years, and not strong.

"Darn me if I couldn't eat 'em," said the man, with a threatening shake of his head, "and if I han't half a mind to't!"

I earnestly expressed my hope that he wouldn't, and held tighter to

(45) the tombstone on which he had put me; partly, to keep myself upon it; partly, to keep myself from crying.

"Now lookee here!" said the man. "Where's your mother?"

"There, sir!" said I.

He started, made a short run, and stopped and looked over his

(50) shoulder.

"There, sir!" I timidly explained. "Also Georgiana. That's my mother."

"Oh!" said he, coming back. "And is that your father alonger your mother?"

"Yes, sir," said I; "him too; late of this parish."

(55) "Ha!" he muttered then, considering. "Who d'ye live with,—supposin' you're kindly let to live, which I han't made up my mind about?"

"My sister, sir,—Mrs. Joe Gargery,—wife of Joe Gargery, the blacksmith, sir."

"Blacksmith, eh?" said he. And looked down at his leg.

(60)　After darkly looking at his leg and me several times, he came closer to my tombstone, took me by both arms, and tilted me back as far as he could hold me; so that his eyes looked most powerfully down into mine, and mine looked most helplessly up into his.

"Now lookee here," he said, "the question being whether you're to be
(65)　let to live. You know what a file is?"

"Yes, sir."

"And you know what wittles is?"

"Yes, sir."

After each question he tilted me over a little more, so as to give me a
(70)　greater sense of helplessness and danger.

"You get me a file." He tilted me again. "And you get me wittles." He tilted me again. "You bring 'em both to me." He tilted me again. "Or I'll have your heart and liver out." He tilted me again.

1.　Over the course of the passage, the narrator's attitude shifts from

(A)　fear about the future to excitement about it.
(B)　doubt about a stranger to belief in him.
(C)　sadness about his family to fear for his safety.
(D)　uncertainty of his surroundings to appreciation of them.

2.　Which choice provides the best evidence for the answer to the previous question?

(A)　Lines 2–4 ("My . . . evening")
(B)　Lines 4–17 ("At . . . throat")
(C)　Lines 18–23 ("A . . . chin")
(D)　Lines 60–63 ("After . . . his")

3.　As used in line 3, "impression of the identity of things" means

(A)　opinion about the world.
(B)　idea about the future.
(C)　feeling about home.
(D)　strong memory.

4. The narrator indicates that Pip is

   (A) an orphan.
   (B) a temperamental boy.
   (C) hostile to the idea of strangers.
   (D) contemplating running away.

5. The phrase in lines 13–14 ("small bundle . . . Pip") mainly serves to

   (A) expose a side of the narrator that he prefers to keep secret.
   (B) demonstrate that the narrator does not think in a scientific manner.
   (C) show that the narrator is thinking back and picturing himself at a place in the past.
   (D) emphasize how long ago this scene took place.

6. The passage implies that the stranger is

   (A) a runaway convict.
   (B) an enemy soldier.
   (C) a poor farmer.
   (D) a circus strongman.

7. What choice provides the best evidence for the answer to the previous question?

   (A) Lines 15–17 ("Hold . . . throat")
   (B) Lines 18–20 ("A . . . head")
   (C) Lines 32–33 ("The . . . bread")
   (D) Lines 34–37 ("When . . . ravenously")

8. In line 12, "lair" means

   (A) cave.
   (B) tunnel.
   (C) place of origin.
   (D) hole in the ground.

9. As presented in the passage, the stranger is described as

   (A) outwardly imposing but inwardly scared.
   (B) naturally generous but frequently imprudent.
   (C) socially awkward but frequently sensible.
   (D) superficially kind but actually selfish.

10. Which choice provides the best evidence for the answer to the previous question?

   (A) Lines 18–20 ("A . . . head")
   (B) Lines 20–23 ("A . . . chin")
   (C) Lines 32–37 ("The . . . ravenously")
   (D) Lines 42–50 ("Darn . . . shoulder")

Questions 11–21 are based on the following passage.

The passage is adapted from *Progress and Poverty* by Henry George. Originally published in 1879.

We have by inference already obtained the law of wages. But to verify the deduction and to strip the subject of all ambiguities, let us seek the law from an independent starting point.

Line   There is, of course, no such thing as a common rate of wages, in the
(5) sense that there is at any given time and place a common rate of interest. Wages, which include all returns received from labor, not only vary with the differing powers of individuals, but, as the organization of society becomes elaborate, very largely as between occupations. Nevertheless, there is a certain general relation between all wages, so that we express
(10) a clear and well-understood idea when we say that wages are higher or lower in one time or place than in another. In their degrees, wages rise and fall in obedience to a common law. What is this law?

The fundamental principle of human action—the law that is to political economy what the law of gravitation is to physics—is that men seek
(15) to gratify their desires with the least exertion. Evidently, this principle must bring to an equality, through the competition it induces, the reward gained by equal exertions under similar circumstances. When men work

for themselves, this equalization will be largely affected by the equation of prices; and between in conditions of freedom, will be the terms
(20) at which one man can hire others to work for him? Evidently, they will
be fixed by what the men could make if laboring for themselves. The
principle which will prevent him from having to give anything above
this, except what is necessary to induce the change, will also prevent
them from taking less. Did they demand more, the competition of others
(25) would prevent them from getting employment. Did he offer less, none
would accept the terms, as they could obtain greater results by working
for themselves. Thus, although the employer wishes to pay as little as
possible, and the employee to receive as much as possible, wages will be
fixed by the value or produce of such labor to the laborers themselves. If
(30) wages are temporarily carried either above or below this line, a tendency
to carry them back at once arises.

But the result, or the earnings of labor, as is readily seen in those
primary and fundamental occupations in which labor first engages,
and which, even in the most highly developed condition of society, still
(35) form the base of production, does not depend merely upon the intensity
or quality of the labor itself. Wealth is the product of two factors, land
and labor, and what a given amount of labor will yield will vary with the
powers of the natural opportunities to which it is applied. This being the
case, the principle that men seek to gratify their desires with the least
(40) exertion, will fix wages at the produce of such labor at the point of highest natural productiveness open to it. Now, by virtue of the same principle, the highest point of natural productiveness open to labor under
existing conditions will be the lowest point at which production continues, for men, impelled by a supreme law of the human mind to seek the
(45) satisfaction of their desires with the least exertion, will not expend labor
at a lower point of productiveness while a higher is open to them. Thus
the wages which an employer must pay will be measured by the lowest
point of natural productiveness to which production extends, and wages
will rise or fall as this point rises or falls.
(50)   To illustrate: In a simple state of society, each man, as is the primitive
mode, works for himself—some in hunting, let us say, some in fishing,
some in cultivating the ground. Cultivation, we will suppose, has just
begun, and the land in use is all of the same quality, yielding a similar

return to similar exertions. Wages, therefore—for, though there is neither
(55) employer nor employed, there are yet wages— will be the full produce
of labor, and, making allowance for the difference of agreeableness, risk,
etc., in the three pursuits, they will be on the average equal in each—
that is to say, equal exertions will yield equal results. Now, if one of their
number wishes to employ some of his fellows to work for him instead of
(60) for themselves, he must pay wages fixed by this full, average produce of
labor.

11. Which choice summarizes the second paragraph of the passage
     (lines 4–12)?

     (A) The common rate of interest is roughly comparable to the common
         rate of wages.
     (B) The common rate of wages can be deduced by studying the
         common rate of interest.
     (C) Wages are different for different people and occupations, but there is
         no real reason this is so.
     (D) Wages differ by place and occupation, but they all must follow a
         guiding law.

12. Which choice does the author cite as the reason people work?

     (A) To leave the world a better place for their children
     (B) To obtain food, shelter, and water
     (C) To fulfill their wants with the least work
     (D) To strive to acquire enough capital so that they can have others work
         for them

13. In line 26, "results" is closest in meaning to

     (A) consequence.
     (B) payment.
     (C) final score.
     (D) solution.

14. According to the passage, which choice describes best how equality of wages is determined between employer and employees?

(A) The employer must always pay the wages that the employees demand.
(B) People will not work for a lower wage while a higher wage for the same work is open to them.
(C) The employees are fortunate if their employer pays a fair wage.
(D) If the employees work hard, they will be rewarded by their employers with higher pay.

15. Which choice provides the best evidence for the answer to the previous question?

(A) Lines 32–36 ("But . . . itself")
(B) Lines 36–38 ("Wealth . . . applied")
(C) Lines 38–46 ("This . . . them")
(D) Lines 50–52 ("To . . . ground")

16. The passage implies that society has progressed because

(A) people study economic problems and benefits.
(B) there are laws governing wages.
(C) people now work for others and not only for themselves.
(D) people can find work in different sectors of society.

17. Which choice provides the best evidence for the answer to the previous question?

(A) Lines 17–20 (When . . . him?")
(B) Lines 36–41 ("Wealth . . . it")
(C) Lines 50–52 ("To . . . ground")
(D) Lines 58–61 ("Now . . . labor")

18. As used in line 36, "product" is closest in meaning to

    (A) outcome.
    (B) artifact.
    (C) multiplied quantity.
    (D) substance.

19. The author most likely uses the illustration of a simple state of society in the last paragraph (lines 50–61) to highlight the

    (A) regularity of modern times versus the uncertainty of primitive times.
    (B) contrast of work in those times to the complexity of the law of modern wages.
    (C) anxiety people had in primitive times about their wages.
    (D) similarities of modern wages to the wages of more primitive times.

20. The author would likely attribute higher wages than average for one company to

    (A) a temporary cause that will soon be corrected back to normal.
    (B) an inability to understand the value of the labor in that company.
    (C) a company trying to quickly expand.
    (D) an increasingly complex society.

21. The main idea of the final paragraph is that

    (A) human history has always involved labor and wages, even in primitive times.
    (B) people work for someone else only when not hunting or fishing.
    (C) people do not want to work for others but are often forced to.
    (D) when people work for someone else, they must make more than if they were working for themselves.

Questions 22–31 are based on the following passage.

This passage is adapted from "Earthquakes" from the National Park Service. *https://www.nps.gov/yell/learn/nature/earthquakes.htm*

Yellowstone is one of the most seismically active areas in the United States. Approximately 1,000 to 3,000 earthquakes occur each year in the Yellowstone area; most are not felt. They result from the enormous
Line number of faults associated with the volcano.
(5)   Earthquakes occur along fractures in the crust where stress from crustal plate movement and volcanic activity build to a significant level. The rock along these faults becomes so strained that eventually it slips or breaks. Energy is then released as shock waves (seismic waves) that reverberate throughout the surrounding rock. Once a seismic wave
(10) reaches the surface of the Earth, it may be felt. Surface waves affect the ground, which can roll, crack open, or be vertically and/or laterally displaced. Structures are susceptible to earthquake damage because the ground motion is dominantly horizontal.

In Yellowstone, earthquakes help to maintain hydrothermal activity by
(15) keeping the "plumbing" system open. Without periodic disturbance of relatively small earthquakes, the small fractures and conduits that supply hot water to geysers and hot springs might be sealed by mineral deposition. Some earthquakes generate changes in Yellowstone's hydrothermal systems. For example, the 1959 Hebgen Lake and 1983 Borah Peak
(20) earthquakes of magnitude 7.3 and 6.9, respectively, caused measurable changes in Old Faithful Geyser and other hydrothermal features.

Yellowstone commonly experiences "earthquake swarms"—a series of earthquakes over a short period of time in a localized area. The largest swarm occurred in 1985, with more than 3,000 earthquakes recorded
(25) during three months on the northwest side of the park. Hundreds of quakes were recorded during swarms in 2009 (near Lake Village) and 2010 (between Old Faithful area and West Yellowstone). Scientists interpret these swarms as due to shifting and changing pressures in the Earth's crust that are caused by migration of hydrothermal fluids, a
(30) natural occurrence of volcanoes.

Earthquakes help us to map and to understand the sub-surface geology around and beneath Yellowstone. The energy from earthquakes

travels through hard and molten rock at different rates. Scientists can "see" the subsurface and make images of the magma chamber and the
(35) caldera by "reading" the seismic waves emitted during earthquakes. An extensive geological monitoring system is in place to aid in that interpretation.

On March 30, 2014 at 6:34 am Mountain Daylight Time, an earthquake of magnitude 4.8 occurred four miles north-northeast of Norris Geyser
(40) Basin. The M4.8 earthquake was reportedly felt in Yellowstone National Park, in the towns of Gardiner and West Yellowstone, Montana and throughout the region. This is the largest earthquake at Yellowstone since the early 1980s and was part of a notable GPS-determined uplift episode of 3 cm at Norris that built up in the 4 months prior to the quake. The
(45) area returned to subsidence in the following 4 months. Analysis of the earthquake indicated a tectonic origin and was part of a sequence of earthquake swarms located north and northwest of Norris that began in Sept. 2013. Notably, the M4.8 event occurred at the same time that the Yellowstone caldera began to experience increased uplift rates up to
(50) +6 cm/yr, among the highest of the Yellowstone caldera uplift in modern history.

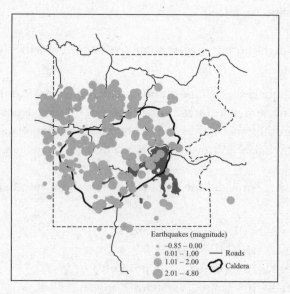

Approximately 2,000 earthquakes occurred in Yellowstone in 2014.
Gray dots = earthquakes.

22. The primary purpose of the passage is to

  (A) present the background of earthquakes and their importance in the Yellowstone area.
  (B) evaluate the research that led to a scientific breakthrough.
  (C) summarize the findings of a long-term research project on earthquakes.
  (D) explain the development of a branch of scientific study.

23. The author's attitude toward earthquakes is best described as

  (A) apprehension.
  (B) ambivalence.
  (C) appreciation.
  (D) astonishment.

24. As used in line 7, "faults" means

  (A) flaw.
  (B) criticism.
  (C) break.
  (D) liability.

25. What does the author suggest about hydrothermal activity and earthquakes?

  (A) Earthquakes lessen the number of hydrothermal features in an area.
  (B) Hydrothermal features can be closed by mineral deposits over time.
  (C) Hydrothermal features and earthquakes have no relationship.
  (D) Earthquakes destroy hydrothermal features in an area.

26. Which choice provides the best evidence for the answer to the previous question?

  (A) Lines 9–13 ("Once . . . horizontal")
  (B) Lines 14–15 ("In . . . open")
  (C) Lines 15–18 ("Without . . . deposition")
  (D) Lines 18–19 ("Some . . . systems")

27. According to the passage, which of the following is true of earthquake swarms?

    (A) Swarms are caused by the movement of hydrothermal fluids below ground.
    (B) Swarms happen over a long period of time.
    (C) Human-made activity has worsened swarms in recent years.
    (D) A swarm can occur over a wide area.

28. Which choice provides the best evidence for the answer to the previous question?

    (A) Lines 15–18 ("Without . . . deposition")
    (B) Lines 25–27 ("Hundreds . . . Yellowstone")
    (C) Lines 27–30 ("Scientists . . . volcanoes")
    (D) Lines 31–33 ("Earthquakes . . . rates")

29. The primary purpose of the final paragraph of the passage (lines 38–51) is to

    (A) illustrate an abstract concept with a concrete occurrence.
    (B) provide an instance of a significant recent earthquake.
    (C) describe how the Yellowstone area was affected by an earthquake.
    (D) clarify a misconception about earthquakes in the Yellowstone area.

30. According to the figure, earthquakes in Yellowstone are

    (A) only near roads that go through the park.
    (B) more concentrated in the caldera than anywhere else.
    (C) only solitary events that do not occur near one another.
    (D) mainly bunched in earthquake swarms.

31. Data in the figure provide most direct support for which idea in the passage?

    (A) Earthquakes are becoming more common in Yellowstone.
    (B) Earthquakes keep hydrothermal features open.
    (C) More than 3,000 earthquakes occurred in 1985.
    (D) Earthquake swarms are likely in the Yellowstone area.

Questions 32–42 are based on the following passages.

Passage 1 is adapted from *The New York Times*, "The Little Horn Massacre: Details of the Battle" from July 7, 1876. Passage 2 is adapted from Chief Two Moon told to Hamlin Garland, "General Custer's Last Fight as Told by Two Moon." From *McClure's* magazine, September 1898.

Passage 1

Gen. Custer left the Rosebud on June 22, with twelve companies of the Seventh Cavalry, striking a trail where Reno left it, leading in the direction of the Little Horn . . . . On the morning of the 25th an Indian
Line village, twenty miles above the mouth of the Little Horn was reported
(5) about three miles long and half a mile wide and fifteen miles away . . . . When near the village it was discovered that the Indians were moving in hot haste as if retreating. Reno, with seven companies of the Seventh Cavalry, was ordered to the left to attack the village at its head, while Custer, with five companies, went to the right and commenced a
(10) vigorous attack. Reno felt of them with three companies of cavalry, and was almost instantly surrounded . . . .

The day wore on. Reno had lost in killed and wounded a large portion of his command, forty odd having been killed before the bluff was reached, many of them in hand to hand conflict with the Indians, who
(15) outnumbered them ten to one, and his men had been without water for thirty-six hours. The suffering was heartrending. In this state of affairs they determined to reach the water at all hazards, and Col. Benton made a sally with his company, and routed the main body of the Indians who were guarding the approach to the river. The Indian sharpshooters were
(20) nearly opposite the mouth of the ravine through which the brave boys approached the river, but the attempt was made, and though one man was killed and seven wounded the water was gained and the command relieved. When the fighting ceased for the night Reno further prepared for attacks.
(25) There had been forty-eight hours' fighting, with no word from Custer. Twenty-four hours more of fighting and the suspense ended, when the Indians abandoned their village in great haste and confusion. Reno knew then that succor was near at hand . . . . Soon an officer came rushing into camp and related that he had found Custer, dead, stripped naked,

(30) but not mutilated, and near him . . . 190 men and scouts. Custer went into battle with Companies C, L, I, F, and E, of the Seventh Cavalry, and the staff and non-commissioned staff of his regiment and a number of scouts, and only one Crow scout remained to tell the tale. All are dead. Custer was surrounded on every side by Indians, and horses fell as they

(35) fought on skirmish line or in line of battle. Custer was among the last who fell, but when his cheering voice was no longer heard, the Indians made easy work of the remainder. The bodies of all save the newspaper correspondent were stripped, and most of them were horribly mutilated. Custer's was not mutilated. He was shot through the body and through

(40) the head. The troops cared for the wounded and buried the dead, and returned to their base for supplies and instructions from the General of the Army.

Passage 2

While I was sitting on my horse I saw flags come up over the hill to the east. Then the soldiers rose all at once, all on horses . . . . They formed

(45) into three bunches with a little ways between. Then a bugle sounded, and they all got off horses, and some soldiers led the horses back over the hill.

Then the Sioux rode up the ridge on all sides, riding very fast. The Cheyennes went up the left way. Then the shooting was quick, quick.

(50) Pop-pop-pop very fast. Some of the soldiers were down on their knees, some standing. Officers all in front. The smoke was like a great cloud, and everywhere the Sioux went the dust rose like smoke. We circled all round him—swirling like water round a stone. We shoot, we ride fast, we shoot again. Soldiers drop, and horses fall on them. Soldiers in line drop,

(55) but one man rides up and down the line—all the time shouting. He rode a sorrel horse with white face and white fore-legs. I don't know who he was. He was a brave man.

Indians kept swirling round and round, and the soldiers killed only a few. Many soldiers fell. At last all horses killed but five. Once in a while

(60) some man would break out and run toward the river, but he would fall. At last about a hundred men and five horsemen stood on the hill all bunched together. All along the bugler kept blowing his commands. He was very brave too. Then a chief was killed. I hear it was Long Hair

[George Armstrong Custer], I don't know; and then the five horsemen
(65) and the bunch of men, maybe so forty, started toward the river. The man
on the sorrel horse led them, shouting all the time. He wore a buckskin
shirt, and had long black hair and mustache. He fought hard with a big
knife. His men were all covered with white dust. I couldn't tell whether
they were officers or not. One man all alone ran far down toward the
(70) river, then round up over the hill. I thought he was going to escape, but a
Sioux fired and hit him in the head . . . .

All the soldiers were now killed, and the bodies were stripped. After
that no one could tell which were officers. The bodies were left where
they fell. We had no dance that night. We were sorrowful.

32. The author of Passage 1 indicates which of the following about the
battle?

(A) The soldiers studied the encampment carefully before executing
their attack.
(B) The Native Americans appeared to be falling back before the battle
started.
(C) The soldiers had expected to find such a large encampment when
they arrived.
(D) The Native Americans attacked before the soldiers could meet with
the leaders to negotiate.

33. Which choice provides the best evidence for the answer to the previous
question?

(A) Lines 1–5 ("Gen. Custer . . . away")
(B) Lines 6–11 ("When . . . surrounded")
(C) Lines 12–16 ("The . . . hours")
(D) Lines 19–24 ("The . . . attacks")

34. The author of Passage 1 indicates that the soldiers

(A) suffered horribly but fought bravely.
(B) could have won the battle but were tricked by their enemy.
(C) suffered fewer causalities than the Native Americans.
(D) were well-supplied but were simply outnumbered.

35. As used in line 18, "company" means

    (A) business.
    (B) concern.
    (C) unit.
    (D) companion.

36. According to the author of Passage 2, the battle

    (A) went badly from the start for the soldiers, but they fought courageously.
    (B) was difficult for both sides.
    (C) caused all the soldiers to break formation and run away.
    (D) was a surprise attack that at first went well for the soldiers.

37. Which choice provides the best evidence for the answer to the previous question?

    (A) Lines 44–47 ("They . . . hill")
    (B) Lines 48–49 ("Then . . . way")
    (C) Lines 52–57 ("We . . . man")
    (D) Lines 58–60 ("Indians . . . fall")

38. The author of Passage 2 implies that the Native Americans were

    (A) different tribes banded together to fight.
    (B) luring the soldiers into a trap from the outset.
    (C) vastly superior warriors to the soldiers.
    (D) not well equipped for battle but made up for it with bravery.

39. Which choice best describes how the author of Passage 2 would most likely have reacted to the remarks about the bodies being stripped in Passage 1?

    (A) With approval, because that did indeed happen as it was reported
    (B) With resignation, because after the battle, the Native Americans became vengeful
    (C) With skepticism, because only General Custer's body was stripped
    (D) With disapproval, because although the bodies were stripped, the Native Americans did not celebrate over the dead

40. Which best describes the overall relationship between Passage 1 and Passage 2?

    (A) Passage 2 strongly challenges the point of view in Passage 1.
    (B) Passage 2 provides an alternate version of the events described in Passage 1.
    (C) Passage 2 elaborates on conclusions presented in Passage 1.
    (D) Passage 2 restates in different terms the events presented in Passage 1.

41. The authors of both passages would most likely agree with which of the following statements about the Battle of Little Bighorn?

    (A) The Native Americans had a distinct advantage of having more horses than did the soldiers.
    (B) The soldiers fought bravely, while the Native Americans used trickery to defeat them.
    (C) Both sides were solemn at the end of the battle for those killed.
    (D) The battle quickly became a rout, and all of the dead soldiers were mutilated.

42. The main purpose of each passage is to

    (A) present a view of an historical event.
    (B) report on the problem of military tactics in the West.
    (C) take a position on Native-American rights in the West.
    (D) make an argument about whose viewpoint of a battle is correct.

Questions 43–52 are based on the following material.
The passage is adapted from *Energy.gov*, "Enhanced Oil Recovery."
http://energy.gov/fe/science-innovation/oil-gas-research/enhanced-oil-recovery

Crude oil development and production in U.S. oil reservoirs can
include up to three distinct phases: primary, secondary, and tertiary (or
enhanced) recovery. During primary recovery, the natural pressure of the
Line reservoir or gravity drive oil into the wellbore, combined with artificial
(5) lift techniques (such as pumps) which bring the oil to the surface. But
only about 10 percent of a reservoir's original oil in place is typically produced during primary recovery. Secondary recovery techniques extend
a field's productive life generally by injecting water or gas to displace oil
and drive it to a production wellbore, resulting in the recovery of 20 to 40
(10) percent of the original oil in place.

However, with much of the easy-to-produce oil already recovered
from U.S. oil fields, producers have attempted several tertiary, or
enhanced oil recovery (EOR), techniques that offer prospects for ultimately producing 30 to 60 percent, or more, of the reservoir's original oil
(15) in place. Three major categories of EOR have been found to be commer-
cially successful to varying degrees:

Thermal recovery, which involves the introduction of heat such as
the injection of steam to lower the viscosity, or thin, the heavy viscous
oil, and improve its ability to flow through the reservoir. Thermal tech-
(20) niques account for over 40 percent of U.S. EOR production, primarily in
California.

Gas injection, which uses gases such as natural gas, nitrogen, or
carbon dioxide (CO_2) that expand in a reservoir to push additional oil to
a production wellbore, or other gases that dissolve in the oil to lower its
(25) viscosity and improves its flow rate. Gas injection accounts for nearly 60
percent of EOR production in the United States.

Chemical injection, which can involve the use of long-chained
molecules called polymers to increase the effectiveness of waterfloods,
or the use of detergent-like surfactants to help lower the surface tension
(30) that often prevents oil droplets from moving through a reservoir.
Chemical techniques account for about one percent of U.S. EOR
production.

Each of these techniques has been hampered by its relatively high cost and, in some cases, by the unpredictability of its effectiveness.

(35) In the U.S., there are about 114 active commercial CO_2 injection projects that together inject over 2 billion cubic feet of CO_2 and produce over 280,000 BOPD (April 19, 2010, Oil and Gas Journal).

CO_2 Injection Offers Considerable Potential Benefits

The EOR technique that is attracting the most new market interest is CO_2-EOR. First tried in 1972 in Scurry County, Texas, CO_2 injection
(40) has been used successfully throughout the Permian Basin of West Texas and eastern New Mexico, and is now being pursued to a limited extent in Kansas, Mississippi, Wyoming, Oklahoma, Colorado, Utah, Montana, Alaska, and Pennsylvania.

Until recently, most of the CO_2 used for EOR has come from naturally-
(45) occurring reservoirs. But new technologies are being developed to produce CO_2 from industrial applications such as natural gas processing, fertilizer, ethanol, and hydrogen plants in locations where naturally occurring reservoirs are not available. One demonstration at the Dakota Gasification Company's plant in Beulah, North Dakota is producing
(50) CO_2 and delivering it by a 204-mile pipeline to the Weyburn oil field in Saskatchewan, Canada. Encana, the field's operator, is injecting the CO_2 to extend the field's productive life, hoping to add another 25 years and as much as 130 million barrels of oil that might otherwise have been abandoned.

Average Oil Recovery by Type

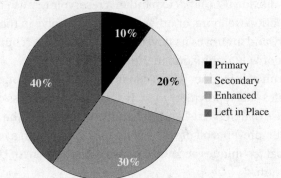

Primary 10%
Secondary 20%
Enhanced 30%
Left in Place 40%

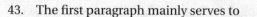

43. The first paragraph mainly serves to

   (A) explain how a scientific process works and to define its terms.
   (B) note a common misconception about production method.
   (C) describe two stages of a production process to introduce a third.
   (D) present a recent study and summarize its findings.

44. As used in line 52, "productive" means

   (A) creative.
   (B) expressive.
   (C) inventive.
   (D) fertile.

45. Over the course of the passage, the focus shifts from

   (A) a criticism of a scientific model to a new theory.
   (B) the use of EOR in oil fields to a new method used in natural gas fields.
   (C) an introduction of EOR to the drawbacks of using it.
   (D) an overview of EOR to a focus on one kind of EOR.

46. According to the passage, enhanced oil recovery most likely can extract up to

   (A) an additional 20 percent of a reservoir's oil.
   (B) an additional 40 percent of a reservoir's oil.
   (C) an additional 50 percent of a reservoir's oil.
   (D) an additional 60 percent of a reservoir's oil.

47. Which choice provides the best evidence for the answer to the previous question?

   (A) Lines 3–5 ("During . . . surface")
   (B) Lines 7–15 ("Secondary . . . place")
   (C) Lines 17–21 ("Thermal . . . California")
   (D) Lines 22–26 ("Gas . . . States")

48. The author implies that among the oil-producing states, the least likely state to use CO_2 injection is

    (A) Alaska.
    (B) Oklahoma.
    (C) Texas.
    (D) California.

49. Which choice provides the best evidence for the answer to the previous question?

    (A) Lines 17–26 ("Thermal . . . States")
    (B) Lines 35–37 ("In . . . Journal)"
    (C) Lines 38–43 ("The . . . Pennsylvania")
    (D) Lines 48–51 ("One . . . Canada")

50. Which concept is supported by the passage and by the information in the chart?

    (A) CO_2 injection is the most promising of all types of EOR.
    (B) Even with EOR, large amounts of oil remain in the ground.
    (C) The United States leads the world in enhanced oil recovery techniques.
    (D) Almost 40% of EOR production occurs in California.

51. How does the graph support the author's point that EOR is important to U.S. oil production?

    (A) It illustrates that the oil fields must use CO_2-EOR to be financially successful.
    (B) It reveals that the primary recovery phase is the most important in the production of an oil well.
    (C) It demonstrates that when primary and secondary recovery techniques have been exhausted, most of the oil is still in the reservoir.
    (D) It shows that all the primary and secondary techniques combined far exceed the potential recovery of EOR.

52. Do the data in the chart provide support for the claim that CO_2 injection offers considerable potential benefits?

(A) Yes, because the data provide evidence that CO_2 injection is the most effective type of EOR.

(B) Yes, because the percentage of oil recovery by type is highest for EOR and CO_2 injection has the most potential benefits.

(C) No, because the data do not provide specific evidence about CO_2 injection as having potential benefits.

(D) No, because the data do not indicate whether EOR is an effective type of oil recovery.

If there is still time remaining, you may review your answers.

WRITING AND LANGUAGE TEST

35 MINUTES, 44 QUESTIONS

Turn to Section 2 of your answer sheet to answer the questions in this section.

> **Directions:** Each passage below is accompanied by questions. For some of those questions, you will revise the passage to improve the expression of ideas. For other questions, you will correct the passage for errors in sentence structure, usage, or punctuation. A passage or a question may be accompanied by one or more graphics (such as a table or graph) that you will use as you revise and edit.
>
> Some questions will be from an underlined portion of a passage. Other questions will take you to a location in a passage, while others will ask you to think about the passage as a whole.
>
> After reading each passage, choose the best answer to each question. The answers will most effectively improve the quality of the writing in the passage or will make the passage comply with the conventions of standard written English. Many of the questions include a "NO CHANGE" option that you will choose if you think the best choice is to leave that portion of the passage the way it is.

Questions 1–11 are based on the following passage.

Teaching Is Changing in a Changing World

The only sure thing about the future of teaching is that it has experienced rapid ❶ changings and will eventually look little like the traditional classroom that has been the foundation of American education for centuries. ❷ However, as techniques and technology changes, education is changing with it, and the role of the teacher is changing, too.

Some things that were traditionally taught for decades, like spelling, ❸ has been de-emphasized

1. (A) NO CHANGE
   (B) changes
   (C) changed
   (D) charged

2. (A) NO CHANGE
   (B) Indeed
   (C) Nevertheless
   (D) Previously

3. (A) NO CHANGE
   (B) which has
   (C) which have
   (D) have

with the advent of computing and
the Internet. Rote memorization
is increasingly viewed as less and
less important in a world where
information is always at the ready.
That is not to say that students should
not be taught how to spell; students
should have an understanding of basic
spelling rules and math tables ❹. But
taking those concepts and ❺ things
to memorize to extremes while
students will always be able to access
the information has been brought into
question.

So what will it be like to be a
teacher in a decade or two? There
are intriguing possibilities. One is
that the teacher becomes more like a
personal trainer, working on students'
weaknesses. With technology, a
teacher can find a student's strengths
and weaknesses and ❻ concentrate
on the weaknesses only instead of

4. At this point, the writer is considering adding the following
information.

—basic addition, subtraction,
multiplication, and division
tables

Should the writer add this here?

(A) Yes, because it provides
specific examples of the
materials discussed in this
sentence.
(B) Yes, because it illustrates
the reason for the de-
emphasis mentioned
earlier.
(C) No, because it interrupts
the flow of the sentence by
supplying irrelevant and
repetitive information.
(D) No, because it weakens the
focus of the passage by discussing mathematics rather
than education.

5. (A) NO CHANGE
(B) things to be memorized by
them
(C) things for their memorizing
(D) memorization

6. (A) NO CHANGE
(B) will concentrate
(C) to concentrate
(D) can concentrate

spending time, as a traditional teacher would, covering a concept with an entire class at once. ❼ Even with technology to assist the teacher and students. This role might prove difficult as a teacher would have to create paths for learning for every student instead of the traditional one lesson per class.

Another view is more of a hybrid between the traditional classroom teacher and the individual teacher-as-personal coach role. In this concept, instead of lecturing the class about a concept on one day and then

7. Which choice best combines the underlined sentences?

(A) Even with technology to assist the teacher and students; this role might prove difficult as a teacher would have to create paths for learning for every student instead of the traditional one lesson per class.

(B) Even with technology to assist the teacher and students, this role might prove difficult as a teacher would have to create paths for learning for every student instead of the traditional one lesson per class.

(C) Technology will assist the teacher and students, however, this role might prove difficult as a teacher would have to create paths for learning for every student instead of the traditional one lesson per class.

(D) Even though the teachers and students have technology to assist them, this role, in fact, could be found to be difficult if a teacher would have to create paths for learning for every student, and not just one path of learning for one class.

discussing it the next, ❽ but the teacher might assign students a video of the lecture, and then the teacher would lead the discussion of it the following day. This would enable the teacher to cover more material than the traditional classroom teacher. Students would also spend more time interacting with their fellow students and teachers in this hybrid role rather than in the personalized approach to education.

There are other possibilities, of course, such as a teacher as a personalized coach for one unit and a traditional classroom teacher for the next unit. ❾ But some teachers are already changing, for example, some teachers never see their students in person. Instead, they conduct all their teaching ❿ on the Internet on computers.

8. (A) NO CHANGE
   (B) and
   (C) for
   (D) DELETE the underlined portion.

9. Which choice sets up the clarification given at the end of the sentence most effectively?

   (A) NO CHANGE
   (B) In the future and right now, there will be changes;
   (C) Still other possibilities are already here:
   (D) When it comes to changes in education, some have arrived already; for example,

10. (A) NO CHANGE
    (B) online.
    (C) on Internet-enabled devices to access each other.
    (D) over the Internet.

As new technologies develop, education will develop with them. ⓫ <u>Although their roles have changed, teachers will continue to be employed for years to come.</u> It will be an exciting time to be a teacher in the coming decades.

11. Which choice ends the passage with a restatement of the writer's primary claim most clearly?

(A) NO CHANGE

(B) Like students, teachers have been around for a long time, but they will not be the same in the future.

(C) And as education changes, the profession of teaching will change with it.

(D) As long as teachers keep up with their training, those teachers who are cut from schools can find other means of employment.

Questions 12–22 are based on the following passage.

The Dutch and Their Influence in America

- 1 -

When students study American history, the emphasis on the colonization of what would become the United States is on the English. **12** For instance, focusing so much on this **13** one group, discredits another country's settlers. The Dutch explored and colonized the Mid-Atlantic region of North **14** America, and they're settlements in New York changed our country and our language.

- 2 -

Just eight years after the English settled at Jamestown, the Dutch established Fort Nassau on Cattle Island in what is now New York. In 1626, Dutch leader Peter Minuit purchased Manhattan Island and established New Amsterdam. Even

12. (A) NO CHANGE
    (B) However,
    (C) On one hand,
    (D) Similarly,

13. (A) NO CHANGE
    (B) one group, discredits another countrys' settlers.
    (C) one group discredits another countrys' settlers.
    (D) one group discredits another country's settlers.

14. (A) NO CHANGE
    (B) America; and their
    (C) America, and their
    (D) America: and there

though the English took over and changed its name to New York in 1664, the Dutch settlers forever changed the language of Americans. **15**

- 3 -

Our common place names have Dutch influences. Even though the colony became New York, the name *Brooklyn*, Dutch for "broken land" because of all the creeks in the area, stayed. *Coney Island* is from the Dutch *Konijn Eiland,* which means "Rabbit Island." But an even bigger name refers all the way back to the original Dutch fort on lower Manhattan Island. The fort and settlement was on the lower tip of the **16** island, a wall was built across the island to protect the settlement from attack from the north. The street that ran along that wall, of course, was and still is *Wall Street*. From its humble origin from a crude wooden wall, the term has been elevated far beyond that, now meaning the world's center of trade and commerce.

15. At this point, the writer is considering adding the following sentence.

The Dutch did continue to colonize the Caribbean, South America, Africa, Asia, and Indonesia.

Should the writer add this here?

(A) Yes, because it provides historical context for the end of the Dutch colonization of North America.

(B) Yes, because it explains why the Dutch were so quick to withdraw from New York.

(C) No, because it goes off topic from the paragraph's message that the Dutch left but their legacy lives on.

D) No, because it implies that the Dutch left because they had other motivations to leave.

16. (A) NO CHANGE
    (B) island and a wall
    (C) island, and a wall
    (D) island and

- 4 -

Other Dutch words replaced inferior English words and have made the language more specific. For example, in English there are savory biscuits and sweet biscuits, but the Dutch had a better term for a sweet biscuit: the *cookie*. **17** A *wagon* is from the Dutch word for cart, *waghen*. But perhaps the biggest word from the Dutch is a word that is now used for New Yorkers and Americans in general. *Yankee* is from *Jan* **18** *Kees*. This was a term that was

17. Which choice gives a second supporting example that is most like the example in the previous sentence?

   (A) NO CHANGE
   (B) *Coleslaw* is from the Dutch word *koolsla*, meaning cabbage salad.
   (C) A ghostly image in Dutch, and now English, is a *spook*.
   (D) *Knapsack* is from the Dutch word *knapzak*, literally a snack bag.

18. Which choice combines the sentences at the underlined portion most effectively?

   (A) *Kees*; a term
   (B) *Kees*, a term
   (C) *Kees*, but the term
   (D) *Kees*, whereas the term

used to mockingly describe first Dutch settlers and then English settlers in New York. In time the term came to mean people from New York, and one of the city's baseball teams even taken the once derogatory term as its name.

19. Which choice matches the stylistic pattern established earlier in the sentence most closely?
    (A) NO CHANGE
    (B) and then settlers from England who moved to New York.
    (C) and then the English settlers in New York were called that, too.
    (D) and then after that English settlers in New York.

20. (A) NO CHANGE
    (B) citys baseball teams even took
    (C) city's baseball teams even take
    (D) city's baseball teams even took

- 5 -

㉑ Even though the English overtook their colonies, the Dutch's strong influence was on one of America's biggest cities and on the English language, and their contributions to the country should not be overlooked in history class.

21. (A) NO CHANGE
    (B) Even though their colonies were ultimately overtaken by the English, one of America's biggest cities and the language had a strong Dutch influence
    (C) Though their colonies, ultimately overtaken by the English, the Dutch had a strong influence on one of America's biggest cities and on the English language
    (D) Even though their colonies were ultimately overtaken by the English, the Dutch had a strong influence on one of America's biggest cities and on the English language

Think about the passage as a whole as you answer question 22.

22. To make the passage most logical, paragraph 2 should be placed

    (A) where it is now.
    (B) after paragraph 3.
    (C) after paragraph 4.
    (D) after paragraph 5.

Questions 23–33 are based on the following passage.

The President's House in Philadelphia

The White House has not always been the home of the U.S. president. The president also resided in New York City for the first two years after the ㉓ Constitution, and then, from 1790–1800, the president lived in Philadelphia. That historic house is long gone, though, and until recently, largely forgotten.

In 1772 Mary Masters married Richard Penn, the Lieutenant Governor and the grandson of William ㉔ Penn—the colony's founder. Mary's mother gave them a house on Market Street a block from the Statehouse, now known as Independence Hall, as a present. ㉕ While the Revolutionary War, British Generals William Howe and Benedict Arnold headquartered here.

23. (A) NO CHANGE
    (B) Constitution and then from 1790–1800, the president lived in Philadelphia.
    (C) Constitution, then, from 1790–1800, the president lived in Philadelphia.
    (D) Constitution and then, from 1790–1800, lived in Philadelphia.

24. (A) NO CHANGE
    (B) Penn,
    (C) Penn;
    (D) Penn:

25. (A) NO CHANGE
    (B) During
    (C) After
    (D) Following

In 1781, Robert Morris 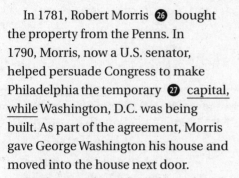 bought the property from the Penns. In 1790, Morris, now a U.S. senator, helped persuade Congress to make Philadelphia the temporary **27** capital, while Washington, D.C. was being built. As part of the agreement, Morris gave George Washington his house and moved into the house next door.

Washington brought eight enslaved Africans with him to the house in 1790. They worked in the house, including Hercules, Washington's favorite chef. The Washingtons were careful to **28** take the slaves out of Pennsylvania since slaves were allowed to stay for only sixth months. Two slaves, Oney Judge and Hercules, escaped to freedom. Oney ran away from the house in Philadelphia.

26. At this point, the writer is considering adding the following information.

   , called the financier of the American Revolution,

   Should the writer make this addition here?

   (A) Yes, because it further explains who Robert Morris is.
   (B) Yes, because it explains the key role Robert Morris played to get the British commanders out of the house.
   (C) No, because it contradicts the fact that the house was occupied by the British.
   (D) No, because it mentions the American Revolution, blurring the focus of the paragraph.

27. (A) NO CHANGE
   (B) capital—while
   (C) capital, "while
   (D) capital while

28. (A) NO CHANGE
   (B) rotate
   (C) dispatch
   (D) dispose of

After Washington left office, Philadelphia offered President John Adams a huge mansion, but Adams decided instead to move **29** <u>their</u> family into Washington's residence. He stayed until May 1800, **30** <u>when they moved into the White House.</u> In total, the house was home to the president of the United States for ten years.

[1] After Adams left, the house was converted into a hotel. [2] Then the hotel became homes for merchants. [3] In the late 1800s, the block became filled with stores. [4] By the 1900s, the neighborhood started a slow slide. **31**

29. (A) NO CHANGE
    (B) they're
    (C) his
    (D) its

30. (A) NO CHANGE
    (B) when Adams moved them into the White House.
    (C) when Adams moved his family into the White House.
    (D) when the White House got moved into by Adams and his family.

31. Where is the most logical place in this paragraph to add the sentence below?

    In 1832, a new owner tore down the house and replaced it with stores.

    (A) After sentence 1
    (B) After sentence 2
    (C) After sentence 3
    (D) After sentence 4

In the 1940s, the city of Philadelphia wanted to create a green space for a park in front of Independence Hall. When the park was built, the planners decided **32** <u>that the President's House would not be excavated or reconstructed.</u> Instead, a women's bathroom was built in that place.

In 2002, a new Liberty Bell Center was planned. The entrance was placed over the grounds of the house. This created interest in Washington's slaves and in excavating the house. In 2007, the site was **33** <u>excavated; and in 2010,</u> the interpretation of the house opened to the public.

32. (A) NO CHANGE
     (B) that there would be no digging up or putting back together the President's House.
     (C) that the President's House would not be dug up and rebuilt.
     (D) that President's House wouldn't be excavated or put back together.

33. (A) NO CHANGE
     (B) excavated, and in 2010
     (C) excavated, and, in 2010
     (D) excavated, and in 2010,

Questions 34–44 are based on the following passage and supplementary material.

Efficient Lightbulbs

34 From which Thomas Edison invented the lightbulb in 1879, no one would have guessed that the technology would not essentially change for more than a century. By the beginning of the twenty-first century, the demand for more efficient forms of light led to the phase out of Edison's incandescent bulbs for, **35** first, the compact fluorescent light (CFL), and then the LED light.

It is estimated that a **36** regulation house spends 14% of its electric bill on traditional lighting. With all the homes and businesses across the country, if the nation could create the same amount of light with less **37** electricity, than the savings could be huge. Furthermore, the demand for electricity would drop, **38** thus lowering the greenhouse gases produced by coal and natural gas power plants.

34. (A) NO CHANGE
    (B) Whereby
    (C) After
    (D) When

35. (A) NO CHANGE
    (B) first—
    (C) first;
    (D) first

36. (A) NO CHANGE
    (B) averaged
    (C) usually normal
    (D) typical

37. (A) NO CHANGE
    (B) electricity, then
    (C) electricity then
    (D) electricity than

38. Which choice provides information that best supports the claim made in the sentence?

    (A) NO CHANGE
    (B) thus raising the greenhouse gases produced by coal and natural gas power plants.
    (C) and therefore coal and natural gas power plants can make more electricity.
    (D) but greenhouse gases produced by coal and natural gas power plants will be as much a problem as they ever have been.

[1] The compact fluorescent light, **which are** also known as the CFL, was the first bulb to replace the traditional incandescent bulb. [2] Although it was designed in **1976;** it was not until the late 1990s that the bulbs were produced cheaply enough to compete with incandescent bulbs. [3] Although they are meant to last much longer than incandescent bulbs, if CFLs are turned on and off frequently, **its** lifespan may significantly drop. [4] Also, over time, CFLs will produce less and less light, so in time, they might only be producing 75% of the light they once did. [5] CFLs are also problematic to dispose of since they are all made with mercury, which is poisonous to humans. [6] While CFLs use only about one-quarter of the energy of an incandescent bulb to produce the same amount of light, they do have drawbacks.

39. (A) NO CHANGE
     (B) who is
     (C) which is
     (D) whom is

40. (A) NO CHANGE
     (B) 1976
     (C) 1976:
     (D) 1976,

41. (A) NO CHANGE
     (B) it's
     (C) they're
     (D) their

42. To make this paragraph most logical, sentence 6 should be placed

     (A) where it is now.
     (B) before sentence 1.
     (C) after sentence 2.
     (D) after sentence 4.

The LED bulb has in recent years started to eclipse the CFL as the best choice for low-energy lighting. Unlike CFLs, LEDs do not contain mercury. Also, they use slightly less electricity than CFLs. **43** <u>An LED that is equivalent to an incandescent 60-watt bulb uses about 10 watts (versus about 14 for a CFL)</u>. What's more, an LED bulb has a life span of about 25,000 hours versus 8,000 for a CFL and 1,000 for an incandescent bulb. And, unlike CFLs, they do not warm up to their full light output and do not lose light output over time like CFLs. Since the demand for these bulbs has increased, supply has too, and, while far more expensive than an incandescent bulb, an LED bulb will more than pay for itself over its lifetime by lasting far longer and requiring far less electricity.

43. Which choice offers an accurate interpretation of the data in the chart?

(A) NO CHANGE

(B) An LED that is equivalent to an incandescent 60-watt bulb uses about 18 watts (versus about 20 for a CFL).

(C) An LED that is equivalent to an incandescent 60-watt bulb uses about 20 watts (versus about 25 for a CFL).

(D) An LED that is equivalent to an incandescent 60-watt bulb uses about 24 watts (versus about 46 for a CFL).

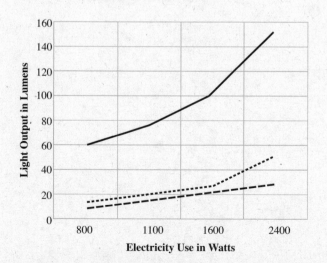

Lighting has changed drastically over the past twenty years after changing very little for more than a century. The benefits of that change mean lower electricity bills, less greenhouse gas from lowered demand for electricity, and, with longer-lasting bulbs, fewer trips to get the stepladder to change the bulb **44** on top of that.

44. (A) NO CHANGE
    (B) in addition.
    (C) likewise.
    (D) DELETE the underlined portion, and end the sentence with a period.

If there is still time remaining, you may review your answers.

MATH TEST (NO CALCULATOR)

25 MINUTES, 20 QUESTIONS

Turn to Section 3 of your answer sheet to answer the questions in this section.

Directions: For questions 1–15, solve each problem and choose the best answer choice. Then fill in the corresponding circle on your answer sheet. **For questions 16–20,** solve the problem and then enter your answer in the grid on the answer sheet. Refer to the directions before question 16 about how to enter your answers in the grid. You may use the open space in your test booklet for your scratch work.

Notes:
1. A calculator is **not permitted** on this test.
2. Unless otherwise indicated, all variables and expressions used represent real numbers.
3. Unless otherwise indicated, figures provided in this test are drawn to scale.
4. Unless otherwise indicated, all figures lie in a plane.
5. The domain of a given function f is the set of all real numbers x for which $f(x)$ is a real number unless otherwise indicated.

REFERENCE INFORMATION

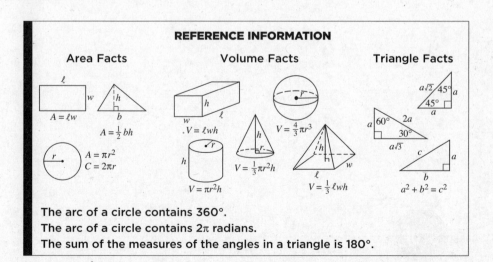

The arc of a circle contains 360°.
The arc of a circle contains 2π radians.
The sum of the measures of the angles in a triangle is 180°.

1. If $\dfrac{x-4}{5} = -1$, what is x?

   (A) -1
   (B) 1
   (C) 4
   (D) 9

2. Which of the following ordered pairs (x, y) satisfies the system of equations below?

   $$x - y = 4$$
   $$6x + y = 10$$

   (A) $(2, 2)$
   (B) $(2, -2)$
   (C) $(4, 0)$
   (D) $(1, 4)$

3. If $4x = 16$, what is $2x - 8$?

   (A) -8
   (B) 0
   (C) 8
   (D) 16

4. On Saturday, Grace baby-sat for x hours and was paid $9 per hour. Willow baby-sat for y hours and was paid $8 per hour. Which of the following expressions represents the total that they were paid together?

   (A) $72xy$
   (B) $17(x + y)$
   (C) $9x + 8y$
   (D) $9y + 8x$

5. If $\dfrac{2}{x} = \dfrac{-4}{x+6}$, what is $\dfrac{x}{2}$?

   (A) -1
   (B) 1
   (C) 4
   (D) 6

6. In the xy-plane below, the point $(4, 0)$ lies on the circle. What is the ratio of the circumference of the circle to the area of the circle?

   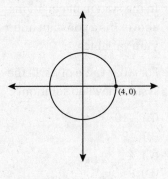

   (A) 2:1
   (B) 3:1
   (C) 1:2
   (D) 8:5

7. $$(a^2b + 2)(a^2b - 2)$$

   Which of the following is equivalent to the expression shown above?

   (A) $2a^2b - 4$
   (B) $a^4b^2 + 4$
   (C) $a^4b^2 - 4$
   (D) $2a^2b - 4ab + 4$

8.
$$\sqrt[3]{2k^2 - 8} - x = 0$$

If $k > 0$ and $x = 2$ in the equation above, what is k?

(A) $2\sqrt{2}$

(B) 4

(C) $4\sqrt{2}$

(D) 8

9.
$$kx + 2y = 5$$
$$3x - 3y = -7$$

In the system of equations above, k is a constant and x and y are variables.

For what value of k will the system have no solution?

(A) −10

(B) −2

(C) 4

(D) 8

10. If $f(x) = x - 4$ and $g(x) = -2x^2$, what is $f(g(-3))$?

(A) −24

(B) −22

(C) 14

(D) 18

11. If $2(x^2 - 6x + 2) + 4 = 0$, what is x?

(A) 2

(B) $3 \pm \sqrt{5}$

(C) $2 \pm \sqrt{15}$

(D) 10

12. A bacteria colony grows at a rate of 11% per year. If the initial sample had a mass of 500 grams, which of the following functions models the size of the colony in grams t years later?

(A) $f(t) = 500(0.89)^t$

(B) $f(t) = 500(1.11)^t$

(C) $f(t) = 11(500)^t$

(D) $f(t) = 11(1.5)^t$

13. If $\dfrac{8^{2x-1}}{2^2} = 2^{y-3}$, what is y in terms of x?

(A) 6

(B) $18x$

(C) $6x - 2$

(D) $6x + 5$

14. The expression $\dfrac{3x+6}{9x^2-36}$ is equivalent to which of the following?

    (A) $\dfrac{1}{3x-6}$

    (B) $\dfrac{1}{3x+6}$

    (C) $x-2$

    (D) $3x^2-9$

15. What is the sum of the values that satisfy $4m^2-11m-3=0$?

    (A) 2

    (B) 2.75

    (C) 3.25

    (D) 4

Grid-in Response Directions

In questions 16–20, first solve the problem, and then enter your answer on the grid provided on the answer sheet. The instructions for entering your answers follow.

- First, write your answer in the boxes at the top of the grid.
- Second, grid your answer in the columns below the boxes.
- Use the fraction bar in the first row or the decimal point in the second row to enter fractions and decimals.

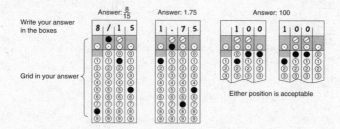

- Grid only one space in each column.
- Entering the answer in the boxes is recommended as an aid in gridding but is not required.
- The machine scoring your exam can read only what you grid, so you **must grid-in your answers correctly to get credit**.
- If a question has more than one correct answer, grid-in only one of them.
- The grid does not have a minus sign; so no answer can be negative.
- A mixed number *must* be converted to an improper fraction or a decimal before it is gridded. Enter $1\frac{1}{4}$ as 5/4 or 1.25; the machine will interpret 11/4 as $\frac{11}{4}$ and mark it wrong.
- **All decimals must be entered as accurately as possible.** Here are three acceptable ways of gridding:

$$\frac{3}{11} = 0.272727\ldots$$

 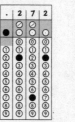 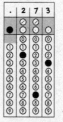

- Note that rounding to .273 is acceptable because you are using the full grid, but you would receive **no credit** for .3 or .27, because they are less accurate.

16. $$3x(-x+1) - 2(x+4) =$$
$$ax^2 + bx + c$$

In the equation above, a, b, and c are constants. If the equation is true for x, what is b?

17. $$|x-3| \leq 1$$

What is one possible solution for x in the equation above?

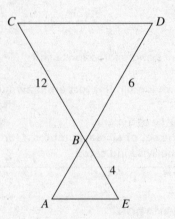

18. In the figure above, $AE \parallel CD$ and segment AD intersects CE at B. What is the length of segment AD?

19. $$3x + 5y = 50$$
$$ax + by = 10$$

In the system above, a and b are constants. If the system has infinite solutions, what is $\dfrac{a}{b}$?

20. If $a = 2\sqrt{3}$ and $3a = \sqrt{3x}$, what is x?

STOP

If there is still time remaining, you may review your answers.

MATH TEST (CALCULATOR)

55 MINUTES, 38 QUESTIONS

Turn to Section 4 of your answer sheet to answer the questions in this section.

Directions: For questions 1–30, solve each problem and choose the best answer choice. Then fill in the corresponding circle on your answer sheet. **For questions 31–38,** solve the problem and grid in the answer on the answer sheet. Refer to the directions before question 31 about how to enter the grid-in answers. You may use any space in the test booklet for your scratch work.

Notes:
1. A calculator **is permitted** on this test.
2. Unless otherwise indicated, all variables and expressions used represent real numbers.
3. Unless otherwise indicated, figures provided in this test are drawn to scale.
4. Unless otherwise indicated, all figures lie in a plane.
5. The domain of a given function f is the set of all real numbers x for which $f(x)$ is a real number unless otherwise indicated.

REFERENCE INFORMATION

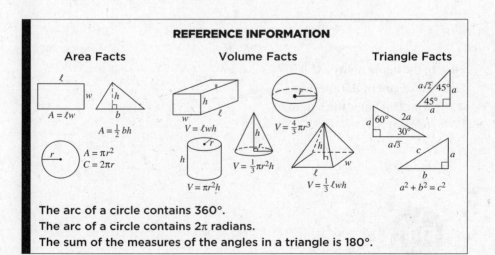

The arc of a circle contains 360°.

The arc of a circle contains 2π radians.

The sum of the measures of the angles in a triangle is 180°.

1. If $y = kx$, where k is a constant and $y = 12$ when $x = 2$, what is y when $x = 4$?

   (A) 2
   (B) 12
   (C) 20
   (D) 24

2. If $12 - 3x$ is 8 more than $7x$, what is $5x$?

   (A) −1
   (B) 1
   (C) 2
   (D) 5

3. A paper clip factory estimates 1 out of every 500 paper clips produced is defective. If in a 24-hour period 20,000 paper clips are produced, how many are defective?

   (A) 10
   (B) 30
   (C) 40
   (D) 400

4. $(3x^2 - 5x + 1) - (-x^2 + 2x + 7)$

   Which of the following is equivalent to the expression above?

   (A) $4x^2 - 3x - 6$
   (B) $2x^2 - 7x - 6$
   (C) $4x^2 - 7x - 6$
   (D) $4x^2 - 7x + 8$

5. The table below shows values of the linear function f. Which function defines f?

n	1	2	3	4
$f(n)$	0	2	4	6

   (A) $2n - 2$
   (B) $n - 2$
   (C) $4n - 2$
   (D) $n + 4$

6. If $-\dfrac{2}{5}a = \dfrac{3}{2}$, what is a?

   (A) $-\dfrac{15}{8}$
   (B) $-\dfrac{15}{4}$
   (C) $\dfrac{15}{4}$
   (D) 15

7. Kevin jogs 50 meters in 12.1 seconds. If he jogs at the same rate, which of the following is closest to the distance Kevin jogs in 7 minutes?

   (A) 1,500 meters
   (B) 1,650 meters
   (C) 1,750 meters
   (D) 1,800 meters

8. What is the sum of the solutions to $x - 2 = \sqrt{x + 4}$?

(A) 0

(B) 5

(C) 10

(D) 15

9. Last week, Beth worked 6 more hours than Alice. If together they worked 68 hours, how many hours did Alice work last week?

(A) 30

(B) 31

(C) 37

(D) 61

Time	Population
0	10
5	100
10	1,000
15	10,000

10. The table above shows estimated bacterial growth over a 15-week time period. Which of the following best describes the relationship between time and the estimated population of bacteria during the 15 weeks?

(A) Linear increase

(B) Linear decrease

(C) Exponential growth

(D) Exponential decay

11. In an xy-plane, the graph of function f has x-intercepts at -4, -2, and 2. Which of the following could define f?

(A) $f(x) = (x - 4)(x - 2)(x + 2)$

(B) $f(x) = (x + 2)(x - 2)(x + 4)$

(C) $f(x) = (x - 2)^2(x - 4)$

(D) $f(x) = (x + 2)^2(x + 4)$

12. Which of the following numbers is NOT a solution for the inequality below?

$$5x + 4 < 6x + 3$$

(A) 1

(B) 2

(C) 3

(D) 4

13. Given the system below, what is the sum of x and y?

$$-x + 3y = 4$$
$$6x + y = 14$$

(A) -2

(B) 2

(C) 4

(D) 8

14. $$E = mc^2$$

What is the equation above when c is written in terms of E and m?

(A) $c = \sqrt{\dfrac{m}{E}}$

(B) $c = \sqrt{\dfrac{E}{m}}$

(C) $c = Em$

(D) $c = E^2 m^2$

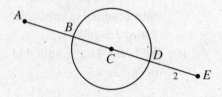

15. Circle C has radius BC and radius CD. If $DE \cong AB$ and $AE = 16$, what is the radius of circle C?

(A) 4

(B) 6

(C) 12

(D) 16

16. Jennifer has a savings account that contains \$450. Her sister, Kim, has a similar account worth 20% less than Jennifer's. What is the amount in Kim's account?

(A) \$300

(B) \$360

(C) \$420

(D) \$480

17. If $5x - 3 \geq 2$, what is the least possible value of $4x + 3$?

(A) 5

(B) 7

(C) 11

(D) 17

18. $$y = mx + b$$

In the slope-intercept equation shown above, what is x in terms of y, m, and b?

(A) $x = y - b - x$

(B) $x = y + b - y$

(C) $x = \dfrac{y - b}{m}$

(D) $x = \dfrac{b - y}{m}$

19. John bought a new cell phone for \$120. The price was after a 20% discount. What was the original price of the phone?

(A) \$96

(B) \$140

(C) \$144

(D) \$150

Questions 20 and 21 refer to the following information.

Cars Per Household

Number of Cars	High School	Middle School
0	10	5
1	30	15
2	20	20
3	30	10
4	30	30

For this survey, 200 students were surveyed.

20. If there are 900 students total between the middle school and high school, about how many have 4 cars per household?

(A) 60
(B) 120
(C) 250
(D) 270

21. What percentage of surveyed students in the middle school had 0 cars in the household?

(A) 2.5%
(B) 6.25%
(C) 7.5%
(D) 15%

22. A bank offers 4 types of savings accounts. Which option below would yield exponential growth?

(A) Each year, 3% of the initial savings is added to the account.
(B) Each year, 2% of the initial savings plus $100 is added to the account.
(C) Each year, 1% of the current value is added to the value of the account.
(D) Each year, $100 is added to the account.

23. In right triangle ABC, AC is the hypotenuse and is $\frac{5}{4} AB$, and $AB = 8$. What is $\cos C$?

(A) $\frac{4}{5}$

(B) $\frac{3}{5}$

(C) 1

(D) 6

24. $$\frac{x^2}{x^k} \bullet \frac{x^{-4}}{x^{-6}} = x^{y+2}$$

What is the value of y if $k = 4$?

(A) −2
(B) −1
(C) 1
(D) 2

25. $$x^2 + y^2 + 2x - 6y = -1$$

The equation of a circle in the xy-plane is shown above. What is the value of the radius of the circle?

(A) 3

(B) $2\sqrt{2}$

(C) $2\sqrt{3}$

(D) 8

26. A line has coordinates $(3, k)$ and $(-4, -1)$. What value of k would allow this line to have a slope of 0?

(A) -1

(B) 0

(C) 1

(D) 4

27. A rectangle with an area of 16 square units was altered by increasing the length by 50% and decreasing the width by 50%. What percentage of the old area is the new area?

(A) 50

(B) 75

(C) 80

(D) 100

28. $$f(x) = (x + 3)(x - 4)(x + 5) =$$
$$x^3 + kx^2 - 17x - 60$$

What is the value of k?

(A) -4

(B) 1

(C) 2

(D) 4

29. If $-\dfrac{8}{5} < -3t + 2 < -\dfrac{2}{5}$, what is one possible value of $8t - 1$?

(A) 5

(B) 7

(C) 9

(D) 11

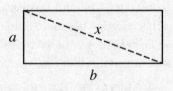

30. If the length of diagonal x is 10 and if b is twice the length of a, what is the value of a?

(A) $\sqrt{5}$

(B) $2\sqrt{5}$

(C) 5

(D) 10

Grid-in Response Directions

In questions 31–38, first solve the problem, and then enter your answer on the grid provided on the answer sheet. The instructions for entering your answers follow.

- First, write your answer in the boxes at the top of the grid.
- Second, grid your answer in the columns below the boxes.
- Use the fraction bar in the first row or the decimal point in the second row to enter fractions and decimals.

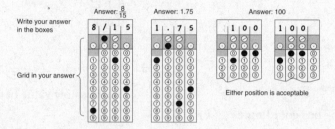

- Grid only one space in each column.
- Entering the answer in the boxes is recommended as an aid in gridding but is not required.
- The machine scoring your exam can read only what you grid, so you **must grid-in your answers correctly to get credit**.
- If a question has more than one correct answer, grid-in only one of them.
- The grid does not have a minus sign; so no answer can be negative.
- A mixed number *must* be converted to an improper fraction or a decimal before it is gridded. Enter $1\frac{1}{4}$ as 5/4 or 1.25; the machine will interpret 11/4 as $\frac{11}{4}$ and mark it wrong.
- **All decimals must be entered as accurately as possible.** Here are three acceptable ways of gridding:

$$\frac{3}{11} = 0.272727\ldots$$

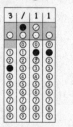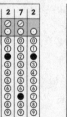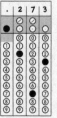

- Note that rounding to .273 is acceptable because you are using the full grid, but you would receive **no credit** for .3 or .27, because they are less accurate.

31. $$\frac{8}{x+1} - \frac{6}{x-1} = 0$$

    What is the solution for the above equation?

32. If h hours and 20 minutes is equal to 380 minutes, what is h?

33. In the xy-plane, the point $(2, 5)$ lies on the graph of

    $$f(x) = 2x^2 - bx + 4$$

    What is b?

34. In a circle with center O, central $\angle AOB$ has a measure of $\frac{\pi}{2}$ radians. The area of the sector formed by central $\angle AOB$ is what fraction of the area of the circle?

35. $$A = 16t + 25$$

    Alma made a deposit into a savings account. Each week thereafter, she deposited a fixed amount into the account. The equation above models the amount in dollars, A, that Alma has deposited after t weekly deposits. According to the equation, how much was Alma's original deposit?

36. $$y \le -10x + 200$$
    $$y \le 15x$$

    In the xy-plane, if a point with coordinates (a, b) lies in the solution set of the system of inequalities above, what is the maximum possible value of b?

Questions 37 and 38 refer to the following information.

Julia opened a bank account that earns 3% interest compounded annually. Her initial deposit was $500, and her account uses the expression $\$500(x)^t$ to find the value of the account after t years.

37. What is the value of x in the expression above?

38. After approximately how many years will Julia have doubled her money? (Round your answer up to the nearest whole year.)

ESSAY (OPTIONAL)

Directions: In this assignment, you will demonstrate your ability to skillfully read and understand a source text and to write a response analyzing the source. In your essay, you should show that you have understood the source text, give proficient analysis, and use the English language effectively. If the essay is off topic, it will not be scored. You will have 50 minutes to complete the assignment, including reading the source text and writing your essay.

Read the following passage and consider how the author uses:

- Evidence, such as examples, to help the argument
- Reasoning to demonstrate logical connections among facts and ideas
- Rhetoric, like emotional and logical appeals, to help the argument

The following is from the inaugural address by President Barack Obama on January 21, 2013. From *https://www.whitehouse.gov/the-press-office/2013/01/21/inaugural-address-president-barack-obama*

1   Each time we gather to inaugurate a President we bear witness to the enduring strength of our Constitution. We affirm the promise of our democracy. We recall that what binds this nation together is not the colors of our skin or the tenets of our faith or the origins of our names. What makes us exceptional—what makes us American—is our allegiance to an idea articulated in a declaration made more than two centuries ago: "We hold these truths to be self-evident, that all men are created equal; that they are endowed by their Creator with certain unalienable rights; that among these are life, liberty, and the pursuit of happiness."

2   Today we continue a never-ending journey to bridge the meaning of those words with the realities of our time. For history tells us that while these truths may be self-evident, they've never been self-executing; that while freedom is a gift from God, it must be secured by His people here on Earth. The patriots of 1776 did not fight to replace the tyranny of a king with the privileges of a few or the rule of a mob. They gave to us a republic, a government of, and by, and for the people, entrusting each generation to keep safe our founding creed.

3   And for more than two hundred years, we have.

4   Through blood drawn by lash and blood drawn by sword, we learned that no union founded on the principles of liberty and equality could survive half-slave and half-free. We made ourselves anew, and vowed to move forward together.

5   Together, we determined that a modern economy requires railroads and highways to speed travel and commerce, schools and colleges to train our workers.

6   Together, we discovered that a free market only thrives when there are rules to ensure competition and fair play.

7   Together, we resolved that a great nation must care for the vulnerable, and protect its people from life's worst hazards and misfortune.

8   Through it all, we have never relinquished our skepticism of central authority, nor have we succumbed to the fiction that all society's ills can be cured through government alone. Our celebration of initiative and enterprise, our insistence on hard work and personal responsibility, these are constants in our character.

9   But we have always understood that when times change, so must we; that fidelity to our founding principles requires new responses to new challenges; that preserving our individual freedoms ultimately requires collective action. For the American people can no more meet the demands of today's world by acting alone than American soldiers could have met the forces of fascism or communism with muskets and militias. No single person can train all the math and science teachers we'll need to equip our children for the future, or build the roads and networks and research labs that will bring new jobs and businesses to our shores. Now, more than ever, we must do these things together, as one nation and one people.

10 This generation of Americans has been tested by crises that steeled our resolve and proved our resilience. A decade of war is now ending. An economic recovery has begun. America's possibilities are limitless, for we possess all the qualities that this world without boundaries demands: youth and drive; diversity and openness; an endless capacity for risk and a gift for reinvention. My fellow Americans, we are made for this moment, and we will seize it—so long as we seize it together.

11   For we, the people, understand that our country cannot succeed when a shrinking few do very well and a growing many barely make it. We believe that America's prosperity must rest upon the broad shoulders of a rising middle class. We know that America thrives when every person can find independence and pride in their work; when the wages of honest labor liberate families from the brink of hardship. We are true to our creed when a little girl born into the bleakest poverty knows that she has the same chance to succeed as anybody else, because she is an American; she is free, and she is equal, not just in the eyes of God but also in our own.

Write an essay in which you explain how Barack Obama builds an argument to persuade his audience that the citizens of the United States must work together to overcome the country's challenges. In your response, analyze how Obama uses one or more of the following: evidence to support his claims; reasoning to connect claims and evidence and to develop ideas; rhetorical elements, such as logical appeals, emotional appeals, and word choice; and/or other features. Be sure your analysis focuses on the main ideas of the passage.

Your essay should not simply explain Obama's speech or explain whether you agree with Obama's claims but, rather, explain how Obama builds an argument to persuade his audience that the citizens of the United States must work together to overcome the country's challenges.

ANSWER KEY
Practice Test

Section 1: Reading Test

1.	C	14.	B	27.	A	40.	B
2.	B	15.	C	28.	C	41.	C
3.	D	16.	C	29.	B	42.	A
4.	A	17.	C	30.	D	43.	C
5.	C	18.	A	31.	D	44.	D
6.	A	19.	B	32.	B	45.	D
7.	B	20.	A	33.	B	46.	B
8.	C	21.	D	34.	A	47.	B
9.	A	22.	A	35.	C	48.	D
10.	D	23.	C	36.	A	49.	A
11.	D	24.	C	37.	C	50.	B
12.	C	25.	B	38.	A	51.	C
13.	B	26.	C	39.	D	52.	C

Number Correct _____   Number Incorrect _____

Section 2: Writing and Language Test

1.	B	12.	B	23.	A	34.	D
2.	B	13.	D	24.	B	35.	A
3.	D	14.	C	25.	B	36.	D
4.	C	15.	C	26.	A	37.	B
5.	D	16.	C	27.	D	38.	A
6.	D	17.	B	28.	B	39.	C
7.	B	18.	B	29.	C	40.	D
8.	D	19.	A	30.	C	41.	D
9.	C	20.	D	31.	B	42.	C
10.	B	21.	D	32.	A	43.	A
11.	C	22.	A	33.	D	44.	D

Number Correct _____   Number Incorrect _____

ANSWER KEY
Practice Test

Section 3: Math Test (No Calculator)

1. **A**   6. **C**   11. **B**
2. **B**   7. **C**   12. **B**
3. **B**   8. **A**   13. **C**
4. **C**   9. **B**   14. **A**
5. **A**   10. **B**   15. **B**

16. **1**

17. **2, 3, or 4**

18. **8**

19. **3/5 or .6**

or

20. **36**

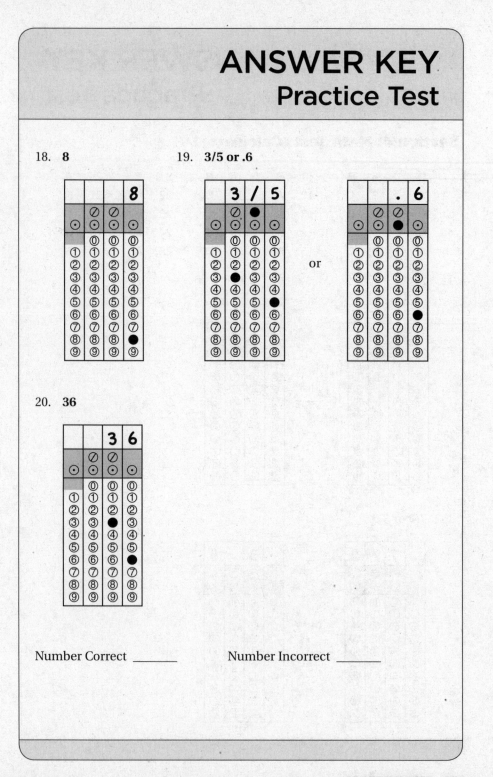

Number Correct _____   Number Incorrect _____

ANSWER KEY
Practice Test

Section 4: Math Test (Calculator)

1. **D**	6. **B**	11. **B**	16. **B**	21. **B**	26. **A**
2. **C**	7. **C**	12. **A**	17. **B**	22. **C**	27. **B**
3. **C**	8. **B**	13. **C**	18. **C**	23. **B**	28. **D**
4. **C**	9. **B**	14. **B**	19. **D**	24. **A**	29. **B**
5. **A**	10. **C**	15. **B**	20. **D**	25. **A**	30. **B**

31. **7**   32. **6**

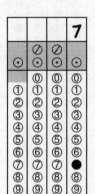

33. **7/2 or 3.5**

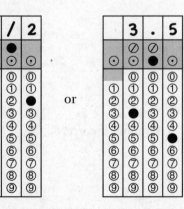

or

ANSWER KEY
Practice Test

34. **1/4 or .25**

35. **25**

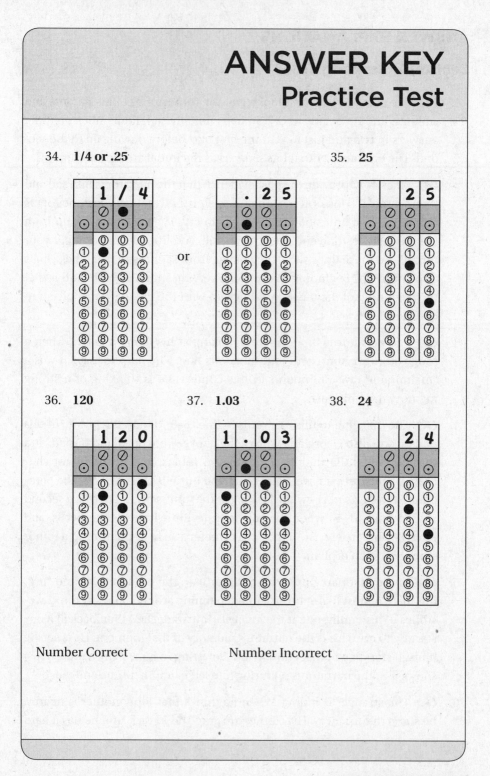

or

36. **120**

37. **1.03**

38. **24**

Number Correct _____   Number Incorrect _____

ANSWER EXPLANATIONS

Section 1: Reading Test

1. **(C)** The narrator is at first looking at the tombstones of his parents and siblings, and he begins to cry. So he is initially sad. Remember, split the answers in two and just look at the first part before moving on to the second. The only answer that has sadness as the initial attitude is choice C.

2. **(B)** Lines 4–17 provide the best evidence that the narrator is first sad and then scared. Pip looks at the lonely cemetery and at the tombstones of his father, mother, and siblings. He starts to cry. Then a man pops up from behind a gravestone and says, "Keep still, you little devil, or I'll cut your throat!" So these lines show the change from sadness to fear. These lines also show Pip "beginning to cry." Since crying shows sadness and it is at the beginning of the passage, it lines up with the first part of choice C in question 1.

3. **(D)** The narrator is in a cemetery looking at his family's graves when a rough stranger jumps out and threatens him. The narrator says it was a "memorable raw afternoon." In this context, he is thinking of a strong memory from his past.

4. **(A)** The first clue to this answer is in lines 6–9, "Philip Pirrip, late of this parish, and also Georgiana wife of the above, were dead and buried; and that Alexander, Bartholomew, Abraham, Tobias, and Roger, infant children of the aforesaid, were also dead and buried." At the end of the paragraph, Pip starts to cry while looking at the tombstones. There is a second clue in lines 51–54 when the convict asks Pip where his mother is, and Pip tells him "There, sir!" Pip is in a cemetery, so he is pointing at a tombstone. Pip is an orphan.

5. **(C)** In the first paragraph, the narrator uses the pronouns "I" and "my" but then, almost like a movie camera panning around, looks at the gravestones of his family, out at the lonely countryside, and then back at a boy starting to cry. This is the narrator's memory of that moment. He is seeing himself standing in that churchyard. Referring to himself by name ("Pip") shows that the narrator is picturing himself in another time and place.

6. **(A)** The stranger is hiding. When he thinks that Pip's mother is nearby, he starts to turn away. His clothes are gray and in rags, and he has a hard

demeanor. Most of all, he has "a great iron on his leg." He is an escaped convict.

7. **(B)** In these lines, the narrator describes the stranger. His clothes are "coarse gray." This might indicate a convict's clothes, but not necessarily. The real giveaway occurs later in the sentence with the words "a great iron around his leg." The shackles show that the stranger must be an escaped convict.

8. **(C)** Go back to the sentence containing "lair," cross out the word, and create your own sentence, ". . . that the distant savage _____ from which the wind was rushing was the sea." A good fit would be the words *starting place*. Look at the list; all the choices are places. Only choice C, though, includes *origin*. That makes choice C correct.

9. **(A)** Split the choices in half and look at just the first part of each. The stranger is not generous or kind, so eliminate choices B and D. Now look at the second part of choices A and C. The stranger is not sensible, so eliminate choice C.

10. **(D)** Although other selections show that the stranger is outwardly imposing, only lines 42–50 show that he is also inwardly scared. Lines 49–50 state, "He started, made a short run, and stopped and looked over his shoulder." The stranger is fearful that he will be spotted, making him fearful despite his gruff demeanor.

11. **(D)** In the paragraph, the author states that wages vary by person and occupation, but "there is a certain general relation between all wages." They differ, but they must follow a certain law. Choices A and B are meant to grab the attention of people who only flip back and look at the key words of the first sentence. Choice C is only partially correct.

12. **(C)** In lines 39–40, the author states that "men seek to gratify their desires with the least exertion." People work to fulfill their wants by doing the least amount of work. Choices A, B, and D are never mentioned in the passage as possible reasons.

13. **(B)** Here it helps to use line 26 as the bull's-eye on the target. Then expand that target by reading a little more. Specifically, read into the next sentence, "Did he offer less, none would accept the terms, as they could obtain greater **results** by working for themselves. Thus, although the employer wishes to **pay** as little as possible . . . ." *Results* must refer to

payment, which is choice B. The other three choices are all synonyms of *result*, but none of them are how the word is used in that sentence.

14. **(B)** This is the first of a set of paired questions. Additionally, this question and the wording of its answer choices are challenging. So it is probably best to use the answer choices for question 15 to work backward through the answer choices for question 14. Choice A of question 15 only says that earnings do "not depend merely upon the intensity or quality of the labor itself." This does not give a reason for any of the choices in question 14. Choice B only says of wages that the "given amount of labor will yield will vary." There is nothing about wages varying in any of the choices for question 14. Choice C of question 15 says that people "will not expend labor at a lower point of productiveness while a higher is open to them." Thus, people will not work for a lower wage when a higher wage is open to them. Choice B is correct for question 14, and choice C is correct for question 15.

15. **(C)** See the explanation of the answer for question 14 to understand the answer to question 15.

16. **(C)** This is the first of another set of paired questions. So go to the choices for question 17 and work backward to find the answer for question 16. Choices A and B in question 17 do not imply any of the choices for question 16. Choice C of question 17 says, "In a simple state of society, each man . . . works for himself." Since the passage is about the wages of people working for others, society must have progressed beyond the primitive state where men work only for themselves. Choice C is correct for both question 16 and question 17.

17. **(C)** See the explanation of the answer for question 16 to understand the answer to question 17.

18. **(A)** The sentence says that "wealth is the **product** of two factors, land and labor, and what a given amount of labor will yield will vary with the powers of the natural opportunities to which it is applied." In this context, the author is stating that wealth is the *outcome* of land and labor.

19. **(B)** Focus on the main word in each answer choice. The last paragraph does not show *regularity*, *anxiety*, or *similarities*. It does show a *contrast* to modern times and the law of wages. In the paragraph, the author states that "in a simple state of society, each man, as is the primitive mode, works for himself." Since the rest of the passage is about the law that governs how people work for one another, the last paragraph must illustrate the point by offering a contrast, making choice B correct.

20. **(A)** In lines 29–31, the author states, "If wages are temporarily carried either above or below this line, a tendency to carry them back at once arises." So if a company is paying higher than normal wages, they will be carried back to normal at once, making the situation temporary.

21. **(D)** The passage is an illustration of why people work for others. It uses a primitive society as a contrast to show why people work for others. In the last sentence, the author states that if one person hires someone else, "He must pay wages fixed by this full, average produce of labor." Thus, the main idea of the paragraph is to show that when people work for others, they must make more than if they worked for themselves.

22. **(A)** When you are presented with a main idea question first, remember to mark it and then come back to it after trying all the detail questions for that passage. Focus on the key words in each answer choice, and then narrow down the choices. Choice A says "present the background." Choice B says "evaluate the research." Choice C says "summarize the findings." Choice D says "explain the development." Since there is no evaluation, eliminate choice B. Since there is no summary of findings, eliminate choice C. Now look at choices A and D more closely. Choice D is about a branch of scientific study. Choice A is about the background and importance of earthquakes at Yellowstone. Choice D is too broad, so eliminate it. Therefore, choice A is the correct answer.

23. **(C)** The author appreciates earthquakes and describes them as helping to "maintain hydrothermal activity" and to "map and to understand the sub-surface geology around and beneath Yellowstone." When asked a tone or attitude question, first decide if the passage is positive, negative, or neutral. In this case, it is positive. That eliminates choices A and B. Compare choices C and D. Choice C is correct because choice D is too positive. The author appreciates earthquakes but is not astonished by them.

24. **(C)** In the passage, the author is using geology terms to describe earthquakes. Go back to the passage, and reread the sentence before the one that contains *faults*. That sentence states that "earthquakes occur along **fractures** in the crust where stress from crustal plate movement and volcanic activity build to a significant level. The rock along these **faults** . . . ." The previous sentence uses the word *fractures* to describe where the earthquakes occur. A *fracture* is a *break*.

25. **(B)** First eliminate the choices that are obviously incorrect. Choices C and D are incorrect since earthquakes help keep hydrothermal features open. Since earthquakes are helpful to hydrothermal features, choice A is also incorrect. That leaves choice B as the correct choice.

26. **(C)** Now that you have choice B for question 25, look at the answer choices for question 26. Find the one that states mineral deposits can close hydrothermal features. Choice C states, "Without periodic disturbance of relatively small earthquakes, the small fractures and conduits that supply hot water to geysers and hot springs might be sealed by mineral deposition." This is the only choice that mentions mineral deposits, so it is the correct choice.

27. **(A)** In lines 27–30, the author states that "scientists interpret these swarms as due to shifting and changing pressures in the Earth's crust that are caused by migration of hydrothermal fluids, a natural occurrence of volcanoes." Choice B is incorrect because swarms occur over a short time. Choice C is incorrect since swarms are "a natural occurrence." Choice D is incorrect since the swarms are described as localized.

28. **(C)** Since question 27 is choice A, the evidence for that answer is lines 27–30. There the author states that the swarms are a result of a movement of fluids below ground.

29. **(B)** The earthquake of magnitude 4.8 occurred in 2014, so it is recent. It was felt throughout the Yellowstone area, so it was significant. Choice B describes this, making it the correct choice. Choice C is incorrect because it does not give details about damage to the area. Choice D is incorrect because there was no misconception noted in the passage.

30. **(D)** Look at the figure and the lines representing roads. The figure shows that sometimes earthquakes occur near roads and sometimes they do not. So eliminate choice A. The outlined sector represents the caldera. The figure shows that earthquakes occur both in and out of the caldera, eliminating choice B. Since the dots are often stacked on top of or close to each other, choice C is incorrect. Since choice C is the opposite of choice D, choice D is the correct answer.

31. **(D)** The passage never indicates that earthquakes are becoming more common, which eliminates choice A. Although choices B and C are true based on information found in the passage, the figure does not confirm either statement. The dots representing earthquakes in the figure show

that the earthquakes frequently occur in swarms, making choice D correct.

32. **(B)** In the first paragraph, the author states that "the Indians were moving in hot haste as if retreating." They appeared to be retreating, making choice B correct.

33. **(B)** The words stating that the Native Americans appeared to be retreating are in the sentence that begins on line 6. None of the other answer choices mention retreating.

34. **(A)** In the second paragraph, the author states that even though "the suffering was heartrending," the soldiers were able to rout "the main body of the Indians who were guarding the approach to the river." This shows that the soldiers suffered but fought bravely. Choice B is incorrect because there is no mention of deception. Choice C mentions only the casualties of the soldiers. Choice D states that the soldiers had not had water for thirty-six hours, making them not well supplied.

35. **(C)** The passage is about an army of soldiers in battle. It mentions different leaders and their companies. A *company*, then, must be the group of men under that leader. The best synonym among the choices in the list is *unit*.

36. **(A)** Two Moon states that the soldiers were surrounded and picked off, with their horses falling on top of them, but that they fought on. He notes different soldiers for how bravely they fought despite the situation. Choice A describes the situation best. Be careful! Choice C might look good, but it says "all the soldiers" ran away. The author does note one soldier running away, but not all of them. This makes choice C incorrect. Watch for words that proclaim absolutes!

37. **(C)** Two Moon describes the battle throughout the passage. However, the lines that best describe and support question 36 are lines 52–57. Two Moon states, "We shoot, we ride fast, we shoot again. Soldiers drop, and horses fall on them. Soldiers in line drop, but one man rides up and down the line—all the time shouting. He rode a sorrel horse with white face and white fore-legs. I don't know who he was. He was a brave man." The swirl of battle and the description of the brave soldier provide the best evidence from among the answer choices.

38. **(A)** The author mentions the Sioux went to fight in one direction and then the Cheyenne went in another. He does not refer to the Native

Americans as one group because they are from different tribes. There is no information about choice B in Passage 2. Choice C is incorrect because the author boasts about the abilities of any warrior and, in fact, mentions some soldiers for their bravery. Choice D is incorrect because there is no lack of weapons mentioned in the passage.

39. **(D)** The last paragraph of Passage 2 does mention that the bodies were stripped. However, it goes on to say, "We had no dance that night. We were sorrowful." So Two Moon would have disapproved the statement in Passage 1 that implies that the bodies were purposely stripped and mutilated in some sort of savage victory celebration.

40. **(B)** Passage 1 describes the battle as soldiers bravely fighting and scoring small victories but then eventually succumbing to the onslaught. Passage 2 describes the same battle from a different point of view. In Passage 2, Two Moon provides an alternate version of the events. He never challenges the point of view of Passage 1, elaborates on conclusions in Passage 1, or restates the events in different terms. He simply has an entirely different viewpoint of the events.

41. **(C)** Passage 2 mentions horses but does not mention an advantage in number for either side, so eliminate choice A. The first part of choice B is true. However, the second part is not, so eliminate choice B. Choice D looks good, but note that it says *all* of the dead soldiers were mutilated. That makes choice D incorrect. Choice C is correct. In Passage 1, the soldiers bury the dead. In Passage 2, the Native Americans did not dance that night because they were "sorrowful."

42. **(A)** Both passages showed one side's view of the Battle of Little Bighorn: one from the soldiers' point of view and one from a Native American's point of view. Choice B is incorrect since the passages never discuss any military problems. Choice C is incorrect because neither passage takes a position. Choice D is incorrect as both passages simply tell their sides of the story but never state whose version is better.

43. **(C)** The first paragraph states the three stages of oil production. It then goes on to explain the primary and secondary stages fully. This is all to get to the main point of the article: tertiary production. Choices A, B, and D are incorrect. Just look at the main words in those answer choices; scientific process, misconception, and recent study are all off topic.

44. **(D)** The sentence is about extending the life of an oil field. So *productive* must mean getting as much oil out of the ground as possible. *Fertile* is the

closest synonym since it means getting as much out of the ground (usually farming) as possible. Choices A, B, and C are all synonyms of *productive*, but those words are used for people. An oil field cannot be *creative*, for example.

45. **(D)** Since each choice has two portions, split them up and focus on one part of an answer choice at a time. Eliminate choice A since there is no criticism of a scientific model in the beginning of the passage. Now look at the second half of choices B, C, and D. Eliminate choice B because there is no mention of the new method being used *in natural gas fields.* Eliminate choice C since there is mention of drawbacks. Choice D is correct.

46. **(B)** This answer requires you to take two pieces of data and put them together. Since this is a paired question, it is easiest to see which choices deal with percentages. All of the choices mention percentages, but only choice B of question 47 deals with additional percentages of oil that can be recovered. Now that you have found the evidence, read it carefully. The biggest mistake is to jump at the second set of percentages and pick choice D since it has the exact same numbers. Read the sentences again. After secondary recovery, 20 to 40 percent of the oil has been taken from the field. After EOR, 30 to 60 percent has been taken. Therefore, the most additional oil EOR can most likely recover is 60 **minus** 20 already recovered (the two numbers farthest apart), or 40 percent. Choice B is the correct answer.

47. **(B)** See the explanation of question 46 for the answer explanation.

48. **(D)** You can go back and scan for each of the four states listed in the choices and then find the clues. Since this is a paired question, the choices in question 49 show you where to look. Go to lines 17–26 first (choice A of question 49). Those lines state that thermal techniques of EOR account for 40 percent of EOR, "primarily in California." The next paragraph states that nearly 60 percent of EOR is CO_2 injection. Therefore, since 60 percent plus 40 percent is 100 percent, there cannot be much, if any, CO_2 injection in California. Choice D is correct.

49. **(A)** See the explanation of question 48 for the answer explanation.

50. **(B)** The key to this question is that the answer must be supported by both the passage and the chart. Since the chart is simpler, read it first. It shows the average oil recovered by type. Now go back to the first and second paragraphs, which state what each type of recovery each method yields. Since after EOR a reservoir could have 60% of its oil recovered, 40% of the

oil must still be in place. Choice B is correct. Be careful! Choices A and D are both stated in the passage. Since they are not in the chart, though, they are incorrect.

51. **(C)** Choice A is incorrect because the chart reveals nothing about the finances of oil recovery. Choice B is incorrect because primary yields only about 10% of the oil in a reservoir. Choice D is incorrect because primary and secondary combined yield only 30% of recovered oil, the same as EOR. Choice C is correct because when primary and secondary are combined, only about 30% of the oil has been recovered. So most of the oil must still be in the ground.

52. **(C)** First, look at the chart. Does it show in any way anything about CO_2 injection? Since it does not, eliminate choices A and B. Now look at choices C and D. The chart does indicate that EOR is effective since it greatly increases the amount of oil recovered, so choice D is incorrect. Since the chart does not show evidence that CO_2 injection has benefits because it only on focuses EOR in general, choice C is the correct answer.

Section 2: Writing and Language Test

1. **(B)** Choice B provides a noun, "changes," creating a grammatically coherent sentence. Choices A, C, and D are incorrect because each provides a verb or a gerund, while the sentence requires a noun.

2. **(B)** The transition required for this sentence needs to emphasize the statement. *Indeed* is a transition used for emphasis. Choices A, C, and D are incorrect because those transitions are used for other purposes.

3. **(D)** This is an error in subject-verb agreement. The subject of the sentence is *things*, which requires a plural verb. The trick is that *spelling* is put in a phrase just before the verb. *Spelling has* sounds correct even though it's not because *spelling* isn't the subject. Choices B and C create clauses that then create sentence fragments.

4. **(C)** First, decide whether the addition makes the sentence better. In this case, it does not. So rule out choices A and B. Now compare choices C and D. Choice C is better because the phrase is obviously repetitive. Note how the sentence already says *basic* and *tables*, yet those words are in the phrase.

5. **(D)** Choices A, B, and C are all wordy. Those choices include an unnecessary pronoun, either *them* or *their*. It is more concise simply to use *memorization* at that point in the sentence.

6. **(D)** This is a mistake in parallelism. Go back and circle the two verbs. The first is *can find*, and the second is only *concentrate*. Circling the parts when confronted with a problem like this makes it easy to spot the correct answer.

7. **(B)** Remember the rules for combining sentences. Choice A uses a semicolon where a comma is needed because there is an introductory phrase attached to a sentence and not two sentences. Choice C uses a comma with *however* where a semicolon is needed, and choice D is awkward and repetitive.

8. **(D)** Delete *but* because no conjunction is necessary to communicate the relationship between the clauses in the sentence. *Instead of* at the beginning of the sentence already creates the relationship. This is not a compound sentence (two sentences written as one), so there is no need for a comma and a conjunction. Choices B and C are also conjunctions, so they would create the same problem as *but*.

9. **(C)** For clarification, a colon is used. Choice C provides one. Choice A uses incorrect punctuation. Choices B and D are awkward and redundant.

10. **(B)** *Online* is concise, and it is consistent with the language of the passage. Choices A, C, and D are incorrect because they are either wordy or use language that does not match the tone of the passage.

11. **(C)** This choice restates the writer's primary argument, which is that teachers' roles will change in the future. Choices A, B, and D are incorrect because they do not restate that claim.

12. **(B)** *However* is the correct transition for this sentence. The previous sentence states that studying colonization focuses on the English, but the sentences that follow say the Dutch are important, too. Choices A, C, and D do not connect the ideas in the sentences correctly.

13. **(D)** There are two rules being tested here: commas and apostrophes. First, there is no reason to pause after *group*, so no comma is needed. That eliminates choices A and B. Next, the apostrophe is placed before *s* when the word is singular. Choice C is incorrect for that reason.

14. **(C)** This is a compound sentence that contains a conjunction, so a comma is needed with the conjunction. Eliminate choices B and D. Next, the possessive form of *they* is needed, which is *their*. Choice C is correct.

15. **(C)** The sentence is not necessary. Eliminate choices A and B. Now look at the two remaining choices. Adding that sentence would detract from the main point of the paragraph, so choice C is correct. Choice D is irrelevant to the paragraph.

16. **(C)** Choice A creates a run-on sentence. Choice B correctly adds *and* but does not include a comma, so it is incorrect. Choice C correctly has a comma plus *and*. Choice D removes the subject of the second sentence, *a wall*, changing the meaning of the entire sentence.

17. **(B)** All the choices show Dutch words that are now in English. You have to find the example most like the one in the previous sentence. The previous sentence is about the cookie, which is a food. Choice B is the only other detail about a food.

18. **(B)** The most efficient way to combine these sentences is to take the second sentence and make it into a clause, adding a comma and deleting *this was*. Choices A, C, and D are incorrect because they either provide incorrect punctuation (choice A) or are awkward or wordy (choices C and D).

19. **(A)** The term was used to describe two things. Look at the first thing: *first Dutch settlers*. The second thing should match *first Dutch settlers*. The first term is short and to the point, so the second should be, too. Choice A is a close match with *and then English settlers*. Choices B, C, and D do not match as well because they are wordier than choice A.

20. **(D)** Break the problem in two. First, check the apostrophe rule. The city possesses the team, so an apostrophe *s* is needed. Eliminate choice B. Now check the verb. The sentence is past tense, and the simple past tense of *take* is *took*. Choice D is correct.

21. **(D)** This sentence has an introductory phrase (*Even though . . .*) that must modify the noun after it. Who were overtaken by the English? The Dutch were overtaken, which means this word must start the main sentence. Choice D does that. Choice A is not about the Dutch but about the Dutch's strong influence. Choice B has the wrong word being modified (*one*), and choice C splits the opening phrase unnecessarily with a comma after *colonies*.

22. **(A)** Paragraph 2 gives a brief history of the Dutch colonizers coming to America and ends with *the Dutch settlers forever changed the language of Americans.* The following paragraphs then explain those changes. So paragraph 2 is in the correct place. Choices B, C, and D are incorrect because they propose placing the paragraph in a place that prevents the passage from developing logically.

23. **(A)** The sentence is compound, meaning it is two complete sentences joined together. Choice A properly joins them together with a comma and a conjunction. Choices B, C, and D drop the comma (choice B), the conjunction *and* (choice C), and the subject of the second sentence, creating an illogical sentence (choice D).

24. **(B)** The phrase after *William Penn* gives extra information about him. This is called an appositive. More importantly, appositives are surrounded by commas. Choices A, C, and D use incorrect punctuation for an appositive.

25. **(B)** The correct transition for this sentence is *during. After* and *following* are sequentially illogical, and *while* is awkward.

26. **(A)** Choice A is best because the additional information helps the reader understand the importance of Robert Morris and, since he owned it, of the house itself. Choice B is incorrect because that statement is not true. Choices C and D are incorrect because the additional information is useful.

27. **(D)** The clause *while Washington, D.C. was being built* does not require a comma because the sentence has no interruption. Choices A, B, and C all interrupt the sentence in some way, making those choices incorrect.

28. **(B)** Since the sentence says that the slaves were allowed to stay for only six months, the Washingtons must have taken slaves out of Pennsylvania and then brought them back. *Rotate* is the most accurate word. Choices A, C, and D are not as accurate and are therefore incorrect.

29. **(C)** John Adams was one person. The singular pronoun *his* agrees with *Adams.* Choices A, B, and D are incorrect because they provide the wrong pronoun.

30. **(C)** In choice A, *they* is unclear, as is *them* in choice B. Choice C is correct because it makes clear who moved into the White House. Choice D is incorrect because it is passive and awkward.

31. **(B)** The key here is the words *in 1832*. That means it occurs before the late 1800s, eliminating choices C and D. Look again at sentence 2. It mentions *then the hotel became homes for merchants.* Since the first sentence states that the home became a hotel after Adams left, sentence 2 must follow sentence 1. Therefore, the new sentence should be placed after sentence 2.

32. **(A)** This is the best choice because its clear wording and formal tone correspond with the style of the passage. Choices B, C, and D lack the tone of the passage, particularly by using phrases like *dug up* or *put back together*.

33. **(D)** Two commas are needed. The first comma is needed after *excavated* because the sentence is compound and has the conjunction *and*. So a comma must precede the conjunction. The second comma is needed after the interrupting phrase *in 2010*. Note that there are two other interrupts with years (*in 2002* and *in 2007*) in the paragraph, and they both end with commas. Choices A, B, and C are incorrect because they use the wrong punctuation or place the punctuation in the wrong spots.

34. **(D)** *When* provides the correct word to start the opening clause of the sentence because it indicates the time that Edison invented the lightbulb. Choices A, B, and C are incorrect because those words miscommunicate the relationship between the opening clause and the rest of the sentence.

35. **(A)** The word *first* interrupts the sentence and must be surrounded by commas. Note that there is a comma before the word, too. Remember that English is balanced, and a second comma balances the punctuation. Choices B, C, and D all provide incorrect punctuation.

36. **(D)** *Typical* accurately describes the *house* that spends 14% of its electrical bill on traditional lighting. Choices A, B, and C are incorrect because none provides a more accurate word or a word that matches the style of the passage.

37. **(B)** The word *if* is followed by *then*. The word *than* is used with comparisons, eliminating choices A and D. Choice C is incorrect because there is a pause after *electricity*, which requires a comma.

38. **(A)** Since there would be a lower demand for electricity, power plants would not have to produce as much. Therefore, fewer greenhouse gases would be produced. Choices B and D are incorrect because they state more or the same amount of greenhouse gases would be produced.

Choice C is incorrect because power plants making more electricity does not logically connect to the rest of the sentence.

39. **(C)** A light is a thing, and the word *which* is used with things. The words *who* and *whom* are used with people. A light is singular and requires the singular verb *is*. Choices A, B, and D have either the wrong pronoun or a plural verb.

40. **(D)** *Although it was designed in 1976* is an introductory clause. So it needs a comma. Choices A, B, and C are incorrect because they provide incorrect punctuation.

41. **(D)** The pronoun refers back to *CFLs*, which is plural. That eliminates choices A and B. Choice C is incorrect because *they're* means *they are*.

42. **(C)** The paragraph starts with the advantages of the CFL and then shifts to CFL's drawbacks. Sentence 6 is the transition from advantages to disadvantages. So it must be placed after the advantages and before the disadvantages. Choices A, B, and D are incorrect because they place the sentence in an illogical spot.

43. **(A)** It is important that you find the correct column when looking at the chart. The sentence states that the incandescent bulb uses 60 watts, so locate the correct column by finding where the incandescent line is at 60 watts. Since that is all the way to the left, go down that column and see that both CFL and LED are between 0 and 20 watts. This quickly eliminates choices C and D. Look closely at where the LED line is. Since it is about halfway between 0 and 20 watts, choice A is correct. Choice B places the LED line very close to 20 watts, making choice B incorrect.

44. **(D)** No other wording is needed to convey the benefits of the change of new lightbulbs. No other words or phrases are needed to clarify the point, so choices A, B, and C are incorrect.

Section 3: Math Test—No Calculator

1. **(A)** First, multiply both sides by 5. Now add 4 to both sides. You are left with $x = -1$.

2. **(B)** To satisfy this system, first rewrite each equation, setting each equal to y. Once you set both equations equal to y, set each equation equal to each other. This makes your equation $x - 4 = -6x + 10$. Solve for x. Its value

is 2. Plug $x = 2$ into either equation to calculate the value of y to be -2. This makes your final answer $(2, -2)$.

3. **(B)** To solve this problem, start by solving for x in the first expression. This will give you $x = 4$. Plug this value into the second expression and solve. You will find that $2x - 8 = 0$.

4. **(C)** You are told that x stands for the number of hours that Grace worked and y stands for the number of hours that Willow worked. You can then multiply those assigned variables by the amount each person earned per hour working. Grace is represented by $9x$ and Willow by $8y$. Putting their earnings together means adding them. So their total earnings are represented by $9x + 8y$.

5. **(A)** The first step is to solve for x in the proportion. In order to do this, you must cross multiply, giving you the equation $-4x = 2x + 12$. From here, solving for x gives $x = -2$. Remember to plug this back into the fraction $\frac{x}{2}$. The final answer is -1.

6. **(C)** The key is realizing that you are being asked for a ratio between the circumference of a circle and the area of a circle. You will need the radius of the circle. Based on the diagram and the information provided in the question, the distance between the center and the given point is 4 units on the x-axis. So the radius is 4. Using this information, calculate the circumference by using the formula $C = 2\pi r$. Plugging in 4 for r will give 8π as the circumference. Now you must calculate the area by using the formula $A = 2\pi r^2$. Again, plug in 4 for r. The area is 16π. Finally, find the ratio of circumference to area. You will get $8\pi : 16\pi$, which reduces to 1:2.

7. **(C)** Use the FOIL method to solve this. Pay special attention to the exponents that you must add since you are multiplying. After distributing, you should notice that your middle two terms cancel each other, leaving you with $a^4 b^2 - 4$.

8. **(A)** To solve this problem the most convenient way, you must first replace x with the given 2. You must now add 2 to both sides to leave just a radical on the left side of the equation. Now you must **cube** both sides to eliminate the radical. Be sure to cube both sides, not square them! Doing this will eliminate the radical, leaving you with the equation $2k^2 - 8 = 8$. Once here, isolate k by first adding 8 to both sides, then dividing both sides by 2, and finally taking the square root of both sides to eliminate the squared term. This last step will leave you with $k = \sqrt{8}$, which equals $2\sqrt{2}$ when simplified.

9. **(B)** The key here is to realize that for a system to have no solutions, you must eliminate both variables at the same time. This will leave you with the constant k on the left side of the equation set equal to a different number on the right. Remember that for a system to have no solution, the values of x and y in each equation must be different. Start by multiplying the top equation by 3 and the bottom equation by 2. To eliminate the x-values, you must set $3kx = -6x$ (the opposite of the bottom equation's x-term). Once this is done, solve for k. The final answer is -2.

10. **(B)** The key here is to work from the inside out. First, plug -3 in for x in the $g(x)$ function. By doing this, you will find the value of the $g(x)$ function is -18. From here, take the -18 and replace that for x in the $f(x)$ function, allowing you to arrive at the final answer of -22.

11. **(B)** To find the value of x, you must use the quadratic formula. In order to use the formula properly, you must get the equation into standard form. Start by distributing the 2 inside of the parentheses and simplifying your whole numbers to obtain the equation $2x^2 - 12x + 8 = 0$. From here, you can apply the quadratic formula, which will yield $\dfrac{12 \pm 4\sqrt{5}}{4}$. Stop here and look at your answers. The only choice with $\sqrt{5}$ is choice B, which must be the answer. If you divide both 12 and $4\sqrt{5}$ by 4, the answer reduces to $3 \pm \sqrt{5}$.

12. **(B)** This description represents exponential growth. To create an equation for exponential growth, start with the original mass (500 grams). This value is then multiplied by the percentage growth shown as a decimal (0.11) and added to 1.00. Finally, the new value of 1.11 is raised to the power of t, representing the number of years that have passed. Putting this all together gives a final answer of $f(t) = 500(1.11)^t$.

13. **(C)** To solve this problem, you must know how to work with exponents. First, you must change 8 into 2^3. By using exponent rules, the exponent 3 can now be distributed into $2x - 1$ to make the new exponent $6x - 3$. The next step is to bring the exponent of 2 from the denominator to the numerator, remembering to change the sign when bringing it up. This will make the new exponent in the numerator $6x - 5$. Since you now have a standard base, you are able to set the exponents equal to each other. Finally, by adding 3 to both sides, you reach the final answer of $y = 6x - 2$.

14. **(A)** Start by factoring the denominator. The expression will now be in this form:

$$\frac{(3x+6)}{(3x+6)(3x-6)}$$

Notice that the numerator and one of the binomials from the denominator will cancel, leaving you with $\frac{1}{3x-6}$, which is choice A.

15. **(B)** To solve this problem, you must use the quadratic formula. After inserting the values given into the quadratic formula, you will get answers of 3 and $-\frac{1}{4}$. The final step is to add your answers together, making the answer to this question $2\frac{3}{4}$, which equals 2.75.

16. **1** This problem can quickly get confusing. However, if you realize that the problem is just asking for the constant connected to the x-term on the left side of the equation, you will find the question much easier. You must now distribute into the parentheses and combine like terms, leaving you with $-3x^2 + x - 8$. So the b-term is equal to 1.

17. **2, 3, or 4** In order for the left side of the inequality to be less than or equal to 1, the term inside the absolute value must total between -1 and 1. For this to be true, x must be greater than or equal to 2 and less than or equal to 4.

18. **8** You can approach this problem in several ways. However, the easiest is to apply proportions to the two triangles that have been created. Since the lines creating the triangles are parallel, the two triangles are similar. So you can use proportions to find the length of BA: $\frac{12}{4} = \frac{6}{x}$. After cross multiplying, you get $24 = 12x$, making x (or the length of BA) equal 2. Finally, by adding the length of BA (2) and the length of BD (6), you will find the final length of AD is 8.

19. **3/5 or .6** Look at the constant on the right side of each equation. The constant in the bottom equation is $\frac{1}{5}$ the constant in the top equation. Since the system has infinite solutions, this $\frac{1}{5}$ ratio applies to all parts of both equations. Look at the first equation. Divide the coefficient of 3 by 5 to obtain the value of a in the second equation, which is $\frac{3}{5}$. Go back to the first equation. Now divide the coefficient of 5 by 5 to get the value

of b in the second equation, which is 1. To find the final answer, divide a by b: $\frac{3}{5} \div 1 = \frac{3}{5}$. The final answer is $\frac{3}{5}$.

20. **36** If a is $2\sqrt{3}$, then $3a$ must be $6\sqrt{3}$. Find a number beneath the radical that is equal to $6\sqrt{3}$. That number is 108. Dividing $108 \div 3$ gives the value of x, which is 36.

Section 4: Math Test—Calculator Permitted

1. **(D)** Replace y with 12 and x with 2. This will leave you with the equation $12 = 2k$. Solving for k you will get an answer of 6. Now that you have k, insert 6 for k and 4 for the new x to get the final answer of $y = 24$.

2. **(C)** You must first create an equation from the information. This will give you $12 - 3x = 7x + 8$. Solving for x will give you an answer of $\frac{2}{5}$. Plugging this value into $5x$, you will get a final answer of 2.

3. **(C)** To solve this problem, you must use a proportion. By using the proportion $\frac{1}{500} = \frac{x}{20,000}$, cross multiplying, and solving for x, you will get an answer of $x = 40$.

4. **(C)** The only trick here is to remember to distribute the negative through the entire second trinomial. Once that is done, combine like terms. You will get the expression $4x^2 - 7x - 6$.

5. **(A)** The most efficient way to find this answer is to use the answer choices and plug in values for n until you find the correct equation. You have to check only two values to determine that the correct answer is $2n - 2$.

6. **(B)** To find a, you must divide $\frac{3}{2}$ by $-\frac{2}{5}$. Remember that dividing by a fraction is the same as multiplying by its reciprocal. To find your answer, you must multiply $\frac{3}{2}$ by $-\frac{5}{2}$. Multiplying both the numerators and denominators straight across gives the answer: $-\frac{15}{4}$.

7. **(C)** First convert the 7 minutes to seconds by multiplying by 60. Now that you have 420 seconds, set up this problem as a proportion: $\frac{50}{12.1} = \frac{x}{420}$. From here, cross multiply and solve for x. You will find the value of x is about 1,735. The closest choice is 1,750 meters.

8. **(B)** Square both sides of the equation to remove the radical sign. Then multiply the two binomials of $x - 2$. You will now have the equation $x^2 - 4x + 4 = x + 4$. Setting the entire equation equal to 0 will leave you with $x^2 - 5x = 0$. Factor x from this equation. The result is $x(x - 5) = 0$. So the solutions to this equation appear to be 0 and 5. However, note that zero is NOT a solution because $0 - 2 = -2 \neq \sqrt{0 + 4} = 2$. Thus, 5 is the only solution to this equation.

9. **(B)** To answer this question, you must assign variables to represent each girl. If Alice is represented by x and if Beth is represented by $x + 6$, you can create the equation $x + (x + 6) = 68$ to represent the entire problem. Once you create this equation, you can solve for x, which leads you to the correct answer of 31.

10. **(C)** Look at each time interval. While time passes in regular intervals, the population growth increases by a power of 10 each time. Since this change is exponential and the population is increasing, the bacteria are undergoing exponential growth.

11. **(B)** The x-intercepts occur when each binomial is set equal to 0. Because of this, you must reverse the signs of the given x-intercepts to create the final equation, which is $f(x) = (x + 2)(x - 2)(x + 4)$.

12. **(A)** The key is to focus on the term NOT in the problem. Since you are looking for a solution that does not satisfy the inequality, use the choices to help find the solution that does not satisfy the inequality. Remember to stop when you find the first choice that does not work. In this case, it is choice A.

13. **(C)** You must find a way to eliminate one of the variables from the system in order to solve the entire system. The most efficient way to do this is by elimination (also known as the addition method). With this method, you must find a way to add the two equations vertically in such a way that one of the variables will be equal to 0. The most convenient way to carry out this method with this system is to multiply the first equation by 6. Then add the equations vertically, which eliminates the variable x. You are left with $19y = 38$. Solving gives $y = 2$. Substitute 2 for y into either of the original equations, and solve for x. No matter which original equation you use, you will get $x = 2$. Finally, find the sum of x and y. The answer is 4, choice C.

14. **(B)** First, be aware that this is a real-world problem. E refers to an amount of energy, m refers to the mass of the particle or particles in question, and

the constant c represents the speed of light in a vacuum. Since this is a real-world problem, disregard the negative answer formed by taking the square root. To find the final answer, manipulate the variables so that c is isolated. To do this, first divide both sides by m. Then take the square root of both sides to get $c = \sqrt{\dfrac{E}{m}}$.

15. **(B)** Break down the description, and write the values directly into the diagram. First, mark down the length of AE as 16. You know that DE is 2 and that AB is congruent to DE. By the transitive property, you can say that AB is 2 as well. Next, by subtracting AB and DE from the entire length of the segment, you are left with 12 as the diameter of the circle. Finally, since you know that C is the center of the circle and that BC and CD are radii, divide that diameter in half to get the length of the radius, which is 6.

16. **(B)** Jennifer starts with $450. Since Kim's account is 20% smaller, you must multiply $450 by 0.80 (100% − 20% = 80%) to find the size of Kim's account, which is $360.

17. **(B)** Finding the least possible value of $4x - 3$ requires you to calculate the least possible value of x in the inequality. This can be done by changing the inequality sign to an equal sign and solving for x. In doing so, you will get a value of $x = 1$. Now that you have the value of x, plug that back into $4x + 3$ to get the final answer of 7.

18. **(C)** To set this equation equal to x, start by subtracting b from both sides. Then divide both sides by m to get the final answer of $x = \dfrac{y - b}{m}$.

19. **(D)** By recognizing that the original price will be greater than what John paid eliminates choice A immediately. To find the original price, you must divide the price, $120, by 80% or 0.8 in order to find the original price of $150, choice D.

20. **(D)** This problem must be done using a proportion. Since 60 of the 200 students surveyed have 4 cars per household, make the proportion $\dfrac{60}{200} = \dfrac{x}{900}$. By cross multiplying and solving for x, you will find that the answer is 270.

21. **(B)** You must realize for this question that you are looking only at the middle school students. Because of this, you are looking at a sample size of 80 with 5 of those students having 0 cars. In order to solve the problem,

you must divide 5 by 80 to get an answer of 0.0625. Finally, multiply by 100 to change this decimal number to a percent: 6.25%.

22. **(C)** To find exponential growth, you must identify which option increases its value by using the growing value of the account and not a standard flat rate. The only option that fits this requirement is choice C. Each year, it adds a percentage of the total value of the account (the current value, not the initial value). The other options all add a flat rate.

23. **(B)** Start this problem by sketching a right triangle and labeling the side that you know, AB, as 8. Now calculate the length of the hypotenuse by multiplying $8 \times \frac{5}{4}$. The length of the hypotenuse is 10. Use the Pythagorean theorem to find the length of BC, which is 6. The final step is to find the cosine of C, which means dividing the adjacent side by the hypotenuse (CAH). The adjacent over the hypotenuse is $\frac{6}{10}$, which reduces to the final answer of $\frac{3}{5}$.

24. **(A)** First, substitute $k = 4$ into the equation. Then multiply the numerators and denominators on the left side of the equation, remembering to add the exponents since you are multiplying. This will leave you with $\frac{x^{-2}}{x^{-2}}$ on the left side of the equation, which is equal to 1. Now the real question becomes what will make the right side of the equation equal to 1. The answer to that is found in the exponents. The exponent $y + 2$ must be equal to 0 in order for the right side of the equation to be equal to 1. For this to be true, y must be equal to -2, choice A.

25. **(A)** To solve this equation for a circle, you must create two perfect square trinomials with the variables provided. You can create a perfect square trinomial for x by adding 1 to each side. To create a perfect square trinomial for y, you must add 9 to both sides. Once you do this, you have the equation $x^2 + 2x + 1 + y^2 - 6y + 9 = -1 + 1 + 9$. Simplify this to $x^2 + 2x + 1 + y^2 - 6y + 9 = 9$. This format is very important since the 9 on the right side of the equation is equal to the radius squared, based on the standard equation for a circle. Finally, to find the radius, you must take the square root of 9. The final answer is 3.

26. **(A)** For the points given to be on the same line and for that line to have a slope of 0, the y-values must be equal. The only choice that meets that rule is choice A, -1.

27. **(B)** The most reliable way to answer this question is to create a rectangle that satisfies the area requested first. A convenient size for the rectangle is a length of 8 and a width of 2. (To keep the problem simple, make sure you choose even numbers since you will be changing them by half.) Increasing the length by 50% will result in a new length of 12, and decreasing the width by 50% will result in a new width of 1. By multiplying the new length by the new width, you have a new area that is 12. Dividing your new area (12) by the original area (16) tells you that the new area is 75% of the old area, choice B.

28. **(D)** To solve for k, you must FOIL the first two binomials, giving you $(x^2 - x - 12)(x + 5)$. From there, you must now distribute both items from the second binomial to the trinomial. This will generate the expression $x^3 - x^2 - 12x + 5x^2 - 5x - 60$. After combining like terms, you will have the expression $x^3 + 4x^2 - 17x - 60$, making k equal to 4.

29. **(B)** First, you must isolate t inside the compound inequality. So subtract 2 from both sides. This gives you $-\frac{18}{5} < -3t < -\frac{12}{5}$. Then divide all three parts of the inequality by –3, remembering to reverse the direction of the signs since you are dividing by a negative number. You now have the inequality $\frac{18}{15} > t > \frac{12}{15}$, which means that t has a value of between 0.8 and 1.2. The only answer choice that can be calculated with the expression $8t - 1$ when using a value between 0.8 and 1.2 is choice B. Substituting 1 for t yields 7.

30. **(B)** You must realize that the diagonal with length x creates a right triangle. So label length a as a and length b as $2a$ since side b is twice the length of side a. Now you can label the diagonal x with the length of 10 that is given in the question. Since all three sides now have values, use the Pythagorean theorem to solve for a. This gives the equation $a^2 + (2a)^2 = 10^2$. Solving this equation for a results in $\sqrt{20}$, which is $2\sqrt{5}$ when simplified.

31. **7** To make this equation true, each fraction must be equal. The only value of x that makes both fractions equal is 7, for which each fraction equals 1.

32. **6** First, subtract 20 minutes from 380 to get 360 minutes. To solve from this point, you must convert 360 minutes to hours. So divide 360 minutes by 60 minutes (the number of minutes in an hour). The final answer is 6.

33. **7/2 or 3.5** To solve for b, substitute the given values of x and y into the function. This creates the equation $5 = 2(2)^2 - b(2) + 4$. Solving this equation for b gets you to the final answer of $\frac{7}{2}$ or 3.5.

34. **1/4 or .25** The central angle measures $\frac{\pi}{2}$ radians. You must remember that the entire circle measures 2π radians. Since $\frac{\pi}{2}$ is $\frac{1}{4}$ of 2π, the area of the central angle is 25% or $\frac{1}{4}$ of the area of the entire circle.

35. **25** According to the equation, the constant of 25 in the equation represents the original deposit.

36. **120** Set the two inequalities equal to each other, and solve for x. You will get a value of 8 for x. Once you have that value, you can plug this into either inequality to get the maximum value of 120.

37. **1.03** The x represents the rate of growth of the initial amount. Since Julia is earning 3% interest, this amount must be added to the amount she is starting with (which is represented by 1.00 or 100%). So the value of x is 103%, which is 1.03.

38. **24** The most convenient way to find the point in time that the original $500 will be double, or $1,000, is to use the equation provided in the problem. Keep changing the variable for time until you reach your final answer. In this case, that final answer is 24 years.

Essay

Below is one student's example of marking up text, arranging ideas into an outline, and writing an essay in response to Barack Obama's inaugural speech.

SAMPLE ESSAY TEXT MARKUP

1 Each time we gather to inaugurate a President we bear witness to the enduring strength of our Constitution. We affirm the promise of our democracy. We recall that what binds this nation together is not the colors of our skin or the tenets of our faith or the origins of our names. What makes us exceptional—what makes us American—is our allegiance to an idea articulated in a declaration made more than two centuries ago: "We hold these truths to be self-evident, that all men are created

equal; that they are endowed by their Creator with certain unalienable rights; that among these are life, liberty, and the pursuit of happiness."

2   Today we continue a never-ending journey to bridge the meaning of those words with the realities of our time. For history tells us that while these truths may be self-evident, they've never been self-executing; that while freedom is a gift from God, it must be secured by His people here on Earth. The patriots of 1776 did not fight to replace the tyranny of a king with the privileges of a few or the rule of a mob. They gave to us a republic, a government of, and by, and for the people, entrusting each generation to keep safe our founding creed.

3   And for more than two hundred years, we have.

4   Through blood drawn by lash and blood drawn by sword, we learned that no union founded on the principles of liberty and equality could survive half-slave and half-free. We made ourselves anew, and vowed to move forward together.

5   Together, we determined that a modern economy requires railroads and highways to speed travel and commerce, schools and colleges to train our workers.

6   Together, we discovered that a free market only thrives when there are rules to ensure competition and fair play.

7   Together, we resolved that a great nation must care for the vulnerable, and protect its people from life's worst hazards and misfortune.

8   Through it all, we have never relinquished our skepticism of central authority, nor have we succumbed to the fiction that all society's ills can be cured through government alone. Our celebration of initiative and enterprise, our insistence on hard work and personal responsibility, these are constants in our character.

9   But we have always understood that when times change, so must we; that fidelity to our founding principles requires new responses to new challenges; that preserving our individual freedoms ultimately requires collective action. For the American people can no more meet the demands of today's world by acting alone than American soldiers could have met the forces of fascism or communism with muskets and militias. No single person can train all the math and science teachers we'll need to equip our children for the future, or build the roads and networks and

research labs that will bring new jobs and businesses to our shores. Now, more than ever, we must do these things together, as one nation and one people.

10 This generation of Americans has been tested by crises that steeled our resolve and proved our resilience. A decade of war is now ending. An economic recovery has begun. America's possibilities are limitless, for we possess all the qualities that this world without boundaries demands: youth and drive; diversity and openness; an endless capacity for risk and a gift for reinvention. My fellow Americans, we are made for this moment, and we will seize it—so long as we seize it together.

11 For we, the people, understand that our country cannot succeed when a shrinking few do very well and a growing many barely make it. We believe that America's prosperity must rest upon the broad shoulders of a rising middle class. We know that America thrives when every person can find independence and pride in their work; when the wages of honest labor liberate families from the brink of hardship. We are true to our creed when a little girl born into the bleakest poverty knows that she has the same chance to succeed as anybody else, because she is an American; she is free, and she is equal, not just in the eyes of God but also in our own.

SAMPLE ESSAY OUTLINE

I. Introduction: Obama reelected in 2012.

   A. Made second inaugural speech.
   B. Used the inaugural as a chance to bring the country together: "We continue a never-ending journey to bridge the meaning of those words with the realities of our time."
   C. Argued that Americans must work together to ensure freedom and to meet the country's challenges.

II. Speech uses pathos (emotional appeal).

   A. Paragraph 1 stirs the audience by reminding them that a belief in equality sets them apart: "What makes us American—is our allegiance to an idea articulated in a declaration."
   B. Paragraph 2 tells the audience that they must work for freedom: "Truths may be self-evident, they've never been self-executing; that while freedom is a gift from God, it must be secured by His people here on Earth."

C. After each challenge, he said about the nation: "We made ourselves anew, and vowed to move forward together."

D. Paragraph 10 tells the audience they are exceptional: "We possess all the qualities that this world without boundaries demands."

III. Speech uses ethos (building credibility).

A. Paragraph 1: Mentions Constitution as part of swearing in office.

B. Paragraph 1: Quotes the Declaration of Independence: "We hold these truths to be self-evident, that all men are created equal" to lead into his idea of working together.

C. Paragraph 2: Quotes Lincoln's Gettysburg Address: "A government of, and by, and for the people" to remind the audience of a time when the nation had to come back together.

D. Paragraph 11: Quotes the Preamble to the Constitution: "We the people" in order to again bring the country together.

IV. Speech uses repetition.

A. From Paragraph 1 on, Obama repeats "we" over and over.

B. Paragraphs 5, 6, and 7 all started with "Together, we" to emphasize that the nation must work together to face challenges.

C. In paragraph 9, says: "But we have always understood that when times change, so must we" to bring home the idea of rising to new challenges together.

D. In paragraph 10, repeats "we" and "together" again to stir the audience to rise to the current challenges: "My fellow Americans, we are made for this moment, and we will seize it—so long as we seize it together."

V. Conclusion.

A. Use of pathos, ethos, and repetition is an effective rhetorical mix for the speech.

B. Uses one to build on the other and bring his ideas together effectively.

C. Paragraph 11 brings all his rhetoric together: "We are true to our creed when a little girl born into the bleakest poverty knows that she has the same chance to succeed as anybody else, because she is an American; she is free, and she is equal, not just in the eyes of God but also in our own."

SAMPLE ESSAY

In 2012, Barack Obama was reelected President and presented his second inaugural speech that persuaded the American people using ethos, pathos, and repetition. He argued that Americans must work together to ensure freedom and to meet the country's challenges. Obama used this as an opportunity to bring the American people together when reminding the people that "we continue a never-ending journey to bridge the meaning of those words with the realities of our time."

Obama made an emotional appeal to his audience by reminding them that it is their belief in equality that sets them apart from others. "What makes us American—is our allegiance to an idea articulated in a declaration." He reminds the audience that they must work for their freedom. "Truths may be self-evident, they've never been self-executing; that while freedom is a gift from God, it must be secured by his people here on Earth." After each challenge, Obama told the nation, "We made ourselves anew, and vowed to move forward together." He stressed his use of pathos when he posited that "we possess all the qualities that this world without boundaries demands."

To build credibility, Obama used ethos within his speech by referencing critical documents in our nation's development. He includes the Constitution from the beginning of his speech to validate his swearing in. He quotes the Declaration of Independence when stating: "We hold these truths to be self-evident, that all men are created equal" to lead into his idea of working together. Obama also calls upon Lincoln's Gettysburg Address when stating, "A government of, and by, and for the people" to remind

the audience of a time when the nation had to come back together. He further solidifies his foundation when quoting the Preamble to the Constitution: "We the people" in order to bring the country together again.

Obama also persuaded people through the use of repetition. He confidently repeats "we" throughout his speech. Paragraphs five, six, and seven all started with "Together, we" to emphasize that the nation must work together to face and overcome challenges. In paragraph nine, Obama continues the theme when stating: "But we have always understood that when times change, so must we" to emphasize the idea of rising to new challenges together. In paragraph ten, he repeats "we" and "together" to stir the audience to rise to current challenges. Obama stressed unity when stating, "My fellow Americans, we are made for this moment, and we will seize it—so long as we seize it together."

In his second inaugural speech, Barack Obama used pathos, ethos, and repetition to effectively persuade his audience to embrace his message. Each technique built upon the other and helped create a cohesive argument. Paragraph eleven demonstrates these techniques and brings his message together: "We are true to our creed when a little girl born into the bleakest poverty knows that she has the same chance to succeed as anybody else, because she is an American; she is free, and she is equal, not just in the eyes of God but also in our own." Obama's approach was direct and effective, and he passionately persuaded his audience.

SCORING THE SAMPLE ESSAY

Before discussing how this essay is scored, remember that there are three categories—Reading, Analysis, and Writing—and that each category is scored on a scale of 1 to 4 for a total of between 3 and 12. (Since the essay is scored by two different people, the total possible score ranges from 6 to 24.) Let's see how this essay scores in each category.

Reading: 4

This essay shows a strong comprehension of the source text, Obama's speech. It shows an understanding of both the central claim and the details of the speech. The opening paragraph stated the speech's central idea, that Americans had to work together to ensure freedom and meet the country's challenges. The essay then breaks down the speech's details in the supporting paragraphs. The evidence ties the central idea to the details. This essay shows advanced reading comprehension.

Analysis: 4

This essay demonstrates a good analysis of the speech. The writer breaks the speech into pathos, ethos, and repetition and then shows how each helps build Barack Obama's speech. The essay utilizes many quotes from the speech, and this provides great evidence to back the ideas in each paragraph. The analysis does connect the three ideas in the supporting paragraphs in the conclusion. This connection in the conclusion helps the analysis score.

Writing: 3

This essay demonstrates a generally effective use of language. The essay's structure is solid, and the ideas flow well. There are good transitions between sentences and between paragraphs. The writer also structures the essay to build the analysis of the speech so that the conclusion brings the ideas together with the final quote (starting with "We are true . . ."). There are some minor flaws in punctuation (for example, a comma precedes a quote, not a colon). The writer also writes in the past tense but occasionally lapses into the present tense. These minor flaws keep the score from being a 4. The essay shows good writing.

Overall Score

Reading: 4

Analysis: 4

Writing: 3

Total: 11 out of 12 (Remember, the essay is scored twice, so this essay would score a 22 out of 24.)

SCORE ANALYSIS

Reading and Writing Test

Section 1: Reading _____ = _____ (A)

                      # correct   raw score

Section 2: Writing _____ = _____ (B)

                      # correct   raw score

To find your Reading and Writing test scores, consult the chart below: find the ranges in which your raw scores lie and read across to find the ranges of your test scores.

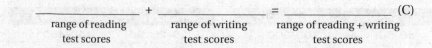

_____ + _____ = _____ (C)

  range of reading   range of writing   range of reading + writing

    test scores   test scores   test scores

To find the range of your Reading and Writing Scaled Score, multiply (C) by 10.

Test Scores for the Reading and Writing Sections

Reading Raw Score	Writing Raw Score	Test Score
44–52	39–44	35–40
36–43	33–38	31–34
30–35	28–32	28–30
24–29	22–27	24–27
19–23	17–21	21–23
14–18	13–16	19–20
9–13	9–12	16–18
5–8	5–8	13–15
less than 5	less than 5	10–12

Math Test

Section 3:   _____ = _____ (D)
                 # correct   raw score

Section 4:   _____ = _____ (E)
                 # correct   raw score

Total Math raw score: (D) + (E) = _____ .

To find your Math Scaled Score, consult the chart below: find the range in which your raw score lies and read across to find the range for your scaled score.

Scaled Scores for the Math Test

Raw Score	Scaled Score	Raw Score	Scaled Score
50–58	700–800	20–25	450–490
44–49	650–690	15–19	400–440
38–43	600–640	11–14	350–390
32–37	550–590	7–10	300–340
26–32	500–540	less than 7	200–290

Appendix A:
List of BIG Strategies

BIG STRATEGIES: OVERVIEW

BIG Strategy #1: You'll Gain More Points by Improving on the Writing and Language Test than by Improving on the Reading Test

The Reading Test and the Writing and Language Test are each worth 400 points. However, the Reading Test has 52 questions, while the Writing and Language Test has 44 questions. Therefore, each of the questions on the Writing and Language Test is worth more points (about 9.1 points each) than each of the questions on the Reading Test (about 7.7 points each). This means that you can gain more SAT points for each question you get correct on the Writing and Language Test than for each question you answer correctly on the Reading Test.

BIG Strategy #2: When to Take the SAT and How Many Times You Should Take It

The SAT is administered on Saturday mornings throughout the school year. Testing occurs:

- In the beginning of October
- In the beginning of November
- In the beginning of December
- In the middle of March
- In the beginning of May
- In the beginning of June
- In late August

Knowing when the test is given is important as you make your study and testing plans. You should plan on taking the test more than once because doing so will help your chances of getting accepted into more colleges.

BIG Strategy #3: Don't Get Competitive with Scores

Remember what the SAT is—a test that colleges use to help decide who to accept. Once your scores are in the range you need to get accepted to a college, you've reached your goal.

Students often lose sight of that. When you hear friends talking about their SAT scores at the lunch table, don't start thinking of your scores versus theirs. Their scores are theirs; yours are yours. Getting into a bragging match about SAT scores is worthless and pointless.

Your only goal with the SAT is to do the best you can to give you the most opportunities with college. Once you've earned the scores you need to get into the college you hope to go to, you've met your goal.

BIG STRATEGIES: WRITING AND LANGUAGE TEST

BIG Strategy #4: Read the Passage!

Read the whole passage. You can't skim the passage on the Writing Test.

Remember, these passages are short, only 400–450 words. Since you will be asked to perform several different editing and revising tasks, it's important to have a sense of the overall main point of each reading passage. You cannot just read the questions and look at the sentences in isolation. Also, you might be asked questions that deal with the whole paragraph or the whole passage.

So read a paragraph. Then stop and answer the questions in that paragraph. Once you get to questions in the next paragraph, keep reading. As you read, think about the main idea, its support or examples, and errors you see in the passage. That way when you get to the questions, you will already be thinking about the answers. The Writing and Language Test is an editing test. Without reading the passage carefully, you will struggle with questions that are specifically designed to punish students who do not read the passage or who do not understand the main idea of the paragraphs and of the passage.

BIG Strategy #5: Don't Listen for the Answer; Look for It!

Don't go with the answer that "sounds" best. Most people who take the test will do this. The College Board test makers know that is what most people will do. The test will often have a question choice that sounds great but is wrong, or it

will have a question choice that sounds wrong but is right. So don't *listen* for the answer; *look* for it!

BIG Strategy #6: Eliminate Like a Coach Making Cuts

The SAT is mostly a multiple-choice test. Use that to your advantage. On some (and hopefully most) questions, you will know the answer. However, there will be other questions where you're not sure or have no idea. What should you do then?

There is no penalty for choosing wrong answers, so answer every question. To get a higher score, pretend you're a coach making cuts before the season. Coaches don't simply make one cut and then form the roster. They make first cuts, eliminating those who don't know on which hand to put the mitt. Then the coaches take a look again and make second cuts, eliminating those who are close but not quite right.

If you can eliminate any choices, you increase your chances of getting the question correct and therefore increasing your score. For example, say you take a wild guess on 10 questions on the English portion of the SAT. Each question has 4 choices. If you eliminate none of the answer choices, you have a 1-in-4 chance of getting each question correct. Over 10 questions, that means you probably get 2 or maybe 3 correct, raising your score by 20 to 30 points.

If you eliminate one bad choice from each of those questions, you now have a 1-in-3 chance of getting each of those questions right. Now you probably answer 3 or possibly 4 correct, boosting your score by 30 to 40 points.

If you eliminated two choices, you now have a 50-50 chance of getting those 10 questions correct. So you probably answer 5 questions correctly, which boosts your score by 50 points.

Instead of adding up to 20 points to your score by taking wild guesses, you can raise your score by up to 50 points simply by eliminating answer choices.

Eliminating choices before guessing can add up to a big increase in your score!

BIG Strategy #7: Don't Be Afraid to Choose "NO CHANGE"

Remember that the SAT is not like a test made by teachers. When teachers write tests, choices like "None of the above" or "All of the above" are rarely correct. The SAT carefully balances its choices, though. So there is as good a chance the correct answer is choice A ("NO CHANGE") as it is choice D. Remember

to answer every question. Leave no answer spaces blank. After all, there's no penalty for guessing!

BIG Strategy #8: Don't Overthink the Questions!

Often, juniors and seniors use the same process while taking the SAT as they use in English class every day. In class, their teachers say, "OK, here's what the author said in chapter 12. But what did he *really* say?" Those students then have to take what they've read and apply it to another idea to create a new thought. In other words, the teachers try to get students to use higher-level thinking skills to create ideas. That's great, of course. However, the SAT doesn't do that! When the SAT asks what the author said, it is referring to what the author said. Do take an inch and make it a foot. The test questions do not run very deep. This does not mean that the Reading Test is easy! It just means that the Reading Test questions are asking only about what is on the page and not about anything beyond it.

BIG Strategy #9: If You've Eliminated A, B, and C, Choose D and Move On

If you are working through the answer choices and you eliminate choice A, then choice B, and then choice C, choose choice D and move on to the next question. You know that choices A, B, and C are not correct, so why bother reading choice D? It must be the answer! We have a tendency to want to make sure we are right. On this test, though, that tendency can hurt you. If you eliminate the other choices and then read choice D, you are possibly second-guessing yourself and talking yourself out of choosing the right answer. You are also taking precious time when second-guessing. That time might be needed for another question, so don't give it away. Keep moving!

BIG STRATEGIES: READING TEST

BIG Strategy #10: Come Up with Your Own Answer

Think of the answer before you look at the answer choices. The Reading Test will try to trick you into choosing wrong answers. To avoid this trap, you have to decide what the answer is before you look at the choices offered by the test. Imagine going to a restaurant wanting a steak. Then you read the menu and, after getting caught up in the description of a dish, you order the chicken. As

you are eating the chicken, you realize that your meal has been ruined because you did not get what you wanted. This is how the SAT Reading Test is designed. The only way to avoid choosing the wrong answer is to decide what you want first and then search for it. Remember: that applies to every question, not just the vocabulary questions.

BIG Strategy #11: If You Are Asked Something You Already Know, Be Careful!

Remember, the SAT is a test of your reading skills, not of your knowledge. Often, the test will have questions that seem to be common knowledge. If read carefully, though, the information is actually different from what you learned in school. This is most true on vocabulary, where a word you studied may not be used with the definition you studied.

BIG Strategy #12: Read One Paragraph at a Time

Most people who take the SAT feel that the reading selection is very difficult to focus on and to understand. The test wants you to read the whole passage at once. When you do, though, staying focused is difficult because you are reading a random page from the middle of a book you have probably not read. Who reads like this? Since this is a completely unnatural way of reading, the material is, by its very nature, difficult to absorb all at once. To make the reading selection easier, you should read one paragraph at a time and answer whatever questions you can. Then read another paragraph and answer more questions.

BIG Strategy #13: Always Look Back on the Reading Test

The SAT is the best kind of test: open book! You are not being asked to immediately memorize what you have read. You are also not being asked to be an expert on what you just read. Instead, you are being asked some questions that pertain only to the text on the page when the page is still right in front of you. If you do not look back to search for or confirm your answer, you are giving away your biggest advantage. If you neglect to look back at the passage for your answer, you are reducing the number of questions you will get correct. Use the passage to find the answers!

BIG Strategy #14: You Won't Completely Understand the Passage

When reading a passage, know that you will not 100% "get it." Accept that fact! You are reading random information. For this reason, the passage won't make perfect sense to you. However, this does not matter because all of the questions are based on information right there on the page. The answers do not extend beyond the passage. So relax. Even though you won't understand the passage completely, you will be able to answer the questions.

BIG Strategy #15: Look for the Argument

The biggest advantage on the essay is that the prompt will always be the same: How did the author persuade the audience? So look for elements of persuasion as you read the test and underline those elements. Then jot a note in the margin once you've read the paragraph about what kind of persuasive writing it was.

This process will save you an enormous amount of time and effort from having to go back and search for how the author persuaded the audience. It will also keep you focused on the topic of your essay. By finding and underlining specifics, you will also be finding specific evidence to include in your supporting paragraphs. The work you do before you write the first word of the essay is the key to getting a good score!

BIG STRATEGIES: MATH TEST

BIG Strategy #16: Work Faster at the Beginning of the Math Test So You'll Have More Time for the Harder Questions at the End

The math questions become increasingly harder as you work through each section. In other words, the questions at the end of each Math Test section are more difficult than those at the beginning. (More specifically, the math questions go from easy to hard on the multiple-choice questions and then reset back to easy on the grid-in questions.) To use this to your advantage, work at a faster pace at the beginning of both math sections so that you have a little more time for each of the harder questions at the end. If you simply give each question equal time, you will have trouble conceptualizing and solving the more difficult questions in the time remaining. Working a little faster on the questions you know

are easier will buy you more time to answer those tougher questions toward the end of the test. Only the math questions are presented in order of increasing difficulty, not the English questions. So make this a math strategy approach.

BIG Strategy #17: Use Your Calculator Whenever Possible

One of your biggest enemies while testing is time. So do not waste your most valuable resource doing calculations by hand, which is time consuming. In the section that permits it, use your calculator! Do all but the most basic of calculations using your calculator. You are given that resource for an important reason; take advantage of it!

BIG Strategy #18: Never Do More Work than Necessary

Once you have eliminated three of the four choices as possible answers, choose the remaining answer. You should not complete the rest of your work to be sure the last-remaining answer choice is correct. Remember that time can be either your friend or your enemy. If you have an extra minute at the end of the test that you need to complete a hard problem, you will be grateful that you saved 20 seconds on one problem and 30 seconds on another by not doing unnecessary work on earlier problems. Do what you can to conserve the valuable resource of time so that you can give every question the time and effort it needs.

BIG Strategy #19: Work Backward from Answer Choices

Take your time reading a problem. If you can generally grasp what is being asked, you might want to look at the answer choices and work backward. Many times, this method can get you to the correct solution quickly. The answer choices will often reveal either the solution itself or the path to the answer. Sometimes plugging in the answer choices to see which one works is the fastest way to finding the solution.

BIG Strategy #20: Make a Quick Sketch

Say that you have a problem that mentions a triangle, but there is no triangle on the page. You must sketch it! Making a sketch will help you see the problem. As you have heard your teachers tell you for years, don't try to do the problem in your head! Sketching will make the problem easier to see and therefore easier to solve. You do not have to be an artist to make a useful sketch that will help you solve a problem. In many cases, adding a visual component to a problem that doesn't originally include one can be the difference between finding a correct answer quickly and wasting your most valuable resource—time. Your sketches need to be accurate. At the same time, they must be done quickly. This is not the time to create a masterpiece. You are simply putting the image onto the page to help you see what the problem is asking and what it wants you to solve.

BIG Strategy #21: Focus on the Basics

To excel in geometry and trigonometry on the SAT, you do not have to be a master mathematician. Instead, focus on being a master of the basics, such as the Pythagorean theorem; sine, cosine, and tangent properties; and the basic attributes of geometric shapes (area, perimeter, and volume). Mastering these topics will help you succeed with these types of problems on test day.

BIG Strategy #22: Use Common Sense to Break Down Mathematical Logic

When encountering problems rooted in the real world, break them down into simpler problems. How can you do this? Just use your common sense. Real-world problems require you to draw on personal experiences to understand fully what the question is asking and to find the correct answer in the easiest way possible. Making complicated problems into much simpler problems is the key to success when tackling real-world problems.

Appendix B:
Important Math Facts

USEFUL MATH FORMULAS, POSTULATES, AND THEOREMS

Area of a Triangle

$$A = \frac{1}{2}bh$$

Cross Multiplying Proportions

$$\frac{a}{b} = \frac{c}{d} \rightarrow ad = bc$$

Converting Degrees to Radians

$$180° = \pi \text{ radians}$$

Equation for a Circle

$$(x - h)^2 + (y - k)^2 = r^2$$

Pythagorean Theorem

$$a^2 + b^2 = c^2$$

Quadratic Formula

$$\frac{-b \pm \sqrt{b^2 - 4ac}}{2a}$$

Converting Roots to Standard Form

$$\sqrt[n]{a^m} = a^{\frac{m}{n}}$$

Finding the Slope of a Line Using Two Points

$$m = \frac{y_2 - y_1}{x_2 - x_1}$$

SOH-CAH-TOA (Trigonometric Functions for Right Triangles)

$$\text{sine} = \frac{\text{opposite}}{\text{hypotenuse}}$$

$$\cos = \frac{\text{adjacent}}{\text{hypotenuse}}$$

$$\tan = \frac{\text{opposite}}{\text{adjacent}}$$

Slope-Intercept Formula of a Line

$$y = mx + b$$

Standard Form of a Quadratic Equation

$$y = ax^2 + bx + c$$

NOTES